First
Communication

(Book I in the Nelta Series)

J.P. Osterman

First Communication

(Book I in the Nelta Series)

Copyright © 2013 J.P. Osterman

All rights reserved.

CreateSpace, Charleston SC

Published by J.P. Osterman.com

ISBN-10: 0615975089
ISBN-13: 978-0-615-97508-5
Date of Publication: August 12, 2014
Printed in the United States of America

Cover Photo: Bruce Rolff | Shutterstock.com

DEDICATION

To Drew, Andrew and Jennifer. Thanks for your faith in me.

ACKNOWLEDGMENTS

I thank my editor Drew and Bruce Rolff for my cover art.

First Communication

Part I: First Communication

First Communication

Chapter 1 - Ozone Strike

In a 1998 hearing before the U.S. Senate, General Alexander Lebed, Russia's former National Security Advisor, testified that more than 100 nuclear weapons had "disappeared." Most were suitcase-sized nukes that he believed were in the hands of terrorists. The weapons were *each* capable of producing anywhere from a single kiloton to over a 1-megaton explosion.

Six decades passed. We forgot about those bombs. ...

It was Sunday, June 10, 2057 in the United States when extremist groups came out of deep hiding and launched a combined strike on the world. They detonated 47 of the missing nukes high in the atmosphere, where much larger amounts of ionizing gamma radiation and x-rays would cause the most damage to our ozone.

A week after the attempted holocaust, it was clear we had entered into World War III against an army of jihadists and anti-Western militants whose hatred had been seething for decades! Those terrorists struck us *hard*. Back in 2051, the northern ice sheet had exhaled its last vapor due to global warming, but the radiation created by the explosions on that global day of devastation produced a chain reaction that began

J.P. Osterman

destroying the ozone layer and deteriorating our air quality.

Institutions collapsed. Governments and nations toppled. Communicating through the internet, we survivors reached out to one another other through a new, One World social media site. We took refuge in beehive communities, many underground with protective solar lighting.

Unite! Survive! Rebuild! motivational signs were tacked up *everywhere*, and the survivors did just that!

Scientists and engineers in Russia and China united their terraforming projects and installed an electron manipulation system on the old International Space Station. That Earth-directed device with its particle accelerators began stabilizing gases in the ozone layer, but only to minimum levels. With the help of private companies like SpaceX, Area 51 astrophysicists launched *four* cloud-seeding devices on solar powered, unmanned aerial vehicles. The technology people had been developing for a manned mission to Mars began saving Earth!

Not enough.

Realizing that if we were going to survive and thrive, we had to consolidate *all* our resources. On January 2, 2058, in what would be the first of *many* democratic on-line elections, we voted for and approved a global government, United Earth, and a 50-member team of representatives: The Regency. The next day, our media site posted nominations for those positions; and the following day, we voted the *first* United Earth officials into office. They had to have known what they were getting themselves into because on any day we, The World, could vote them out of The Regency!

On Monday, April 1, 2058, we approved our Global Constitution. The next Monday, we approved the Enforcer Agency that merged all of Earth's fragile police forces. That Thursday, we voted in favor of a unified military—Stealth Force, bestowing on them the power to bring our terrorist enemies to justice.

"Justice? Justice for what!"

That's what some of us kept arguing about through our One

First Communication

World site. After all, our delicate ozone layer was now a sieve. No global unity, passionate pursuit of technology, or intense hunt-and-strike strategy against terrorists would stop Earth from eventually becoming a mostly uninhabitable zone. What many of our scientists believed was humanity's extinction-level event was looming in our faces as people died daily!

Three months later, in an intensive campaign, one of our representatives, Regent Thornton Manning, implored us to approve a quick set up of an advanced radio telescope array and link it with the Very Large Array in New Mexico, the SETI Institute, and the observatories in the Atacama Desert. Harnessing energy from the particle accelerator at the Space Station, he had already begun a preliminary quantum transmission into the Virgo Cluster of galaxies but needed more optics to complete his experiment. He said that he and his team had picked up "a strong signal from the M84 galaxy, one of *many* galaxies in that Virgo Cluster." He kept interrupting all our TV entertainment programs to update us on the frequencies they were hearing that sounded like high-pitched revving engines alternating with long flatline noises at one-minute intervals. He contended, "The sounds *must be* spacecraft emissions, and advanced aliens."

"What a waste of time!" many reporters and his Regency colleagues scoffed, claiming that his plan, "to message aliens and ask for help," was throwing away money and scarce resources. Even if an advanced civilization had the technology to help us, no *one* or *thing* could *ever* travel at light speed or harness enough energy to journey through wormholes to save Earth before our ozone would bleed out. The distance between the Virgo Cluster and the Milky Way was too great. "Cleaning up cities and stopping terrorism *are* priority," people maintained, trying to stop Regent Manning's ideas from flourishing as the day to vote on his Observatory Measure approached.

Yet, two weeks later, in a short ten-minute speech, he convinced 86% of us voters that humanity's ultimate survival might depend on aliens hearing the message and answering his cosmic call for help. Based on Dr. M. Suhail Zubairy's Counterfactual Quantum Communication Principle back in 2013, we found it difficult to understand how *anyone* could communicate *without* data traveling through time and space. That's radio, satellite, the internet and fiber-optic communications. Regent Manning's quantum SOS experiment appeared like a psychic reading! He said his new orbital observatory would allow immediate communication anywhere - across the street - across the World - or across the Universe - instantly. "The speed of light is no longer a limiting factor!"

Then he showed us a small model of his outer space invention that looked like a six-foot round particle accelerator with tentacles. When he turned on the model, its yellow laser lights lit up, hummed, lifted in the air, blasting sounds and an image of Earth *right* into our portable devices. We saw the data appear on the Mars probes and the Titan probe! The SOS would reach the Virgo Cluster once he had the necessary optics to quantum-transmit the SOS.

But the most convincing part of his speech came when he showed us pictures of our deteriorating ozone, thinning *worse* than anyone had anticipated, with solar radiation beating out hot spots around Earth. Desperation clinched an 86% vote to move forward.

One month later on November 17, 2058, Regent Thornton Manning made a special appearance at the Arecibo observatory. With breaking news, he interrupted all The Regents' recorded speeches on our One World Campaign and Voting site to demonstrate his Decagon Communications Platform connected to the renovated Space Station that was also linking with *every* observatory on Earth. Harnessing particle accelerator energy, the two-mile wide, ten-armed, "octopus" station was concentrating electron-embedded data at precise locations at M84 and the surrounding Virgo Cluster. Accessing the facility's home page, *we* could see, hear and monitor the SOS. Regent Manning had interwoven our message with the transmission we were *still* receiving and

First Communication

scenes of Earth—destructive scenes from our deteriorating ozone, and clips of some of Earth's most beautiful scenery, combined with images of the people who volunteered to be a part of his SOS endeavor. He ended his special broadcast by saying: "This is quantum communication, transmitting data as atomic particles that exist in multiple places, even across the universe. They *will* hear us! Now we can only wait, hope they answer, and are willing to help us."

Chapter 2 - The Anomaly

The time was around noon on Thursday, August 23, 2060. I was sitting in my old, fourth floor office in the Levine Science and Research Center at my alma mater, Duke University, checking over data and results on a new optics sensor when the sky darkened under heavy cloud cover, just like that. The atmospheric pressure was slowly dropping, and the humidity was at five percent as if a hurricane was approaching the East Coast. I'd never seen or heard of such a condition! I felt a static cling in the air. My tongue dried. Drinking water didn't even begin to quench my thirst!

With a shocked expression on her face, Dr. Lynn Altmin, an old research colleague of mine, ran into the lab and began pointing out the big picture window at the center of the west wall. "Thornton, is this an eclipse? The Global Weather Service messaged us downstairs saying that something big was incoming but they can't make it out. Whataya think?!"

The fourth floor had a Top Secret Security designation. I couldn't leave until the right technician with the proper credentials could relieve me. That person wasn't Lynn, yet she

First Communication

was there. I wondered why; but before I asked and risked sounding stupid, I remembered that she had a few military experiments in the south section of the lab. "A new type of terror attack maybe?" I asked, pointing at several areas in the sky, trying to spot drones. I couldn't. "I don't know, but I'll find out right now." I tried to get a landline connection to General Mark Bernstein, the Four Star hero I swore into office in Argentina after he captured a group of militants and saved the heart of Buenos Aires from destruction. At my giant work area at the south section of the room, all my transparent screen processors, Smart stands, and portable working areas were dark and nonfunctional. Everything had shut down! No luck reaching The General. When I couldn't spot any sort of attack or strike maneuver outside, Lynn and I began gathering more instruments to analyze the air both inside and outside.

I couldn't stop from examining Lynn too! Some things about her had changed; some hadn't. The last time we spoke was May, 30, 2058 when I accepted my Regency position after that day's vote. She accused me of bailing out of hard science to play high-stakes politics. Huh! I left, and a rift began that I believed would never mend.

Memories of her flashed through my mind like the static causing confusion and chaos.

Lynn had full rosy lips and shoulder-length, sun-bleached blond hair she wore either in a ponytail or in a penciled bun at the back of her head. Her large hazel eyes had a dazzle to them. I saw her as a man magnet, and I told her that once, although she laughed off my assessment. I think the splash of bright green in the lower corner of her right eye startled people, made *everyone* take a second glance at her. But Lynn always laughed off—or waved off—the extra attention, calling the second takers "idiots," "ignorant" or "creepy" for not understanding the term *sectoral heterochromia*. I think kids bullied her in middle school or high school, and she withdrew from social opportunities that could have made her popular 'cause she was just so darn beautiful! But she was also sensitive, and had the personality type that made it hard for her to brush off

J.P. Osterman

insults. Thus, she pursued optics software research, and helped advanced military apps in the early months of World War III. With her slender figure, almost eidetic memory, and outgoing personality, Lynn really had the potential to become an actor or model. She *definitely* had spotlight potential— always juggling instruments in the lab or impersonating some classic TV personality like Pauley Perrette from *NCIS*. But if she woulda taken that route, I'da never met Lynn Altmin. As then, she still had a dark tan, and healthy physique.

"Are you still running marathons?" I asked softly, picking up pencils that toppled to the floor when the sky broke out in a long rumble. It was darkening like dusk, but also bright in spots, which hadn't been the case since the ozone attacks. Whatever was occurring high in the atmosphere was definitely altering molecules in the air…for the better.

She gestured at me as if I was nuts. "You *really* wanna play catch up at a time like this, Thornton?" Her sun basted appearance made her look like a cross between a die-hard athlete and an island tourist. She gave me a sudden sad blank stare. She looked lost, but then quickly sprung back to peering out the window, and the bedlam occurring in the university quad with all the windblown students and faculty. Then she began sifting through my old desk, pulling out all types of phones and turning them on.

"I know this isn't the time for catching up," I began, "but I hope we can visit later on after this storm passes. Will you consider it? For—for uh old times?" I asked as I gleaned environmental readings so we could stream them to other labs when a connection activated.

She stopped abruptly, exhaled an obvious angry puff of air, and then continued rifling through apps on one old iPhone that flared on but then jingled off. "Damn!" she shouted.

I grabbed her shaking hand. "It'll be okay, Lynn, I—"

She pulled away, turned away, and kept on frantically working to find another mode of internet connectivity. I felt stupid, but then, I suppose I deserved that silent bashing. I'd

8

First Communication

been forwarding her Skype calls to my Automated Response app. Working up close to her to help rig a phone connection, I noticed that she still exuded the smell of scented soaps and walked with a light bounce and a *flip-flop*.

Years ago, when the same spot we were standing in had been a giant lab, she said she purposely wore flip-flops so our team would know her location at all times. Even after I left Duke, I believed I heard those *flip-flop* sounds off and on— echoes of her everywhere, disorienting me a bit and making me ache a bit until I found another piece of hardware for the Decagon Platform into which I could throw my experiment-driven attentions. I missed her!

Lynn was the Data Mapper of our research team. After I consolidated the results of an experiment and our team input all the data, she would generate the statistical probabilities. Only then could we draw conclusions, but not without Lynn's blessing because she was also the editorial genius behind our publications.

Another thing I remember about Lynn is that she liked donning the newest surfer fashions. Sometimes, coming into work early, she'd have a green energy drink in one hand, open up her lab coat with her other hand as if flashing bare skin, and announced, "Look at this great deal I found at the outlet store last night *real* cheap!"

I'd laugh, reach into my stash of confetti I kept in a baggie in my lab drawer, and fling a few specks of it at her. We were always clowning around, always playing little pranks on each other.

She was perfect, and I couldn't stop my self-loathing as I kept thinking: God—I blew it when I left! Then I wondered: But did I really? After all, she was *right* there beside me even though we were experiencing a potential calamity! Maybe I had a chance to reverse the past.

That's what I realized as I stood there beside her at the picture window after over two years of being so far away from her. I then noticed that she hadn't taken down the awards we had won for our research projects. They were dusty, but still hanging perfectly the way I left them on the far south wall behind several bleeping Smart-screen processors. I pushed them away and blew off the dusk.

"Oh yeah, I forgot to take those down months ago before the new Smart systems arrived," she laughed. "I've been working on hologram technology in that area, converting wall screens and ceiling processors to link with portable tablets to generate room-wide virtual reality capability!"

"That's brilliant, Lynn," I said.

Then she sighed, and her excitement seemed to morph into dark recollection of our past argument. She turned her attention back to the abnormal weather patterns lifting tree branches and shrubbery like a magnet manipulating paperclips.

That's when I realized that without Lynn, my *entire* bright political future felt dead. Maybe I had a chance to change that! I tried to say those words as she kept talking about the temperature, atmospheric readings, and leaving our secure fourth-floor facility. My tongue felt like cork! I drank more water that she gave me, but I still couldn't say the words that might soften her hardened attitude toward me: "I'm sorry. Come on...forgive me." Tapping stalled apps on a bunch of weak portable tablets was diverting my attention to an escalating outside current of wind. I must say, I never saw Lynn *once* become unhinged over anything, except now, as we watched yellow and white clouds gathering at least fifty miles high! They were circulating and conveying energy, but the air and space around them were still and calm.

"Those can't be storm clouds...no way," she cried, her chest moving so rapidly I thought she might hyperventilate. "A tech downstairs said this atmospheric condition started at exactly 12 p.m. Strange, the precise time, huh, Thornton?"

I agreed. "I don't think we're due for an eclipse, but let me bring up this morning's paper and check it out." One of the outmoded iTablets suddenly powered on and I picked it up. I told Lynn that mine was out for service; and when I found Duke's website, I logged in to the secure page, entered my

First Communication

Regency code and gained access to Duke's Siri Network. Hitting the darn iTablet several times because it stalled through so much interference, I *finally* received a clear signal and called on the *Star* app. "Gosh, I didn't realize I've been stuck in here since 6:30 a.m. I'm starving." As Lynn threw me a power bar and I chomped it down, I noticed the 3D newscast on my iTablet was blurry and hardly audible. "Pixels are moving all over the place…weird," I said. Then I received a buffer time…two minutes to *Clear View*. "I never hearda such a thing, not since 2040!" She was shocked at that bad buffer return as well. The time was 12:12 p.m. "Damn cloud network." I called for a download of an outmoded signal so I could at least message my Arecibo team my location. "The darn iTablet says it's gonna take ten minutes for a system reconfigure…damn! What a time for something like this to happen. I have so much data to upload from flash drives. The processing time alone from flash drive to storage clouds to Arecibo is gonna take until two in the morning if this doesn't stop!"

Huffing out a chuckle, she said: "You always were so precision oriented, Thornton, always sticking to the clock. Not much has changed."

"Huh?" She seemed perturbed, no—angry.

"Never mind," she said, and then she returned to inspecting the sky. She kept switching hand-held instruments to do it…some so bulky she had to Velcro them to a special vest. "Experimental," she called the instruments.

I coulda swore they were her armor. Waiting for the right moment to ask her if we could stop all our game playing and just talk to each other, I peeked up at the convection, now really enlarging. "It's definitely changing, Lynn, and getting brighter around the edge!"

"Rapidly!" She clutched my arm.

"There isn't a downdraft or updraft with the disturbance. This is definitely *not* normal."

"Maybe gravitational? Magnetic? But the round black interior isn't expanding. Oh—dark matter contracting against dark energy—"

"The center of a black hole? *Naaw*," I said.

"Then a polar reversal is starting," she screamed. "My God—we hear that something like this could happen because of the sudden ozone depletion, or residual effects of the terrorists' bombs!" She whimpered a bit and added slowly, "We're good as dead, Thornton."

"No, wait!" I looked her in the eye. "Let's not go to death-and-destruction just yet, Lynn. Let's do a little more investigating." As she calmed, I continued: "That's what you were always good at, remember? Ya got all this stuff around us. So let's keep scanning the air with these instruments, downstream the data, and see what the lab computers downstairs toss back to us." I was forcing myself to sound light hearted...trying to stay calm. I coulda raced right outta there. I didn't. Looking back, I should have, 'cause what happened later on, maybe I coulda prevented. But at that time, I knew she would never have left the block's worth of experimental equipment unsecured in that fourth story facility.

"Yeah, you're right, Thornton," she breathed, picking up another small detector and then studying the air. She activated a weak downstream to the lab. "Here goes...I'm sending info."

I began hearing chaos coming from the outside quad. People were shouting and screaming the words I was thinking:

"Is that a new type of terrorist bomb exploding up there?"

"We're being attacked!"

"My God—a new type of nuke!"

"Lord help us!"

"Aliens are invading!"

One man hollered, "The Rapture is here!"

The widespread panic sounded like that day on June 10, 2057 when those terrorists detonated their nukes in the ozone.

Rolling closed the long line of windows, I said to Lynn as the noise muffled: "We can't conjecture worst-case scenarios. We have to ascertain the facts...find out the composition of

First Communication

the disturbance first. Then we'll know what we're dealing with." Hoping that an alien had heard my SOS and was answering, but not yet accepting that possibility 'cause we hadn't received cosmic noise at the Decagon Platform for over a year, I grabbed her shoulders, steadying her. Then I saw her hands on my elbows. She was helping me! I exhaled—the deep breathing helping us both. I said, "Then we can deal with that air frisbee up there." I remembered the past. She sometimes proposed outlandish experiments that scared our team. One was a gamma, face-frying, nano-weapons patch that we could program to make terrorists "sing" while punishing 'em. Fear. We were used to feeling the unnerving emotion every day because of those 2057 ozone attacks. Fear motivated us to develop more technology. Wild technology! Now, we were two lone souls fending off fear.

"Strange though, huh, Thornton?" she laughed shyly "*You* were the one who *usually* did all the catastrophizing over contamination-this-and-threat-to-validity-that."

Oo that hurt. Should I change the subject? I said, "Gosh— I haven't even met with the research team assigned to Arecibo yet."

"Really?" she asked, sarcastically as she pocketed a Geiger counter and hoisted up a spinning radiometer. Then she stopped everything and said, "I *heard* you were here."

That's when it hit me: She was wondering why I hadn't conferenced with her. "I've been trying to stay focused. Sorry, Lynn," I replied. "I've been concerned about protecting some new data from corruption. I wanted to remain completely unbiased."

"*Hm*, yeah." She shook her finger jokingly in my face. "See? Just like I said…you *haven't* changed."

I felt so taken off guard and so undeserving of it. She was probably the only one, outside of my dead parents, who I'd *ever* let talk to me like that without telling them off on the spot. Trying to deal with that churning disturbance above and her confusing gestures, I felt my mind beginning to fog. I also felt depleted of energy. I didn't want to argue, but God I felt as if we were spinning 'round in a bad communication cycle that if gone unchecked, we'd be in forever, getting nowhere! "Okay, Lynn...I get your point. You're pissed off at me."

"You're reading *that*? From me?"

I saw feigned innocence and that ticked me off. "Yeah! Sure am!" A sudden deep droning sound from the sky shut me up. Her too. I said softly, "Look, let's save all of this tension between us for later, until after we figure out what that thing is in the sky and can stop it, okay?"

"Fine, yeah, you're right." She turned away, continuing to scan the sky while intermittently trying to reach people in the downstairs lab on her iTablet.

Softly, I said: "Can you try getting a visual of Team-2 for me? I was supposed to meet them right about now, and in here, but obviously that's not happening." I had sent them an outmoded A-Okay emergency message but never heard back.

"Sure, *Regent* Manning," she said, emphasizing my title. "If I can get a good link. I guess you're used to people doing things for ya now. Maybe ya lost how to do things for yourself, being a *Regent* and all."

Now I heard distaste. I had to dodge the jab. "If you do that, Lynn, I can investigate if there's any solar flare or geomagnetic activity. I have a precarious connection to the Solar Dynamics Observatory (SDO) that'll admit me right away without jumping through hoops, and I'm trying to get some answers using an old program." As she began trying to get a visual of my Team-2 in another part of the lab, a planetary show hosted by the famous astrophysicist, Jacque Léglise appeared on my iTablet. He gave a brief tour of the sky with an exact latitude and longitude precision. After the show ended, I said as she dashed back next to me: "He's not predicting an eclipse. And SDO shows no solar prominences. He also had the current position of the Decagon Platform. It's increased its orbit and scanning Earth in depth. I need it to be scanning space!" I called in that message to the orbiting facility through a sliver of a connection.

First Communication

Lynn stopped me from closing the app entirely when she spotted something troubling. "Wait, this is unusual."

I zoomed in on a long line of light stretching from one of our solar satellites into the heart of disturbance. SDO showed the light to be a network of undefinable, elementary particles, aligning. "Wow—that convection is absorbing and altering solar energy! Using light! Maybe manipulating light?" I checked the iTablet. Scientists at the Decagon Platform had received the message but not replied. That's when I felt a lump of irrepressible excitement begin to well up inside of me. An alien contact...could it be?

"The central point in the storm *is* the locus of concentration." Lynn showed me images of the sky that people were streaming into social media sites. "And the anomaly is gradually enlarging..."

"But other than *it*, nothing else is up there." The screen went black. I wanted to end that sentence with the word, "yet," but forced myself to keep my mouth closed.

"Nothing? No way, Thornton! Photons don't behave that way unless they're being bombarded with antiparticles. *An, ti, par, ti, cles,* Thornton," she said. "From where?" Her eyes were wide, the splash of green in her heterochromia concentrated.

I was feeling overwhelmed too. "Damn, I hope that thing isn't going to affect the iTablet towers, lines, and I-Clouds or—"

"The electrical grids," she said. "Oh no! Everything's gonna shut down!"

I grabbed her and held her tightly, smelling the fruit smell of her hair. "Lynn—stop!" I let her go. She was trembling. I could see goose bumps on her arms. I scurried around to find a jacket. "This whole thing's probably a drone test gone bad, or a test pilot at the Nevada Test Range leaving one helluva bad contrail, or a little CERN mishap that scientists are probably working on to rectify." I knew we had nothing like that in the works. "Worst case, another foiled terrorist attack."

"Bastards! Damn terrorist bastards!" She put on the jacket and began crying.

J.P. Osterman

"I can't disagree with ya there," I said. "Hey, were you able to reach my Team-2? Maybe they have some news about what's going on. They work solely for The Regency and have access to restricted information." I wanted to give her something kinesthetic to do to divert her emotional mind.

She shook her head no. "One-World Media Site is down. I have a message pending in the Out Box though, but we have to wait until the connection opens in order for it to send. I bet people are concerned about you, Thornton, for your safety especially, even though I told them I was here with you…but that was before all *this* started happening."

For seconds, we riveted ourselves to the windowsill, glancing at the disturbance and everything outside growing more chaotic by the moment. People were bolting from buildings, staring at the sky, standing like statues in the quad, pointing at the cycling yellow and white disturbance. Some people dashed to their cars while crying out the names of their husbands, wives, children, and parents. Distant roads were turning into a honking traffic jams. There were car crashes and fender benders…buses and trucks running off the road. Drivers were trying to bypass all the long lines by speeding through grassy divides and barreling through fences. Helicopters and small planes from the nearby airport were sky bound, their abrupt launch sounds vibrating our windows.

What I had just conjectured was wrong. The anomaly was no weapons experiment or fighter pilot demonstration. Perhaps a CERN disaster then? A high altitude experiment of the General's or Stealth Force gone awry? But no one had informed The Regency of a pending atmospheric experiment or drone test. Then again, I had been busy for days with my project and research that I hadn't paid any attention to messages from the military or The Regency! I wished I had. Then again, the anomaly seemed centered almost directly above us…but Duke was way outside the approved experimental zone.

"Should we make a go of it too? Get outta here while we

First Communication

have the chance?" she asked, obviously concerned about exiting the city and not just the fourth-floor lab.

"No, I think we're better off staying here and at Duke," I answered. "We have one of the best science teams on the globe right here. Cutting edge. And this place is solid, the best renovation for experimental conditions. So don't worry, okay?"

Sighing, she said, "Yeah, you're right, sure."

Suddenly, my skin felt cold and tingling. "*Whew...burr*—it's chilly in here. Can't be the air system 'cause I haven't received any verbal update or warning."

Shivering, Lynn pointed at the phenomenon as if tracing a sign of the zodiac in the night sky. "What *is* that...that silver shape that's forming inside the cycling clouds? It looks like a heating element on an electrical stove. It's—it's rotating counterclockwise—"

"Cyclogenesis," I began, "definitely high-atmospheric dynamics are at play up there. Photons and cyclogenesis."

"Yeah, and something else," she said, her expression inquisitive.

I found two thick jackets, and we donned them as we continued watching the mesospheric anomaly. "That's no eclipse. That cyclone *has* to be magnetic, and electric, and definitely interacting with the solar wind. Wait—there *are* particles inside the disturbance!"

"Those particles we saw streaming in from the sun, and I bet they're attracting and interacting with dark matter. A gravitational anomaly!"

I agreed, and put those ideas into another Alert Image Message to send immediately to the lab downstairs. "See the spin force? That thing is affecting gravity. I think we're about to be hit with something big...really enormous."

"Yep." She tried activating a conference call on the iTablet.

But the Connectivity app kept flashing, "*Busy*; then, *Forwarding.*"

Lynn said: "Whatever the silver force is, it's gathering elements...a dust-grain formation, and the force of the formation is generating energy. Any second now, or a few minutes, we should be feeling its gravitational effects."

"Energy from where and that'll do what?" I tried Skyping with my on-site team at Arecibo or the Decagon Platform via the downstairs lab's IMAX transparent screen. "The cosmologists and astro-engineers *there* are probably assessing that thing *right now*! I bet they have this disturbance playing out in our graphics program and simulators. They're probably analyzing it *right now* with *every* electromagnetic spectrometer and device available." I was exaggerating hopefulness—a *real* defense mechanism to avoid facing the possibility of the world really ending.

"Well? Can't you get through to anyone using your Secret Regency connection?" asked Lynn, her shoulders rapidly rising and falling.

"Nothing, dead noise." I felt a twinge of helplessness—my mind slamming into a wall. I believed I could survive anything! Realizing I might be wrong, I said, "I remember the time you told me that I could solve problems faster than anybody…remember, Lynn?" I chuckled, trying now to be an entertainer.

Lynn waved at me and exhaled. "Oh—I was just a little mad that day. No, jealous." Suddenly, she stood straight up. The instruments on her lap clanked to the floor.

Terrified cries were coming from the halls outside our fourth floor lab. It was a rampage—people stampeding to the exits.

"We should get outta here…get downstairs to the main lab," I gestured. "That's the place where our best will be setting up." I glanced at several outside walkways where professors, students and security were carrying in and rolling in high-tech equipment. They were fighting against the exiting crowds as golf carts, bicycles, scooters and revving jeeps were speeding across the quad. Security and Enforcers were wielding batons and unleashing their guns at a few violent individuals who had no regard for people in front of them. "I

First Communication

never thought an emergency could come to this! People are ready to kill *anyone* in their path!"

She screamed; then she said, in a sad tone of voice that sounded as if she was giving up: "Thornton, I don't think there's a place on Earth, or below Earth, that we can hide and be safe from that cosmic thing. But I'm ready for it…whatever it's gonna do to us. Even if that storm means the end of the Earth." She dabbed her teary eyes. "You're here with me, Thornton, right now, and one of the few people I know who I'd want at my side when I die, even though you *are* a Regent."

I felt all ˙m breath leave my chest. That sounded derogatory, but I also felt relieved that she didn't hate me. "Lynn, really, we're *not* going to die. You're exaggerating."

Her face brightened like a haloed angry angel as static raised her blond eyebrows. A new type of energy was wafting into the room; and she wrapped her jacket tighter around her waist, pushed away her clumpy blond bangs, and stuck her hands on her hips. "This feels like the end," she said defiantly.

I guess I upset her. Looking like a titan avenger, she was definitely mustering up strength as a bristling animal to fight the turmoil in the sky. Then I received an old broadband converted e-message from the downstairs lab on the iTablet. Scientists and the military were aware of my location, but they needed me to stay put.

Lynn said: "I'm not giving up until I take my last breath, Thornton Seth Manning. Let's find out what that cosmic disturbance is and confront that hounding cosmic storm in the sky!"

In the distance, I spotted waterspouts. "Pillars of lake water…but they're not moving…"

Her panicked breaths were puffs of warm air in the chill. "Damn—I take back what I just said! That thing might have the power to lift up the Atlantic if it amasses enough energy. Hell with fighting it like I thought we could…we're all dead!" She ran out of the office.

"Lynn—come back!" No use. She was gone. I yelled into

the large screen to open up a conference feed again, but all I got was a repeat, *beeeeee...*" Useless. My Confidential iTablet that coulda secured me a top-line connection was out for virus removal. God what a day for *that* to happen! I wished we had some type of a global quantum computer system where I could access information instantly, bypass problem connections, eliminate the Ethernet, eradicate buffering, and interface with cloud servers.

Dr. Elisa Holton stuck her face inside the lab, shocking me. She was a Biomedical Engineer who had graduated at the top of her class from Duke's Pratt School of Engineering. I had just hired on a temporary basis to help me with my research results. After she told me she had bypassed Lynn in the hallways, she quickly said: "Regent Manning, the energy is altering space and matter, creating some type of channel. That's what NASA and DoD-International believe thus far. Duke University is on lockdown and implementing emergency protocol."

Running back into the room and bumping into Dr. Holton, Lynn said: "Elisa, what about the vaults containing experimental tissues and virus samples? If those vaults erupt, we could have a global breakout. That dry wind is at times roaring outside." She obviously knew Dr. Holton from another project because they were on a first-name basis.

Dr. Holton looked calm under the pressure-cooking event. "Every grad student is working to protect and move those samples, Lynn. I know they're important to you. Last year, Pratt finished an underground, T-2 storage facility in case we should experience another terrorist attack." She rubbed her pale face and the whites of her brown eyes reddened. It was obvious she hadn't seen sunlight in days. She'd been working for me that hard.

Two universities had hailed Dr. Elisa Holton a stickler for detail and an astute nerd of the absolute type. She told me she valued that label while some might interpret it as an indication that she'd devoted her life to running away from life by

First Communication

exchanging her past-time for innovation and research. They and everything matrix appeared to be her home and security. She had straight, shoulder-length, shiny brown hair and was wearing a starch-cream blouse and black A-line skirt. I met her over a conference call and hired her two days ago after receiving her transcripts from the College of Nanoscale Science and Engineering and Lynn's recommendation. Elisa Holton had been under tight quarantine there for two months while conducting research on bio-cellular nanobotics.

"Who woulda thought an emergency would be coming from the cosmos, huh, Lynn?" she asked.

"What's the protocol in the downstairs lab, Dr. Holton," I asked after Lynn and she exchanged words of comfort. If Lynn had confidence in Dr. Holton and knew her so well, I could trust Dr. Holton to give me the straight facts. Suddenly, I began worrying about the other forty-nine Regents. Had they found shelter? The Regency had its headquarters in Moscow this year. "Is the cosmic event manifesting only above the east coast or above other places around the globe as well, Dr. Holton?" I told her to inquire into their safety and their whereabouts.

As Lynn placed a few conference calls trying to get some answers, Dr. Holton began informing me of everything happening in the burgeoning downstairs lab. "We have just about every faculty member at Duke there, Sir." She fastened the Velcro straps of her iTablet to her wrist and glanced at the time. "The lab is emergency expanding. Its subterranean anterooms are rising and will connect with the main facility in two minutes." She tapped her iTablet. "When all rooms unite, we'll gain eight-thousand square feet for high-tech utilization." When she connected her iTablet to my center screen, hardware began synchronizing, and the downstairs lab began streaming information to me via the giant screen I had so much trouble activating. Still, we were receiving a bit of white intermittent fuzz—and a scrolling down of a horizontal line.

"This stuff *is* a Deep-Field scream of cosmic interference," I said as Dr. Holton and Lynn continued to connect my lab with the huge burgeoning facility downstairs. "I'm sure glad the lab's expanding. We're gonna need every bit of the best equipment to analyze that atmospheric anomaly and all its noise and nuances." When a face finally appeared on my giant lab screen, I ordered the temporary facilitator: "Please fly in General Bernstein. He's *the best* at streamlining data, assembling personnel and maintaining order. If not for General Bernstein, those terrorists back in 2057 woulda exploded ten *more* nukes in the stratosphere!" After three minutes of not seeing General Bernstein's face to confirm his whereabouts, I felt my patience wearing thin. I wanted to scurry down to the main lab—to take charge o'the place myself. But because of security protocol—that perhaps this cosmic anomaly was truly some type of new and high-tech terrorist attack—I needed to stay on the top fourth floor.

Roy, the temporary Lab Facilitator ordered me: "Regent Manning, The World needs you to broadcast your presence through the One-World Media Site ASAP. We have the Regency's standard Stage-1 Emergency alert going strong globally, but people need you, Sir, and the Regency, for guidance, leadership, and to instill hope. They need to see you're all right, Sir, even though you can't address them verbally because of the strong interference."

"That's why I'm doing my best to interconnect all the hardware in here to you people in the lab, Roy," Dr. Holton snapped back at him. She took several flash drives, adaptors, Rip Jaws, graphics darts and recovery pins out of her backpack and tossed some to Lynn. We began pushing, pulling around, and linking desktops, portable processing systems, and small cloud storage towers. We looked as if we were assembling a systems warehouse for a window display! Dr. Holton was moving so quickly; she was obviously familiar with the most advanced systems, software and connectivity devices...much of which were in the experimental stage 'cause they flared on right away.

"Nothing, *nothing* can happen to you, Sir," Roy said, when

ten images of him flashed on in the room. "Where you're at, on the fourth floor, is the best location. Please, Regent Manning, remain in that location." The he faded off-screens.

Now half the lab resembled a U-shaped computer facility.

"Roy is right, Thornton." Lynn's lips had a nippy bluish blush. The air was frosty cold.

"I agree, Sir, and I've also been ordered to give you this firearm." Stopping what she was doing, Dr. Holton handed me a semiautomatic revolver. "I was instructed by General Bernstein, in a message that died before I could channel the feed over to you, to give this gun to you to use just in case all of this is some type of terrorist attack."

I think I gave Dr. Holton and Lynn the most helpless look as I glanced from them to the gun. I didn't have the guts to tell them that I had never fired a weapon. "Fine, I'll take it, but I pray I don't have to use it." After a stun-faced and lost student peeked into the lab and asked for fire extinguishers, Lynn left to help people across the hallway.

In addition to being an *outstanding* research leader—from what several of her references depicted, including Lynn's—Dr. Elisa Holton carried herself with confidence as if she had spent years in the military, although she appeared shy around me, with a tendency to look downward when I talked to her instead of looking me in the eye. Bashfulness or insecurity? Around Lynn, Elisa Holton was different. If I hadn't ever met her, I would have thought she was General Bernstein's assistant, except for her white lab coat. And if not for her brown hair, slightly taller physique, and pale face, I would have mistaken her for Lynn's sister, although I remember Lynn telling me that she only had one sibling, a brother, Norlin Altmin. He was a Washington, D.C. Enforcer whom I personally appointed a few years ago after The World voted to eliminate all law enforcement agencies and established the Global Enforcer Agency on April 8, 2058.

After Dr. Holton finished as much as she said she could accomplish, she pulled open the door that a strong breeze kept trying to close on her. She kicked the door open and it thudded into its metal knocker. The wall shook. "I received a message from a scientist in the downstairs facility when our outgoing ones sent."

"What does it say?"

"Faculty are assembling all sort of high-tech equipment from their departments to add to what's already down in the lab—3D screens, portable tablets, glass monitors, cube data bases, table monitors—the best," Dr. Holton said.

Then I thought about a possible power outage that had to occur at any moment. "What about generators?"

"Two of them are working right now, Sir, and ten more are being bused in," she replied. "I just received a secure link between my iTablet and the lab and I'm downloading the special app. In a minute or so, depending on connectivity and lack of interference, we should have full-figure conferencing."

First Communication

Chapter 3 - Nowhere To Hide

Lynn returned and out of breath. "What a mess out there! People are racing everywhere in search of places to hide from the anomaly." Then she told Dr. Holton that IT techs needed her to synchronize with the Pratt center. "We have no idea of the long-term effects of that cosmic anomaly on DNA. The biology department needs you, Elisa, to stream incoming information to the global database." As Dr. Holton was about to leave, she toppled back into the office to escape a crowd of charging students. Lynn helped her to her feet as she received an urgent message on her iTablet. Lynn read it like Lotto numbers. "Experts from NOAA and TTNWeb are on their way here to Duke, Thornton. And planes with probe devices and slicker drones are heading toward the—" She paused with a look of confusion on her face. "Well, thus far, everyone's been calling the stratospheric event 'the phenomenon,' or, 'the cosmic anomaly,' or, 'the disturbance'."

"Those terms are mild for it and what we're experiencing," chimed in Lynn.

Affirming the slight joke, Dr. Holton said, "Anyway, craft have launched from carriers and bases around the globe and are heading straight for it." She showed us a launch on her iTablet. "Langley, Hanscom, Bolling, Taverny and Osan launched fifty craft."

Several sophisticated sites were streaming to me their responses. But what I found most interesting was a quick interruption from the Decagon Platform. Right that very moment, they had the Rio Scale of alien contact at *3* with an *Intermediate* level of importance! That meant that several scientists on the station believed that the anomaly was a directional beam designed by someone or something to draw attention. My hand shaking, I messaged them back: *Let me know when you bump it up to Outstanding.* After I closed out that site, I read more messages to Lynn and Dr. Holton: "Cyber Command International's pointing every global scan toward the sky for Very Long Baseline Interferometry to obtain a 3D image of the phenomenon's composition."

Logging into another of her science websites, Lynn said, "Observatories are exchanging data and sending *us* data as they're positioning JWST, ATLAST, and Cosmic Quest to analyze the anomaly as well. That's *your* specialty, Thornton."

"And I just communicated with the Decagon Platform. So all our *best* technology is in action *everywhere* and synchronizing *everywhere*," I said. "Please, Dr. Holton, check on The Regency. I wanna know how my colleagues are doing. A global-wide response the likes of what we just received *had* to have originated from one or more of them. We also need measurements of that cosmic mass…and are there any others manifesting anywhere else?"

"I'll check, Sir," she said, "and then I'll leave for downstairs after I find an answer."

Lynn said: "Recon craft are on course to designated locations, but the officials directing and craft from several sites around the globe are having them do an Alpha Check, just a survey of the anomaly from a safe distance. We're trying to get as many readings, images and measurements as possible so we can know what we're dealing with, what's driving the thing, and what we need to do to stop it, *if* we need to stop it at all."

First Communication

"Hey—maybe we don't even need to be stopping it at all," Dr. Holton said.

"What?" Lynn exclaimed.

"Just hear me out for a second," she replied. "There are so many effects, and hazards, and ramifications…consequences!"

"Hurry," I said, "because we really don't have *five* seconds."

"Well, maybe the high-altitude storm's just that," Dr. Holton began. "An innocent mixture of conflicting streams that haven't surged for centuries…and no one ever noticed because the phenomenon either occurred during the night; or if it occurred, no one bothered to document it." Her iTablet blasted out a jingle and she answered it. More chaos was breaking out on the outside quad. Her face contorted in a puzzled expression. "Oh gosh…*ahh*, whooo?"

"Who, *what*, Dr. Holton?" My chest was starting to feel heavy as if I was diving in a hundred feet of water. "Damn, I wish at least that I had an outdated iPhone!"

She showed me the special DoD app that was still in the process of initializing video conferencing and gestured that the military's Skype stream should connect us to the lab soon. "I just heard, Regent Manning, that the Regency is safe. However, a small group, grounded in Moscow, has put Enforcers around the world on alert *and* our Global Oceanic Forces too."

Lynn peeked over her shoulder from one of the large screens she was monitoring that was streaming in vital data. "Telescopes scattered throughout the solar system as well as the Taurus-Littrow lunar array are showing the anomaly blending in with space. Only the unstable energy—and force—swirling around the anomaly is unstable."

"It's blending in with space?" I asked.

"Lynn said, "Another dimension intruding on this one maybe?"

Competing with the outside noises, I said loudly, "Or a Schwarzschild wormhole. Perhaps a Lorentzian wormhole, but from what we know about wormholes, any one would have blown out our sun before we even realized it was there."

J.P. Osterman

My head began aching from having to synthesize answers to questions that theorists have been sweating over for years.

"Sir—everyone assembling downstairs in the lab is as stunned as you are," Dr. Holton said, showing a satellite image of the phenomenon streaming globally. "The backside view *is* imaging space. The front of the anomaly is spiraling. It's emitting energy and absorbing energy simultaneously."

"Definitely Magnetic and electric but without radioactivity," Lynn said. "Otherwise, we'd all be fried."

"It's like something is cutting into *our* space," Dr. Holton said. "But that's impossible. That would mean the act is causative...with an effect as a goal."

That scared me. "Part black hole then? Could someone have initiated it?" I checked the long line of transparent monitors that were displaying Top-Secret facilities and the Ground Penetrating Radar Center. "No one generated a black hole. Not terrorists...not anyone in the scientific community...and *not* the Global Weapons Institute. And CERN would have requested that The World vote on such a project as that." I knew the threat was real—and tangible.

Dr. Holton said: "Earth is like a lamb out in space, no—a delicate Gaia. Anything—anyone or any force—could pluck the petals of life right from under us...leaving us a floating cinder, like Mercury."

"Don't say that, Elisa!" Lynn snapped. "That sounds so hopeless! That *can't* happen!"

"Sorry," she said softly, sighing.

After running a few sentences of calming interference, I said: "So the scientists downstairs *do* believe the atmospheric anomaly *is* dangerous, or at least they've found *some* evidence that it's destructive, huh?"

Outside, a slow, low thunderous rumble resounded like the flow of a sonic boom.

"That answers that question!" I said.

Lynn gasped. "We have to presume so! Look at the darkness out there...and the weather's definitely changed for the worse." She gestured toward one weather screen after she

First Communication

blew warmth into her fingers. "Pulse-Doppler radar is tracking the formation of the mass. Data is translating in the downstairs lab." She continued to search the internet—downloading visuals and data that she then streamed downstairs.

Dr. Holton's Skype app initialized, and we began video conferencing with scientists, the military, and our top-level global officers down in the lab. I began downstreaming them the results of all my cosmic research from multibeam arrays all over the world. Before all this happened, I was working to stream those same results to specific astronomical sites so they could access all the cosmic data my team had collected from all the high-orbiting telescopes and ground multi-beam receivers. Streaming the most important results to the downstairs lab was taking longer than I wanted. Our internet connection was as unpredictable as a worm on an angler's hook! I remember getting so frustrated when a line of processor screens froze that I just about toppled the cylinder systems to the floor when I was trying to shake them to active mode!

That's when I noticed an important reading...a measurement so unbelievable. "The barometric pressure dropped 4.3 pounds per square inch but then returned to its former reading. Gust-fronts and rear-flanking winds are superimposing, but without all the destructive winds." I asked the team responsible for atmospheric measurements: "How many miles up is the anomaly? Where's its center over Earth? How far away are the planes from those gray streaks that seem to be creating a—a space whirlpool?"

Lynn launched another video-conferencing app, and General Bernstein's face appeared on the large middle screen in the quad-shaped monitor assemblage.

"Finally...I see the best there is!" I said. It was the first feeling of security I had felt in hours! "General, stream everything that's going on in the atmosphere and between us to the One-World Media Site. People need to see, here, and know *everything* that's happening while you're also streaming them the Emergency Alerts."

J.P. Osterman

After General Bernstein called out the order to a small camera crew in the background, he replied: "I hope I live up to that compliment you gave me, Sir, but now on to the urgent matter."

"Yes, please!" I pressed him.

"The epicenter of the cosmic anomaly is 120 kilometers south of D.C., but it's *not* like a hurricane, Sir," The General began. "There is no eye-of-the-storm. The planes and drones that are analyzing the anomaly are keeping their distance of a minimum of ten kilometers. At this point, they're only surveying, accessing, measuring and recording data. There is *no* directive yet from anyone in the Regency to proceed with a nuclear launch."

"Nuclear! No!" Dr. Holton shouted, coming in between us. I motioned for her to wait.

The General said, "The anomaly is holding at fifty two miles above Earth."

"Good," I said, "and for now, let's *not* consider anything nuclear, General."

Lynn and Dr. Holton sighed in relief as they continued to work with our computer hardware, expand our lab's Ethernet connections, and activate picture-in-picture apps. The monitors in the U-shaped, quad formations began to look like tall, multi-picture walls with eye-activated surround sound.

I had to agree that a nuclear solution, at least for now, was completely wrong. "Those terrorist have done enough ozone damage, and that layer's still bleeding out."

"Yes, Sir." General Bernstein took off his cap, and a few strands of his salt-and-pepper hair sliced the air. He was a tall thin man who looked nerdish, bookish, and harmless. However, after I observed him interrogating terrorists, I realized I was fortunate to be on his good side.

"Please inform the Regency about what's happening, General," I said. "I want to know several things about that anomaly. Is it just above Virginia? Or are there other of these—these cosmic channels materializing around the globe?"

"Just above Virginia, Sir," said General Bernstein. "But

First Communication

that doesn't mean that more can't appear. I think we're realizing that what we believed was impossible is very real. Anything can happen where physics is concerned, Sir. But we're working on solutions."

"Keep problem solving then…and I want to be in full sight of all those screens in the background, General," I said. "That's all any of us can do—think and work—until we discover more about that anomaly." I knew I should be down there with them: all the scientists, some of my old colleagues, the military, and a few famous and not so famous Chief Technology Officers (CTOs), the brightest and best from around the globe. Then I remembered *my* data. I couldn't leave that! I needed it downstreamed into Duke's database. Abandoning years of results on satellite imagery, electromagnetic frequencies, and graphics would have been a waste of billions of dollars. I told him, "General, as soon as I can enter all my passwords and begin streaming all the secondary data I didn't stream to cloud systems, I'll get right down there."

"Yes, Regent Manning," he said.

The sounds of swirling helicopter blades began reverberating through the walls and into my chest. Grabbing the desk, I realized that the vibrations were nothing compared to what that cosmic anomaly could wield should it penetrate Earth's atmosphere. It was numbing anxiety, nearly uncontrollable. I grabbed Lynn's hand. She hugged me. Dr. Holton screamed. One of the towering screen systems was inching its way to the toppling point. Lynn began helped her hold up the conglomeration of screens that were blaring images from all around the world. No sooner did one piece of hardware stabilize but then another dislodged. We couldn't keep propping 'em all back up. We had to let some topple to the floor where they cracked into pieces of glass that crunched like brittle under our shoes.

"We have more defense personnel and CTOs landing right now to help, Sir," Bernstein said loudly, through the noises of helicopters landing and then launching. "I feel like you look right now, Regent Manning." He cleared his throat, and the muscles under his jaw appeared to thicken in anger as he continued softly: "We're all on edge down here, so are people around the globe. Regents are appearing on several networks, broadcasting the anomaly alongside the media. They're also streaming live through our One-World Media Site, trying to calm the public, until connections go haywire. Luckily, all those revamped fiber optics and cell phone towers have By-Pass and Alternate connectivity so if someone can't receive an individual live-stream, he or she can learn what's happening in a safe-haven community setting. All satellite TV, GPS, and *anything* satellite driven is disabled. Everyone feels as if they're standing at Death's door with that thing cycling in the air! It's not visible from everywhere, but it might as well be with all our optics homing in on it. But we're working our hardest with the best-of-the-best to discover what that anomaly is and stop its expansion—"

"Or control it," I interrupted. I had quickly begun inputting my security codes into the cylindrical super-computer pads next to the office. Finally, Upstream-mode activated!

The wind was intensifying. The windowpanes began rattling hard. That anomaly's forces could blow the choppers right into the quad, turning them into flying shrapnel that could kill students and faculty. We were at the onset of a strong gravitational and electrical effect, the beginning of something great even though the disturbance was over fifty miles high.

"Empty those craft, General, and tell the pilots to take off fast!"

"Yes, Regent Manning," Bernstein said. "Sir—I need to leave now to usher them to their positions. Do you need anything—any guards or campus police?"

I couldn't even think about my own safety, and Lynn and Dr. Holton suddenly refused to leave. Then I noticed expensive and rare objects all around us: rows of cylindrical server farms, vital experiments, and delicate prototypes on shelves. Researchers must have been working on everything so

First Communication

hard and for so long in the Materials section. "General, I don't need guards to protect me, but I could use a few people to help me secure some delicate things in here."

"I'll see what I can do," he said. Then campus guards began inundating him with messages from students and faculty who were crying and vying for assistance. In the background, several engineers were disassembling the new body scanner the FDA had just approved. Several software writers were arguing with scientists over vital components. They were grabbing wafers and ionizers out of one another's hands. They all appeared to be inventing probes to send up in the next rocket launch.

"General, I'm putting you in full charge of that entire Floor-1 center so you don't have to request Regency approval for every decision you make," I said, streaming to him my code.

He had a shell-shocked expression on his face. "Sir—I—I—"

"That's a directive, General. I'm the only Regent around who really knows what's happening, so I can confer that authority on you."

"Yes, Sir," he said in a humble low reply.

"I trust you'll do what needs to be done in case our connection severs. Furthermore, I can't do what I need to do here *and* manage Floor-1 simultaneously."

"Yes, Sir." General Bernstein began enlarging a picture-within-a-picture showing several problems. "The biology department's fighting with the physics department over parts and equipment. Seems everyone has an idea, along with a *huge* ego, on what he or she believes should be developed! I sure could use an expert to mediate between the two departments. I could use someone who knows these scientists and researchers here at Duke and who's a bridge builder and problem solver."

I noticed Dr. Holton was about finished propping up screens that were showing views of the anomaly from several incoming perspectives. A few large screens were projecting color lines and static, but I knew they were on Wait mode until another source could send information or measurements. "I'm sending down Dr. Holton to help you, General. The biology department also needs her, so she can be the mediator between them and that physics department."

"Elisa knows the physics behind the scanware of that C-Body Imager," Lynn added.

"I sure do," she said, proudly.

I said to Dr. Holton who was rubbing warmth into her covered arms, "It seems that *everyone* needs you now, and fast!"

After giving out a shy laugh, obviously feeling uneasy with compliments, she drank some water and said into one of the conferencing screens: "I know that imager, General. We conducted clinical trials with it last year. I can convert the body app to a data-stream program. It's just a software re-write, Sir. They don't have to dissect the entire walk-through machine!"

Lynn turned her networking iTablet my way, so both Bernstein and I could get a view of some downstreaming information from space. "Dr. Holton needs the data from these drones. We're receiving abstract code, 3D shapes, and multi-faceted fractal expressions. Molecular? Biological? *Hmm*…you'd sure know if you could analyze these, Elisa!"

"But I don't have clearance to access the genetic databases so I can compare what's in storage to what I find and disseminate, General," she said, helplessly sighing.

General Bernstein straightened up tall, apparently taking pride in the duty of his authority. "Regent Manning's order is as good as a Black Ops Clearance, Dr. Holton. Come on down!" Lynn patted her goodbye on the shoulder, and Dr. Holton raced out of the office.

Before the door closed, I noticed that the halls were becoming treacherous waters. From several security screens, Lynn and I could see that students and faculty were crowding the stairs, elevators and lockers. Going to the doorway, I tried to slow down several panicked and bloodied people, but they didn't even acknowledge me in spite of my Regency insignia.

First Communication

The General called me back over to the screen so he could convey an emergency. "Regent Manning, I'm keeping our video conferencing on Live-mode so you can continue to see what's going on down here, but I have to go. I'm needed for drone programming and to manage another launch." His screen presence extinguished, revealing scientists assembling hardware and techs racing around the Floor-1 facility to obtain parts. Dr. Holton walked into the lab and began assisting engineers.

Turning back to my job in our fourth-floor lab, I lifted up toppled processors and screens on my way to the tall rows of server farms containing all my data. The downstream had begun, but I still had more codes to enter. I was running out of time. With all the wild vibrations occurring, I realized my data would soon corrupt. Two cylindrical processors had already shattered! I had to have given Lynn the saddest dog eyes ever as I asked her: "Can you help me? I know you want to go, *need* to go, but—" The words, 'I need you,' stuck like pizza cheese on my tongue as I gestured to the line of green flashing, long flowing data collectors. In the past, we were a good team. I was hoping she might feel sentimental and help me. Still, from the sarcastic words she had said earlier, something had changed. What exactly? I was clueless.

The power of the choppers' engines launching out of the quad vibrated our building as lightning cracked through the air. Luckily, the aluminum hardware of the server farms stopped the lightning from striking our building. Outside, people weren't as fortunate as us inside! Now-and-then, the bolts struck a high pole, generator, or cell tower, causing aerial arcs and flashes, loud cracks and pops. Sparks were flying as shrieking students and faculty raced through the quad seeking refuge. Some were diving to the ground and clinging to grass, shrubs, and tree trunks. Some people were dashing behind cars and vehicles. Electrocutions were happening right and left!

Dr. Holton ran back into the room and said through coughs and deep breaths: "Regent Manning, the internet's down, again, and *ha*—I, *ha*—downstairs, we're measuring sferics, attenuation, impulse-response from the magnetosphere. Floor-1 is linking with the two lab drones that are right up next to the phenomenon, circling it, analyzing it, the Zephyr and Solar Eagle. They've linked with the Space Weather Prediction Center. Very Long Baseline Interferometric images are starting to come in. But we only have an outline. The scientists at data collection centers need more time to process what we're receiving." Her face took on a pained expression. "We're thinking…as hard as it is to believe right now…that we're receiving signals from *beyond* our solar system," she whispered, those last words sounding emphatic.

When she ran inside and re-aligned the main U-shaped screen, General Bernstein's image materialized. "We're hitting the anomaly with infrared and ultraviolet Ems to see if those wavelengths affect it."

I added, "And include the visible spectrum!"

Dr. Holton jabbed her iTablet against her waist a few times because the connection fizzled. After Bernstein's image re-solidified, she said, "Regent Manning, based on what they receive from the Zephyr and Solar Eagle, General Bernstein might initiate a strike along the perimeter of the anomaly to try to dissipate it."

"A *friendly* strike I hope, General," Lynn said, in a cautionary tone of voice. "After all, we really don't know what that atmospheric thing is. To strike it and eliminate it could prevent us from learning something profound about the universe."

I had to shout through another loud rumble. "Lynn has a point, General. Whatever that phenomenon is, we have to agree that nothing on Earth, or from Earth, or around Earth could have started it."

General Bernstein's straight nose wrinkled—a baffled expression. "You mean alien—"

We were getting cut off, again. "Don't attack, General!" I shouted into the screen. I don't think he heard me through the interference. I also didn't want to face the possibility of an

First Communication

alien appearance just yet. "Tell General Bernstein not to attack, Dr. Holton." In the time she was gone to Floor-1, I tried to call him another way, but the black, outdated office phone wouldn't work in spite of Lynn's genius skill at wiring and re-routing things.

After returning from her mad sprint to the lab, she said: "The General's not striking the anomaly, Sir. He told me to tell you that he wouldn't do that—*never* without your consent, even though you did put him in complete charge of the place."

"That's good news," I said as Lynn and I continued to input stream commands so my data could finish its complete transfer.

"Sir, there's more." We stopped everything when I heard her urgent tone of voice. She continued: "Floor-1 is now streaming live on a secure, high-resolution, fiber-optic network to Goddard, Georgetown, and Columbia—but with a serious precaution." Dr. Holton tapped her iTablet and then swept the 180° view of the downstairs lab on to a large transparent screen.

"What's so serious?" I asked as Lynn raced to the screen and began inserting more Ethernet pins. The static was wild, the screens flaring on but then extinguishing—so frustrating! But Lynn's interventions were helping to correct the ebbing and eddying reception.

Several 3D shows flared on inside all four U-shaped screen zones. Floor-1 was sending a Red Alert and Attack bar around the shows they were streaming.

Her iTablet streaming with Floor-1's systems, Dr. Holton began sweeping more images from Earth's orbit, atmosphere, and military bases to the large screens. "Every high-tech university around here is analyzing that space convection. Everyone's waiting for more incoming results from the planes and drones. And we're video conferencing with just about every agency—the DoD, CIA, NRO, NSA."

Workers inside each bustling facility appeared on more screens. They were retrieving printouts, conversing through ear buds, and conferencing with General Bernstein and scientists in the downstairs lab.

"In case we're way off base and this anomaly is a WMD of some sort," Dr. Holton began, "our military has Global COINTELPRO pointing all its hardware at it. For this reason, General Bernstein is coding the downstairs lab *Floor-1* for security purposes. Any Top-Secret or Confidential information should go through *Floor-1-at-Channel200-dot-military*. That's Floor-1's Black Ops address. If you give the A-Okay, he says he'll activate a separate Live Stream with The World and Regents who are calling in. That way, people can see what's happening."

I opened up the secure line Lynn initialized and said, "General, Floor-1 Live-Stream is a Go. But continue the Emergency Broadcasts. People around the globe should move to their specified Safe Havens they've been using during emergencies since the attacks."

"Yes, Sir," General Bernstein replied, and then Dr. Holton left to return to Floor-1.

Suddenly, the entire research center began vibrating. I heard loud cracks, like guns firing, and thunder that sounded as if it was right up against my ears. Lynn and I raced to the wall and glued ourselves it. I watched helplessly as my cylindrical server farms came tumbling down like dominos. The towers of U-shaped screens that we had worked so hard to prop up finally fell, whacking the splitting floor. Plaster from the ceiling began spraying everywhere like candy spilling out of a piñata. I thought the earth might split open as I once saw in one of those Photo-shopped cataclysmic movies! Clasping hands, we stumbled toward the door while dodging books and plaques.

Lynn and I both called to droves of people scattering in complete disorder in the hallways: "Everyone—stop! Get to a room!" We were enmeshed elbow-to-shoulder in the stampede toward multiple exits.

In the center of the hallway where we found ourselves stuck, we noticed people stuffing themselves into the distant elevators. Shouting officers were pushing horror-stricken

First Communication

people back, forbidding them to enter the overcrowded boxes. Sputtering while closing, one elevator wrenched as it skipped a notch downward—its pulley snapping. I could hear whipping noises cracking through the air…then terrifying screams. I knew that steel box hit bottom at full speed four floors down…most likely crashing at the rim of Floor-1. Those people there were safe…that tungsten facility capable of sustaining the energy output of two nuclear bombs! All around, people were dying exponentially since the onset of the cosmic anomaly. Then, several spots along the floor split open, sending screaming and shrieking students and faculty into a dust-bellowing abyss.

Lynn and I had no choice but to retrace a careful path back to the lab office. In no way could we leave the building or make it to Floor-1. As Lynn and I continued to ram against terrified people, we noticed a smoking lab and flaming Bunsen burners. Lynn heard screams coming from inside.

"We have to help them," she maintained, trying to heave open the door that stampeding people were closing.

I said, "We have to get to those shut-off values behind the instructor's desk first!"

Safely inside, and while turning off the gas, we noticed two crying students huddling inside a long open closet. They said they weren't hurt, just terrified. I covered them with thick layers of white coats while Lynn rubbed their arms, talked to them, and comforted them with her uncanny ability to encourage people. One student an old iPhone he had taken apart but just reassembled. The other student figured out a way to activate an old email icon and send out an S.O.S. text. Lynn praised them for their fix-it prowess!

Meanwhile, the air turned to a weird frigid frostiness. A strange static began rippling across our skin. The students huddled deeper into their tight ball as Lynn and I sat between them and the open lab. Items on the tables, lab implements, plates—*everything* metal—began rising and then slamming back down. We thought some objects might strike us and do some horrible damage! The entire lab—the whole *building* from what we were overhearing people scream outside—had become like a knife throwing performance, only the force behind the wielding implements was invisible.

After minutes of taking cover—protecting ourselves with any plastics we could get our hands on—Lynn and I had an idea. If fluctuating magnetism was responsible for the levitation, perhaps wild electricity might stop it. Racing around the room while dodging flying instruments, we gathered several Tesla coils and positioned them at strategic points throughout the lab, creating a counterforce, and hoping that act might stabilize the metal-tossing event. Turning our experimental system on, we saw that the electrical safety net worked. The room calmed, the objects fell softly to the floor. We then returned our attention back to the cosmic anomaly prickling our skin with static and a stinging chill. We had to get back to the office where we could reconnect with Floor-1. After tossing the students a medical kit, typing in Floor-1's secure channel into their old iPhone, and assuring them we'd return to help them if someone else didn't, Lynn and I secured the gas and water lines. At least we believed we had stopped one horrible explosion from occurring.

Standing in the doorway on our way out, I held in my breath tightly and began sidling along the wall toward the lab. I had an idea and kept shouting for Lynn to follow me. "Take the shortcut through room 10!" She had to have remembered that! I traced the art deco wall trim with my fingers toward room 10. The lights were flickering. Crying, screaming, shrieking people were charging the main exits. I heard metals tanging and clattering from the wild changes in gravity. I saw shiny metal keys and trinkets bobbing in the air like wind chimes. Then I stopped dead when I heard a loud snapping sound. Then more cracking! The ceiling and roof were rupturing! I was at the top of the stairs—paused, with my breath in my throat and my heart beat under my ears—waving for Lynn to join me. Her face looked like the head on a Jack-in-the-box. She kept jumping up and down, obviously trying to keep her eyes on me.

First Communication

"No—that way will kill us!" she kept yelling.

"No—come on!" I believed I knew more than she did, but I hadn't been in those hallways for years. I hadn't considered any type of renovation.

In the thick of our argument, I heard a giant snapping sound under my feet. The floor began jolting like tectonic plates clashing. I was bouncing off screaming people right and left! Someone clawed my face! I could hardly breathe. For a second, I thought my arm snapped. Unable to hang on to anything to keep from plunging down a flight of collapsing steps, Lynn grabbed me. I started seeing her as tiny spots in my eyes! Someone hit me.

"This way!" she shouted. Then she began coughing. Bits of ceiling were striking our heads like a hard rain.

We were holding on for dear life to a handicap railing, but it was splintering off the wall like a toothpick. The granite steps were lifting and colliding. The mortar was pulverizing into plumes of dust. Suddenly, the wall and room in front of us blew out. All I could hear was the howling brisk wind and the screams of people falling to their deaths. All I could feel was Lynn's tight grip on my forearm. I held on to her for my life as she pulled me back to safety. Trying to keep her hair from whipping into my stinging eyes, I looked into at the sky. High in the atmosphere, I could see swirling, bright, yellow-and-white arms of clouds that looked like a small galaxy spiraling in the darkness.

Lynn shouted, "It's like we're at the center of some type of chamber!"

I shouted back: "Hold on! The air'll stabilize soon!" I had noticed a pattern in the magnetic and gravitational output of the anomaly.

Grabbing on to rebar and holding on with all our energy, we saw helpless people fly right by us...soaring uncontrollably to their deaths. If not for Lynn, one of them woulda been me! They were screaming for help, but we couldn't do anything to save them. There wasn't enough rebar to grab on to before the suction swept them away like an ocean rip tide. Part of the upper three stories had broken apart. Letting go meant we'd be swept away along with them. I saw pained, agonizing, and terrified expressions on victims' faces. Their bodies were like spirits wafting into a vacuum of an abyss. Clawing our way over globs of debris—my fingers numb and bleeding from trying to cling on to brick and mortar—we ran through water from ceiling fire extinguishers. Finally, we reached the lab and I kicked the door shut behind us.

I grabbed a support beam and breathed in relief. "We made it—but *whew* am I thirsty."

"Me too," Lynn said. She began kicking planks of wood, obviously in search of the small refrigerator. "There!" She took out two bottles of water, threw me one, and we began gulping down the cool liquid.

Feeling overwhelming relief in spite of my stinging fingers, sore arm, and cramping muscles, I said, "These structural beams you said you hated because they always interfered with our experiments. They saved this room from collapsing! *Whew*...we're safe!"

Laughing, she shrugged as she patted a bandage on her arm. "Okay...so I was wrong 'cause I didn't have eyes that could see into the future, Thornton." For seconds all we could do was to gulp down the refreshing liquid as if we were quenching a desert thirst.

Looking around in the frosty chill of the disheveled lab, I took stock of the damage. The data cylinders I had tried so desperately to protect and stream the remainder of my data were gone. I was so pissed off! In the time since we had attempted an escape, a quarter of the ceiling had fallen. I could see a few two-by-fours, pipes and wire. The smoke alarm was still intermittently blaring, so I picked up a board and slashed it out of its socket. As that extinguished, another high-pitch whirr began wreaking havoc on our inner ears. Wincing, Lynn fell down and covered her head.

I spotted blood on my shoulder. "Something's changed with that cosmic anomaly."

"Sound waves!" she shouted. "High-frequency! My ears!

First Communication

Feel, exploding!"

"Hold on!" I hollered. I had to think of something…began looking around for something to help her; and I felt stupid, like a failure. I hated feeling so vulnerable for not being able to solve that damn cosmic puzzle! I kept touching and stepping through dust, wood splinters, glass, silicon hardware, and beeping exposed processors! I remember thinking: "If I ever make it outta this, I'll make sure I set everything in place…do as much as I can in advance to prepare for disasters and to predict the possible effects for each and every *possible* scenario. Then, perhaps I can stop disasters before one ever happens again.

Just as I was about to give up the hunt, I remembered several good earphones I had seen on the wall, straddling over a crate full of equipment. Running over, I picked up two new Shure prototypes, put one on and threw the other to Lynn. I saw the purest look of relief waft over her face as all the pain seemed to fade away. I was becoming grateful for every bit of luck, fortune, divine intervention…*whatever* that was coming our way and saving us. Still, we had no conferencing connection for the iTablets we discovered buried under two large busted screens. Everything with a sensor was dead or *beep-beeping* calls of malfunctioning. Through an obviously experimental ear-bud connection, at least Lynn and I could talk to each other and hear each other without our eardrums exploding from all the high-frequency vibrations.

Then, I recognized real armor from my past—my $7,500.00 oak William IV writing table inside my small old office. Before I left, I gave the antique desk to the research team as a thank you gesture after finishing another one of my satellite projects for Arecibo. I don't know how I managed to muster up a laugh at a time like that, but I remember chuckling after Lynn and I kicked through piles of debris and slid under that sturdy safe-haven.

I said, "God—I'm glad I spent my last bit of my dad's inheritance on this!"

Lynn said, "You had a giving spirit then, Thornton."

J.P. Osterman

What? What does she mean by 'had'? I was about to voice my irritation until the air grew suddenly colder. Feeling terrified of leaving our huddle but needing to find out what was happening with the cosmic anomaly, we slowly came out from under the desk and peeked out the long picture window overlooking a bit of the quad. We had to be on guard for flying metals and occasionally dodge falling debris. Gravity was levitating what we perceived as innocuous iron-infused objects into tumbleweeds or projectiles! Outside on the quad, we could see dislodged poles, crashed cars, and people careening through the darkness to avoid lightning strikes and tiny ionized restrikes that cracked through the air like Spiderman's white webs. I felt so helpless and powerless, again. Neither Lynn nor I could do a thing to help them…or the poor howling dogs and alarmed whining cats.

"Thornton, you are a Regent, "Lynn began, in a matter of fact tone, "and people will need your leadership when we do finally contact Floor-1. You should remain under cover…out of harm's way." She was just trying to protect me, but I believed she was seeing me as weak.

The windowpanes began rattling, again. The huge picture window I just had "to have" while visiting the research team last year was morphing into our firing squadron. I wished I woulda opted for the office down the hall without a view. But then again, that place was just off the stairs, probably rubble and open to the brutal outdoors. I realized that Lynn and I had only seconds before we'd encounter a cut-glass eruption.

Then Lynn pointed at a reflective material at the opposite end of the lab. "I took an idea you had two years ago, Thornton, and a few of us developed a nano-repellant cloth. Maybe it'll work against glass. We programmed it to do that, but the processor running the app is down. What a way to get results, huh, than to put an experiment into action!" Crawling over debris, she retrieved a large colorful blanket. It was shining and silk soft…as if the fabric was exuding 3D, reading my biometrics, and constantly morphing to accommodate my physical needs. I told her that such a material might have been

First Communication

like Joseph's coat of many colors from the Old Testament. She whispered and winked, "God works in mysterious ways, I guess."

I cocooned us in the large blanket. "Only time'll tell if this stops a flood of glass!"

As dust began pinging off the cloth, she shouted happily and said, "This blanket *is* a working repellant, but I hope it can also save us from frost bite 'cause cripes am I cold!" Her teeth were chattering and her fingers quivering when she stuck her hand out of our cover.

Hearing the double pane windows clanking and crackling, I said: "The window's breaking! Duck!"

She shouted, "If this fabric protects us, Thornton, you can write me a recommendation to fund further research *if* we make it outta here alive...*if* we survive the anomaly." She laughed, but it was a half-frozen guttural chuckle from being so nervous and scared.

I held her closely. "You bet, Lynn." I wanted to keep thinking positively while also being reassuring. I wanted us to believe there still might be another tomorrow. But I began having doubts as to whether we'd make it out of the lab alive. That force in the sky was morphing into an energy that could rip apart the Earth! I couldn't feel my fingers or toes, only that static electricity that was half-driving me crazy and sending metals and slivers of glass hurling over the desk. Every now and then, I stuck my head out of the covers. I told Lynn: "Wow, how human nature sure can make a person fight to live. I'm running on some type of unexplainable energy and strength 'cause I'm exhausted, hungry, and sore all over."

She agreed. Waddled up in the experimental blanket I jokingly named after her, *Altmin Guard-L*, we were feeling disoriented, stunned, and beginning to believe that the world was ending. It was just about as chaotic as that bedlam-filled time of 2012, when some people hunkered down for weeks, preparing for the Mayan apocalypse they believed would hurl the Earth out of orbit on December 21.

Crouching next to me with her arms wrapped over her

head, Lynn said in between picking dust out of her teeth and spitting dirt off her tongue, "Well, Thornton, this is it. I guess I better tell you now...I love you." She exhaled.

"What?" Cold air hit the back of my throat. My stomach knotted. I thought: So this is what all the derogatory comments were about. Maybe she said that before but I didn't hear her. But why now!

A second fluctuation of gravity suddenly struck the Earth. Bandying some glass off our blanket, we cautiously peeked out the window after hearing metals clash and bumpers ram. Again, cars were levitating off the streets—their bumpers and fenders scraping across the pavement like tiptoeing feet. A fire hydrant dislodged, sending a jet of water into the air until a cement truck fell on top of the gushing geyser, stopping its overflow. Everything iron based became dribbling objects over the courtyards of Duke University. They were reflecting the bright light from the cosmic anomaly and looked like menacing flying saucers.

Lynn kissed me, and then hugged me—clasping her arms around my neck. I felt her ribs move as she inhaled and exhaled quickly. Then, she let go of me and looked me straight in the eye. "Goodbye, Thornton. But first, I had to tell you that." She began crying.

Her warm breath in the frigid air curled passed me, and I smelled its sweetness like the peppermints we used to pop after eating lunch in the cafeteria. I was speechless as I held her tightly, smelled hints of strawberry in her blond hair, and felt the nick of her pearl pierced earring that stuck me under my chin. Then I told her: "We're not dead yet, Lynn. Just hold on. We'll find out what's going on and make it outta this. You'll see. We have a whole lot of life ahead of us to talk about the future." She coughed, and I detected embarrassment as I touched her hand. It felt like a cold branch. I wasn't sure what else to say, how to act or how treat her. I didn't want to hurt her either, so I said: "You'll see. We'll be all right. We'll have lots of time to discuss what you just brought up, *ahem*." I let out this giant breath and felt suddenly disconnected from

First Communication

her. I bet she believed I was avoiding her. Uneasiness, and like wanting to get drunk, swallowed me up.

Her lips open, she was about to say something more but then turned away. She always did that, she told me, whenever she felt she couldn't relate to someone emotionally but only intellectually. That's when I realized why we hadn't connected in the past...right here, while working in this very lab and in *this* spot. We were two researchers—doctors—who had become completely swallowed up in conducting experiments, increasing the world's technology, and trying to stabilize Earth after the terrorist attacks. Then again, so were others who had dedicated their lives to squelching terrorism for good. That's how I always saw Dr. Lynn Altmin: smart, energetic, optimistic, and like me, *completely* dedicated to innovation. Now, however, I was seeing her through that cosmic reflective light—as beautiful. Images flashed through my mind as the Spectroscopic Enhancer swept a cerium light-blue color line across Lynn's face.

I remembered the day I met her in the lab, July 7, 2057, a little less than a month after the terrorist attacks. We were both graduate students at Duke and embarking on a new research project. Fate threw together our two fields of study. Lynn and her research friends were returning from celebrating lunch on her twenty-fourth birthday. She had on a party hat, and they were teasing her for not including pin-the-napkin-on-the-booze label as one of the bar games. She disliked me at first—actually, we disliked each other.

The adopted lab cat, Mercury, changed all that after International Workforce Day, September 4. Lynn and I started fighting over who was going to take of the tabby-alley critter because the scruffy thing turned up pregnant. That night, it darted into the parking lot where someone hit it and ran, killing Mercury. Gosh, Lynn didn't speak to anyone for days, obviously crying on the inside, except she talked to me after hours at Wagner's Bar-N-Grill, over drinks.

Several days thereafter, an old girlfriend showed up at the lab unexpectedly, calling me "dirt," "freak," and "ditcher," because I left her a year ago at the altar. That horrible exchange—in which my ex tossed just about every lab instrument at me—made Lynn and I begin to share our bad life stories, but only to a certain point. That's when we put every ounce of our spare time into the lab, often times until two or three in the morning. We became research-addicted glue buddies! "Thorn-n-Altmin" is what our team called us. The name matched the fact: The outcomes of our experiments conducted in parallel always yielded the same results; and we were always high-fiving each other, celebrating our successes over drinks. We were close, but I never even considered taking our dedicated working relationship to another level.

Often times in the lab, another researcher would sneak up on me, behind Lynn's white coat, and joke around with me, saying, "Yeah right—another project...*sure*, Manning, ha!" Then he'd wink. The next morning he'd ask me: "Well? Ya get a piece yet?" Or, "Thornton, didja get your Schlenk flask inta 'er centrifuge tube yet?" After I told him, "No way," he'd mouth the word, "gay." *Oooo* I hated that scumbag!

Finally, I'd had it. Early one morning, I examined a few of his results on an experiment he'd been touting and I found falsified data. A week later, after a review, the board ousted him. A few months thereafter, I ran into him at Wagner's.

Through hate-filled eyes, he said to me: "I'm gonna kill you. One day, you'll see."

I never saw him again. I *heard* he managed to pass the test to join the first Enforcer Regiment and wound up battling some terrorists on the front line. *Ah-hem.* I have no idea what ever happened to Jonas Arlate, *ah-hem.*

Another memory of Lynn flashed through my mind. It was the last time I saw her, Monday, June 3, 2058, that global-wide languishing day when two northern haboobs swept through Europe and the USA, downing the electricity for days. That morning, the entire coastal population was experiencing an upheaval of magnitudinal proportions! People living in the Midwest had already taken refuge in shelters, and everyone at Duke was scavenging for supplies to hit the bunkers before the

First Communication

final Stage-1 Alert. The Regency and the press had scheduled me to accept my Regency position at our Tokyo headquarters. They were flying me out on the last jet scheduled for takeoff at 11:00 a.m. from Raleigh-Durham. I didn't have time for a long-winded goodbye. I didn't think she'd mind if I left her a little bowl of purple orchids she liked so much with a nice note of, *Farewell until next time*, below the flowers…all on our lab table. On my last gulp of coffee and chomping down my last bit of toast, she crept up on me at Café Cluck, the quaint coffee shop overlooking the quad where I was eating breakfast.

She said jokingly, in her light, upbeat, and bubbly way: "Last night, I drank the *best* wine ever, Thornton. You should come with me next time when I buy it so you can buy one too. You won't re*gret* it."

That sounded enticing! Especially the subtle coy roll of her shoulders as if she was sliding off her blouse! So unlike her…as if she had something planned for us…soon. She obviously hadn't read the note I left her in the lab. I didn't tell her about it. We talked a few seconds more. I told her I'd call her later. I gave her a quick hug. I left. She knew…she knew something was up…that something was different. I saw pink sad tears in the whites of her eyes as she inspected my suit before I walked away from her. From that point until today, I hadn't received but a few visual messages from her. Whenever I thought of Lynn Altmin throughout the years, her last words began a shadowy circulation through my head like champagne bubbles: "regret" and "it." I always wondered the possibilities of what "it," the untraveled pathway, could have taken us into the future. …

J.P. Osterman

Chapter 4 - The Altmin Guard-L

Now, huddled with her under the desk, swaddled in the *Altmin Guard-L*, I saw a hot blush drench her cheeks. I wish I had noticed and followed through with that alluring invitation when she had said it! I wished I had noticed *all* the clues: the winks, soft talk, her subtle body language in each strawberry scent and breath mint. How could I have missed *all that*? *Believed* we were colleagues while she was a blaring siren hinting for more? Love. Now—*now* I was feeling the hot realization like a deep cream burning through sore muscles. Why not way back then? What the hell was the matter with me?! I sighed and felt watery eyes when the answer boomed through me like the car horns trumpeting outside. Most likely, being a Regent squashed everything when I chose to leave Duke—to abandon *her* important and vital project that she kept saying was *our* project—to compete for a Regency position. It was "the job," wherein I believed I could save Earth from rampant terrorist destruction. My research and innovation weren't working...weren't enough for me.

She said as she spit out a corner of the crinkling flapping blanket: "You wanted the Regency more than anything,

First Communication

Thornton." Her tears were turning to frost as they hit her shiny cheeks. "But it's alright, even though the Regency has changed you, even though I really don't know you anymore." She shrugged, although her sadness was real. "I just had to come out and say how I felt. *You* never would."

I could have said *that* myself, but she was right: *I can't.* I dabbed the corner of her eyes with the *Altmin Guard-L.*

"Maybe," she began softly, "I just want to capture the way things were before...those *happy* times we used have when we met after hours and joked around."

I remembered and chuckled along with her.

"We laughed so much," she continued, her faced bent down low. "In between the pressures we faced to invent new weapons and enemy deterrents." She chuckled. "So many good times." An expression of loss and isolation weaved over her face. "Silly me...*naah*, stupid." She began fanning away what appeared to be little invisible fireflies of desire. "That's all gone, Thornton, sorry about everything I just said, all just history—right, Thornton?"

"Um—"

As I was about to tell her everything welling up inside me, the old purple orchid tree outside the office snapped, followed by a loud and intense *crraaaaaaccckk*. The noise was so loud that the earphones couldn't eliminate it. Lynn and I flung them off our heads. The tree trunk broke—the crunching and splitting noises sounding like lightning strikes. The scent of wood was pungent. Then smoke! The force had set the tree on fire! I saw small reflections of flickering flames on ceiling panels. "Fire!" I shouted. If not for the cold air meeting hot air and dew beading heavily everywhere, extinguishing the flames, I think the building mighta ignited. A small branch smashed through more of our windowpane, the wind propelling glass into the office like a cannon discharging a nail bomb. The *Altmin Guard-L* saved us!

Now, the office was completely open to the elements; and Lynn and I were at the mercy of every flying leaf, twig, and piece of garbage that began pummeling the desk like sharp

J.P. Osterman

darts hitting a board. It took us ten minutes to fight against that rabid wild nature...to scavenge for pieces of aluminum and tin, and then nail them over small sections of open window. All the while, cold raced inside, a real midnight frost in the middle of the summer afternoon! The office became like an F1 tornado zone! After we mended what we could, Lynn and I covered up again under the sturdy table legs and shielded ourselves with the *Altmin Guard-L.* Again, we believed we might lose our lives. After two minutes of enduring another gravitational fluctuation, the outside pressure equalized with the office, and the wind eased to a continuous swooshing—the sounds akin to waves lapping on a beach.

Just when we believed it was safe enough to look outside, we noticed that the tree—the purple orchid tree—had split in half and partially uprooted. It looked like a person torn in two! That was *the tree* she loved so much...now mostly gone. I told her I'd save it. When she cried like the moon was exploding, I shook her a little bit and said firmly. "Lynn!—I will save it!"

The tree's branches, purple flower pedals, and mashed blossoms were flying in all around us as the building began to shake mildly.

"Another earthquake!" she exclaimed, drying her tears.

Shards of brick flew in on us, battering the desk. Lynn moaned in pain. I yanked on the high-back chair, pulling it under the desk as tightly as I could, hoping the thick wooden bars might shield us from incoming larger pieces of brick and flying rubble. I thought the whole façade of the building might dislodge, the walls crumble, and that silver event horizon of that cosmic cyclone high in the sky suck us up into eternity.

After the vibrations stopped and everything calmed, that's when Lynn and I slowly crawled out of our protective cover and saw the stratospheric phenomenon distinctly for the very first time. The white-and-yellow swirling clouds cycling around the silver disc had dissipated.

Almost right above us, there it was—I guessed it must be at least one-hundred miles in circumference, emitting the luminosity of a bright full moon at the ecliptic zenith. Only its

First Communication

color was a bright silvery luminescence...like a swirling pool of mercury. Lynn said the phenomenon looked like all the artistic renditions she had seen of a black hole. I told her that if the anomaly really *was* a black hole, then before it even *appeared* in our mesosphere, we would have died. However, the anomaly *did* look like a black hole—minus an accretion disk. It had a swirling gravitational lensing effect, like water spinning down a drain, and its tiny white singularity had to be at least twenty miles in diameter.

Outside, people were screaming, crying, shrieking, and shouting for help. They were doing what *we* were doing: gaping with terror, speculation and awe at the cosmic anomaly slowly enlarging in the sky. I heard horrible moans and writhing calls of pain coming from the hallway. People were terribly injured, needing help; but bricks, wood, and plaster were mounds and pillars blocking Lynn and I from reaching the door. Sirens were blaring on fire trucks and Enforcer cars. Brakes were squealing and engines revving as ambulance drivers were trying to avoid crashing into uprooted trees, debris, and wrecked cars. Just about every emergency alarm, car horn, tower bell and megaphone were sounding off. I saw taxi drivers arguing with bus drivers, and passengers tumbling out of smoking vehicles. Forget about finding fault in an accident! They were ordering one other to disable their horns and alarms so they could watch the changing cosmic anomaly and predict its behavior!

Then all sounds suddenly stilled...except for the droning hum rolling across the sky, and the wind. "Is that coming from some type of device that's emitting an EMP?" I asked Lynn.

A few more cars on a distant street collided, and I could see candles ignite into flames in buildings in the distance. "It's not a weapon or a device cause it's not solid," I said, "but gas appliances and electrical equipment are exploding where ever that force touches it." A man was shouting that his radio wouldn't work. "Everything with a circuit or containing a computer chip is toast," I added.

J.P. Osterman

Lynn said, "At least the anomaly isn't levitating metals right now."

Gesturing toward metals impaled into buildings, I said, "I hope *that* stopped!" But I knew it'd be only a matter of time before everything iron-based would start flying again. That force was like on a timer, and synchronizing with some sort of clock. Someone controlling it? I wondered. Again, I blanked "aliens" outta my head!

"That anomaly is definitely electromagnetic, Thornton," Lynn said.

I debated whether to tell a joke about aliens while grabbing a cracked iTablet and working on it so we could contact Floor-1 and General Bernstein.

After kicking away debris, she walked over to a shelf full of hardware and took down one of the center's newest devices. "Dr. Tom Bennett calls this thing *Magi Fifta Fugafuf.*"

"Huh?" I laughed.

Glowering at me jokingly, she said, "It's an acronym for Magnetic Field, and Ion, Beta, Gamma Flux with a photon reader." She turned it on, without needing electrical power or sensor support. "This works on an absorption principle. It should sift out all air molecules and measure *all* electromagnetic signals that are turning this place almost upside down!"

Not believing the device could work by sifting the air, I asked Lynn to show me the results. I marveled at the improbable physics: "All those readings are cancelling out!" I couldn't understand the contradicting electron volts and energy yields. "I wish the internet would connect so we can stream these results."

Lynn joked, "Or we might just have to find bungee cords, repel down to Floor-1 and knock on the door."

Spotting another crimpled blanket buried under two damaged hardware processors, I unearthed the *Altmin Guard-L* and scrunched into her jacket around her veined cold neck and shoulders. "There." I found paper-thin tape and quickly wrapped each of her fingers, her hands, and her wrists. She

First Communication

kept fighting me at first, but then when the warmth obviously set into her muscles, and she moaned as if in a hot tub.

"Thanks...that's better," she breathed. "So cold," she chuckled.

For a moment, I kept her fingers in my hands.

"Everything's gotten so quiet," she suddenly said, letting go of me.

Stepping through dust-spewing debris, we ducked down and looked over the broken windowsill to the outside quad. Everything and everyone had become way too quiet, way too still, except for throng of people ooing-and-ahing.

"Snow!" Lynn exclaimed.

We couldn't believe it...snow, in August!

"*What* could explain this?" she asked, putting her hand out the window. Tiny flakes of snow lighted and then melted on her palm. She tasted the liquid in spite of my trying to stop her. "It's just water, Thornton! The atmospheric circulation is wild up there. A polar cell must be converging with a Hadley equatorial cell or vice versa."

"But the magnetic force the anomaly is emitting is changing the conversion," I began. "That means it's also changing space/time." Now I was beginning to think—not say—that the anomaly was some type of wormhole or space/time altering conduit. But I needed more evidence before I'd stake my reputation on such a theory as an extraterrestrial entity activating a wormhole to communicate with Earth. It was a *great* claim that I believe demanded *great* proof.

We sat through seconds of exchanging thoughts and ideas while the sky continued to darken and the snow suddenly stopped. Streetlights were flickering as if someone was firing rampant shots of EMPs. Metal objects began bobbing in the air—and intermittently colliding—as if levitating on a magnetic field. "Here it comes again," I shouted, ducking, pulling her down with me so we could make a fast entrance under the study table.

"You act like the force or energy is right on time," Lynn said. "You know something you're not telling me? Out with it, 'cause your intuition generally is always right."

I didn't yet want to say the words "alien" or "extraterrestrial." In the past, when we talked about intelligent life on other Earth-like planets, Lynn concluded that there was probably life, but not life beyond at or beyond human cognition or we would have really seen some concrete evidence by now. I had already secured funds for the Arecibo array by convincing The World that perhaps extraterrestrials could exist and could save Earth's ozone. What fights over *that* she and I often had!

I began shouting over escalating noises, "Yep, the levitation is right on time, Lynn, like clockwork, but I don't see any sort of intergalactic machine propelling it." I had the iTablet I was trying to fix tucked inside my jacket. "Broken." I threw it down.

Her eyes rounded with shock. "We need more data...need contact with Floor-1, *now*."

Nighttime and cries of panic and pain began engulfing the afternoon landscape. The wind was blowing, bending branches, flipping green leaves into the streets and flinging flowers off stems. We thought we were at the edge of an endless hurricane with the silver, cycling phenomenon morphing space and time high above us.

Lynn began crying and wiping her eyes. She pulled out her iTablet, picked up the one I tried to fix, linked them, and tried to contact Floor-1 and access the internet, but everything was down. Even the screen processor we managed to stand up, turn on, and stabilize wouldn't connect. Once, for about a minute, the internet flashed on. She sent the downstairs lab our recorded A-Okay image and an attachment containing the results gleaned from Dr. Bennett's *Magi Fifta Fugafuf* device. Her iTablet showed that everything streamed successfully; and from the green light on the bottom of the Sent icon, we believed the computers on Floor-1 had sufficient time to add our results.

Lynn said, "Now, we just need to hear from General Bernstein."

First Communication

"Any time now," I added.

The coldness began to abate. The oxygenated air was in an obvious fight-or-flight state of equilibrium but atoms were trying to achieve homeostasis.

Wade Farstel, a researcher who had worked on several of my Arecibo projects and Dr. Holton dashed into the office, calling out our names.

"Over here!" Lynn shouted and then warned them about sparking electrical connections.

Breaking through debris, they finally reached us.

Lynn hugged Dr. Holton who was also crying tears of happiness. "Elisa—thank God!"

After telling them that Lynn and I were about to make a mad dash out of the office and find a way to repel down to Floor-1, I asked, "What have they discovered in the lab?"

The ceiling cracked, opening up a small fissure. The floor rumbled.

"Get down!" I grabbed Lynn's hand and we dove under the desk.

Beams snapped in two. Dollops of drywall collapsed like apples dropping off a tree.

Wade Farstel and Dr. Holton scampered under the desk after us as the ceiling ripped open, exposing more of the turbulent sky.

We all began huddling together, questioning one another about what the military, the scientific community and scholars were doing to discern the nature of the anomaly.

Wade Farstel had a thin layer of frost on top of his short black frizzy hair. The frost looked as crisp as the whites of his black eyes and accentuated his black skin. Dr. Elisa Holton had a red tipped nose and her cheeks looked chaffed as if she had just come inside out of a frigid, dark, January evening. After screaming for help, we realized that no one could hear us. When the chaos stopped, we hunted and pecked for protective cover for our heads, found some, and began craning our necks upward, trying to get a good view of the cosmic anomaly through the giant hole in the roof.

J.P. Osterman

That's when we spotted satellites that had dislodged from orbit. They were blazing and streaking away from the swirling silver cosmic disc with its pin-white singularity.

Wade Farstel said, "It looks like the Fourth of July up there!"

"Did something strike 'em? Shoot 'em down?" I asked.

The satellites were balls of fire and arcing on a crash-course to Earth. However, some satellites remained steadily in orbit around the anomaly. They were shining brightly, flashing radiantly, as if their hardware were switching gears…reconfiguring.

Dr. Holton said: "Is someone *inside* the anomaly? Around it? *Using* the satellites? That's the *only* way something like this could be happening." Her tone was one of stern conviction.

Setting the timer on her watch in an apparent move to gathering more evidence, Lynn said, "No way, Elisa. That would mean that someone *is* there or accessing those *specific* locations…someone *not* from anywhere *here*." Gesturing at the space around us, she shook her head no. "I'm having a hard time believing that. In spite of everything *Hollywoodesque*, that *you* people *wanna* believe, I just can't wrap my logic around an alien super-intelligence. Life? Yes. But advanced *intelligent* life? Like us? Or *more* advance? I don't think so."

I felt insulted—and forced back in time—to rehash our stale old argument even though it was a waste of time. "Lynn—all my work on the Decagon Platform…and the SOS project I fought for that The World approved to hunt for aliens who might be able to help us. Years ago, you, *you*, encouraged me—"

Wade and Dr. Holton had puzzled stares on their faces as well.

"*Ahhh* forget it," I waved. I couldn't have done *anything* to convince her of my theoretical position: No great proof, up until now, perhaps…but I needed a lot more to state for sure that extraterrestrials were behind the cosmic anomaly. In the recesses of my soul, I still couldn't solidly accept the reality that advanced aliens really existed myself even though I

First Communication

championed their existence! Interrupting their debates, I said: "It's human nature not to believe in what we can't tangibly experience. People continued to doubt that water was on Mars even after those drills exposed a pocket of it like a Texas well spouting oil! When SpaceX bought some back to sell and people began buying Martian water, only *then* did they believe water was on Mars. Now, we're encountering another such debate...disputing what might *really* be true and exist even though we can't experience aliens first hand."

Everyone laughed.

"Aliens heading for *Earth*? Really!" Wade was huffing and puffing. "Maybe it'll be like aliens transporting down here right next to us...*ahhh*!" Shaking, he dove under the blanket, and Lynn began talking him through his panic attack.

"I believe Floor-1's gathering enough evidence to say that a Being somewhere in space, or inside that channel—or force, or conduit, or tunnel—*someone* or some 'thing' *is* using the satellites," Dr. Holton said in a matter-of-fact scientific tone of voice.

"But the power needed to accomplish such a cosmic reach would have to be magnified by fusion energy," I said. "The Decagon Platform hasn't streamed me an indication that it's received *that* type of energy expenditure. That's the only reason up, until now, that I haven't been jumping for joy that aliens could be arriving to meet us!" Then I bounced in my shoes! I thought about dark energy, dark matter, and harnessing neutrinos for manipulating space/time. "I think I've been wrong!"

"About what?" Elisa and Wade asked.

"Aliens could be using a type of energy or power that we've only heard of but never believed possible to use in space travel!"

"That data eliminates the terrorists for sure, Regent Manning," Wade whispered.

On her iTablet that Wade partially fixed, Lynn called on several images of solar satellites and showed us their readings and measurements that the computers on Floor-1 had compiled and translated. "This is what solar satellites transmitted. See all the finely tuned cosmic wind that we believed was only a solar flare? This cosmic wind is interacting with our working satellites."

I felt overwhelmed as pieces of the puzzle were coming together to form a picture of real alien contact; but I still couldn't believe it, even though I advocated so hard for years to convince everyone that advanced aliens *do* exist! My eyes would have to see a *real* extraterrestrial image, and my ears *hear* a nonhuman voice. My lead astrophysicist at Arecibo who was in constant contact with the Decagon Platform would have to announce to The World, "We struck cosmic gold!" That was our agreed upon proclamation should we ever discover an alien signal. I didn't want to tell Lynn that people at Arecibo might be close to announcing that right now if they were seeing what we were seeing right. Instead, I said: "The satellites are being set in *perfect* three-dimensional positions around the anomaly. Someone, or thing, or device, or being—whatever—*is* communicating with our satellites, setting them in their proper locations and synchronizing with them. That's the evidence...a fact."

Lightly pouting, Lynn sat back with angry arms folded across her chest.

"Some type of preparation is being made high in the mesosphere," Dr. Holton said. She had a thoughtful sheen in her eyes that were reflecting light from the anomaly as she tapped her lower lip with her forefinger. "Lynn, I think we need to begin to consider a real alien presence even if *you* believe it's too soon for us to announce it to The World."

"Then...we are experiencing first contact—first communication?" Wade questioned, coming out of hiding from under the blanket.

A state of massive panic was still sweeping through the campus. People were throwing everything metal out of their pockets and flinging objects out of windows. We could hear crying and hysterical screams as individuals were stomping out new paths through the university rubble.

First Communication

I heard one professor yell, "Everyone—keep together...listen up!" She picked up a megaphone that someone handed her. As a strong anomalous gale hurled around her, she said through it: "On the Rio Scale of a possible alien contact, we're at a 4! Take cover where you can find it! Don't come out! Keep trying to access websites on what's happening!"

That meant that people everywhere were hunkering down for a possibly alien contact, and an Emergency Broadcast alert was on all TV stations, directing the public to prepare.

Another professor was pushing students to one of Duke's underground bunkers. However, from what I remembered, that space was limited. On the pathways beyond a large field, I saw that I was right. People were shouting and crying that they needed another place to hide in besides the ones the university assigned to them. It was like a huge blaring sign: No Room Anywhere At All! Everyone outside and exposed to the new Nature was behaving in desperation, despondency or anger one second; and, curiosity, authority or sympathy the next second. It seemed they were reflecting the swinging polarity of the anomaly itself!

Dr. Holton said through the ebbing and eddying wind, "I do believe we are being visited by aliens, Regent Manning." After stopping Lynn who began arguing with her, Dr. Holton added: "Lynn, the evidence is mounting. Look at your watch. I've been observing mine, and counting the times in between levitations, meticulously."

"Levitation time is right on," I said, glancing at my watch.

"I'm beginning to believe that this *is* a *real* alien contact...a first communication," Dr. Holton said as Lynn shrugged with a conceding expression on her face. "The evidence for such a contact is yielding tangible results."

"God!" Wade shouted and buried himself again under the *Altmin Guard-L.*

Suddenly, a booming swooshing noise combined with a strong wind struck the outside air. The glassy-swirling cosmic modulation solidified into a transparent white ball. The land vibrated softly.

I could see a frightening hue reflecting in Dr. Holton's brown eyes as she grabbed Lynn's arm and said, "I hope that thing isn't altering Earth's precession or changing its orbital position!"

"Good point," I began. "We have to inform everyone working on Floor-1 of that. I just wish I had a connection!"

While glancing at the swirling cosmic vortex with its yellow gravitational lensing, Lynn had an excited expression on her face. It was as if she finally believed that intelligent life *did* co-exist with humanity in the universe, and that she could *see* into the future, actually foresee some alien species. Too bad things went so wrong.

"The minute *I* have proof of alien intelligence," she said adamantly, perking up, "and the *second* we get outta here, I'm gonna tell our astrophysicists to make sure that they tell, or signal, whoever or whatever begins communicating with us, that they take into account Earth's orbit, gravity *and* magnetosphere. We_don't_want another anomaly winterizing or dehydrating our planet, throwing us out of orbit, or altering Earth into a free-floating space ball." She continued to work on the internet and then cussed when it fizzled out.

"A death ball—my God!" Dr. Holton gasped.

"Not *you* panicking, Dr. Holton," I said. "You've been the calm one through all this."

Shaking but then composing herself through a moment of silence, she said, "Sorry, Regent Manning, I—I guess a person can only fathom a little-at-a-time. My mind feels, well—"

"Scattered? Disoriented? I *completely* understand," Lynn said, patting her on the shoulder. "I just sent that concern you just voiced, our position, and an S.O.S. icon to Floor-1 on an old internet connection I vamped up. We should hear from Floor-1 and be able to stream on full speed soon, I hope. They should be able to spare us some help...soon."

Electrostatic currents were still dancing across my skin. After lifting my shirt off my arms, I said: "We need to remain level-headed on all this alien speculation and stay grounded in

First Communication

the here-and-now. If we don't, we'll go nuts and waste time conjuring up attack scenarios and invasion disasters when nothing horrible—outside of a few tossed trees and hovering metals—has happened."

"Except for all the people who've died," Dr. Holton said in a lamenting tone of voice.

Wade began hitting his arms. "This electrostatic action on my skin feels like a razor's moving over my body! When's this gonna stop? My God—help!" His respiration rapid, his hot breaths were curling in spouts of steamy panic. "It's like ants—no, gnats landing on me—biting me!" He was flinching, the large blanket crinkling and flapping like a sheet in the wind.

Lynn slapped his face. "Wade stop! Breeeathe...thaaat's it."

Dr. Holton began flicking water on his face. When Wade passed out, his head dropping on Lynn's shoulder, a brief calmness wafted through the air. Dr. Holton said, "Well, static's not a killer from space even though he's knocked out by it."

Lynn laid Wade down gently. "You're like a relief pitcher, Elisa." Turning to me, she said: "Thornton, you don't know her, but I do. Elisa's a real builder upper."

"*Aa*, come on—"

"You really are able to get along with everybody," Lynn maintained. "That's the only way I can describe how she can interface with so many people and departments and even prevent interdepartmental fights."

"Elisa—please!" She was reddening.

"Thornton, if you ever need an objective ear to decipher a hard dispute that could jeopardize your career, Elisa's your answer." Lynn sniffled, and our small warm quarters felt cushioned, safe, but eerily foreboding. "She keeps *any*thing *any*one says confidential."

"So you're no gossip, Dr. Holton," I chuckled.

A look of irritation swept across Lynn's eyes. "This is serious. Listen to me."

"Okay, okay...Dr. Holton, I approve of you," I whispered.

J.P. Osterman

Lynn wiped away a tear. "Thornton, you can count on her, depend on her should—if—" She inhaled and a vein in her throat bulged. "Anything happens to me."

"But nothing's going to happen to you, Lynn," Dr. Holton said, waving off the praise.

Shadows from outside flashlights and battery-operated floodlights were dancing on the walls. People were still crying and moaning for rescue.

"I'm feeling pretty grateful for my life right now," Dr. Holton began, "but I feel so stupid for always having been so hard on myself, for not being famous like some of our colleagues Lynn and I know." As Lynn touched her arm in a comforting gesture, Dr. Holton had a wide-eyed death stare written on her face. "Dr. Manning, are you happy? I mean, happy with what you're doing? Happy as a Regent?"

I knew what she meant. The Regency position was prestigious. I had money, daily recognition in the media, the best food-clothing-and-shelter, my name in every archive for posterity, and access to *every* technological innovation—both Black Ops classified and prototypes. In spite of my daily trudging-of-the-polls, I had *everything* any survivor after a near apocalypse could want. After a long pause where I couldn't take my eyes off Lynn—as electrostatic energy danced like balloons over my skin—I said, "Well—yes and no."

Lynn's head was low and she was biting her thumbnail. Dr. Holton's questions were obviously uncomfortable for her.

I was wondering if, at some point, she would be able to tell me how she grew to love me…and if we'd ever be able to have such an intimate conversation again. I finally said softly after I nudged Lynn, "Dr. Holton, I wouldn't trade my job for anything, but then again, some mornings I feel like I wanna give it all up." I felt suddenly released from a terrible ball of uneasiness. I felt light and uplifted as I breathed in a new type of fresh air. When I looked at Lynn, I remembered the time I almost asked her over to my place one night after our research team finished our drinks. I didn't. From the shy expression she gave me—a slight grin and coy glance from behind her

First Communication

thin blond bangs—I believed she was remembering that moment as well. "No matter what we do with our lives, Dr. Holton," I continued, "what choices we end up making or waving off like crap...our lives are really just a countdown, a scroll of various possibilities, a complicated network of paths and choices. Most times, especially when we're young, we're forced to make decisions without the luxury of learning from the past. In the future, when we look back on our lives—assess where we've been, whether our paths have been good or bad, and whether we ended up great or small, happy or miserable—we can't do a damn thing to change the past."

"No time machines to start over," Lynn chuckled, peeking up at the round silver anomaly in the sky. The shining satellites were bright lights like stars surrounding it.

"At that point, we can only hope for enough courage to push ourselves on to another tomorrow without pounding ourselves with all our mistakes, failures and regrets." I shrugged.

Wade woke up with a ghastly pale expression on his face. "By then, there's death's door, Regent Manning. Guess I better think twice about every decision I make now 'cause there's not a damn thing I can do to change it!"

"*Oo* that's grim," Dr. Holton cringed, and then she perked up. "But I think my future still looks good." She shoved her fist at the anomaly. "Bring it on! Come on down! I'm right here!"

Lynn stoked the sky right along with her. They were both challenging vessels I wouldn't want angry at me—two sister types who seemed to be imbibing from the universe the power and energy to defeat *any* force.

When I looked into the sky, I saw the remaining satellites beaming light straight into the silver conduit. "No one likes death...no one."

"Even as we face, Thornton, we still have to live every moment," Lynn said, wiping tears away. She touched my hand. "I wanna live. I'm *going* to live!"

Dr. Holton shouted, "That's right...thata girl!

J.P. Osterman

An aura of acceptance appeared on Lynn's face—and a sudden beautiful sheen of rainbows began reflecting across her cheeks. I kissed her as Dr. Holton and Wade kept shouting words of fire and brimstone at the swirling phenomenon.

When Lynn and I finally parted, I felt energized, the frosty atmosphere imbibing my breaths with wild oxygen. I whispered to her that we were right smack in the center of what people had been anticipating for centuries. "We—you and me!—are in the throng of history-in-the-making!"

Dr. Holton and Wade exclaimed, "Any moment now!"

I felt as if I was standing behind a door with the bell ringing. I was always told, "Don't open it! You could die!" As an adult, I always tried to anticipate danger and shield myself with the best possible protection. But now, watching the anomaly, I realized we were defenseless and facing an uncontrollable situation. The unknown was behind the door...somewhere within that phenomenon...and we as a human species were about to take our next great step in the universe, make our presence known in the universe, and meet extraterrestrials.

As the anomaly generated another fluctuation in gravity, car parts careened and flying tools clashed right outside our window. The levitation force was beginning again.

Lynn and Dr. Holton stopped challenging the anomaly like it was some sort of a celebration, and I began trembling. The levitating force was stronger than before.

Lynn exclaimed, "The iTablet's up!" After hailing General Bernstein, she established a conference connection to Floor-1 through an outdated but secure Video-Siri stream. "They're all safe, *whew*! That lab is *definitely* a fortress."

"That's why the bottom did yank out from under us, just most of the roof," I said.

"I streamed General Bernstein our attachments and concerns about the anomaly affecting Earth's orbit, again," Dr. Holton said. "I'm telling them to code the satellites with a Proceed with Caution message, translated into a mathematical language...and a Danger signal, in every computer

First Communication

language…stop sign images too, so that any advanced intelligence will realize that we're experiencing trouble with its incoming cosmic wormhole."

"If in fact we *are* dealing with extraterrestrials," Wade said. "The Intelligence could be computer hardware, robotic, cyborg—"

"Stop!" Lynn heaved. "Please Wade."

As Wade calmed down, I told General Bernstein: "Interface with my Arecibo team. They'll be able to confirm any extraterrestrial signal."

"Yes, Regent Manning," he replied. After expressing words of relief that we were all alive and surviving, he said: "We received the simulations Dr. Holton sent and we're writing counter programs and working on codes and several wave messages. Those satellites should receive all signals in about five minutes. Then they'll send our communications directly into the conduit." He appeared worn out and yawned. Behind him was a table filled with C-Rations and bottles of water. Around the table, scientists were integrating equipment. Some were still arguing over right and wrong logic, and engineers were assembling a large high-tech satellite for a launch that had a countdown of ten minutes.

"Translate the Danger and Caution messages into musical notes, sound waves, and radio frequencies too," Lynn suggested, speaking into the iTablet. "We don't know what we're dealing with, so blasting the conduit with every program and signal will help us get our messages across to them."

"Or it," Wade interjected. "Hey—please send us some help when ya can, General."

The iTablet began streaming Regent Ruth Stein's face.

I was glad and shocked to see her. She looked a bit disheveled in her Regency business suit, and her blonde-haired bouffant was lightly tilting like frosting about to slide off a cake. She was wearing only one of her diamond-stud earrings. Her other ear was bleeding, making me believe that the gravitational tug-of-war or some accident had ripped the jewel right off of her. She always presented herself as a Marilyn

J.P. Osterman

Monroe type, but I now I couldn't see the resemblance even in the hard hue of her black eyeliner. "Ruth! How—where—"

"I arrived at Duke this morning, Thornton," she began, "to present my team's findings on our genome project. I was going to call you and talk to you. I heard you were in the building, but I just got terribly busy, and then all *this* started happening." Using her smooth hand and red fingernails, she delicately brushed away her blond bangs that bristled over her dark-brown penciled-in eyebrows. She exhaled in condescension as if someone was forcing her to experience something she hated. Standing beside a line of military officers, she nodded distastefully at them and then turned and smiled at an image of the anomaly they had playing alongside her. "I believe that gravity and magnetism are fluctuating for control, Thornton. See?" She stepped aside so we could see an aerial view playing out on another screen. That's when I realized that she hated working with The Military.

She and other scientists began showing us data from the planes and drones. There were so many screens displaying conflicting readings. Not all of us together could make sense of all the fluctuating atmospheric currents, ionosphere waveguides, barometric readings, whistler signals, magnetosphere resonances, charged particles, ground-colliding electromagnetic wavelengths, and incoming charged radiation.

General Bernstein showed us three other displays—particularly one from the Defense Advanced Research Projects Agency—that were also linking with several agencies, as well as our Moscow-based Regency, in an attempt to isolate the structure of the anomaly. He began to address everyone who was conferencing with him, but whom we couldn't see. "We detect a gravitational pull but then the force reverses. That's the time stamp we've been noticing."

"A time signature," Regent Ruth Stein added, "a strange gravitational time signature."

"Gravity and anti-matter mixing at light speed," General Bernstein said. "That anomaly is feeding on *our* gravity…working to stabilize and solidify itself."

First Communication

Regent Stein said: "Physics is completely twisting beyond our understanding. Absolutely no one here in the lab…and no one at the most advanced military level, knows what theoretical concepts are at work. We are all open to ideas, *anything*."

One MIT hotshot said, "Maybe this is what happens beyond the center of black holes and in places we can't study."

I thought I'd inject my opinion. "Definitely, something, or as Dr. Elisa Holton said, *someone*, an alien presence or advanced technology *is* interfering with *our* four forces. *Earth* is fighting for equilibrium. After all, the universe is mostly a vacuum. *We* are the anomaly."

Lynn finally was able to activate the big transparent screen she had been working hard to interface with our new iTablet. "Check these plasma experiments I'm downloading to you. What we're seeing, experiencing and feeling *is* a gravity problem."

Regent Ruth Stein's face popped into our discussion and she said: "We've been able to image the data we received the drones and the craft analyzing the cosmic anomaly. The disturbance *is* a conduit of some type."

"Confirmed by my Arecibo team?" I asked.

Nodding an affirmative, Regent Stein said, "They told me to tell you these words: 'We struck cosmic gold'."

For a moment, I lost my balance and couldn't see. "Yes! Proof!" I hugged Lynn while forcing myself to think clearly and not react fearfully. "A signal! History in the making!" I forced myself to bottle up all my exciting emotions. "Tell the astronomers and astrophysicists to fine-tune our transmitting signal. They have translation programs in place…research we've been consolidating for years combined with what I've been sending them today. Tell them to stream all my data into their mega-cloud processors and then into the satellites and the Decagon Platform that the extraterrestrials are using. The Integrate Signal apps won't fully complete because of some destruction that happened here, but I believed three-fourths of the app is ready. Use it! They contain every imaginable mode of relational relating possible, from mathematics, frequencies, and images. You name it and the Integrated Signal has it. Transmit using the Integrated Signal, now! Communicating with them should work."

"The scientists at Arecibo are interfacing with all hardware on Floor-1, Regent Manning," Regent Ruth Stein said. "Those satellites you see are around the phenomenon *are* streaming connections right now."

"What kind of connections?" I asked her.

She replied, "All global-wide computer systems, server farms and cloud facilities have linked and are streaming the Integrated Communications Signal through a tortoise coordinate, the latter being for buffering and counter-communicating purposes so *they* don't blow out our entire world-wide streaming capability when they talk back to us!" She wafted back her bangs again and exhaled through the tedious task. "The satellites are nulling the geodesics of the conduit." She stopped moving and held her hand up at the screen. "Wait!"

Floor-1 went silent.

"Waaait—" Ruth Stein's light blue eyes widened and her lips parted like those on a sculpture fixed in permanent shock. "We *are* receiving code. We *are* receiving a signal!"

"What kind of signal?" Lynn, Wade, and Dr. Holton asked simultaneously.

She answered: "Lines, and one frequency. I think whoever's sending the signal's trying to figure out who we are as much as we're trying to discern them."

"And the Decagon Platform, Ruth?" I asked.

"We launched an absorption-reflective Blank Screen that contains a Blank Slate Cloud Computer with energized interferometers," she began. "Functioning together, they're comparable to a modern-day *Voyager-1* that an intelligent race of beings can utilize to communicate with us. It, along with your Decagon Platform station, have formed a perfect communications conduit and are streaming our messages to them—it, or whoever—"

"Or whatever," Dr. Holton said. "An extraterrestrial

First Communication

message—wow!"

"But *not* a voice...not yet," Lynn said in a cautious intonation. "That's what I wanna hear, followed by a face, then I'll believe, then I'll get excited and wanna meet 'em myself. Chances are that a ground-zero contact point will be somewhere close above us."

Wade was checking stats on a graphics program that was running possible contact points and directional landing locations. "The tropopause above us is where they should show themselves I'm sure."

"A transmission...an alien communication...*everything* I've been working toward!" I could hardly breathe as I patted him on the back in support. All the while, my five senses kept deadening and rushing back to me, and palpitations of anxiety kept numbing my arms in waves until the reality of a *real* alien presence jolted me back to thinking clearly. Glancing at Lynn, Wade Farstel, Elisa Holton and everyone I could see in the lab on Floor-1, I noticed shell-shocked faces as if peoples' hearts were skipping beats. We were experiencing a communal pang of trauma! And completely defenseless, powerless, and helpless!

Regent Ruth Stein said: "Regent Manning, our colleagues in The Regency are going on networks worldwide. I think just about everyone on the planet is seeing this in some form or another. Several of our colleagues have said that *everyone* is in the process of trying to make meaning of the alien signal. People *are* panicking everywhere...and retreating to places they believe they can find safe shelter."

After General Bernstein assured us that shelters and safe-havens were filling up around the globe and that support networks were activating inside them all, I asked, "Do we know where this conduit is coming from, Ruth?"

"Definitely this is an advanced signal that we're trying to track at the entrance to the conduit," she shouted as a sudden wind flooded the university. It was another levitation sequence. From the automatic barricades and Yellow Warning flash that activated in Floor-1, I could see that people were becoming more prepared to handle the fluctuating force. "A code we can't understand, Thornton, but we're trying to translate the code through your Arecibo Integrated Communications Program. Programmers at Rosetta Stone are also contributing. We also have sound specialists working with particle physicists who are analyzing all incoming electromagnetic frequencies. A 3D message is forming, but a word will take some time."

"That means that the beings behind the signal *are* advanced," Dr. Holton exclaimed.

"Yes, we agree," replied Regent Stein. "The satellites are in the process of tracing the transmission inside the conduit…'the communications conduit,' a scientist is calling the cosmic anomaly now." After a moment, wherein lines and shapes began rippling across the huge transmission screen, she stepped away and appeared to stumble back until General Bernstein caught her, preventing her from falling. "We *are* receiving shapes! These are forming words!"

Everyone continued to shout that phrase. Some people were cheering; a few scientists fainted. One man vomited in a basket while several reporters began screaming into their iTablets. Camera crewmembers began a frantic dialogue with their stations. Internet, One-World media specialists began to stream the event live for The World. On screens in the background, I could see 3D lines slowly forming words out of colliding musical notes and sinusoidal waves. Sometimes, we could hear the dissonance on the fourth floor! The flats, sharps, and intermittent frequencies all merging and then suddenly splitting apart made us grab those earphones, huddle, and share them the best we could! In those few minutes, I realized we were doing everything we could—through years of dedicated research—to communicate with the extraterrestrials. Finally, the Integrate Translation Signal focused on one harmony and one mode of communication, and the loud attempts to converse with them dissipated.

Through a network that Dr. Holton secured at Regent Stein's suggestion, and from a swept up area in our fourth

First Communication

floor lab, I began addressing The World about the alien transmission. With Lynn, Dr. Holton, and Wade standing nearby with several iTablets linking as media cameras, I took a deep breath and said to people around the globe:

"This is what humanity has been anticipating for centuries…what we have been waiting for and hoping for: a communication, a *real* transmission from another species on another planet. Yes, intelligent life on another planet. Where? That's what we are attempting to discover right here at Duke University with the best specialists and scientists from around the globe."

I paused for a few seconds to allow the reality of the situation to sink in, but I didn't want people to panic. As Lynn and Dr. Holton continued feeding me visual events transpiring around the globe, I continued:

"*Please*—don't panic, pleeeaase." I took a deep breath, hoping The World was inhaling and exhaling calmness along with me. "Please, remain in your shelters, or go to the nearest shelter or safe haven if you haven't already. That's where you can find support and comfort, as you once did after the terrorist attacks."

Several green screens ignited in the background, and I knew that local stations were outlining safe-havens and shelters with directions on how to get there. I continued:

"We must *all* remain calm." Again, I paused and made sure I was looking into the cameras while projecting an aura of confidence and peacefulness. "As of now, we are receiving satellite information streaming in live from drones and craft surrounding the conduit. Our best-of-the-best are gathering all the data from the communications conduit and Arecibo's special Integrate Signal Translator is working to solve the incoming messages. We are proceeding with caution." I repeated that several times. I was also trying to stay collected. I couldn't let The World detect any feelings of self-alarm or uneasiness. "Some of you have been concerned about an invasion or an attack. That's not happening." I repeated that too. "No one or no thing is invading us or attacking Earth. If so, that conduit would have expanded to a full-blown wormhole and destroyed all life hours ago."

I repeated with confidence that Earth was all right...that we were safe. I had to project a stable persona for each man, woman, and child looking to me for safety, security and stability. Yet people were wildly messaging us, wanting to know the facts of Earth's dire atmosphere so they could assess the ozone and cosmic occurrence for themselves. After ordering General Bernstein to convert two military channels to public viewing, to stream every Video-Siri TV station live, and to stream live to The World each-and-every bit of data from the drones and craft, I said as I looked sternly into the camera:

"In an effort to maintain transparency, please stay tuned to all networks and live-streaming stations. Most of all, stay calm. Go to, or remain in, your shelters and safe havens. I know that I'm repeating myself, but as one of your Lead Regents, that's my job...to make sure that we all stay together and remain calm. That's my priority—for everyone, everywhere."

I looked at Lynn. She was crying and patting her chest. She was mouthing words I couldn't make out...like the confusing alien lines and sounds we were receiving that we couldn't' understand but were so desperately trying to translate!

All I could discern from her moving lips were, "I've...wrong...sorry."

Chapter 5 - Shining Conduit

I looked back into the iTablet lenses and told all the watching souls around the world, who were tuning into my live streaming broadcast, that scientists were working hard to establish a solid connection with the conduit and the extraterrestrials. After that, we hoped to open up a dialogue with the advanced beings. As part of my closing, I said: "When we acquire that fine line of mutual communication, you will hear every word and see every image. Full transparency." I pointed into the lens. "Rest assured...full transparency."

On the Floor-1 lab, I heard whispers of awe. I also wanted to acknowledge their feelings of terror as I continued: "Yes...you're probably feeling like I'm feeling right now...excited and also frightened. But that's why we began the SETI project in the first place, to discover if there might be another cosmic voice in the universe besides our own."

Images, faces, and events flashed on screen as I mentioned each scientific milestone.

"SETI began with Frank Drake's Project Ozma, to Big Ear in 1963, to Suitcase SETI, to our Microwave Observing

J.P. Osterman

Program, and then on to the Arecibo Array. Scientists built these projects on the firm foundation that one day, humanity would hear an intelligent voice in the universe. Friends, that day is now. We *are* receiving a word, right now. It's a strange cipher, but still a communications…a *true* extraterrestrial transmission. The signal is not a voice—not yet. We're working to translate the signal and stabilize that conduit that many of you are seeing above the east coast."

Elisa Holton handed me another tablet showing panic breaking out in several cities.

Believing we were in trouble more from ourselves than from any extraterrestrial interference, I said, "Everyone, please remain calm!" I showed them the display screen with that horrible chaos breaking out everywhere. I said: "Feeling overwhelmed is understandable, but I am putting out an order for everyone to follow the same emergency procedures as after the terrorist explosions. If you are experiencing distress, please stream to the Global Counseling network, where several Regents, psychologists, and counselors have assembled to talk you through your discomfort or confusion. It's understandable…but not a reason to loot or become violent when we need more than ever to rally together and help one another. I know we set up shelters and safe-havens to meet the needs of people who were experiencing life-or-death situations from the terrorist attacks. Now, I believe this extraterrestrial transmission falls into the same category. As such, we need to remain on a Stage-1 Emergency Alert. Thus far, around the globe, we are experiencing no harm from the communications conduit, except for fluctuations in gravity and severe weather disturbances, but these abnormalities appear to be abating. The levitations occurring on the East Coast also appear to be less severe than when they first appeared. That means, in my observation, that the beings trying to communicate with us must realize that this wormhole is unstable, and they too are working to help us." I tapped on an image of the conduit that was receding into a safe space above the mesosphere. I showed the screen image to The World, and

First Communication

then added: "As soon as the communications conduit stabilizes, we anticipate communicating with the advanced beings. At this point, we are treating the beings, who are trying to communicate with us, as friendly and *not* hostile. I repeat...we believe that the extraterrestrials *are* friendly, *not* hostile." I paused and stared firmly into the iTablets' lenses that were streaming my broadcast to The World. "It is so important, so crucial that right now that everyone remain indoors. Keep your PCs, Siri, community processors, Smart phones, and iTablets devices streaming live with this Emergency Broadcast Network."

General Bernstein initiated several conferencing network links; and then I said: "We are stopping all regularly scheduled programs to stream this Emergency Broadcast Network. Around the globe, our Regency is opening up *all* shelters in *all* major institutions as before, including schools and churches. If you had a job at a shelter or recovery center after July of 2057, please go to that site and resume your former position at that facility. At any moment, you should be receiving your previous activation code. After receiving that code, go to that facility and resume your previous position. All major universities and high-tech companies are setting up scientific labs, like the one here at Duke, out of which I am broadcasting, to analyze all incoming data from the cosmic conduit. Again, keep streaming live to receive the most current information regarding the alien communication. For now, I will remain at Duke University in a protected area, assisting our best scientist as we make progress in communicating with the extraterrestrials. Thank you, God bless you, and remain in Live-Stream mode and following emergency protocol. Until then...God keep planet Earth."

The camera crew on Floor-1 ended my speech, but reporters began interviewing scientists and translators who were displaying images of the conduit and the illuminated satellites the aliens were using to communicate with us. The scientists had positioned the satellites in perfect synchronization around the conduit and named the satellites and my interfacing Decagon Platform: the Decagon system. The conduit interacting with the shining Decagon system looked like a giant, sparking dice with a white shimmering diamond in the center that someone could pick up and roll on a board game!

I stepped away from the iTablets that were broadcasting my speech from the fourth floor lab, and Dr. Holton began disassembling the portable tablets to take with us when General Bernstein would give the A-Okay signal for me to head down to Floor-1. They had quite a bit of building repairs to make yet in order for me to make that next step! Meanwhile, Lynn had managed to salvage some screen processors from our previous, giant, U-shape tower that had toppled down. Now we had a small line of screens that were allowing us communicate and monitor Floor-1 as well as locations around the globe.

Outside, a platoon of Enforcers stopped picking up debris and suddenly began screaming, pointing at the conduit, and unleashing their weapons like gunslingers. Through loud speakers, General Bernstein ordered the energized soldiers to hold back on all gunfire, saying: "The alert demands we prepare for a counterstrike should we experience some type of enemy fire. Keep troops assembled, but stand down and wait for my next order." Then he activated the link to me and said through several hard sighs, "Not that using *our* weapons would do any good, 'cause from what we're receiving—a photon net wrapping around the entrance of the conduit—the extraterrestrials are extremely advanced...their capabilities incomprehensible to us."

Dr. Elisa Holton enlarged the image of the conduit. A white-bright line of that photon energy was extending from the white singularity to the Decagon system. The extraterrestrials were using the satellite system as a giant accelerator to absorb various types of electromagnetic energy and a new type of energy into the conduit. Scientists were displaying neutrino streams interspersed with dark matter pulses coalescing around the singularity. "The photon net *is* acting as a stabilizing force

First Communication

for the wormhole," she said.

"That means that at any moment, someone, something, or some force will be coming out of it," Lynn exclaimed as Wade Farstel zoomed in on a visual depicting a sound frequency melding with light. "The Decagon system *should* initiate a communication soon."

General Bernstein ordered tanks to roll in an experimental, Directed Energy Plasma Burst Cannon. His top officers were calculating an optimal spot for a laser launch on the anomaly. "These aliens are highly advanced. We need our best—and our max!—to protect ourselves if they land or attack," he said sharply.

I demanded he hold all fire. "General, Earth's only about five billion years old...modern humans about thirty-five thousand years old." The General huffed in what I saw as derisive patience! "The universe has been around for about fourteen billion years. Do the math...that's nine million years before Earth and like yesterday on the Acquisition of Intelligence scale!" He turned to answer urgent calls from his subordinate but put them on hold in obvious respect of my passive, waiting position. "Their measure of intelligence is most certainly *very* advanced. But that doesn't mean they wanna kill us, General...by all means no! That's too hasty an assumption that if followed through by our military prowess could incur their wrath...don'tcha think?"

"Well, *ahem*, you, you have a strong point, Sir, *ahem*, but it's my job as Lead General and Commander—"

"Don'tcha think a laser strike on our part will be a measly flicker on a candle to them?" He folded his arms and gave me a stern glance. "You belief their intention is to conquer us. But remember...Regents are scientists at heart. We don't hold your belief of a conquering and needy alien species. Perhaps scientific wonder is at the heart of their advanced culture." I showed him several ideas that Regents had sent me, ideas for communicating and exchanging visuals that I should include in the translation program streaming through the Decagon system. "Send these suggestions and perspectives to *all* leaders and TV and radio stations." As he quickly sifted through my attachments, an expression of metamorphosis appeared on his face. "We believe that we'll be shaking hands with explorers, General. That's how we handle this first communication, with caution, and without showing 'em long sharp claws and pointy fangs!"

"Yes, Sir," he said, standing up straight and tall—his military pride exuding as he donned his hat and saluted me. "I'm just giving you protocols of caution, Sir. That's my job, , but I see your point...and that's how we respond to the aliens."

"Nothing yet suggests that the extraterrestrials are evil, invasive or conquering," I said. We need to translate a message first. Then we make inferences, and then acquire a first impression. *Then* we can begin compiling interpretations and assumptions." He kept nodding as he continued sifting through our suggestions of friendly sayings and graphic handshake images. "Just think of this first communication as the time when Columbus encountered the indigenous people of the Americas." That's when I had the idea for historians to join us. I ordered several university administrators who were present on Floor-1: "Fly in those experts! They might have very good suggestions on how to proceed once we finally establish contact with the aliens."

"From all the messages we've been receiving, people seem to be wondering one thing...what the aliens might want," Lynn interjected.

General Bernstein paused from his pensive perusal to deflect a rush of negative comments to our Regency's "friendly gesture" broadcast. Behind him, his officers were barking orders to troops on all continents, telling them to stand down. He said, so that everyone could hear his acquiescing tone of voice: "Then God help us, and I hope you're correct that they're friendly. The force behind this cosmic contact had better be explorer-oriented 'cause our weapons will look like plastic toys to these beings." He pointed at images of tanks and laser cannons. "Still they're all we have." He rolled his

First Communication

shoulders tall in an expression of his eager willingness to die first in the presence of the cosmic visitors.

Lynn broke the atmosphere of dejection. "General, they might *really* be friendly. God, everyone is *immediately* predicting an invasion scenario...*oooo* brain-sucking, Earth-conquering ETs!" She made a facetious frightful gesture. "*That* type of conclusion's nonsense."

"Yeah, but those themes have raked in money!" Dr. Holton said. "Since the nineteen fifties when astrophysicists began discovering more about the universe, attack movies have indoctrinated people into responding to first contact scenarios with fear and retaliation."

Regent Ruth Stein then announced on a campus loudspeaker from Floor-1, "Everyone—your attention." After the facility stilled, she continued: "We're trying to join with their sophisticated photon net, but the naturally occurring cosmic interference of time/space is hindering our efforts. The static keeps eating away at their photon weave and de-stabilizing the Decagon system powering the translation hardware. Slowly, we're integrating a stable connection. Like alphabet noodles surfacing in a murky soup, a word, or symbol, *is* coalescing."

"*Real* language...an inter-galactic voice," Lynn said, marveling at the sky.

"Soon, The World will hear their words...their message," Dr. Holton added.

On a large screen, measurements of radio signals in blue and white began bleeping. Frequencies from C to E mingled in 3D. A spider-web network formed. The giant two-mile wide accelerator on the Decagon platform flared white as images streamed from the conduit, into the satellites, and then into the IMAX screen on Floor-1.

Scrolling words and numbers like crisscrossing calculations and algorithms appeared. Hardware and devices were accelerating exponentially—their humming and whirring sounds intensifying—as graphics programs processed the new language.

J.P. Osterman

An intergalactic map began forming on the huge screen that looked like galaxies spinning white expansive roadways!

"We activated a global social site where hackers can help us if they have the technical savvy to do so," Regent Stein said. "We need people from every culture who can speak that particular language. You never know what intonation might spark a translation so we can understand what these— people—" She suddenly looked puzzled. "*Ah* I mean 'beings,' ah…what *should* we call them, Regent Manning? I wouldn't wanna make a reply and insult them. Thornton, whata we *say?*" She had a frightened expression in her tired blue eyes. Her eyebrows and thin eyeliner matched the black color of the screen's changing deep field. Every muscle in her face appeared frozen like a schoolchild terrified of failing grades.

The only thing that came to my mind was the word, *manners*. "Regent Stein, we talk to them as if we're meeting someone for the first time. We be polite. We greet them as we'd treat a stranger even though we can't see facial expressions or body gestures, and we might not even get that! Only maps and letters…from what we're translating now."

Dr. Holton said: "Body language is ninety percent of the way people *truly* communicate. If we could see them, we could at least *read* them."

Lynn replied, "But that's assuming they're like us…readable."

"Voice and possibly intonation are all we'll have of them, at first," Regent Stein said. "So at least we're prepared linguistically and with Relational Communications Specialists."

I thought of another consideration. "As we present their language and possibly their faces to The World, I think we should refer to 'them' as Advanced Beings, or Intelligent Beings, or Advanced Intelligent Race, or Extraterrestrial Beings…until they tell us who they are. Don't call them 'aliens.' I could taste the repulsion. "We already have a mess on our hands with *that* terminology! The media are streaming and broadcasting *Alien* and *Thing* images. I show community

First Communication

leaders and facilitators in just about every shelter and safe-haven working hard to dispel the terror that those old shows are igniting in people."

"*And* some of the *new* attack and conquer movies from exospheric worlds in far off galaxies," Dr. Holton said. She showed us an image of a giant flesh-devouring amoeba. "If the media are connecting alien critters to the action occurring inside the conduit, experts are going to have to counter that with practical and grounded facts to stop peoples' fright and horror."

Lynn enlarged a news alert showing people around the world gathering in front of TV screens and PC centers inside shelters. They were also doling out supplies and obviously comforting and caring for one another. "I suggest we send scenes like these around the world. This will also allay peoples' fears because they'll see that we're all connecting to one another."

Dr. Stein followed her suggestion, and then said: "Enforcers are also calming people down, preventing riots. Our Emergency Network is allocating brief time slots for religious leaders to deliver assuaging messages. Anything else that some wacky cult leader might broadcast, we've ordered to shut off immediately!" With a puzzled expression on her face, she then whispered, "What do you want us to call the extraterrestrials if we don't say 'alien'?"

"Intelligent Beings for now," I said. "Until we discover what they call themselves.'

General Bernstein intervened and showed us a view of Earth's atmosphere. The silver wormhole appeared round and bright. An intense intercommunication was streaming between it and the star shimmering Decagon system. He said: "As we're stabilizing the conduit, it keeps expanding and contracting from the thermosphere to the exosphere. We're experiencing *global* tidal forces. It's taking more time than we expected to interface with their sophisticated photon net…time we might run out of if we can't solve some serious equations and stop that conduit's wild fluctuations!"

J.P. Osterman

Dr. Holton opened an app with a sound frequency translating into Morse code. "I entered a mathematical model that morphed an old telegraph signal into a musical modeled Stop-and-Hold wave. Send this to the Decagon system to stream into their photon net. If the musical model works, it'll also be a communication foundation."

General Bernstein laughed, but Regent Stein said: "Might work! It's worth trying."

"So primitive! They might think we're either children or that we're insulting them," General Bernstein argued.

I felt caught between the wisdom of an old owl and the practical understanding of a brilliant high-tech artist. I had to go with Dr. Holton. "Send the SOS into the conduit, General. If the extraterrestrials are as intelligent as we believe, they'll pick up the musical Help formula—from where ever they're transmitting—and they should stop their intense transmission."

"And stop our oceans from rippling beyond our shores," Lynn said.

General Bernstein gave the order, and Floor-1's scientific team scattered to their high-tech stations to comply.

Keeping my eyes on the conduit that looked like a shining silver disc with a gold rim and small diamond-white center, I said, "Well, if that wormhole doesn't pull back soon, that gold edge that's fanning out into an expanding mine is going to blast Earth to bits." Then I remembered what Lynn and I had done that had helped the two injured students in the lab across the hall. "Check for quartz on the satellites! You can create a magnetic current! That should synchronize better with their photon net than the carbon-based devices. *Then* stream Dr. Holton's message. Together those two changes may be all we need stabilize the forces in the photon-tuned event horizon."

Lynn jumped up in excitement and said, "It'll work!" She had two pieces of metal in her hands, exchanging equal amounts of energy via a contained Tesla stream using a small floor cone device. "But the current powering the SOS through the quartz is going to have to be strong! Use solar power.

First Communication

That's it! The experimental cyclotron!"

Dr. Holton gave her the high five. "Harness energy and concentrate it into the conduit!"

Astrophysicists and plasma physicists began working eagerly on the solution as several techs called up blueprints of the Decagon system around the anomaly, and the experimental cyclotron powered by solar satellites.

General Bernstein said, "We're ready for implementation."

I watched the blueprints enlarge—their designs morph into 3D cosmic expansion bridges—on large screens as mathematicians began connecting our solutions with new algorithms, frequencies, equations and software codes.

A hologram of our galaxy illuminated on every large screen. It began connecting with a shining network of several globule clusters and several golden spiral galaxies. Together they were forming a cosmic road map into a faraway galaxy. The ending was still a blur until the musical note F-flat major resounded throughout the building, shaking us. The vibration even rippled the trees outside Duke! Several workers ducked as if dodging an enormous bird until a technician was able to tone down the volume.

General Bernstein yelled, "The point of origin is fifty-five million light years!"

"If you can distance the satellites by fifty meters then," I began, "the quartz medium should absorb the extra output of their photon net and stabilize the singularity. Use Eddington-Finkelstein coordinates when you're directing power from the accelerator. The magnet output should generate null geodesics, refract the photons, and stabilize that conduit so we can initiate a *real* communication."

After five minutes of waiting, while metal objects continued to hover—gently bobbing up and down over the streets and campus quads—another rocket launched. The ground rumbled. More debris slipped off the roof and sprayed into our lab. It felt like as if Dr. Holton, Lynn, Wade, and I were under a shower. I could feel static vibrations rolling from my toes through my chest as rocket engines boomed thunderous reverberations. As the rocket vaulted toward space to deliver more hardware to the Decagon system, we could see white-hot flaming contrails.

The General said: "The rocket contains a miniature cyclotron, programmed to absorb, convert, and deliver more solar energy into various electromagnetic waves and elementary particles the aliens might be using. In one minute, the cyclotron will jettison quartz crystals around the event horizon. They'll act as buffers for the extraterrestrial photon net and anchor our gravity. Now we just have to wait and see if they hear us, end our gravitational problems, and direct the conduit to stabilize in the exosphere."

Lynn's iPhone then went dead. Our screens died.

"Damn!" I yelled. "All we can do now is pray that what we did in the lab on a much smaller scale will work on a larger scale."

Dr. Holton said, "From all our scientific calculations, that quartz-induced net should settle the fluctuating forces in their photon net."

Looking up into the blackness while waiting for results, we saw a giant whirlpool surrounded by bright gold lights—our satellites. They were activating, creating orange beams of light that looked like corpuscular dawn, illuminating the night sky into a burgeoning sunrise.

Outside, people began tiptoeing out of their hiding spots. They were marveling at how gravity was still levitating objects; but at least now, the metals weren't deadly knives and darts. After shouting for people to take cover, Lynn, Wade, Dr. Holton and I noticed some students darting under cars and twirling poles. They were snatching metals out of the air and bandying the objects as if they were inventing a new game of Hover Dodge Ball.

Lynn kept shouting at them so much that her red face turned sweaty. "When gravity equalizes, those metals could impale you! Drop what you're doing and get somewhere safe!"

Then the missile that had launched exploded along the edge of the conduit. Everyone stopped to behold the heavenly

First Communication

outbreak that filled the sky with a rainbow burst of color. Behind the conduit, the afternoon sun suddenly appeared like a giant bronze ball. Daylight returned, along with blue sky.

Feeling relief wash through every inch of my body, I told Lynn as we saw an electromagnetic field stabilize the photon net around the conduit: "The experiment worked! The quartz rim worked! They heard us!"

People everywhere were cheering in elation and screaming words of amazement.

Our big screens turned on; all our hardware illuminated; and once again, we had contact with Floor-1.

"We did it!" Dr. Holton cried, hugging Wade Farstel.

Lynn had her fingers over her mouth in obvious astonishment. "My God—my God—a *real* window into another galaxy! A *real* fold-in-space leading to another galaxy! *True* quantum communication!"

She hugged me as if the touch might be her last. She then began talking to Elisa Holton while General Bernstein began conversing sternly with Wade Farstel. They were still debating the *right* words to use, and when we should stream them into the intergalactic window, but I told them we needed the aliens' words first in our Decagon system translators and then in our Floor-1 IMAX screen.

"What do you think, Elisa?" Lynn asked, her eyes fixed longingly on the burgeoning window into another world. "God—I wish I were up there right now to greet them!"

"That's bold. I never believed you'd say that," Elisa replied. "I'm taking a cautious approach. Not drastic like The General over there...but guarded and on the lookout for ways we can make this whole outcome better."

"Ya think someone or something'll *actually* come through? Whataya think? Aren'tcha *completely* excited?" Lynn seemed to be blocking out everyone.

"Totally!" Elisa replied, wiping away tears. "I might not act like it, but I am."

Lynn was beaming with happiness—occasionally jumping up and down. Normally, I woulda felt disgusted by such a display, calling the person "emotionally unstable." But everyone around me was dancing or hollering or ranting in the same way. Maybe I was the unusual one...me, the unemotional outlier.

Dr. Holton reached around Lynn's arm and held on to her tightly as she activated her conference app on her iTablet. "Wait—General Bernstein's Rosetta team sent this message. Let's see what we can make of it," she said.

We listened to General Bernstein's assessment of what was transpiring in the exosphere. "The incoming transmission is a holographic cipher. We're repeating the cipher, with a few additions from Rosetta, and transmitting our reply into their spacefold field. Continue to stay upstairs in your secure lab, Regent Manning. As the campus settles down and we receive more Enforcers and workers, we'll get you outta there. Just a precaution, Sir, in case this is—*ahem*, I know you don't like my saying it—an attack."

We continued to link screens with old Ethernet connections to Floor-1. I kept telling Lynn, "I wish we had a network that didn't buffer, with instantaneous processing that wouldn't fail in emergency situations."

She replied: "That's a quantum computer, Thornton, and all prototypes have failed. But if we can quantum communicate with beings fifty-five million light years away, a quantum computer streaming on Earth should be no problem. I bet they'll help us...I *bet* they will!"

Dr. Holton said with an awestricken expression on her face as she stared at the basketball-size, yellow wormhole in the exosphere: "Who knows what technology they have."

"They must be millennia ahead of us," Wade said as he struck two HDMI cables like wet whips through the air.

We had various opinions about the technological prowess and genius of the extraterrestrials, but we pretty much agreed on one thing: The beings could fold space and manipulate the four forces in the universe.

Wade became panic-stricken. "Kaboom swoosh—we're toast! What else can they do? Lord help us all!"

First Communication

"Again—stop Wade!" I breathed an exaggerated heave of peacefulness and grabbed him by the shoulders. "Let's stay calm and not entertain any type of invasion."

Wade was holding his stomach as if someone had slugged him.

Dr. Holton scavenged through a file cabinet, found a small medical kit she obviously was familiar with, and gave Wade a pill that he swallowed like candy. "That'll calm ya down in a minute but not knock ya out. After he thanked her and leaned on a chair to rest, she said, "Getting all hyped up about the unknown only makes people argue and panic, which only leads to wasting energy." She threw the kit to Lynn who shoved it back in place.

I told her, "Dr. Holton, if ever the time comes when I need you to be a part of any team of mine, you're in."

She smiled at me as if I had just awarded her a Regency Honor, which I was considering. "Thanks, I'll count on that in the future, Regent Manning."

As the silver event horizon surrounding the brilliant conduit suddenly turned transparent like a mirror, reflecting areas of the Earth, General Bernstein assured us that the Decagon system was interfacing perfectly with the wormhole's photon output. At any time, we'd be hearing from the aliens fifty-five million light years from Earth. Then, all the levitating objects began drifting to the ground as gravity settled.

Outside, people were reacting in several ways. Some were holding each other as if the dirt might split under their feet and the air might slurp off the Earth. A few crying students were lying on the ground, gripping tall grass or clutching barren bushes.

Several people were stranded in high places, hanging on for dear life to branches and electrical poles: "Help—get us down!" After I asked how the hell they managed to get that high up, they cried, "We were Z-surfing!"

I recognized them. They were the students who had invented that new game and were bandying metal objects. They said they were trying to see who could surf on the thinnest piece of metal and soar to the highest spot. Now, they were in trouble, but Enforcers were helping the injured and had to leave the kids stranded.

"You have to wait your turn," Dr. Holton said, calling the Red Cross for them.

A man was puking on the street next to a smoking crunched up car. When I yelled that there were lose electrical wires popping and dancing on the street and that he could be electrocuted, he said, "Gravity did this! Trapped me in my car!" I told him to get on the dirt path away from all the water. He said, "I just gliding over a river in this damn tin car!" He began racing down the street, repeating, "We're all gonna die!"

I hailed an Enforcer, ordered him to apprehend the disoriented man and take him to the nearest shelter. "Probably we'll have a lot more trauma cases we're gonna have to deal with," I shouted to the officer. "On my order that I'm streaming now to the Emergency Broadcast Center, tell Helping Professionals at the shelter to be prepared for more traumatized people."

In the distance, we could see smoke from all sorts of land explosion and midair collisions. Cars were crashing-landing on rooftops and patio covers, flagpoles piercing aluminum siding, and mailboxes exploding like grenades as they hit ground. A fire hydrant plowed into the hood of a yellow school bus, and children ran out screaming for their moms and dads. Lawn chairs were striking walkways and fences splintering as car and truck horns continued blaring. Engines *everywhere* began revving and lights *everywhere* popped, fizzled or hissed as the electricity droned on, but many electrical components began catching fire. I could see frantic people spraying small flames with extinguishers. TVs, computers, and alarms flared on in just about each room in every building. The entire world was becoming a giant audio environment blasting! General Bernstein was considering implementing Top-Secret EMPs to put everything electrical out of commission since the conduit's electromagnetic force stagnated, thus giving us this chaotic and bellowing global situation. Luckily, after we broadcast our

First Communication

concern worldwide, most debilitating systems de-activated before he ordered the strike.

Lynn kept shouting through the decrescendo as if her eardrums had burst: "Has Floor-1 translated the extraterrestrial message yet?"

"Real alien contact now!" Wade exclaimed groggily, yawning. He was like a limp rag but at least calm. The medicine had worked, but not for long. "'Bout time! I bet they're back like they said they'd return on those megalithic rocks of Pedra Pinta." Wade had always been a true believer in extraterrestrials visiting Earth. He told me that last year when he helped me on one of my new Arecibo receivers. Half African American and half Native American, he told the lab team while tweaking a wave on a gamma gun experiment: "Several cavern walls in the desert where I'm from are testaments to alien visitations. Come with me sometime and see for yourself the ancient pictographs and petroglyphs."

A minute thereafter, I believe the time was around 4:00 p.m. but I'm not quite sure because our watches had quit several times during the fluctuating gravity, all horns stopped. People began shouting from all directions: "Turn on your TV," and, "Stream to The Regency," and, "An alien word!" That hum was still thick in the air, lifting the hairs on our skin as if we were in the center of some giant anti-polarity experiment. I didn't care what The General had said. I needed to leave the fourth floor lab. I had enough of feeling caged in and fighting with precarious computers, huge screens and wacky Ethernet connections.

A student stuck his face through a small hole above the doorframe just as we were kicking wood and plaster to try to get out the door. It was one of those unforgettable faces of a lifetime. "An alien word, Regent Manning!"

I'll never forget that horrified white expression on his face that made him look as if he was on drugs. He asked me the same questions that terrified people around the globe were asking: "Who are they? Whata they want? Where're they from? Why're they here?"

J.P. Osterman

Everywhere around the world and appearing on several screens, people were congregating for comfort, scurrying for survival, and praying. Children were singing hymns their parents were singing. Churches were packed. I spotted several individuals kneeling down and chanting toward the conduit. Family members were holding one another, kissing one another. I never saw so many iTablets flare up in my life as people began searching for missing relatives and friends. Buffering and lag times were awful! I, and several Regents, began pleading with CFOs of major utility companies to add additional workers to restore power and repair fiber optic cables. The conduit had gone viral through the internet. It was also in perfect geosynchronous orbit in the stratosphere. People had been recording the wormhole and posting their experiences. Some people streamed right away to vote that August 23 become a holiday.

I remember what that agitated student kept repeating as he kicked his way to us through piles and columns of rubble. "We're about to translate a symbol into a word, Regent Manning. General Bernstein needs you now!"

Ten agents burrowed through to us and led us into the hallway where two physicians examined me to make sure I was okay. Then we began the climb down to Floor-1.

When we entered the bustling facility, Lynn asked, "Has anyone been able to solidify an image of the extraterrestrials?"

"No, not yet," General Bernstein replied. "We're receiving symbols and ciphers as the Decagon system responds with our translation programs streaming into the conduit."

Dr. Holton connected her iTablet to the IMAX screen and created some 3D images that appeared folded. She was maneuvering and manipulating the alien signs and symbols as if creating an origami project. "When these do begin to make some sense, it's gonna take an hour before we can begin communicating at the level of a six month old infant."

The IMAX screen began illuminating a long, vivid white row of the number 5. The number kept repeating, in columns. The accompanying noise was piercing at first, until our Sound

First Communication

Engineers began adjusting the volume. In response, they sent the number 5 through the translation program at the Decagon. Everyone stood breathless in the waiting game.

More 3D number sequences continued streaming in, but this time, from Dr. Holton's portable tablet that she had repaired and expanded while we were in the upstairs lab. She had linked it to downstream data into the IMAX screen. It was morphing into a new type of device, uniting complex programs from all around Earth. I don't know if the aliens were using power from the satellites, energy from Earth, all our knowledge, or everything! The interconnectivity and systems transformations were happening so quickly and we had no way to monitor the metamorphosis!

Dr. Holton suddenly dropped the iTablet. "My fingers! Burning!"

A doctor ran over to her, washing them. She was okay, but startled.

Ten large screens around the room lit up, interacting through the special iTablet. We began watching more extraterrestrial strings of fives appear—in color—as the Decagon system in the sky intensified. The Decagon satellites looked little stars going supernova around the silver swirling conduit! Its white singularity was interfacing with them. I directed a camera crew to broadcasting the long lines and columns of repeating fives that were appearing around us—in our monitors, spectrographs, and sound systems—as radio frequency 10.966, C major, and the primal number 137.

When a computer spit out the number, I said, "Scientists in *several* fields have speculated that this prime number is a type of universal calling card denoting a special link."

One screen began flashing pictures of familiar, and unknown, chambered nautili. Through marveling gasps, Dr. Holton stammered: "The number 137 is a universal symbol...and obviously these types of species are present in viable environments throughout the universe."

"Meaning that life, in its basic forms, is present *everywhere*," added Lynn.

J.P. Osterman

As scientists were activating a Copy command of all the frequencies while sending responses into the Decagon, Dr. Holton said, "But obviously in conjunction with other symbols and frequencies that the aliens are using to communicate with us…and perhaps other species throughout the universe."

We paused to ponder the magnanimity of such a profound cosmic hand grasping gesture. I said, "To them, *we're* the aliens."

First Communication

Chapter 6 - We're The Aliens

General Bernstein, Enforcers, linguists, a group of Regents, and prominent physicists began reading aloud the first number that streamed through a mathematical equation...and the words that followed:

55.21973 million light years—

A fuzzy holographic image of their galaxy appeared on screen, then the imaged fined tuned into a larger view of their solar system: a twin star system surrounded by five planets. The picture expanded, focusing on a giant planet in a Green zone. It appeared as large as Jupiter—its source of energy, two suns! We began calculating its size. The planet had one giant land mass surrounding its entire equatorial zone. The rest was beautiful blue water.

Lynn suddenly exclaimed, "It's circumference at the equator is 81,002 kilometers!"

"Over twice the size of Earth," I said.

Then we all became mystified when we spotted something so magnificent and unusual.

Squinting at the anomaly's bright white, beauteous line of formation, Lynn said, "I've *never* seen *anything* like it." She appeared captured by a spell.

Several cosmologists and astrophysicists agreed. They began taking pictures of the powerful force and speculating on its composition.

"Is it a particle field?"

"A nebula?"

"An energy that's defying physics?"

"An artificial power...or solar force?"

"A controlled extragalactic jet from a black hole?"

The planet appeared surrounded by a glowing, yellow-white ribbon, a million miles long.

The bright strip of force—reading off our spectrographic charts—was defying all physical laws as it stretched beyond one of the planet's two suns. The massive string of intense photons seemed to be infusing their entire, small solar system with energy that looked like a giant solar prominence, except the energy source appeared to be helping their planet and not destroying it with radiation.

An audio sound then materialized with the numbers and words: *We are on Nelta [white noise] 55.21973 million light-years from you [noise] Hello, hello...*

I think *every person* on Floor-1 and outside Duke shout those words...several times!

Pointing at the yellow-white ribbon, I asked so that even people streaming my broadcast could hear me: "Is *that* a *light* beam? Or particle laser beam moving through their solar system? The energy string seems to be in a tight path through the system and around Nelta!"

Scientists had been examining the powerful ribbon with spectroscopic devices. They kept showing me images and molecular structures of energy sources we were familiar with, but *nothing* matched the confined stringy form or fierce elementary particle/photon composition in that force in that Neltan solar system. Everyone was coming more curious about "it," than Nelta and species we named, "The Neltans."

I asked: "Is *that* ribbon-like force helping them? Or hurting their planet?" Right then I said, "Maybe *they* need help as well

First Communication

as us!"

As more words came through the conduit and we translated them, Dr. Holton pointed to the ribbon that looked like an energized jet stream. "The energy is rejuvenating this red-shifted area over their south pole, creating a Mega Doppler green-shift. Green!"

"A creation force is what that stream is, Thornton," Lynn exclaimed. "Our spectroscopic instruments are reading a perfect harmony with all elements...*all* elements. That's the green color source." I've never seen anything like it in all my years of research."

An augmented form of the S.O.S. that Dr. Holton suggested we send into the conduit appeared. They were beginning to reply to us! A diminished chord in G-major blared through Floor-1, severing my special broadcast to The World. Scientists turned down the volume as a team of astrophysicists working on the raw reply streamed in another distorted image.

When I fixed the broadcast difficulty, Dr. Holton ran up to me with a concerned look on her face. "Sir, I think they *are* in trouble." She showed us all an enlarged view of several images they were sending us through the conduit. "There's a Black Blistered area in the galaxy beyond Nelta and its emitting an outlandish amount of radioactivity...enough to destroy our solar system in a second! Send back the image with a photon embedded phrase: *Danger?*"

After an eleven-second lag, we received a holographic cipher that our computers converted into English: *black hole infection.*

The image of Nelta that followed began boiling, depicting the optical flash of radiation—the Black Blister—hitting Nelta, their vibrant planet frying.

I said: "They probably sent *this* image out into the *entire* universe! The optical flash looks like an extinction-level event is about to hit their planet—"

"They sent out a universal visual, Call-for-Help," Lynn exclaimed.

J.P. Osterman

"Yes," Dr. Holton said. "It's a real intergalactic cry for help. The infection area looks like star about to supernova. It's in a galaxy about eight light-years away from Nelta. Something bad *definitely* will happen to their planet and everyone on it in about eight years."

As scientists began measuring the hostile star with instruments, Lynn asked: "I wonder *why* they don't they just leave Nelta or wall out the radiation? After all, if they can manipulate forces in the universe *surely* they can stop a radiation shower."

"I'm sure we'll find out soon," I answered, "but they're obviously experiencing horrible distress, as we are with our failing ozone."

"Maybe the catastrophe will affect their bodies somehow...create some type of permanent genetic damage," Lynn said in a speculating tone.

"Well, whatever is headed their way, they need help. We can understand that!" Dr. Holton said. "There are all sorts of forces we don't understand, like that bright white energy string of theirs we're seeing."

"And all types of good as well as *deadly* organisms abounding in the universe, which no one—not even the most advanced beings—could possibly predict will hit them, or that they can ward off, or protect themselves against." Lynn pointed to the south, to beyond the conduit to the sun's blistering rays bleeding through the thin ozone. "Plagues, mega-twisters, solar flares...we know all about those," said Lynn. "Heck," she waved, "we were *terrified* of that asteroid that bypassed us in 2025!" She opened up an image of MB-3022 that was as big as Boulder, Colorado. "We discovered all sorts of microbes on that thing after we probed it and blew it to smithereens. We even let some of the residuals filter into our atmosphere, hoping those molecules would help our ozone." Her shoulders sagged as she exhaled. "Nope!"

"So that supernova force that appears due to strike the Neltans is so powerful that not even intelligence and advanced technology can stop it," Wade added, wiping sweat away from

First Communication

his eyes. His hands were still trembling and his body lightly shaking.

Dr. Holton patted his back in a calming gesture. "I don't understand. These extraterrestrials obviously have capabilities *way* beyond our understanding. *What* could *they possibly need* or *want* from *us* that they *can't fix* them*selves*?"

Shrugging, Lynn said: "Maybe they just wanna stay on their planet...ride out the storm so to speak, as we've been living underground since the terrorist attacks. After all, home is home...to us *and* to beings living throughout the cosmos, I'd guess. I must admit though," she began whispering, "the fact that they're *not* here is a bit of a relief—*whoow*." She had a suspicious look in her eyes as the spot of heterochromia appeared to burn with caution as well as curiosity. "Their lack of presence *has* to mean that they're not wanting—as what Wade and others have been afraid of—to attack, exterminate us or take Earth."

Dr. Holton nudged Lynn in a consolingly gesture. "I suspect you're right, Lynn, that they woulda done one of those things already *if* that was the motive behind communicating with us."

I had to agree with Dr. Holton as I downed some coffee to try to keep awake. "Our statisticians are on that speculation right now. They're inputting each incoming symbol, word, frequency column, and electromagnetic wave into our *best* computers. I suspect *you're* right, Dr. Holton. And as of yet, until we find out more *from* them and *about* them, we're not going to discover what they *really* want or need from us."

Then we received another blaring signal: *SOS—SOS*...

Each of our fifteen screens *and* the IMAX screen burst alive with the distress signal that pounded the lab as a musical hammer. The bleeping discordant notes rammed our ears until General Bernstein initialized a program to adjust the strong signal the extraterrestrials were utilizing to get their important message through the conduit to the Decagon Platform. As we continued to receive more words that we proceeded to translate, I ordered the creation of WBET, the Nelta-to-

J.P. Osterman

Regency TV channel, so that all people in all locations and using all types of devices could connect and safety see what we were witnessing in our giant Floor-1 facility.

Five minutes later, on the giant IMAX screen, we saw our first pixelated image of a Neltan named Shaesar, but the image was shaky and fuzzy, which was puzzling considering the advanced technology and civilization of the Neltans.

Shaesar had facial characteristic similar to our own; however, his nose was longer, his ears barely discernible, his neck thinner, and his frontal cortex larger.

Lynn said, "He sure looks similar to several artists' renditions I've seen of how an advanced alien species looks."

A laugh stuck in my throat because I was feeling so shocked and excited. All I could was to nod an affirmation and wave in everyone from scientists to select camera crews and reporters.

People in the lab were trying to silence them, "Shhh—shhh!"

I had to shush them back!

"He's not green like that extraterrestrial from *E.T.* the movie, or tall with thin lanky arms and reptilian legs like those attacking aliens from *Independence Day*," Wade said.

At first entrance into the facility, and upon seeing Shaesar, people stopped, mimicking some of Wade's sentiments. They were almost drop-dead mesmerized by Shaesar's large but intermittently blurry image on the IMAX screen. Camera crews were fumbling, adjusted their hardware to the correct aperture and lighting. Reporters were bandying microphones and portable tablets, sometimes dropping them as they stumbled around to gain the best perspective to capture "the advanced alien species," they began streaming to The World in spite of the poor internet connections that kept blacking out, leaving the media feeling frustrated and angry.

Military personnel kept directing them "to stay quiet," "keep calm," and find a location *away* from all the scientists and translators who were working hard to do their jobs. The new, profound alien face, static noise, droning IMAX screen,

First Communication

and stuffy air were rippling stress, disorientation, and a weird sort of stifling madness throughout the giant lab! Soon, however, over time, I knew that people would grow familiar with the aliens, and we'd begin to adjust to the change, and then slowly adapt to a burgeoning relationship over more time. But would this be all there is? Only a quantum communication contact? Or could a more intense interaction be in our futures? Again, only time would tell. *That's* what we needed: time and security, and believing as a species that *we'd* all be okay and Earth *not* attacked, but saved. It's like we were newborn babies seeing for the first time our parents' faces! But that was the problem: the Neltans weren't "parents" but total strangers. We were terrified in this burgeoning quantum-information age. That's what I streamed one of our astrophysicists to tell the reporters. I copied my initial appearance from the Arecibo observatory where I had demonstrated my first working model of Dr. M. Suhail Zubairy's Counterfactual Quantum Communication Principle. His theory was now law! The universe would soon be opening up to us!

Then, through a sudden stable quantum-connection, we could make out Shaesar's features. Several people around me said, "Ask him—'cause he just sent a signal that he's a man—if his species sent anyone to Earth because he sure has overwhelming human characteristics!"

Two scientists threw up and ran out of the room. Several reporters and a few CEOs who had dashed into the lab experienced panic attacks and sprinted out the door. But most other "approved visitors" were crying and holding onto one another.

Then the blasted image blurred again, turned a bit fuzzy. Shaesar and few of his "people" were still manifesting, but I feared that our quantum-connection might blow apart.

"Fix it!" I said. "See if the accelerator at the Decagon Platform can increase energy. That's gotta be the problem!" Lynn rolled her eyes, a gesture telling me that I was not being my usual calm collected self.

J.P. Osterman

Meanwhile, Shaesar had been watching peoples' movements and reactions, and continued to bring in more of his people on his end. They were scrambling to translate *our* language, and most likely more—everything from our moving lips to our body language. Then we began noticing that Shaesar and his entourage had several common characteristics representative of their species as a whole: the long noses, almost invisible earlobes, white skin, and black pupils surrounded by only faint sclera. It reminded me of what The General's assistant had yelled out just before Shaesar's image materialized: "Don't shoot until you see their sclera!" The whites of their eyes were prominent. I wondered about their visual cortex: could they see like us, colors and perception? There was so much to ask them and so much to learn! I felt as if I might blurt out those questions before I could even see them clearly!

Then our camera crew announced that the fuzzy reception problem was on our end.

Meanwhile, Enforcers and security workers around the globe began sending The Regency messages that fear and panic were spreading through cities. Most people were helping one another while some individuals were still confused and terrified in spite of my special broadcast and the famous and popular, expert scientists trying to allay their fears with facts about Nelta and the now stable communications conduit. WBET was helping, but not enough. Enforcers were dealing with suicide threats and pending riots. I ordered our Floor-1's special screen to interface with screens in New York City's Time's Square, Plaza Major in Spain, Zócalo in Mexico, Tiananmen Square in China, and other city squares around the world. I said, "Please remain calm. Now you have direct access to everything *we* are encountering here at Duke University. Together, we can experience the *Exchange of Worlds* broadcast of our first communication with the Neltans as we work to strengthen the signal...that appears quantum oriented...with the Neltan signaling us...Shaesar." I went on to say how we had no idea of whether Shaesar was man,

First Communication

woman, or robot! I left the question-and-answer-information session to those famous and popular scientists whom people had been watching on the news and science channels for years.

When Floor-1 finally reversed the S.O.S., we realized that Shaesar was receiving our words but was experiencing difficulty seeing *us*. Scientists at Floor-1 reduced down their image of Shaesar to our ancient (by Neltan standards) technology in order to transmit to Earth. Hopefully, with some high-tech assistance from *them*, we could establish a better connection soon. That's what we began asking them for right away!

As we waited during the course of the next hour for a better quantum communication, I called into our broadcast more Regents, sociologists, psychologists and scientists to help facilitate our next course of action. During that hour, I said in an Emergency broadcast at 8:30 p.m., that night of August 23, 2060:

"Earth received a signal from a wormhole that stabilized on the Kàrmàn line at 62 miles high at 2:17 p.m. EST. Please, everyone, remain calm. You may return to your homes, or you may also remain in shelters or safe havens. We are safe. Earth is safe! If you need help, we have dispatched more Red Cross volunteers, Global Impact workers, the National Guard, and Enforcers to assist you to your homes or provide you with basic essentials. Ladies and Gentlemen, if you are able, please help others. *Mutual Care* is the foundation of our Global Constitution. *Care* and *Transparency*, which I, and The Regency, are working diligently to provide to you, is our protocol since the devastating terrorist attacks, and what we need to do now more than ever to help one another and maintain order.

We survived the difficult part of this first communication. And as we continue to learn more of the Neltans, we will broadcast our findings on WBET, which you can access now in the One-World Media Site."

I showed an image of a re-purposed, 2056, fighter shuttle— *Brilliance*. Scientists at Duke were busily adding hardware to its insides in order to launch the renovated shuttle to the exosphere, rendezvous with the Decagon system, and strengthen our reception with the Neltans. I continued:

"General Bernstein and a special team are preparing a mission to the conduit on the renovated *Brilliance* shuttle. We first used the *Brilliance* to locate and strike down terrorists in their hideouts from outer space in 2057. This craft, with a little tender care from our best scientists, will be perfect for this new cosmic expedition. Because our visual reception with the conduit is limited, members of this mission will install and activate a special translator, receiver, and imager. The Neltans are transmitting to us cyphers to construct the special equipment powered by a high-frequency cyclotron right now. After this crucial step, we should be able to receive clear images and exchange dialogue more frequently through regularly scheduled wormhole conduits. We are calling this first special mission, *Earth's Advocate*. And the re-purposed shuttle *you* named through the One-World Media Site we are renaming *Greeter*."

Several reporters motioned to me that fifty-million people were streaming in their concerns. The reporters had compiled questions that Regents said I should address and answer immediately. They had a graphics app display the questions, and we tried our best to answer each one. Their biggest concern was, "Could the spacefold wormhole cause damage?"

I answered: "As another mesosphere disturbance, yes, but we have that Decagon system pushing the conduit to the exosphere, where future points-of-contact between the worlds will occur." That's when we learned more about the forces streaming communications between Earth and Nelta: spacefolding. The Neltans were manipulating gravity, "folding space," through several points between them and us, using energy from several event horizons along the spacefolding course, to reach us.

As I learned more about the process, I said: "The entire photonic stream of dialogue and visuals is like light originating at one point, dodging the vacuum of space, energizing with event horizon energy, and then arriving in tact at their

First Communication

destination. I know you're frightened that another catastrophe could occur again. This wormhole is now stable. And soon, we hope to have a clear view of Nelta and what the Neltans look like." I said that four times, and then I opened up visual settings of several of high-tech companies, institutions, and universities where scientists and workers were busy constructing sophisticated equipment for outer space. "We are following their directions and building new hardware and innovative materials to ensure that no weather catastrophes occur again. That's what the new *Greeter* shuttle will be stocked with. The Neltans are pinpointing intergalactic alignments and creating a space/time sequence of black hole energy folds so that we can predict the next time they can activate a wormhole *to* Earth and communicate faster with 3D resolution and clarity. Ladies and Gentlemen, *we are* dialoguing with an advanced race of beings from another galaxy. It's primitive at best…but *very* real! We need time, *and* patience to perfect our interactions."

Each intergalactic passageway that looked like a braid extending from the orbiting Decagon system to Nelta began lighting up on several screens.

"By early tomorrow morning," I said, "we should have a special graphics computer installed on *Greeter.*"

I zoomed in on an image of the shuttle, *Greeter.* Alongside it, I swept over images of the shuttle's construction zones, the exact point-of-contact *Greeter* would engage with the conduit, and other satellites involved in the synchronization of energy needed to stabilize it. I had thirty pictures-within-pictures of the entire mission streaming for The World to see, scrutinize, and message The Regency and scientific communities with their opinions, complaints and suggestions. The media also created several First Communication Visual Cloud Sites where people could videoconference in mass with one another free of charge.

"Tomorrow evening, at 7:41 p.m. Eastern Standard Time, we are scheduling *Greeter* to launch," I continued. "Ten minutes after launch, it will rendezvous with *The Einstein*, our

J.P. Osterman

most advanced optical/reconnaissance satellite developed for the Decagon by the Center for Advanced Research in Space Optics. *Greeter* will position itself at the most intense point surrounding the wormhole and begin another verbal exchange with the Neltans...that is, if an intergalactic alignment will permit, which we should discover when the *Greeter* arrives in position."

Each-and-every simulation—in conjunction with my images and animations—our best scientists, astronomers, military personnel, and communications specialists put on WBET-TV for The World to watch and video conference with the experts. Our Duke University Floor-1 facility received the viewer ratings from TV and social media sites: three-fourths of the population! Without time to sleep and with only short windows to eat, I, and other Regents, continued to inform people around the globe of *everything* that was happening.

First Communication

Chapter 7 - *The Greeter* Shuttle

The next morning of August 24, a panel of expert Regents informed me of their choice of astronauts for *Greeter*. I told The World as information on the astronauts began streaming in to me: "I am about to post on The Regency media site the list of the ten astronauts who are about to participate in the *Earth's Advocate* mission. At 5:30 p.m., approximately two hours prior to launch, I will open a ten-minute, live-stream window for you to send in a visual message wishing them a safe journey, successful mission, and speedy return to Earth."

I saw the astronauts' faces on screens in front of me. There, in the center, stood Lynn Altmin, tall and proud. On her right side was a smiling General Bernstein. I felt my head fog and my body drain of energy. Even though "the experts" were assuring everyone that *Greeter* was safe and the mission, *Earth's Advocate*, meticulously assembling, the journey was risky. However, I also realized that the mission was the opportunity-of-a-lifetime for Lynn. I couldn't even think of asking her to give up that ambition.

Then I realized that in all the rushing around and chaos, Lynn and I never had a chance to say goodbye. Now, all I could do was to send her a farewell and bon voyage message. Damn! I hailed *each* scientist at *Greeter*'s launch site: "Triple-check *every* instrument and connection. Follow *each* Neltan direction *perfectly*. You got it! Understand?"

The expressions on their terrified faces told me they'd *never* dare defy *that* order. One scientist *sent* me back an automated reply. That pissed me off! How *could* he *not visually* and *personally* reply *to me*! But I was so busy running interface between physicists and speechwriters...too occupied to follow through with a proper personal goodbye since Lynn was in solitary preparation for the launch. I intended to send a message.

Two hours prior to launch time, I opened up visuals on each computer station on Floor-1 and activated the orbiting Decagon system at the exact "Earth" time Shaesar indicated, preparing for another spacefold communication.

At 7:01 p.m., forty minutes prior to launch, a Terror Threat, *Stage-2*, resounded at Duke, making me speed away from the launch site next to the university. A spot in The Middle East was under threat of another terrorist attack, and General Rand—General Bernstein's colleague—needed my physical presence in Building 2 to broadcast an Act of Retaliation as per *Global Law V*, Article 1. I missed *Greeter*'s launch while driving back as fast as I could to the launch site. I hoped to catch *Greeter* docking with *The Einstein* and together harnessing power to operate via the Decagon accelerator. Working in unison, the three will have morphed into a new sophisticated system for both our species to communicate. It would be primitive, but capable of evolving into so much more, with help, from *them*.

At 7:45 p.m., I heard people screaming. I was in a subway car, in between buildings at Duke.

"What the hell's wrong!" I kept shouting into my iTablet as I dashed toward the Floor-1 Facility subway platform.

People were gasping in horror, moaning, groaning, crying, and staring into the sky. I could see their distraught faces through security cameras but no view of the sky.

First Communication

"Gone!" shouted someone, kneeling on the ground.

"God help them!" a group of people cried, huddling together.

It took me back to June 10, 2057, seconds after the bombs detonated in the ozone, and their shrill laments rekindled my instinctive smell of that electric static I called Instant Death. I felt it all the way down on the subway platform. This time, I was racing up, not diving for cover.

When I stepped out of the subway elevator just outside Floor-1's facility, I saw Dr. Holton throwing up on the ground. I dashed over to help her as Dr. Wade Farstel kicked open security doors and ran to her as well.

In Wade's eyes, I saw the reflection of pillars of fiery clouds.

"What the hell!" I cried. I looked up into the sky and saw debris from exploding fuel cylinders flying, careening and vaulting through the unnatural atmosphere. "Lynn!" I felt my stomach wrench. "Lynn!" I dropped to the ground. "Oh God…Lynn…no!" I felt as if Instant Death had soul-sucked me.

"Regent Manning," Dr. Holton sobbed, "I'm so sorry! Lynn—"

"Dr. Altmin *and* General Bernstein!" Wade cried. "Our best were on *Greeter*."

"Wait," I said, "maybe she escaped before—" I was trying to glean hope out of the white giant contrails of billowing gases. That hope died.

"No, Sir. They're *all* dead. All ten-o-them—dead." Wade fainted.

Watching the blooms of smoke and debris rain down like a metal shower, I hailed the launch site and saw on screen faces filled with sorrow. Each person in the facility—it seemed from everywhere around the globe—was shouting, moaning and languishing through the explosion that kept trickling down gray and black fragments like dead roses sloughing decapitated petals to the ground in a huge wailing wind.

"What the hell *happened* up there? I wanna know—*now!*"

J.P. Osterman

Numbingly, I kept repeating that phrase...moving on autopilot. Thank God, I left that gun on the fourth floor or I woulda hijacked a car, drove to the assembly site and fired on whoever put *Greeter* together! Several times, I tasted blood. After seeing that explosion that I couldn't stop, I musta scratched my cheek raw and bit my tongue in the fury of it all...the senseless loss of life! Lynn's life.

All that day, the scientists in charge of *Greeter*'s assembly talked with me through either fear-filled or avoidant eyes. They appeared to know what I was thinking: You're gonna pay for this...*pay* for what went wrong. I actually went up to retrieve the gun! Gone. Maybe Wade took it. I was so fatigued and distraught for days...functioning, but like a zombie...that I never thought to confront Wade to ask him.

The next day, at dusk, Lynn's funeral—along with General Bernstein's and the other eight scientists—began in another quad at Duke. During that same time, a prominent scientist who was one of the several experts in charge of assembling *Greeter*, explained in front of the media, and two rows of investigators, what triggered the explosion.

"A fiber-optic bundle in navigation melted into a refractor panel, making the new cyclotron reflect solar energy and not emit energy into the conduit," a chemist named Dr. Darrel Coflin said. The investigation was just beginning, and he was gleaning sympathy from The World because of his profound and emotional displays of apology. I believed he was being too demonstrative, almost bordering melodramatic. With several images and helm measurements to back his statements, Dr. Coflin passed a hearing the next day and assured The World, The Regency, and my *Greeter* Investigative Committee that he was innocent of any type of accidental mishap. He also offered schematics and calculations to the teams at Stanford and BYD in China—locations of the best high-tech manufacturing. He said that scientists there were inventing another thin-film design for the temperature-sensitive cyclotron.

"The same type of accident that down *Greeter* will not

First Communication

happen again!" Dr. Coflin and his team assured *everyone.*

That wasn't a good enough apology for me. Several days later, the investigative committee cleared Dr. Daryl Coflin and his colleagues of all criminal activities. I ordered an immediate suspension of his team. I also input a shadow Black List so all their potential employers would know that I, Regent Thornton Manning, was investigating them, personally. Yes, I began *my own* deep hunting expedition...vowing, until the day I die, to expose the criminal or criminals who downed *Greeter.* I had my own types of "interrogations" in mind.

The last thing I remembered of that funeral day, which I named *Greeter* Memorial Day, was Dr. Holton crying as she told a grieving Wade Farstel: "Someday, if we end up landing on Nelta, we need to erect some type of monument commemorating all those scientists who died." She put a box filled with Lynn's favorite things—including a Snickers bar, jasmine soap and her blue bag of tiny marbles—into a sealed time capsule at the base of Lynn's bronze statue at Duke. Lynn's tiny statue was beyond the purple orchid tree that a lightning strike had sliced in half but was still blooming purple blossoms outside the lab where we first met, where workers were fixing the roof that the anomaly had almost ripped off the building. I picked Lynn's locket out of the box before the pastor could inter it.

"Sir, I suggest you don't look in that," Dr. Holton said in a warning tone of voice, her nose running, her eyes bloodshot.

"Why not?" The metal felt warm as if Lynn had worn it for eons but needed to take it off before donning her space suit.

Wade tapped the locket. "Most ones I know of contain pictures of loved ones, Sir. It was obvious, Sir, that Dr. Altmin, well—*ahem*, liked you, Sir."

Images of Lynn and I *had* to have been memorialized—locked in some still-life past moment—in *that* locket. Try as hard as I could, I couldn't remember anyone taking a picture of the two of us together. I didn't have the guts to peek inside. Pain. I swallowed it...buried it, but not the anger seething inside me. "Someone's gotta be responsible for this—

someone! I'll never believe that explosion was accidental." I think I shouted every curse word imaginable, so unlike me. Dr. Holton and Wade stepped back in fright...Dr. Holton more than Wade. Did she *know* something? *Naaw*! Still, from that moment on, I wondered.

"I'll keep this locket for you, Sir, instead of interring it," began Dr. Holton, gently taking it from me and slipping it into her purse. If there comes a time in the future when you believe it should have a final resting place, I'll give it to you, and you can do with it as you like. Is that okay, Sir? She was, well, my best friend." She began heaving tears, again.

"It's probably hard right now for you to say a final goodbye to her, Sir," Wade added.

Agreeing, I then added: "Who knows...maybe, someday, her locket *will* settle on Nelta. She'll never make it there, but at least a memory of her might." I rubbed the warmth between my fingers. I believed I was feeling her silky blond hair with every nuance still living in my memories of Lynn Altmin. "Yeah...she'd like that. Done."

After a moment's pause, Wade said sorrowfully, "Dr. Altmin was so looking forward to the first clear communication...so excited about bringing extraterrestrial images to the world."

I said, "If there was a way to bring her back...some scientific advancement or computer enhancement—"

"Clone Lynn!—*hm*," Dr. Holton said.

I saw an aha-moment of discovery light up her face. I was getting to know Dr. Holton as the type of person who was quick to notice a problem and whip up solutions. As Lynn had said, Dr. Holton was proving to have a special intellect. "I'd do it. Clone 'er." I closed my eyes and felt grief spread through me like a debilitating flu. "I'd search the ends-of-the-earth to find *any* piece of her I could and bring back Lynn."

Dr. Holton touched my shoulder. "I would too. She was my friend for years. I'm so sorry. So sad—and, and sorry." She cried so hard I believed she'd drop.

I stepped away fast from the funeral procession. I couldn't

First Communication

say anything more except bye to Dr. Holton and Wade. I felt as dead as the murky hot sky accumulating UV strikes from our depleting ozone! I couldn't cry. I had too much to do and time was ticking down. We had to assemble another solution, quickly! On my way to Floor-1, General Bernstein's officers and I video-conferenced about another craft that The General had spotted in storage several weeks ago at Goddard. It was supposed to launch as a manned mission to Mars before the terror attacks of 2057. No one had seen the craft or checked on it since. Hailed by the media as a "money pit and mistake" because the craft wasn't manufactured to heal the ozone or to hunt down and attack terrorists, the military dry-docked it. The reason General Bernstein had learned about the spacecraft was that a scientist wanted to strip it for parts for *Greeter*.

"The General wouldn't have that, Regent Manning," the officer said.

"That was like him, Colonel, always thinking ahead of our time and into the future. Thank God, 'cause if not for that craft that he protected, our last hope for saving Earth would surely vanish as will this quantum-communication with the Neltans if we can't do something fast," I said. With my throat burning and damming up tears, I began the long walk back to the lab to re-group and prepare for another shuttle launch: *The Expression*. My legs felt like clay and I couldn't even feel my feet! I felt that dead...but constantly breathed in to try to get energy into my bones. I had to snap out of my listlessness! Lynn woulda wanted me to. ...

J.P. Osterman

Chapter 8 - Another Change In Human Consciousness

After spending a week translating words between Earth and Nelta and another week deciphering blueprints, astrophysicists built an intergalactic receiver/transmitter and implanted the communications device in wormhole-activation panels embedded in *The Expression.* However, activating and stabilizing another wormhole, gently, was the hardest part to receiving a big enough conduit to generate 3D images—the Neltans only way to communicate with us.

We assembled *The Expression* to do just that. Positioned in three concentric circles in the ionosphere—and utilizing solar radiation and cosmic particles to harness energy—*The Expression*'s energy storage system was directing more energy into the Decagon Platform that was interfacing with the wormhole conduit. The entire quantum communications system in geosynchronous orbit around Earth looked like a series of concentric rings in a 3D dartboard with a glowing gold ball of intense energy at the bull's eye. Concentrating energy at the Target of Singularity, the intense force collapses dark matter gravity and stirs up dark energy into springing

First Communication

particle repellents. The rippling forces—colliding with the sixteen streams of sixteen separated elementary particles—open the wormhole on Earth's end, thus accepting the communications wormhole from Nelta. We named our interfacing system with the Neltans, the Decagon. Through a spacefolding array of intergalactic wormholes, the Decagon holds constant the quantum forces while processors onboard its subsidiary stations translate messages, which in turn Live Stream into the special IMAX transmission screen where The Regency decided *who* can watch or listen to the discussions, and how much of the Knowledge Exchanges the public can view.

Already some "discussion time" The Regency was allocating as "Confidential Scientific Exchange." Then we encountered a power issue. Another, small, atmospheric wormhole accident occurred over Africa that almost effected Earth's precession. The ten-minute disturbance caused an earthquake that split off the Afar Triangle! We determined, and the Neltans calculated the distance, that the Decagon had to maneuver far away from Earth to avoid future problems. The entire, ten-mile wide, glowing Decagon began its slow trajectory past Mars. That location proved to be better, allowing the first of many subsequent craft to launch through a few synchronizing particle accelerators to Mars and us beginning to explore the red planet.

On October 10, 2060, using the first version of the Decagon/*Einstein* system, scientists on Space Station I activated a vortex in space/time and stabilized a large enough wormhole for a more extensive dialogue to be possible with Nelta. For the second time, people heard more voices from the planet fifty-five million light years from Earth. Still, this communication's conduit was of a limited duration and filled with fine-tuning and adjusting the wormhole so that the energy and power the conduit needed from our Decagon accelerator system wouldn't fall forward into the mesosphere. It felt like we were just shaking hands with the Neltans, or tipping our greeting hats.

On December 11, 2060, scientists activated another

J.P. Osterman

Neltan/Earth communications wormhole. This third one was even more stable than the second; and through it, the Neltans sent us a preliminary gift that we couldn't make heads-or-tails of at first because the visuals were cipher networks. Sophistication *way* beyond our comprehension! It wouldn't be until months after Fourth Communication that we'd learn that those schematics were for a quantum-computer matrix. Constructing that, we learned, would help us communicate better with the Neltans because their transmissions were quantum, fractal-photonic.

Three months later, on March 26, 2061, during a three-day period of intergalactic activity in which several event horizons aligned between Earth and Nelta, we were able to communicate more in depth with the Neltans. Each word, idea and concept we had worked on for months to develop a translation program with Rosetta Stone. From what had happened thus far in several communications, we were messing up words and meanings quite a bit. We were hoping that this time, accurate translations might improve.

People around the globe had encamped in city squares and plazas, glued themselves to our emergency WBET channel, PCs, or our One-World Media Site to experience *Information Exchange* segments between scientists and leaders of Earth and those on Nelta. With the flood of new information and visual technology, we were able to reduce Cosmic Microwave Background Radiation noise and diminished lag time in communications to fifteen seconds. We strengthened the space-fold pathway by reducing intergalactic conduits twenty-five percent.

Finally, at 1:22 a.m. on that March 26, advanced holographic images from Nelta transmitted to Earth with precision clarity and verbal acuity. It was like talking to The Extraterrestrial in person! We had implemented *full*, and perfectly fine-tuned, quantum communication. That's when we learned about their government, the Neltan Advancement Committee (NAC), comprised of over one thousand male and female scientists. They named Shaesar—one of their lead

First Communication

scientists and the man who first appeared to us—as their Ambassador to Earth. However, Shaesar was five minutes late for the 2:00 a.m. Exchange Meeting. The NAC didn't explain why Shaesar was late. That made us Regents and most of our scientists nervous. Definitely, there was a problem on Nelta. For some reason, they were holding back in divulging the problem, or problems.

After acclimating to Shaesar and getting to know "him," other beings on Nelta (whom we were now at times referring to as "people" as well even though the Neltans weren't at all human), and images from Nelta, people around the globe were feeling the desire to intensify our Information Exchanges with the Neltans. Fear had kept scientists—and us Regents!—from asking Shaesar the *really* hard questions; for example, "Will you attack? Have you attacked planets before? Do you know evil and if other species in the universe are hostile?"

That day and several times until the quantum communications conduit faded three days later, The Regency allowed Open Mic segments. The visual and verbal exchanges began to bring consciousness awakening throughout The World. People wanted to know *everything* about Nelta, other alien species, and the universe.

Conversely, the Neltans were curious about, "everything Earth and everything human!" They wanted to know about our history, technology, culture, religion, geography, geology, galactic location and cosmic occurrences. Every minute we had to pack with fast-and-furious excitement and exchange of information: from technical discussions to knowledge of our two species, our philosophies and our beliefs. Several times on that first day, the One-World Media Site crashed until we ordered the companies to install more web servers, domain server locations, community routers, and cloud servers. We also added four more particle attractors to our orbiting decagon system and fractal hardware containing a Boost Farm to many servers. Shaesar streamed the technology to Earth in two hours! He said, "The quantum Boost will enhance your current routes of intergalactic traffic by fifty percent." That night of March 26, everyone who had any type of Smart TV, portable tablet, or iPhone could receive at least two 3D body images as they watched Fourth Contact.

It was early in the morning the next day, March 27 when scientists and engineers on both worlds exchanged their reasons for why they were searching the cosmos for intelligent life. Both planets were in trouble. We told the Neltans about all the circumstances surrounding our World War III, and they told us about the deadly radiation that was about to strike their world. For the entire morning, people around the globe watched, listened and streamed their reactions to all the visuals we, The Regency and prominent scientists, were transmitting to Nelta and the visuals of the deadly supernova the Neltan Exchange Board was sending us.

Taking a break from the intense and disturbing dialogue that we had to mandate be rated at times Mature Content, TV-MA; at 12:02 p.m., EST, we ate a virtual lunch with the Neltans. Shaesar showed us what a meal looked like on his planet. The fifteen minute, 3D feast of fish, fruit and drinks set out on both planets, for people on both worlds to see, was almost as good as sharing a real meal with Shaesar and his governing Exchange Board. Several top chefs on Earth were in their famous kitchens trying to create the Neltan meals that cooks on Nelta were taking out of their oven. Except we have no large squid farms, Neltan blue-red large lettuce leaves, or two foot bulbous-prickly pineapple. Still, we did our best to foster a sharing and caring spirit between our leaders and scientists.

Immediately after lunch, Shaesar told us several things about the extinction level event about to pummel Nelta. It was the reason he was late for the March 26, 2:00 a.m. meeting. He said, "In preparation for the radiation that is about to bombard our planet, I accidentally almost killed someone." His thin lips were quivering on his long face and his large brown eyes were wide with fear. He apologized for being so emotional. He continued: "I was late because I am in charge of managing the installation of body chambers in subterranean stasis facilities.

First Communication

One of those body pods malfunctioned, but I repaired the stasis chamber in time to prevent a body fry."

That frightened us! Another glitch in our translation program! "Body fry," simply meant, "overheat to exhaustion," to them. Misinterpretations were happening occasionally, making us at times terrified of their technology; and the deviations in connotations, denotations, idiomatic phrases, inflections, and inferences were frustrating and puzzling to species on both planets. Gradually, translation programs on both planets were advancing and decreasing our states of confusion, but not before generating a bit of panic at times, or bouts of laughter from words or phrases that sounded down right hilarious.

Shaesar showed us a visual of one of the ten-mile wide and twenty-mile long stasis caverns. "These sites seem to be the equivalent of one of your small cities. We have fifty such facilities we are almost through constructing below the surface of Nelta." For the next twelve minutes, he transmitted what one looked like. The deep underground facility was comparable to one of Earth's giant caverns, only the Neltans had obviously spent years building them to modern and technical specifications. As I marveled at the contents of the stasis facility, I remembered the movie *Forbidden Planet*. Except for the deep tunnels and high columns, the Neltan facility contained rows and towers of body pods. In a few antechambers, I detected some stasis pods occupied with sleeping Neltans. Being that Nelta was over twice the size of Earth, I then had no problem fathoming that the entire race of Neltans could go into hibernation underground and avoid the extinction-level event. Shaesar went on to explain their major problem: "We have protective technology, but the thousand years we need to hibernate will have an adverse effect on our genetics. Our primal code will remain stable, however our longevity—"

We received garbled words and struggled for five minutes to translate the next segment. It was another glitch due to *our* inferior technology and terminology coupled with the difficulty translating the phrase. Several other times during our communications, we experienced the same warbled difficulty. It was like someone from twenty thousand years ago suddenly materializing into 2060, and feeling scattered and panicking while trying to make sense of modern civilization. The Neltan quantum transmission devices were so sophisticated and so photon sensitive, and their explanations, instructions and operations so complex! "Overload." That's the only word we had to excuse ourselves when they appeared a bit frustrated with us. Our language, separated by their eons of sophistication and intellect, was like an ancient hieroglyphic puzzle that not even a Rosetta Stone could solve.

Finally, as best we could, we extrapolated images from their quantum designs and translated the following segment that we determined to be the extinction-level genetic problem they would be encountering after emerging from their thousand-year stasis. Shaesar said: "A nanopore sequence of our T-strand will lack an OH group. Eventually, over the course of a few generations, we will die. The deterioration is telomere specific." Ambassador Shaesar repeated that phrase as a group of scientists behind him showed the affected DNA strand.

For the remainder of that day through the early evening of March 27, a few groups around the globe—and hidden terrorist cells!—began hacking into the One-World Media Site. They were trying to incite riots by sending out photo-shopped images and videos of Neltans attacking, exterminating humanity, and overthrowing Earth. As if we didn't have enough to clean up in the months after the conduit's upheaval, now we had to deal with fear mongers, fundamentalists, *more* extremists, and a growing group opposing *everything* new and Neltan: Tech-No protesters they called themselves. Trying to appease the dissidents and those being overly scrupulous, we worked through the night and into the morning of March 28 setting up a special camera crew not only to broadcast, but also to record for research purposes, Shaesar's first revelations to The World. On this special crew, sociologists, biotech engineers, and psychiatrists began analyzing Shaesar's every

First Communication

intonation, expression, and body language. We realized that these aspects were Earth bound and the results couldn't possibly be statistically accurate in assessing the Neltans. Still, we were learning that people everywhere were tense and apprehensive. We had to do something.

With every Neltan who appeared in 3D-form in front of the newly constructed quantum communication screen, our experts were synthesizing statistics and generating probability on Neltan honesty, morality and ethics. We couldn't *fully* quantum-engage with Nelta right away, so software writers— mostly game programmers—had to write the special analytical apps into their portable iTablets, spy cameras, and computers to receive "a good read" of the Neltans. On March 28, at 2:22 a.m., EST, prior to the end of Fourth Communication, I brought up an interesting idea that I voiced to The Regency, our scientific team, and the media who were always present and telecasting the intergalactic communication. After an hour of debate followed by a vote among only us, I said to the Neltans: "I wish we could do something to help with your dire situation since it appears that our genetic makeup is close to yours, and vice versa. At first, they misinterpreted, "makeup," meaning, "constituent parts," for, "makeup," meaning, "face enhancements." Ouch! We fixed that verbal faux pas quickly!

Prior to the wormhole extinguishing, Regent Ruth Stein said: "During the next few months, as we experience a prolonged silence between our two worlds, until July 2, perhaps you can do a further analysis of our genetic information we sent you. Again, we appreciate your giving us that laser-weapon blueprint to help us in our war against terror...and the quantum-computer system gift. For now, please stop streaming to Earth...stop sending...technological plans and blueprints. We're experiencing some trouble because of your generosity, even though most of us are so grateful, and, well, *happy* with all the changes your gifts are bringing to our planet. I know that *I'm* grateful!"

Just as the communications wormhole was about to extinguish, I had an idea. "Wait! Maybe, we can help one

J.P. Osterman

another."

Ambassador Shaesar and the Neltan Advancement Committee listened intently to us. Whenever they voiced any unilateral decision, they had some type of hardware that spoke for them. It looked like a beehive with little glowing cavities and I believe the rainbow cycling around it was the device's processor. After several exchanges with the Committee, it didn't take long for us to ascertain that the device was gathering their thoughts, consolidating them, and then processing the statistically significant results in unison. Our translators interpreted the device to mean, "Mind Speak." The voice reminded me of the wizard's in that Land of Oz, only it was feminine sounding. As the line of their Committee members stood still with their lips not moving, Mind Speak addressed us. Right after I told them that maybe we could help one another, Mind Speak's rainbow processor began cycling wildly. I knew something big was about to happen, because this time a gold virtual pen appeared above the Committee that began writing down the proclamation in Neltan and English. It's as if they were preparing to implant our words in some of time archive...maybe they were "composing a deal?"

Mind Speak proclaimed: "We have a force that can heal your ozone. We must determine the right and wrong concerning the distribution and use of the force, the proper transport of the force through a wormhole, and if—"

"If!" a Neltan scientist shouted. The dissent severed their Mind Speak connection and the rainbow processor dimmed.

The scientist was obviously skeptical of their species communicating with humans. Neither Shaesar nor other members in the Committee appeared perturbed by the outburst. Our Regents often shouted at one another when we disagreed. That dry calmness between *their* committee members made me wonder exactly how they settled their disagreements so amicably.

Shaesar said: "Yes, maybe we *can* help one another, *if* we decide whether we can spare any of the force from our solar system and *if* our genetic compositions are compatible.

First Communication

Goodbye, until your July 2, 2061, at 3:47 p.m., Eastern Standard Time." The wormhole closed.

Prior to the Fifth Communication with Nelta, The Regency met with the special research team that we hired to assess the Neltans at Fourth Contact. It was April 5, 2061. For two days after receiving the team's results, we became embroiled in heated bantering sessions as we tried to decide whether to proceed with further with the Neltans or just hang up on them and destroy the orbiting Decagon-*Einstein* System. After one Regent suffered a heart attack, and Enforcers arrested five Regents for a "time out" between punches and strikes, we determined that we, as a fifty-member Global Advocacy Team, could not make such profound and life changing decisions regarding the Neltan technology ourselves. One or two gifts from them were fine. And *wow* did we appreciate that laser weapon, *and* that blueprint that appeared to be able to evolve our digital networks, cloud servers, server farms and wireless technology into a working quantum-computer matrix. Still, *we* decided that *people* needed to decide what they wanted and didn't want. "Let *The World* vote on everything the Neltans are offering us," we Regents determined. People were already voicing their opinions and attitudes through the One-World Media Site, which in turn, was influencing us anyway; thus resulting in all the spats, name calling, backstabbing and manipulating. Any more of *that* and I believed we might have killed one another! No one among us wanted to make any type of decision that might the next day get him-or-her ousted from The Regency. We were *constantly* revved up on terror juice. We were groveling people pleasers and brownnosers...some of us *ardently* portraying ourselves as "stars". We were sick...for sure! Sick and tired. The *Global Law* of 2058 began unraveling. We added "aliens" to our human global equation.

Therefore, on WBET-TV, the station we still had up and running to conduct business regarding "everything Neltan," we decided to relinquish our power "in this decision" and to empower The World. At those special televised session from the Capital, in Washington, D.C., as leader of the team conducting the *Project Go-or-No* debates, I said on WBET: "Being that this era is at a tipping point concerning the acquisition and implementation of Neltan technology, we need to take a pure, democratic vote to make this critical decision. This is *not* a decision The Regency can make on *your* behalf. Your demonstrations and votes have shown us that! We need The World's vote, *your* eighty-five percent Vote-of-Approval, in order to decide whether we should continue our relationship with the Neltans, or use the Decagon-*Einstein* system to reverse the intergalactic communication stream when the next Neltan/Earth wormhole initiates. It's simple: yes or no. Continue communicating with the Neltans? Or hang up on them by reversing their next incoming wormhole? During the course of the next two days, as scientists present their findings, *you* decide." I and other Regents whom reporters were interviewing kept repeating that simple statement several times. None among us wanted any more in fighting. We told reporters, newscasters, TV hosts, and posted on the One-World Media site: "An 85% Vote of Acceptance will determine what we, *your* representatives, do next concerning the Neltans." It was a complete democratic vote, interspersed with the best internet security to prevent fraud.

We set up our new super-computer system to receive and calculate the population's answers. People over eighteen could vote for or against communicating with the Neltans. There were two bars: one for "yes" and one for "no." As we, and special scientists, presented information we learned from observing and listening to the Neltans, people streamed in their votes that the tally center in China was broadcasting live. That site was receiving millions of votes per second! Prior to receiving "The Network Improvement and Boost" from Nelta that helped us strengthen our Decagon-*Einstein* energy connection—that we used to intensify our internet—the internet would have crashed before one-tenth of the population could sign into the site and vote. That was almost proof enough that we could benefit from more advanced

First Communication

technology, and that what we had received was benefitting us and not detrimental.

By the middle of that voting day, April 9, 2061, I became frustrated. I was barely hanging onto my Regency position because my popularity was bouncing "Re-elect" and "Dismiss" like the dancing ball oscillating over old sing-a-long songs. The global vote was becoming like the *Dance Realm* TV show! The two bars seemed always to race neck-n-neck as if people were manipulating the results on purpose even though our special scientific team was showing people positive results of their experiments. I drove to the WBET, raced in front of the cameras, interrupted seven scientists, and plastered myself in full view of the cameras where people were tuning in before they were going to vote. I waved everyone off stage and explained more of the facts to The World.

On various screens, I opened up several research projects that our best scientists had covertly performed on the Neltans. Those same scientists found *no* statistical link between the Neltans' expressions, body language and verbal intonations and bad intentions, threatening behaviors, deception, dishonesty, intimidation or oppression. None! The Neltans appeared to be high on our ethical/morality scales of decency, compassion, intention, and altruism. They appeared to have no desire, will, drive, or motivation to amass "alien" resources, conquer beings from other worlds, or over-power and enslave life forms on other worlds.

I said on that day, as the sights and smells of tiny cherry blossoms peaked fruity in the air before solar radiation would destroy them the next day: "By God—you're *all* educated men and women but acting like you're in preschool!" I knew *that* could cause me my Regency job, but I really didn't give a damn at that point. I went on...

"Let's wait a little longer before we make such a drastic and impulsive decision to hang up on the Neltans. Let's hear more from Shaesar and then decide what to do. Then, if *you* decide that we don't want any more technology or to communicate with them any longer, let's just be honest and tell them that.

J.P. Osterman

But simply ignoring them when they "quantum phone in" isn't right and doesn't display the character of humanity. Being dishonest, ungrateful, and manipulative are not the impressions we want to send out into the universe. Come on…think about how First Communication has altered us and our position and status in the universe. That's what we're dealing with now, because *they* could be sharing *us* with other alien worlds. Ask yourselves: How do you want other species on other worlds to see us on Earth?"

I opened up a presentation of the images that were most detrimental to Earth. "Look around and look up at our ozone. We need help. And we know that *they* need help. They have a force—we've had a glimpse of it—that they say can possibly help us. Their Matter Stream. Let's learn more about the Neltans and their Matter Stream. Let's vote on this issue later and show them, and one another, that we're *not* impulsive or a callous species that has no care or concern about other life forms in the cosmos."

The bar on the Popularity Graph soared to over ninety percent. Automatically, *Project Go-or-No* expunged from WBET-TV's voting site. Taking a long break while gulping down coffee in the cafeteria, I watched the broadcast wherein the famous newscaster, Tim Wallace announced that I had stopped a Regency walkout and a global-wide meltdown of our entire *Global Constitution*.

Whew—I never realized the situation had become that desperate…that Earth shattering! The next day, we Regents re-enacted *Global Law I*, Article I and resumed our leadership as approved back in 2058. On April 24, two days after Enforcers used a laser-burst channel to stop another attack, The World approved *The Need* for more Neltan technology, especially any technology that could help us win World War III.

On July 2, 2061, at the beginning of a five-day exchange of information between Nelta and Earth, I decided to host the broadcast with a panel of Regents. After we opened the show with a live performance of the *Oedipus* trilogy, I created another

First Communication

open mic segment on WBET-TV and told everyone around the globe: "Today, we are going to be open and honest with Ambassador Shaesar and the Neltan Exchange Committee. As you hear information from Nelta, feel free to stream into this broadcast all your opinions, thoughts and reactions. The new program the Neltans transmitted will consolidate your words into categories, and then our panel will express what you say to our friends in the cosmos."

Two reporters told me right after I said that—during a tiny break, "Regent Manning, we've never seen such a high vote count for you before 4 p.m.!"

In that next hour, we voiced our fears, concerns, and even some expectations to the Neltans. We called the exchange, *Scenic and Serene Contemplations*, and set the next five-days in several places throughout the Seven Wonders of the World. We had ordinary people, eating regular family style meals, addressing the Neltans as if the extraterrestrials were part of their families. Their discussions were so moving, that at times they brought us to tears with their concerns about the ozone bleeding out into space, and stories about some members of their families—and their friends—having died horrible deaths in the terrorist attacks. They talked about their fears of humanity becoming extinct because we couldn't apprehend the attackers who were still in deep hiding and plotting Earth's demise. The years of being afraid of death and having to live under threat of abject terror were senseless—the rampant loss of life pointless. And there was no "sending out messages of persuasion and enlightenment" to change the Jihadists' points of view and religious beliefs. The Neltans at times cried through Power Point presentations and emotional narrations. Internet traffic quadrupled that July 2 as if someone opened a floodgate, allowing any type of flow of emotion to course over the land and through the intergalactic wormhole. Even in the most intensive and angry outburst—some people raging because the Neltans refused to give us weapons that could disintegrate the terrorists—the Neltans were patient, kind and gentle in their responses and reactions to us.

J.P. Osterman

Finally, after two days of participating in the narrative/descriptive style format, The World voted to be transparent with the Neltans in the future. No longer would we hide our suspicions—keep them bottled up and festering. The next day, after The Popularity bars increased over eighty-two percent, we again showed the Neltans the devastating consequences of the bombs that were eating away our ozone layer, depleting—almost irreparably—our atmosphere. We showed the Neltans live images wherein most people were living underground or in fortified structures above ground. We showed them animal carcasses in the cracked earthen desert—our animal control crews working overtime to scrape them off the ground and bury them. Some deserts were water while some lakes were deserts, with the carcasses of ships and boats jutting out of dry beds. We had a global burn ban, *Global Law III*, so cremations and the burning of garbage and wood for fireplaces were illegal, along with arson, which if convicted one would serve Life on Prison Station V. Voters also outlawed pet ownership in all community settings, except for guide dogs: that was *Global Law IV*. Zoos were limited, and highly protected. We eradicated poaching and began preserving the DNA of all wildlife in universities next to the labs developing weapons to defeat the terrorists who had started all this mass destruction subsequent mayhem. Living alone was almost unheard of, cities overcrowded like beehives, and all families were living "in community." I believed I could hear *each* person on Earth cry for the remainder of the *entire* day as I disclosed the consequences of World War III.

After Shaesar and his scientific team listened patiently, and appeared empathetic, they took an hour-long break and returned to *Scenic and Serene Contemplations*. Shaesar said, "We have a cure for your ozone layer, and our governing committee has made a positive decision." He showed us an enlarged view of The Matter Stream that felt as if we were riding through their solar system on a high-speed chase. Their Matter Stream appeared as a long, bright, white-yellow, photon-energy string, a million miles in length, and making regular sweeps around

First Communication

Nelta's two-suns and five sister planets. "If we can make an exchange, we can provide you with a sample of our Matter Stream that can heal your ozone layer. We must negotiate the terms and make a decision within the next few years because we need to contain The Matter Stream prior to entering our underground stasis facilities."

Of course, people around the globe became curious and apprehensive about what we were seeing on that quantum screen—The Matter Stream.

I said, as I had marveled at the sight before: "That force looks like a cross between a solar prominence and a laser beam. It looks destructive, not healing, and deadly—not at all a rejuvenating force or energy."

Shaesar quickly replied: "The Matter Stream is a vital creation force in *this* universe, Regent Manning. It is responsible for stabilizing gravity among the prominent forces."

"Sorry, I didn't understand that before, and we're having trouble understanding the composition of The Matter Stream now as well," I told him. "If it's so rejuvenating, and comprised of creation properties, why can't you use it to stop the radiation that's about to destroy Nelta?" I saw real pain in their eyes.

Shaesar and the Neltan scientists each took turns explaining what had happened in their history but which now they could no longer fix. They said they had taken this type of radiation beating over one hundred and fifty million years ago, and had survived through a period of stasis back then just fine. However, now, something was wrong. "Something our most advanced genetic engineers can't fix. No one is The Divine."

He had said, "The Divine," before; but before we could ask him to explain The Divine to us, a lag in our quantum-communication occurred. The only thing we could discern was a quote, in Neltan, that appeared garbled under a landscape scene of a place that looked like a cross between a wheat field and a cornfield. Beams of light were striking the glowing fields that appeared energized by the photosynthetic

J.P. Osterman

energy of Nelta's two suns. In that ten-second lag time, the translation finally appeared that made several religious representatives drop to their knees in tears and prayer: *He has made everything beautiful in its time. He has set eternity in our hearts. No one will ever be able to fathom God's from beginning to end.*

"That is a *Bible* quote from Ecclesiastes!" Rabbi Weizmann said, his eyes lifting up in prayer. "*The Bible*...this far from Earth!"

Shaesar and two Neltan scientists came back on quantum-stream. Just as I was about to ask them about the striking similarity and introduce the Rabbi to the Neltans, Shaesar said, "We are approaching our end. The Divine cannot help us."

"You mean you're facing absolute extinction?" Several Regents asked.

"There are advanced eugenic manipulations which we cannot surpass," Shaesar said. "We cannot bridge The Divine's most intricate and detailed work in the universe: nano-genetic life...life at its most elementary cellular level." He sent us an image of a virtual cell.

Upon materializing on our screen, the cell broke apart into its fundamental parts until we could no longer see it. Strings appeared in 3D form in front of the large quantum transmission-reception screen. Their vibrational notes sounded musically beauteous as they changed into rainbow that began floating around the room, landing on the walls, and lighting on all the pictures. Where the rainbows touched, images inside pictures seemed to come to life and walk right out of the frames! They were transparent, didn't recognize us, or couldn't see us, but they were there just the same! Historical people began walking among us even though they had long ago died. Several times, I ran my finger through ghosts, but they were obviously locked in the past because when I spoke to John F. Kennedy, tried to touch a dog, and attempted to stop Admiral David Glasgow Farragut from walking through a window, none of the figures responded to me. All around us, *Time*, for those thirty seconds, changed. I wondered if what we were experiencing, if everyone on Earth

First Communication

was experiencing as well! Flabbergasted reporters and the camera crew were telling me no. Then, like a flash of slow moving lightning, a low-pitched vibration resonated through the Capitol, and the historical figures disappeared when the rainbows and strings extinguished.

I think *everyone* inside the Capitol broke out in tears. I touched my chest, felt my arms, moved my jaw and rubbed my eyes. I ran over to the drinking fountain and splashed water on my face. Every drop I drank and rubbed along my skin seemed to absorb into every cell. Every atom of air felt like energy to my sharp senses! Asking our scientists what had happened, we were aghast and concluded that we had no idea what had happened at the molecular level. All any of us could do was to glance in awe between the Neltans and ourselves. Someone, or something, had moved through us…had touched our innermost cells. Yet we knew that nothing, *nothing* we could ever comprehend, could do such a thing.

As people around the globe began streaming wildly their feelings after the Spiritual Contact, Shaesar said, "The Divine." He repeated The Name with such close intimacy that I thought he was like a Moses who had actually seen Holy God. In spite of that spiritual revelation they streamed to us as evidence of their, *The Divine*, our best scientists began conjecturing on plausible scientific explanations.

After we manipulated *their* letters for *The Divine* in our graphics programs, the Hebrew words appeared which our Rosetta program deciphered: *I Am the First and I Am the Last.*

Jewish scholars began streaming the phrase to their religious communities. The Pope and several theologians who had given the Neltans a lesson on *The Bible* before the previous wormhole extinguished concluded, "That phrase *had* to have come from the mouth of God! God *is* The Divine."

I don't think that throughout the course of history, an entire global population had been able to understand a concept through sheer intuition simultaneously. We were experiencing a new Sea of Faith, as Carl Jung called the phenomenon, "synchronicity." At the same time, we also received an answer to another puzzling question. We never did understand why they looked like us—human—with a few small variations, for example, thin nose bones, a tad bit more space in between the eyes than us, and thin lips. If we, on Earth, had evolved from lower primates, why were there other humanoid looking beings in the universe? Our inner voices—our human souls—seemed to want to burst out in unison, "There is a God! *One* God!"

At that point, so many of us believed World War III would stop. For those mystical, few precious seconds, everyone on Earth felt at peace. We even sent out a White Flag peace offering to the terrorists...a real olive branch. It was holy alright, 'cause never before would *anyone* have even considered extending a kind hand to even one of those destroyers!

We began waiting for a reply.

After spending an hour streaming words of comfort to The World, Shaesar and his line of scientists continued to voice their cry for help in a plea to humanity. We particularly wanted to know *why* The Matter Stream couldn't help them resolve their dire genetic problem since The Matter Stream obviously contains intensive curative powers that appear to synchronize with *anything* organic and keep it from deteriorating or dying.

"Just contain some of it somewhere and then release it back on Nelta and it should cure all of you and Nelta," I and several other Regents and scientists said to the Ambassador and his Committee.

They had confused expressions on their long glowing holographic faces, and began looking at one another as if not sure where to begin explaining all the details encompassing their Matter Stream. Finally, after several of their scientists glided holographic balls containing compact images to Shaesar, Shaesar said: "The type of radiation from this large supernova will slowly dissipate The Matter Stream into another spatial dimension. We can already detect the stream's subtle deterioration by the readings we're receiving from several cones we placed in strategic locations throughout our M84 cluster of galaxies and distant galaxies." He enlarged one of those holographic balls that began showing us several

First Communication

monolithic, cone-shaped, gravity detectors that Neltan explorers had seated on or around several planets. "We almost have completed the construction of an artificial sun to contain and protect The Matter Stream. If not, its disappearance from our universe will set in motion destructive rumbles that will spread to *your* part of the universe." He then showed us *two* simulations of possible effects of The Matter Stream fading from the universe. "Your Milky Way galaxy and solar system will slowly break up as planets veer off their orbital pathways. Space could expand or contract. Either scenario can occur, changing matter and altering the Four Forces.

Several of us gasped in horror as Shaesar showed a few more simulations of The End of the Universe.

Making a motion to sever, temporarily, the broadcast, I shouted, "Cut out—now!" I didn't want the tumultuous scenario to keep streaming live to The World. "That catastrophe would mean a state of eternal explosions and instantaneous death!" I began pacing the floor as I wondered: What the hell should I do? Sever our connection? If yes, we might lose an opportunity for a new Earth.

I noticed the camera crew gesturing toward the Popularity bar and ratings meter. The computer program, consolidating all the incoming reactions, was blaring Red in its Panic Indicator. Again, the atmosphere in the room felt like June 10, 1057 all over again but without bombs! I told The World as I restarted the talk show: "Please, people, remain calm." I repeated that petition several times and then paused until I saw the Red in the bar fall at least fifteen percent back from The World's eighty-five percent contagion of fright. I gestured for Shaesar to step forward as well, to help me try to calm down the public.

Then I thought of the past year and all the ups-and-downs people had been experiencing since First Communication: one uprising after another it seemed. After I said that to The World, I added: "No way...*no way*—can we keep up this roller coaster ride-of-an-existence by believing we're *always* in danger of experiencing total cataclysm. Look at us, each one of us." I showed The World their reactions streaming into the talk show. "From looking at these Popularity and Response bars, almost each person around the globe is in a state of hysterics. Now, it's time to put a stop to the rising Bar of Red Fear. The Neltans say they can help us. Let's listen calmly as they explain what their Matter Stream can do for Earth. Let's rally together, remain calm, and stop the overflowing terror that seems to be putting everyone on edge and in a feeding frenzy of alarm."

Then, several of us realized—after consulting with our team of sociologists and psychologists—that the only way to assuage the global population was to put Shaesar and his scientific team back on live broadcast, in Teaching mode, even though other Regents remained terrified of riots breaking out or people charging the station at WBET-TV. People might even fight Enforcers and guards outside the Capitol, break through the guardrails, and destroy the quantum screen thus severing any further communication with Nelta. Even though the simulations were only possibilities and potential scenarios, those shows felt so real. People were obviously experiencing real terror by the unbelievable and incomprehensible power and force of the Neltan's Matter Stream. It seemed like the joyful and peaceful moments we all experienced together just a few hours ago were now colliding back into thunderous rolls of terror, panic, criticism and widespread sorrow and grief. All those strong feelings of kinship and spiritual connection were gone. Even inside of me. I think all our negative emotions squashed those harmonious feelings right out of us. I guess we'd have to experience billions of years more of life and existence to reach the Neltans' spiritual and communal states of consciousness. Even in the midst of believing that their species would soon be running out of time, they were emotional, but not destructive, earnest in their pleading, but not rioting or forcing themselves on us. I wondered what we'd do if the situation were playing out in reverse.

First Communication

Chapter 9 - The Multiverse Explanation

After making a plea, again, for people around the globe to remain calm, to stay indoors, to remain in schools, and to be patient as Shaesar continued to educate us about life in *his* part of the universe, I asked Shaesar and his scientific team to continue to explain the forces at work in their solar system.

Shaesar said: "*All* beings in This Universe and in *every* universe of The Multiverse need The Matter Stream for its vital creation properties. There is a Matter Stream in each universe, stabilizing The Multiverse so that they don't all collapse or inflate out of proportion." He showed us an image of a six-trillion year old universe in its seven-trillionth cycle. Time and space were different there...distortions making everything appear sparkling. The universe was repeating, obviously in the thrall of trying to work some things out until "the work" was complete! He and his Governing Exchange Committee spent the rest of the day and evening of July 4—with only two days remaining in which to dialogue—showing and presenting historic pictures and information on their vital Matter Stream and many universes in The Multiverse.

After The Regency compiled a list of The World's top ten

questions and responses to present to the Neltans; the next day, July 5, in another talk show format, I asked Shaesar: "People on Earth now believe that The Divine most likely is our God as well. Is that where the Matter Stream came from? The Divine? And, if *everything* is proportional and unified as you said, that means that there *is* order in *every* universe of The Multiverse; and without The Matter Stream unifying The Multiverse, the four forces would ignite in chaos, start competing for dominance, and *everything* would completely shatter, implode, explode, or just disappear?!" I thought my head was at impact point just thinking about the vastness of that concept!

Shaesar answered: "For the twelve billion years we have occupied this universe, which is thirteen billion, eight-hundred thousand, ninety-six of your Earth years old, and as much as we have colonized other planets, probed other dimensions, and manipulated space/time, we are unsure as to the exact name of The Matter Stream's creator. Because The Matter Stream *is* a creation force, it had a place of origin and a point of origin which only The Divine can fathom." Again, that quotation from Ecclesiastes appeared from Rabbi Weizmann who was now present at our communication exchanges, helping us. Shaesar continued: "The Divine is beyond *any* Being's comprehension, except for that String of Worship we sent you to experience him/her—the Neltan translation of the androgynous Divine—as we have come to experience him/her over the millennia. The Divine is not bound to any point in space and time. The Divine is present around us all."

A pastor called out, "Christ said that the Kingdom of Heaven is among us!"

As translators paused intermittently in an attempt to interpret more abstract terms, Shaesar continued: "The Divine exists in all interspatial dimensions and created The Matter Stream. If not for The Matter Stream present now in *this* universe, we believe this universe will expand more rapidly than its current path of evolution. The expansion *could* spawn another universal bubble, or implode."

First Communication

"*We need* the Matter Stream in *our* solar system…our exact position of Quadrant Central," one of the Neltan officials adamantly stated.

Seeing a line of questions streaming in from The World, we took a break while programmers compiled another top-ten list of questions, comments and concerns they had for the Neltans.

During that interlude, I met with most of The Regents in the break room. As several propulsion engineers conversed with the Neltans to pinpoint the opening of the next wormhole, I said behind those closed doors: "Shaesar told us that The Matter Stream can fix our failing ozone. But The World is asking and I want to know as well: What's the cost? The price? And why should we *only* get a sample? Shouldn't *they* send the whole thing here in spite of what that other Neltan leader said?" Little did I realize then that those complicated questions would take *months* to iron out before we could come to an agreement with the Neltans.

Regent Sylvia Itonovich, the famous Biotech Engineer who developed a global water purification system after the terrorist attacks said: "'Cause they said we could only have a sample, that's why. The Matter Stream is theirs. I'm not going to argue with Beings who are billions of years more advanced than us, in spite of how peaceful they appear. Will *you*?" She had a look of extreme appreciation on her face that swept over us all. "They're offering to help us I believe. Let's just consider any Earth-saving offer and take what they give us no matter what!"

She had a point, so I said: "No telling *what* the Neltans are really capable of. They've sent us technology we've been implementing, probably as trust-building gestures. *I* wouldn't push them or press them."

"The Spanish and English offered friendship items to the Native Americans before they wiped them out with diseases and took their land," Itonovich whispered.

I waved her off. I had a gut feeling that wasn't the case, especially after having that profound spiritual experience, which was still dissipating quickly, like yesterday's chili I ate, which was the best I'd ever tasted. When I discussed the spiritual purge with my colleagues and the Jewish rabbi who had been there, they both agreed on one thing. The rabbi said: "Obviously, The Divine wants us to choose. We're not puppets. No one should know his or her future. Life is not a predicable pathway. What type of existence would that be?"

I told Regent Sylvia Itonovich: "The Neltans seem to know *right* where we're at as a society, as if they've been where we're at in *their* past, and learned from their mistakes."

"Yeah," Itonovich sighed. "You're probably right. They haven't once threatened us, and our research team who is still evaluating them hasn't detected *any* type of hostility."

Regent Jenkens said: "They're *asking* for an exchange. We don't know yet the *total* extent of their troubles, but they are preparing to enter those stasis chambers in underground facilities."

I said: "I did see what appeared to be several medical centers with genetic codes and jumping DNA strands. The RNA explodes at a certain sequence."

Regent Itonovich said: "They need some type of help, from us I bet, with their gene pool. We need an expert opinion about what could be going on with them to know what they could be wanting from us."

The next morning—one day prior to the fifth wormhole extinguishing—I called Dr. Elisa Holton and asked her to meet me at WBET-TV and to join The Regency's scientific team on a consulting basis.

After introducing her to The Regency as an expert in bioscience, Dr. Holton said after the talk show that last night of July 6: "The Neltans have conducted some extensive genetic engineering experiments on themselves in the past—"

"Although they haven't completely been transparent about their mistakes as a civilization," I interrupted.

"Right, Regent Manning," Dr. Holton said, "but I see a definite mutation that will occur in their future." She opened up an app on her iTablet and inserted genetic codes that the

First Communication

Neltans had quantum-streamed to Earth. The Neltan telomere began shortening in a time-lapsed simulation. "This means their life expectancy will progressively shorten with each generation. Perhaps this mutation is linked to something they did to themselves in the past, what this upcoming stasis period will do to them, or maybe a combination of the both. They did say, however, that the incoming radiation bombardment was unique. No shield or regenerative force can help them, or stop the deathly assault on their planet."

Thanking Dr. Holton, The Regency then dismissed her. I said to my colleagues that night, "Soon, we should ask Shaesar what his people expect from us in exchange for that Matter Stream sample they offered to send us."...

For the next several months, we struggled to obtain a mutually beneficial agreement with the Neltans. The Regency, working with the Neltan Advancement Committee, drafted *The Pact* in its seminal form. The Neltans would quantum-stream humanity a sample of their Matter Stream to heal our ozone and protect Earth from solar radiation, and we would voyage to Nelta with purified human DNA and present our precious cargo to the dignitary who would have revived out of stasis to welcome us to Nelta's rejuvenated world. Most vital are the human telomere and amino acid integrity of our human DNA so that the Neltans can replicate our code and revitalize their gene pool.

By the end of July, as our particle accelerator beyond Mars—the Decagon—improved and our IMAX imaging screen on Earth advanced, we were dialoging through improved quantum-imaging techniques more frequently with the Neltans. Several of our scientists experimenting with nano-organics and electron dispersal at the Decagon attempted to quantum-stream several electron-based genetic segments to Nelta to see if we could avoid the *long*, one-hundred year, spacefold journey to their planet in the M84 galaxy cluster.

Both attempts at teleporting matter failed after the samples streamed out via electron strings through the Decagon.

As we continued to refine the terms of *The Pact*, we learned that we had the correct materials on Earth to build a great ship capable of manipulating space—"folding space"—as the Neltans had been doing for millennia to travel the cosmos. With more blueprints and advanced medical ingenuity from the Neltans, we could spacefold to Nelta and stay young by Regenerating with leftovers from The Matter Stream sample they would quantum-stream to us if only The Regency would approve *The Pact*. As a governing representative and *not* a dictatorship, The Regency couldn't approve *The Pact* verbally to the Neltans without 85% of the voting population first approving it. The numbers daily kept vacillating close to that 85% figure but always fell short. There was always some concern. The biggest issues were time constraint, and arriving on Nelta safely. If we were to agree to the bargain but not make it to Nelta to fulfill our part of *The Pact*, what might they or their alien friends do to the people on Earth? In between our quantum-dialogues with the Neltans, I and several other Regents kept replaying the Neltans' reassuring words to trust them and to have confidence in the schematics of the massive ship that our scientists had received but as of July 19, had not yet disseminated into a working model. We argued to reporters, the media, and through our social sites that the Neltans had helped us advanced our transport vehicles thus far without any adverse effects; therefore, we can trust *them* to provide us the blueprints of a perfect ship that can deliver a crew *safely* to Nelta. Thank goodness that on August 5, another communication day with the Neltans, that our engineers *finally* unraveled a 3D model of a ship—really an astrocity!—capable of gliding through wormholes and gleaning neutrino energy from black hole singularities!

Another day passed and the Voting Facility in China returned the results: 82%. So close! That global-wide persuasive campaigned worked.

However, another problem emerged in the forefront of the daily votes: the time constraint. Could a crew *really* arrive at Nelta on time to present their Advancement Committee with human DNA in sufficient time to fix their genetic problem

First Communication

before their race would become extinct? Even though their life span is twice as long as the human lifespan, by the end of their thousand-year stasis, surely their telomeres will have completely degenerated to allow the survival of only a second generation of their species. "No way can we help them," many people around the globe began asserting through the media.

But I, along with my Regency colleagues and several scientific communities who were Neltan allies kept campaigning and advocating for the 85% vote of approval by saying: "If we don't help them, they *will* die." We continued another staunch persuasive campaign to show them the data that seemed to be the way to change peoples' thinking and voting.

Still, people worried about the time constriction. That September 28 vote appeared bleak, until, in a twist of luck, an old Neltan wise master appeared through the IMAX transmission screen instead of Ambassador Shaesar. People around the world were shocked! He looked so unlike any Neltan anyone of us had ever seen before: tall and lean with white skin, a protruding forehead and white eyes that almost appeared computer generated. He showed us proof that the giant ship we would build—if we follow the specs to the minutest detail —would succeed in spacefolding to Nelta in *exactly* 100 years of Space Fold Time to the 1,000 years Real Time travel period and arrive in orbit around Nelta. Out of his hands as if by magic, he expanded a holographic map of wormholes intersecting, disappearing, and then re-materializing on the approach to Nelta inside their M84 galaxy. One wormhole, a Neltan exploratory team had glided through to spacefold several times to the Andromeda galaxy.

That's how they heard my cosmic call for help in the first place, through one of the particle accelerators their explorers had places in the Andromeda beacons and directional systems. Before walking into one of Nelta's subterranean stasis chambers, the tired man assured us that if we left Earth at the latest by June 10, 2070, we would arrive at Nelta in time to see their planet fully restored by The Matter Stream and greet

J.P. Osterman

Ambassador Shaesar, or another Neltan liaison, and present the liaison with human DNA.

That wise Neltan master and his simple explanations clenched *The Pact* as people around the globe approved the virtual document by 87% on October 4, 2061. Later that night, after the internet Polling Facility in China closed, all fifty of us Regents shook virtual hands with the Neltans inside Parliament House in Canberra, Australia—the Regency's headquarters that year.

With all those heated and sometimes contentious verbal battles, media brawls, and One World media site debates *finally* out of the way, we Regents and scientists could focus on *really* advancing humanity to another level!

During future intergalactic alignments, several agencies, media corporations and learning institutions held forums and symposiums with their counterparts on Nelta. Our engineers, scientists, sociologists, anthropologists, genetic specialists, and other prominent professionals refined our relationships with the Neltans who continued to quantum-transmit technological blueprints and overwhelming knowledge to Earth. As trust and friendship between our species grew, although limited due to the lack of face-to-face contact, friendship most people on Earth welcomed the Neltan-based improvements.

Some people began protesting the influx of alien technology. They were part of the 13% who voted down *The Pact*. That's when the Tech-No Protesters founded their movement and began overtly and covertly stirring up animosity, distrust, and doubt in Ambassador Shaesar and the Neltans.

From that *Pact* signing day until today, February 27, 2068, Neltan-based technology has advanced humanity to a new level of living and experience. As in the past when people acquired an influx of new technology that made life easier and simpler than before, scientists have transformed cumbersome reactors into safe, contained, practical fission-fusion energy devices. Gone was the reliance on plastics, natural gases, and oil as engineers and physicists began harnessing electromagnetic

First Communication

radiation and neutrinos to create self-propagating, energy networks for Smart Biodomes, automobiles, and our quantum-computer, Terra, Version-I.

Nano-technology and robotics melded with biogenetic experimentation and implementation; and all our aerospace industries began building spacecraft out of junk metals and salvage scattered around the globe. Car manufacturers began revamping old automobiles into all sorts of hover cars and hover vehicles.

However, the most giant of *all* space ships, Earth's megaship, *Sagan*, is on a schedule to launch from Space Station I on June 10, 2070, in what The World named Earth's *Friendship Mission* to Nelta.

The only thing left is for our fifty-member Regency team to finalize *The Pact* tonight in a virtual ceremony we have scheduled with the Neltans. The event *has* to go on as planned with *no* interference as per our agreement inside *The Pact*. The Neltans have never threatened us, but we know they have alien friends and allies. They showed us one such race of beings who exist on an exoplanet in the Andromeda galaxy, although that species is centuries behind us technologically and appear incapable of attacking Earth. But, if there's one thing we've learn: time and a little help from advanced beings can alter the perceived expanse of space, even if the vast distance between stars and galaxies appear impossible to reach. We now know differently than what we believed impossible before when the universe appeared too big to explore and our own planets too distant to colonize at will. Now, a flight to the space station orbiting Titan takes one hour via a quick spacefold jaunt. All this advancement…thanks to the Neltans.

Now, since it appears as if *their* part of *The Pact* is working, that The Matter Stream sample is almost finished restoring Earth's depleted ozone, we must begin to fulfill our part of *The Pact*, starting tonight, when we virtually sign the document alongside the Neltan Advancement Committee and Ambassador Shaesar. The last Neltan/Earth wormhole *must* activate at the Decagon Accelerator at 9 o'clock tonight,

J.P. Osterman

Eastern Standard Time, which is 1:00 a.m. Coordinated Universal Time (UTC). At that moment, Ambassador Shaesar's hologram is scheduled to stream from the Decagon into the IMAX transmission screen inside the Press Room of the White House, this year's Regency Headquarters. The translation screen harbors the newest imaging properties that interact continuously with technology on Nelta, that is, until prior to the last of the Neltans entering stasis and severing the quantum connection. The screen takes up nearly *half* of the seventy-foot long wall-zone space of the Press Room's north wall, is in constant synchronicity with the room's ceiling and wall-mount processors, and can read atomic strings inside matter. From those imagers, Terra's matrix will process the quantum-communication for The World to experience through their own personal matrixware systems.

So much is resting on the upcoming final transmission that's scheduled for 9 p.m. Most of the Neltans are already in stasis and all their wildlife in stasis facilities.

Part II: Final Transmission

J.P. Osterman

Chapter 10 - Stage 1 And Holding

Looking at his reflection in the mirror, Thornton Manning lifted his chin, inspecting his neck. "Not a line anywhere...I look twenty-five again. The Regeneration procedure works!"

Suddenly, bright light shot through the Oval Office.

The holographic Smart Bar over his desk showed the alert, a *Yellow Stage 2*, radiation from a solar flare. Not the least of the Yellow Alerts, a *1*, it wasn't as bad as last week's *5* that turned out to be a hardware malfunction in the tropopause shield protecting Earth. Terra automatically streamed the problem and its location to repair crews monitoring the shield on Space Station II. Fixed!

But *this* problem and location weren't even registering on any of his wall zones. Something was wrong with the shield and Terra wasn't "seeing" the problem. Yet the *2* reading was good news. It meant the Matter Stream sample was almost finished healing the ozone as the Neltans had promised in *The Pact*.

He checked the sample's trajectory and stats on one of his

First Communication

wall zones. From its sun-bright appearance, it had gleaned another dark matter layer and infused with sufficient dark energy to propel it towards the sun where it would intensity with life-enhancing plasma, streak back to Earth at the speed of a solar flare, and fortify the ozone one last time. That final *Time of Contact* continued to flash, *4:45 p.m.*, in an hour.

A grid map on another zone displayed the number of people congregating throughout the city: 1,000,252. For several days, people had been streaming out of hovercraft stations and Metros. They had judged the atmosphere safe, trusted the Neltans' promise, and wanted to experience tonight's *Pact* signing ceremony with Ambassador Shaesar and the Neltan Advancement Committee. If that light *2* would scroll up to a *5*, Manning realized he'd have to stream out an emergency action and evacuate people from the surface.

He raced to the window, searching the sky, a cloudless blue pane with a hint of an aurora. In the distance, he spotted a section of the tropopause shield's spider-web array rippling bright orange as if on fire. The wall zone displaying Earth and its biometrics was showing a C3-class solar flare hitting an area over the Atlantic. Not too bad, but bad enough to interfere with a fragile and healing ozone. If he could see it, everyone could, but Terra *still* wasn't registering the problem either on Earth or in space.

"What's *wrong* with the shield, Terra?" He had his system's version on Verbal-mode, not her usual standard Appearance-mode. "Something's happened. What?"

"I am receiving no indication of a shield problem, Regent Manning," the quantum computer replied.

"*No* indication...w*hat*?!" He waited. She didn't answer. "Appear, please."

She materialized alongside him as the graphics version of a woman he had modeled her after years ago.

"Your matrix can detect *everything* from here to Neptune. I don't believe you aren't picking this problem up." He showed her the glowing sky, then called his concerns to Research Station II and ordered another repair crews to the site over the

Atlantic. "Fast! Hurry! You deal with software coughs and glitches, so check for those *and* intrusions." He also copied General Rand on Military Station III. "This blasted problem could be terror related. Search the area from your position." He turned back to his Terra-III, the only experimental matrix version processing on Earth. Everyone else had Terra-II. "Well? Ya figure out what's wrong?"

"I am receiving no indication of a problem, Regent Manning. However I believe *you* are seeing a problem."

He breathed, and again breathed. "You're looking *right at* the affected area but you can't see it?" Again, she said no. "God—we don't need this right now! If this detection problem you're experiencing gets worse, it could stop tonight's ceremony!" He motioned for her to walk with him along the wall zones. "*This* stream bar indicates that some people outside have noticed the problem. Station II just launched two craft on a trajectory toward the problem. *I* see the problem. We're *not* crazy, Terra."

She stopped at several graphic views of Earth, her green eyes flashing in Scan-mode. He knew she was processing *every* person's holosite address, her matrix streaming data as far as Neptune to people on the small expedition there who were receiving live streams from Earth. Her stats scrolling down on another zone showed her processing at its usual perfect 100%. She had eyes on *every* person and *every* location...all but *one* vital spot.

"I don't believe this!" The alert was holding, but the radioactivity striking the shield was still dancing on that one small area. "Okay—okay...let's *do* something." He walked brusquely over to the zone displaying Earth and its graphic readings and tapped on a request for an entire matrix scan that he knew would ignite Matrix Techs in all seven facilities to scramble for a solution. "Let's fix your glitch and get your cosmic vision back to normal. God—something *so* easy is becoming *so* complicated!" As the facilities streamed back an affirmative response, he said, "I don't think this icon's ever been launched, so when they begin asking me why, *you* tell 'em

First Communication

you can't see, Terra, even though you *seem* to be seeing everything outside, inside, and every which way around all the space stations." He plopped down in one of his chairs, his mind cluttering with possible causes and quick fixes. But if *she* didn't have any, he sure couldn't conjure up any himself! "In the meantime, let's circumvent your sight issue. Rely on measurements and objects around it, like searching for a black hole. I did that for a while at Arecibo before the ozone attack. *That* should temporarily help you work with the techs to locate the point of difficulty." After she complied, he ordered her back to Verbal-mode.

A tropopause shield array activated on January 1, 2062, the day Research Station II activated and began infusing it with solar energy. The Neltan Matter Stream sample was healing the ozone; but in the interim, all we had was the fragile array. At night, it looked like interlocking webs; during the day, invisible as starlight. Through portable tablets and wrist devices, people received readings via any one of the four space stations, except Prison Station V. People knew immediately about solar activity, but Terra categorized the severity, and The Regency determined whether to stream an alert to The World.

He thought of the possible damages: heat exhaustion to dome tiles melting. Medical hovercraft and small emergency stations were at quarter-mile intervals. "Terra, stream *all* shelter locations to people in the affected area but not an *Emergency Alert*. Order people to stay under protective cover, but *not* return home. A mass exit could be a problem too! Tell them we're analyzing the shield and will fix the malfunction ASAP. If *that's* what it is...a malfunction...oh, but don't tell them that! If you predict conditions will deteriorate, I'll order people to evacuate the surface completely." He also streamed the problem to his fellow Regents who were incoming and would need additional protection.

As Terra complied, Jane Dirk's ring tone resounded. His Lead Secret Service Agent, she was a young Second Lieutenant when he hired her after the Australian People's Army consolidation into the Global Enforcer Agency, April 8, 2058.

J.P. Osterman

"On," he called.

From the Secret Service booth at the Center Lobby, Jane appeared in a hologram in the center of the office. She had Location icons floating around her waist. Flicking them up and double tapping them would open up views for observation. "Are you alright, Regent Manning? Terra shows no radiation penetrating the White House, but we haven't received an Okay from you." She was short and lean with an upright posture but warm glowing features.

He gestured at his Smart Bar for the room's environmental stats. "Temperature's fine, Jane. The alert's been holding at *Yellow 1*."

"That's a good sign, Sir!"

"Sure is, but not enough," he said. "I sent Station II an imperative to send a crew to it fast. Obviously, the roboticware malfunctioned or experienced a glitch. This ozone reading's not budging either. I don't like what I keep seeing!"

She touched open a graphic globe of the Earth. In geosynchronous orbit were five interspersed space stations and numerous satellites. Astrocraft were vault out of orbit, gliding into launch sites at the various stations, or waiting for permission to pass through the shield to sites on Earth. The shield was shimmering red in one small location over the Atlantic, and the faint Matter Stream sample was bright in the far background on its approach to the sun.

"Soon we should know the problem and fix it, Sir," she began, "and as soon as that sample finishes its job, we won't *need* to depend on that shield anymore. Soon!"

He gestured at the time on the Smart Bar. "Yep, in less than an hour we should receive those stats. We'll have *solid* reproducible measurements—proof that the Neltans kept their word, and we can finalize tonight's *Pact* without being bombarded with arguments and criticisms of our instruments." He felt nervous, suddenly sweaty and took a long drink of cooling water.

She swept up and enlarged a hologram of two craft revving toward a web of laser-lights interconnected with small cubes,

First Communication

the shield's power sources. "Looks like help's on the way up there. But if that temp increases in here, you gotta vacate to below."

"I'm fine, Jane. But I'll be *especially* fine after they fix that shield!" He waved her away. "Just go and make sure the media are protected in the Press Room. We have a slew of reporters setting up in there."

"Yes, Sir...*and* their robotic projectors are *everywhere*, along with those darn robot servers and greeters from maintenance. Careful where ya step if ya go out there!" Closing the view of space, she enlarged an image of the bustling Press Room.

As one of the few sites receiving the Neltan-based IMAX screen throughout the years, voters should have renamed the renovated Press Room the Quantum-Communication Convention Center! With all the interfacing technology, the place looked like a high-tech lab trying to appear homey...for the Neltans' sake, and so that The Regency could maintain a good impression while the Neltans walked around the room as broadly as the quantum-exchange would permit them to roam, usually a twenty-five foot perimeter in front of the screen. Dotting the room with color were fiber optic trees and plants with virtual blooms. Small sparkling chandeliers were functioning not as lights but Concealers, obstructing Terra's beehive ceiling processors that appeared as decorator mistakes, but that Concealer Securityware could magnify the smallest detail from any perspective. Those were Terra's "eyes," with an instantaneous interface to Jane Dirk, Enforcers and Military Station III. Upon entering one of five double doors, maintenance had placed perfect rows of plush high-back chairs in front of a long line of nine hologram stages. Maximum seating capacity was one thousand, with conservative standing room availability. Behind those stages stood the IMAX transmission screen, an entire section of 3D walling framed by a glowing Neltan-based Matrix Interfacer. The Neltans called the glowing Quantum Interfacer with its translation/transcription capability, Encantado. Actually, that was a human inference after someone finished manipulating the program's virtual shape shifter application. At 9:00 p.m., Eastern Standard Time, that huge screen system would ignite, interface with Terra's matrix, and begin translating quantum images from the Decagon accelerator—the crucible through which the Neltan/Earth wormhole spacefolds through galaxies from Nelta. The intricate cosmic connection would last until one of its 47 wormholes unlinks from the wormhole array: the average quantum-communication lasting three hours, fifteen minutes, ten seconds, and eight-hundred and sixty milliseconds.

"Two media crews with their Matrix Techs just arrived in the Press Room, Sir," Jane said.

"It's only 3:48!"

"Yeah well, the crew wants to add extra imagers to the wall zones and the techs say we need more ceiling processors to interface with the IMAX screen. We checked 'em all out. They're legit. We have to give people at home a good show tonight, right, Sir? Us *and* the Neltans. They said they have something special planned for us too, so I guess the additional hardware is necessary. It's gonna be something, Sir. *Everyone* can't wait!" She rubbed her hands together excitedly.

"Yep, that's right." He watched the image of craft dipping and gliding through glistening power cubes of Earth-protective energy as if they were dodging cones. They suddenly slowed, obviously focusing on one ten-mile section. "It's the last communication The World will have with the Neltans for a thousand years."

"We hope, Sir. We *hope* they all make it outta their stasis just fine…that *everything* turns out for them as planned *and* us on The List who'll be spacefolding there to help them." She had a look of anticipation on her face and then flicked off a glowing piece of lint that someone had brought to her attention on the crested pocket of her starch-perfect blue blazer.

He had hired Jane Dirk in May of 2058 after a Judicial Committee swore him into The Regency. As his Lead Secret Service Agent, he trusted her with his life. Still, he hated

First Communication

admitting people into the Press Room even though a special partition was protecting his adjacent Oval Office. The Tech-Nos had all sorts of hide-and-disguise methods, and the terrorists were good at sneaking in little bomb distractions. Thus far, Jane had always intercepted threats and responded with military measures.

"You're right, Jane. We have to make sure that not only *this* ceremony comes off as scheduled but also that we give The World a great experience. The Regency is counting on your focused attention to Security." He turned the Smart Bar and noticed the alert holding at Stage 1. *Still* something was wrong with the shield. "When's this fix gonna happen?!" On a wall zone, he streamed the alert with a request for an update to the crew now scanning several power cubes on the shield.

"I won't disappoint The Regency, Sir." She swept the view of the repair crew in space in front of them. "I can take every precaution for security around here, but sorry I can't beam up and fix that up there," she chuckled. Appearing breathless, she received a message from a fellow agent. "The media wanna bring in more robotic projectors. The solar flare is interfering with optics translators at the seven matrix facilities." She showed enlarged a virtual display of the interconnected centers flowing from all seven continents. "If this continues, individual holosites will receive fuzzy experiences."

"Allow them to add the hardware then," he said, waiting for a response on the repair.

She swept away all the holographic visuals until only her bustling station appeared in the background. "A few reporters would like to talk to you, Sir, since you're the only Regent around, although we just received word that Regent Jenkens is incoming."

"Reporters, pundits, holosite hosts…*uh*." He felt dread.

"They're ready to go live with this ozone dip and coverage on the ceremony. They'd just like a brief face-to-face with you. Whataya think, Sir?" Her voice turned softly cautious. "I know you hate talking to 'em but would you consider saying just a few words? The polls haven't closed yet for the

Executive position." She showed him results streaming in from the facility in China. "You're in a dead heat with several Regents. Talking to the media would only help. It's none of my—"

"Wait a second." On Wall Zone 1 next to his desk, he received a response from the repair crew. They had located the problem, but they needed a few more minutes before they could give him a detailed report. Then he realized why she was still in his office: to secure interviews. The media must have been hounding her, and panicking, even though he hadn't stream out the alert. Jane was just trying to play mediator. "Fine. I'll open up a connection in here, but I have to keep them on hold until I receive word about the shield. It takes priority."

"I understand, Sir. I'll clear them for entry and tell them all to hurry and set up their equipment." Before she faded, she said, "Oh—and Sir, the crowd's now at one million five-hundred. I'm going to consult with our Lead Enforcers to launch more zeppelins for crowd control. We're also streaming out more security avatars and larger icons in and around the Mall so people can easily locate food, protective grandstands, and entryways to shelters and safe havens. GPS apps *could* experience static."

"Good. Keep me informed of what's happening, Jane. But I think it's best to send out the *Metro Closure* notice to everyone around the globe. Stop people from coming into the city. If they're not within an hour's reach of D.C., order 'em back home." After telling her shut down all Sky Lane traffic into the Metro's Park-n-Ride zones, he said, "Use Wall Zone 1 next to my window to stream me visual updates."

"Yes, Sir, good thinking with those ten interchangeable displays."

A small section of the wall to the left of his desk lit up with a green frame. His Smart Bar still had the air quality alert at *Yellow 1*. Nine-hundred grams per cubic meter was the Old Normal, before the detonations of 2057. We're *so* close to that reading! The outside temperature was an abnormal 85° with

First Communication

the time blaring 3:55 p.m.

"Terra, after we fix this shield problem and your detection glitch, it looks like the Earth'll be back to normal!" He felt churning excitement. "Maybe then we could get some winter."

"And we all *can't wait* until we can *finally* spend time outdoors," Jane interjected. "Think this crowd's getting wild now? Wait until the ozone's reading normal. It'll be like getting a week's worth of presents in one day."

"Yeah, and I'll probably be joining 'em," he chuckled, "but back to this." He showed her the screen depicting all the foot traffic in the city. "Depending on where people are at, they need to know to follow those directional avatars and icons, get into subways and head indoors as a precautionary measure until we can fix the problems. Also, keep monitoring those underground wells and reservoirs. People need not only shelter from this flare, but also plenty of water."

A small flash of light hit the room, and he dashed to the window. "Hold...hold—"

A small sparkle illuminated in the afternoon sky like a tiny fireworks.

"What the hell's the problem up there? Can't those techs and engineers fix that one spot!?" On Wall Zone 1, he watched as craft continued hovering over a shield-cube in space, obviously scanning the hardware.

"I just dispatched your orders, Regent Manning," Jane said softly. Her hologram at the center of the room faded but she appeared on the newly activated, Security Screen 2. "The shield's steady, Sir, and people outside appear to be doing fine. There's a little commotion, understandably, but as you can see..." She opened up a hologram over her wrist device that showed a tiny portion of a busy street. "People are following avatar guides and emergency icons. Businesses are popping up Smart Tents around bleachers, benches, and sidewalks. Everyone's taking cover...just in case air quality worsens."

"*Huh*," he exhaled. "We've been through this before and we'll survive again, Jane. Terra is processing at full matrix intensity...but wait. Wall Zone 2 indicates that one panel is

J.P. Osterman

missing. The crew spotted the problem!"

Terra still wasn't detecting the missing hardware, or she would have posited several solutions.

Red on Wall Zone 2 was now flashing the affected area on the shield: *Quad A10, Section 1: Panel Count: 1,009.*

"Jane, a missing panel let in radiation."

"A missing panel...but how, Sir?" she asked.

"A meteor strike...a malfunction that launched it into space...dunno yet, but we're gonna figure it out." He felt sidestepped and reeling a bit from the revelation.

"A theft, Sir...maybe major theft...not good."

"And Terra didn't see that coming? I can't believe it!" he gasped. "Tell the other Regents please while I work with the repair crew to figure out what happened." As Jane streamed the information, he ordered: "Terra, it's a missing panel, so launch supply craft to that area so the crew can fix it."

"Yes, Regent Manning," Terra replied.

Not wanting to think that terrorists could be responsible for yet more chaos, he called the window to Dim-mode and the brightness subsided. "The atmosphere is stable and no deadly levels of radiation are incoming. It's definitely blinding out there, but nothing that's gonna kill us."

"Right, Sir," Jane said. "So now's probably the best time for an interview."

"Let's do it then," he said.

She hailed the media on her wrist device and ordered them to connect to a live-stream channel right into the Oval Office. She whispered to him as the wall connection hummed to Full View-Mode: "People are *sure* to remember this personal touch coming from you, Sir, as they continue to cast their votes for Executive Regent. *Shh*—we're almost live. Good luck!" She disappeared Off-screen.

A hologram of the bustling Press Room appeared in the center of his office. Reports dropped everything and turned to him. With surprised and eager faces, they began greeting him. The wall mounts and quantum-rainbow ceiling processors in both rooms flared on, and the ceiling trim turned green in

First Communication

Activate-mode. Small robots in the Press Room extended tripods into the air. They began to capture the Oval Office projection for people around the globe to activate in their homes, businesses wrist devices, or portable tablets.

After running his fingers through his hair and smoothing down his jacket, he called on his Standard Public Speaking setting, and Wall Zones 11 through 20 on the opposite side of the office morphed into a scene of soothing waves lapping on a Tahitian shoreline. A gentle breeze resounded, followed by a salty smell. He felt as if he was standing on an actual shoreline. "Okay, Terra, Connect."

Hearing faint Hawaiian music, he waited for Terra's Automated Voice to begin her usual introduction: "People of a United World, I interrupt your regularly-scheduled holosite programs for a *Special Report* live from Regency Headquarters." The imagers all around the room were now blasting his face and the tropical scene around the globe. "Here is Regent Thornton Seth Manning, living from his Oval Office."

Manning said, "Ladies and Gentlemen, the tropopause shield has held through several solar events, and Virginia is the place being hit the hardest this time." He gestured out his window. Orange curls of light were rippling over that portion of the shield. Even though the time read 4:02 p.m. and the sun would set at 5:58, Earth's star appeared blinding. "We're experiencing a little malfunction, that's all. As you can see," he gestured to Wall Zone 2, "this is a minor problem but we're almost through repairing Quad A10."

He continued: "Terra's matrix is streaming through Station II at full capacity into the tropopause shield. We detect no buffer issues in the matrix. That's *good* news." He didn't want to tell The World that another terror attack might be pending. He didn't know all the facts even though something was wrong. Holding his usual calm façade, he said: "Please, Ladies and Gentlemen, follow all virtual icons and avatars to safe locations. There, as before, you will have food, available medical care, and water. The Regency has continued to stock all shelters and safe havens to full capacity. Most

J.P. Osterman

importantly—remember that we *will* continue to survive and thrive. Our ozone *is* continuing to remain stable in spite of this little shield malfunction, which is a good sign that the sample has worked as promised! Furthermore, as you can see from information streaming to you on all your devices, it's refortified…and approaching the orbit of Venus, so the locator app is indicating."

Next to him, he called on a hologram of the one-million-mile long, bright-yellow ribbon of energy sweeping through space toward Venus. Traveling close to the speed of a solar flare, the Matter Stream sample was absorbing dark-matter as its dark-energy containment field continued to propel the force through the cosmos like a giant spring.

He said, "We survived several ozone calamities, and now this small solar flare has just passed." He sighed, hoping The World would feel relief along with him. "Techs are now fixing the shield right now, and I'm connecting our One-World grid to that portion of the matrix so you can watch the repair live." He paused, waiting for the hologram of the sample to fade and a 3D-show of the shield in space to begin. "Ladies and Gentlemen, the Neltan Matter Stream sample *is* on its way to strengthen the ozone layer. Terra?"

After he gestured for her to proceed, she said, "Contact projected at 4:45 p.m."

"That's forty minutes," he said forcefully. "Ladies and Gentlemen, keep your devices activated to the Regency's holosite to receive live updates from Terra. And please, follow all avatar guides and directives. They'll lead you to safety, especially those of you entering the city. The rest of you, please remain in the safety of your communities and businesses. As I streamed to you several minutes ago, we are closing down all air-lane traffic into D.C." He nodded to Terra again, and she re-streamed the message. "Until later, good evening. The Regency and I will continue to interface with you through our personal holosites as usual. Farewell."

He peeked up into his rainbow ceiling processor. "Off, Terra."

First Communication

His tropical background extinguished.

He was alone. He looked at the holographic bar above one of the wall zones. The numbers of people—their profiles really—entering The Regency's holosite made him a bit dizzy. He couldn't keep up with the scrolling tally. "Stop, Terra." He read the count, 796,774,002. That was close to half the population, not including children under twelve, people off-Earth, or the extreme elderly. Below the number, he spotted another important computation: the Global Institution/Facility Profiles, which was holding steady at 152,000. Those numbers meant that some people weren't streaming live to the Emergency Alert, and those people were in danger.

He peered up at his Terra hub in the center of his ceiling. "Terra, I want that speech I just made intruding into the holosite world of everyone who didn't stream into this channel. I need to know that *everyone* gets it—from here to our station orbiting Europa."

"Yes, Regent Manning," she replied.

"And if you don't get a retina read from those people, make our Enforcer avatars *scream* it into their faces. Receiving help and direction are more important than any reality someone's creating, editing, or participating in besides mine."

The rainbow-light processor cycled wildly around the Terra hub, and then stabilized to its normal rotation. "Yes, Regent Manning."

Agent Jane Dirk hailed him to enter and when he approved her visual appearance, she said: "Security is receiving an overwhelming response to your speech, Sir. That holosite intrusion you just ordered is a great idea. You *definitely* have a strong way of delivering a message, Sir and making people listen to warnings. *I* feel safe with *you* in charge."

"Thanks, Jane," Manning said. He was still fixated on the changing sky—invisible solar winds splashing the blue with radioactivity. "If not for that sample the Neltans sent us, I can't even imagine where we'd be right now." He rubbed his eyes. "A dust bowl most likely." He felt tired and popped a coffee lozenge into his mouth. "But thank God we're not!"

J.P. Osterman

He aimed the wrapper for the wall that turned into a virtual basketball net that caught it, slurping the small paper into its nano-materials.

"You never panic like most people, Sir, even though we've been through drills and radiation blasts," she added. "I don't know how you keep it all together, Sir. I'm amazed. You're an inspiration."

"Okay, Jane, thanks," he said, lightly laughing and walking behind his desk. "Now, please get back to activating all the Emergency protocols, and make sure you program all the avatars to tell people to remain calm and follow directions. Get together a team to help you. *You're* The Regency's Lead Secret Service Intermediary." He ordered Terra to activate her new position. "Go and take charge, Agent Dirk."

"Yes, Regent Manning!" she said excitedly and her hologram faded.

First Communication

Chapter 11 - Thief

Manning plopped down in his giant chair. "We'll *all* be just fine…I'm sure…I hope," he said to himself, blowing into his fingers as if it was freezing outside. In reality, the outside temperature was showing a blaring *87°* in the Smart Bar. That was a two-degree increase, which meant that Terra's matrix was holding together the tropopause shield array even though one satellite wasn't operating. "*Whew*—close call. Everything looks fine…hot, but fine. Just keep those shield arrays functioning—"

"I detect an arch in Satellite 4 at latitude thirty-eight degrees, fifty-three minutes north; longitude seventy-seven degrees, two minutes west," Terra interrupted.

"Well, now you're detection problem seems fixed!"

"As of 4:14 p.m., Regent Manning," she said.

He was busy conjecturing the complexity of the hardware fix. "An arch means a by-pass is in progress. Good! Oh—and relieving that you're back to Normal, Terra. I hope."

As he waited for a quick positive response, a hologram of the shield appeared in the center of his office. Terra illuminated the array with the orange spectrum of visibility.

J.P. Osterman

Enveloping the exosphere, the graphic representation of the shield was projecting a magnetic net of protective energy interfacing with one hundred thousand, gold-and-silver, quartz-based, cube-shaped satellites. Terra zoomed in on Quad 1A orbiting over the Atlantic and then homed in on one smoking panel.

The shield's strength, 0.00, appeared on the Smart Bar with the time: 4:17 p.m., E.S.T.

"Panel number 1,009 is gone, Regent Manning." Terra's voice was flat.

He felt revved. "Gone!?" He squinted at the cut wires inside the crippled cube. "It looks like the top's been ripped right off! Who—*what* coulda done this? Damn—how?"

"A repair crew is retrieving hardware from a supply craft to fix it, Regent Manning. However, they cannot leave their craft to weld two intricate photon rods that their roboticware can't reach until the solar flare dissipates in two minutes."

On Wall Zone 3's view of the moon and its graphic details, he spotted a faint, yellow line beyond the satellite array. "Show me the distance of that contrail, Terra. That's not ours. And stream this to General Rand on Station III."

Via the matrix connections through space, Terra zoomed in on the foreign craft emission: 100,002 miles away from Earth.

"What type of fuel, Terra? Maybe you can ID the craft that way."

"I'm detecting a propulsion contrail of a 30/70 mix, Regent Manning," she replied.

He felt his chest sink. "Terrorists!" After receiving an affirmative response from General Rand indicating that Stealth Force had also picked up the contrail and were launching craft toward it, Manning said, "How big is the craft and where's it heading? Is it only one...like we're seeing here right now?"

The hologram in his office extended around him. The moon enlarged to three times its size. He felt immediately tiny inside the scene.

"The one craft is on a trajectory to the far side of the moon, Regent Manning," Terra said.

First Communication

He felt his stomach sink. "What kind of craft, Terra?" Waiting for her analysis, he remembered a previous space hunt that ended with no captures or casualties. As then, he now burned with anger as defeat flashed through his mind. "The terrorist cells we've been trying to track down for months musta stole the panel. They must need it for something. What? What the hell for?"

The numbers left of their terrorist enemies were large; but with Stealth Force engaging more of the enemy in space lately, the terrorists seemed to be advancing into various locations throughout the needle-stack quadrants between the moon and Jupiter. Terra had directed astrofighters to search the moon in December. Unable to locate any cells, they abandoned the search. They never did thoroughly investigate that dark far side. Because of past communication difficulties and the intense solar energy needed to maintain satellite-based illumination, everyone deemed that entire section impossible for any type of colonization even though a few brave companies were using robotics to build landfills and mine for dysprosium, lanthanum, and yttrium.

"God...we were so wrong! How could we have been so wrong and missed this?!" He hit his desk and his water tumbled. He brushed the spill onto the floor where fibers slurped it up.

After he ordered Stealth Force on Space Station III to launch an all-out hunt for the craft, he heard Terra say: "The craft's magnetic residuals are barely discernible even through my best optics on Station III. Its propulsion signature shows traces of outdated rocket fuel. Therefore, the craft must be a retrofitted shuttle at least one hundred meters in circumference."

The view of the shield suddenly dimmed. Watching the Matter Stream sample envelope Earth's exosphere right on time and for the last time, he ordered Terra: "Send General Rand my standard Call-to-Attack. He must not have seen this residual fuel emission so that means the terrorists must have some type of blocking frequency they're bouncing off all the stations' detection hardware. Damn! I guess it was just a glitch inside *your* glitch that you picked this thing up, Terra!" He barked swear words that Terra said she filtered out as protocol. "Fine—you're right. I don't want to be perceived as someone losing control." As Terra complied and returned to re-composing the message, he said: "Tell General Rand I'll contact him when The Matter Stream sample leaves Earth. If my hunch is right, terrorists have been covertly moving off-Earth. I wanna know *how*, and why and why we haven't been able to detect their maneuvers." Anger coursed through his body. God—I thought we're were close to finding them all. We've been hunting them down…capturing and killing 'em right and left." As Terra began an exact body count of the enemy, he interrupted her. "We thought their numbers were decreasing! But this intelligence means they've been increasing…to somewhere else." The white surface of the moon burned bright in his eyes as he tried to search each crevice. "No wonder things on Earth seemed a tiny bit calmer lately. General, how could they have managed to sidewind us like this? Go undetected by our newest and best Terra-III matrix?" He hit his desk hard. "How? How!" He took a swig of his water and slammed the bottle on his desk. "You can extinguish the view of the shield now, Terra."

"Yes, Regent Manning."

He trusted this new Terra-III version in his office, but that bad detection glitch that just occurred had him doubting the matrix. Still, Terra's integration with the shield had detected all sorts of problems before, and in time before any damage could wreak havoc. He just needed a little more faith that the quantum system's interface with the shield would hold just a few more hours until The Matter Stream sample could penetrate Earth's atmosphere and completely heal the ozone for good.

"Terra, what's the response to that message I streamed to The World? I hope nothing else happens that could interfere with tonight's Final Transmission with Nelta!"

Terra's rainbow-processor cycled wildly as the she replied:

First Communication

"After The Emergency Intrusion you sent globally, I embedded your message into all Help Avatars and Safety Icons. *Anyone* jumping into your TManningR4@HolositeRegency World will view it before anything else until you instruct me to change your site. I'm receiving statistically significant positive responses. All others I am rerouting to Enforcers to handle as you instructed."

"Great, Terra!" Still, he only felt half-relieved.

From the nano-panels in his walls, he could hear Terra's matrix voice loud and clear. He could even call up the computer's body he had programmed when he first received the updated version a few months ago. But he didn't want her bodily hologram right now in his office until after matrix techs resolved her vision glitch or facility malfunction. Terrorist spies or hacker Tech-Nos could infiltrate the room via any vulnerability in the Wall Zones, wall-processing mounds, or Terra's ceiling beehive processor. Spy-Eyes could be lurking along Firewalls. A month ago, during the last ozone alert, spies managed to infiltrate his office and captured a Black Ops event. They streamed the scene into space, tipping off the enemy. Thus far, Terra hadn't detected any residual shadows or after glows of hackers or spies, but matrix techs were always writing security algorithms and simultaneously streaming them into everyone's Anti-SpyWare apps-and-icons and Firewalls.

"Enemies," he huffed disgustingly, "and they're everywhere. Just make sure you protect the shield, Terra. Tell General Rand to follow through to-a-T my Call-for-Attack, and fire on *anyone* you see even *inspecting* the shield. Not even our own people are supposed to be around that place except that repair crew!"

"Scanning again, Regent Manning."

"And?"

"The exosphere is clear, Regent Manning. I detect only Station II scientists positioned to space walk and fix the shield as you ordered."

"Good—great, Terra," he said. Outside, he noticed throngs of people on the National Mall popping up shiny silver tents made out of protective nano-materials. "That temporary shield arch better hold...*better* work...and the last portion of that sample strengthen the ozone," he said slowly, inhaling air and holding it. He glanced at the shimmering sky and then the tiny bodies.

The sky was sunset orange, still tinged in green, and the sun shone like a gold coin. The strange aurora was gone, but its death-glow was still burning a pattern of red circles over the Atlantic.

The Pentagon blared again the *Yellow Stage 1* that activated more virtual green lines and arrow icons in the air.

Matrix fixtures on high poles and Terra hubs on buildings began shining virtual Help Mate avatars that began communicating to people, conducting them to areas of safety while prodding them to open up their protective umbrellas.

Calling on several holograms that began showing people responding positively to the alert by following bobbing virtual icons, Manning thought the landscape looked like a virtual world gone-viral. Terra showed him images of people calmly conversing with their avatars. "At least they're doing what I told 'em to do, Terra."

Accordion nano-roofs unraveled and clicked into place along the eaves throughout the entire city, sounded like thousands of staple guns firing.

Manning heard Terra's voice echoing up at him from the streets: "Radiation Level 50. Yellow Stage-1 Alert still in progress."

Rubbing his stinging eyes, Manning said: "That means people inside and under protective materials should be fine, if they take cover." When he heard the roof on the White House flap into place, he added, "I just hope the shield holds! I hope those techs—"

"Shield repaired, Regent Manning," Terra said. "The repair is a seventy-five percent efficiency fix only until the technicians can maintain the proper level of safety in space."

A small red-and-white zeppelin left its advertising path and began following someone who had obviously thought that now

First Communication

was the time to convert a patch of his tent into a floating nano-board and ski across the Reflecting Pool in front of Washington's Monument.

"Terra, order guards in that Coke blimp to zap up that stupid idiot!" he said.

The turret at the base of the zeppelin opened and sent out a red beam that levitated the teenager into the craft. Closing, it resumed its advertisement itinerary over shiny pop-up tents.

"Put a detection grid over that water, Terra...no, put one over *any* surface that some idiot thinks he or she might exploit to become a Holosite sensation."

"Yes, Regent Manning," Terra replied.

The Reflecting Pool shimmered as an invisible net swept over the water.

A droning hum trickled through the White House. "I am interfacing with MacroTec," Terra announced. "The CEO, Mitch Algren, says he needs to launch a satellite to the array to repair the panel to one-hundred percent productivity."

A man's low voice resounded when Terra activated a hologram of the L-shaped facility outside D.C. "We can't repair that section with a mere spacewalk, Regent Manning," Mitch Algren said. "That cube needs a replacement."

"Wow—the shield needs *that much more* reinforcement?" Manning asked.

After a second's lapse in time, Mitch's Algren appeared all suited up in white. "Each nano-spatial portion of a cube needs a photon boost of 0.5 megaelectron volts per nanosecond, Sir. The Matter Stream sample is a regenerative, but its intensity is increasing the electrical output of the entire shield, creating an arcing effect, which in turn is interfering with the stable photon output. Bad cycle to start now, Sir! I know you don't like hearing this but we *must* launch another type of panel to replace that one that's damaged. Now. We—"

"Launch then. Damn!—I can't wait to get the person responsible for this *right* into my hands!" He felt his stomach churn with worry as the hologram of MacroTec and Mitch Algren faded from his office. Walking away from his picture

J.P. Osterman

window—away from the muffled commotion of people stepping out of their tents and marveling at a craft launching into space from Dulles—he watched Mitch Algren's small craft docking with the damaged cube on Wall Zone 3. Space was void of sound, but still his imagination filled in the blanks. As he observed the replacement panel perform the exchange with robotics, he imagined hinges grinding, sheets of nano-metals colliding, and nano-fabrics flapping like kites swirling in a wind. When the new panel flashed inside the cube-shaped satellite, showing interface, he exclaimed, "Done—just in time, *whew*."

"I hope that shield holds. Is it *working*? Terra!" He felt dizzy, his eyes still burning. He could feel static fuzz on his skin. It reminded him of the First Communication with the Neltans, but he washed that memory quickly out of his mind when he heard a high-pitch ring tone. It was his Smart Bar, affirming that the nano-roofing was still interfacing with Terra's matrix, shielding the White House from harmful radiation.

"*Whew*," he exhaled, walking away from the Smart door leading into the room. "Terra? Why haven't you answered?" He glanced at her beehive processor at the center of his ceiling.

The rainbow processing-light cycled wildly around the hub and then quickly stabilized into one, calm oscillating emanation—Terra's way of processing an answer. "My matrix is collecting ninety percent of the solar radiation at all fifty hubs throughout the city and all five-thousand, fifty-eight hubs in Virginia. As The Matter Stream sample passes through the shield into Earth's ozone, I am streaming the converted energy globally, Regent Manning. Since MacroTec began oscillating my Electromagnetic Field Matrix three days ago, I have been able to redirect *more* energy to the tropopause cubes and store more energy for use on Earth. I can give you specific joules upon request. And I *can* assure you that The Shield *is working*, more powerfully *than ever*. It *is* holding."

"Great!" Manning exclaimed. Feeling a tiny reprieve in the chaos, he reached for some cold water, gulped down a throat

First Communication

full of the soothing liquid and then set the bleeding bottle on a table by his giant mirror. Even though the chill slaked his dry mouth, he couldn't quell the hatred stirring through his chest. Once again, he felt palpitating hate for the terrorists who had launched that irreversible chain reaction in the ozone on June 10, 2057.

J.P. Osterman

Chapter 12 - *The Spider*, The Best Astrofighter

"Damn!" He pounded his desk. "I wish I could *reach* in and *rip* terrorists out of *each* and *every* fortress…suck 'em out of *every* lunar hideout, and scoop 'em out of their Martian dugouts! Station III and this office are using your version-III, Terra, and your most innovative Firewalls and recon devices. Why *in the hell* are they *still* eluding us?" He tapped on a graphic representation of her matrix processing flow around the globe. An above-Earth image appeared alongside it, showing matrix processing streaming through the satellite array and into Military Space Station III: the LEO, miniature city station housing all Stealth Force personnel and Civil Service employees supporting the global military. Nothing appeared disturbed even though she was taking so long to answer the question. She appeared stymied.

"Team 10 activated a new shield panel to replace panel 1009," Terra said. That meant that the air quality would immediately improve and the alert subside, especially with the sample scheduled to permeate Earth's atmosphere and fortify

First Communication

it further.

Realizing that they had narrowly escaped a serious air quality problem, he sighed, plopped down behind his desk and said: "That panel must be the key to locating the enemy. Terra, if we can locate that panel and track that foreign contrail, I'm certain we'll gain an advantage over the terrorists. We could take them down...completely...their entire army!...and end World War III. They have something that interfered with your best Firewall, Terra. We find that panel, zero in on their stronghold, hack into their systems, upstream their secrets, and then go in for the kill." He was also concerned with the Decagon beyond Mars. That intricate accelerator needed Stealth Force protection to deter an attack. The Neltan/Earth wormhole had to open up at 9 o'clock for Final Communication with the Neltans. "Ahh we're spread so thin!"

After she streamed the directives to General Rand, Wall Zone 2 flashed a green bar, signaling an incoming transmission. General Rand was responding. Station III's large orbital icon had a time signature: 4:20 p.m. He closed the matrix graphics and enlarged General Rand's incoming scene. The moon was in front of him and the sample about ready to engulf Earth. Earth seemed to brighten in a new kind of blue/green energy. It was the ozone, strengthening already even though the stream was only approaching orbit: that potent and powerful a creation force! He enlarged the view of the moon and stepping toward it so that the blackness surrounded him. He spotted a dilapidated biodome on the lunar surface. Over the jagged dome was a giant, Stealth Force astrofighter that looked like the sleek shiny body of a manta ray. The astrofighter was hovering over the large area, probing for signs of life. On the side of the great ship, he read the name: The Spider.

"Captain Bartlet's craft—yes! Now we have a chance to nab those terrorists!" He remembered the day, January 15 of this year, 2068 when he met Robert Bartlet.

It was late that morning at the bow on the bridge of

astrofighter before it launched from its construction site on Space Station I. Robert Bartlet had a live-stream channel all to himself wherein people around the globe could holosite jump into the craft's virtual world and watch the giant ship's christening ceremony. As the craft untethered from the dock and began a slow glide into space, Captain Robert Bartlet encoded his genetic strand into the matrix, activating the Command-Mode of the ship. Until that point, the astrofighter was a Blank Slate personality void of directionality. The special astrocraft needed its captain's personal touch in the ID grid to read its commander into the matrix.

As Captain Bartlet imprinted his biometrics, the Cosmic Directional Grid and Compass illuminated over the large hologram stage. "Turn 10°, 5 minutes northeast, Terra," he began. "Activate spacefold speed in Camouflage-mode." As the ship coasted like wind over water, he gasped. "She soars like an eagle...and 'er fission-fusion dark-matter rods are hot—hot—hot! The best! Maybe I should call 'er, The Eagle..." He had only two of his ten medals on his starch-perfect beige uniform. His black hair was slick behind his ears and his belt buckle and shoe shine flawlessly brilliant. His First-Chair crewmembers were sitting at their high-tech chairs right up close to the hologram stage, waiting for his next order. His Second-Chair crewmembers were in the background, busily directing holographic icons, securityware, recon grids, and incoming navigational directions.

Manning laughed. "Whatever you decide to name her, this ship's the newest and the best, Captain!" He reached up and struck his shoulder proudly. "The best for the best."

Bartlet maneuvered his astrofighter fifty miles toward a safe, spacefold conduit to Mars.

After he glanced at the ship's direction as reflected in the astrofighter's Microwave Background of that quadrant, Bartlet said: "The hull looks like a spider's legs as it camouflages. This is completely new technology, isn't it Regent Manning?"

"Yes...and an experimental Terra-III, one I hope to work with soon." The bright holographic light was giving him a

First Communication

solid reflection of himself alongside The Captain.

The public had nicknamed him Beethoven, claiming that he resembled historic renditions of the composer. To please his voters, he allowed his campaign team to manipulate the composer's intriguing looks to win him The Regency daily. He even had Beethoven as his avatar and wrist device icon. Although he didn't have anger lines and his hair wasn't as untamed as the composer's, he realized, at that moment, that he could be a Beethoven reincarnation.

"I'll call the ship, The Spider." He said loudly: "Here that? That's your name. I christen you, The Spider."

The ship flashed a green light through Navigation, resounding in a slight drone.

Bartlet exhaled, standing tall, arms folded firmly across his chest.

Manning told him: "The Spider it is, Captain Bartlet, and it'll go down as your best commission yet. Now make The Regency proud. Find the terrorists, strike their niches, and end this war. Stealth Force Success! That's our motto, and you're the guy to make it happen." Then he ordered a propulsion engineer to write the words indelible atop the giant archway leading into The Spider's propulsion tubes on Level 3.

The time changed on his desk, bringing Manning back to the present in his Oval Office. He grappled with what to do next: fret over the shield that he couldn't do anything more about anyway, or watch perhaps the last battle scene that could end World War III.

4:25 p.m. Final Communication would commence in four hours and thirty-five minutes. The ozone problem was gone, along with the alert, and new shield panel was functioning at 100%. He thought: I have to do something…or else be stuck watching the frenzied crowds and worrying about espionage. "I'll monitor what Captain Bartlet and The Spider are doing for a while, Terra," he said excitedly. After she affirmed his direction, he said: "Terra, decrease the projection to ten feet high by fifteen feet wide. I'll observe what's happening from my desk so I can keep an eye on both events in case we receive a Tech-No threat."

"Yes, Regent Manning."

In the center of his office, the virtual reality of The Spider gliding over the surface of the moon enlarged. To anyone seeing the astrofighter without Terra's unfiltered perspective, the ship would have camouflage and blending in with the moon or space.

The Spider decelerated. The crew had located something.

A steady flow of messages appeared alongside the giant ship: conversations between Captain Bartlet and General Rand. Rand was streaming Manning's order to track the foreign contrail, locate the stronghold, hack their computers, discover what technology the terrorists were using that was acting like a mirror to all Stealth Force detectors, and then destroy the enemy.

Manning wanted a better vantage point of the unfolding battle. "Terra, connect me to the interior of The Captain's Navigation Center. I only want to listen, so interface my wall mounts to Covert Display, Mute-Mode. He'll know someone from The Regency is watching, but that's okay. He's used to intermittent and impromptu monitoring." That type of open system was part of Global Law V's Transparency Clause to prevent corruption. "He even welcomes it...get that! I'm grateful I'm not an officer 'cause I'd hate that."

"Yes, Regent Manning," Terra said, her matrix zooming in on the interior of The Spider. His entire Oval Office was now The Spider's Navigation Center. He could call off the Covert Display Mute-Mode functions, hail Captain Bartlet, and appear right alongside him.

As the cockpit enlarged, Manning said: "The Spider is one of the best in action. Terra, it's your best matrix in a stealth astrofighter." He quickly added, whispering: "Stop here and keep me at a distance. No affirmative replies necessary from this point forward until I tell you otherwise, Terra."

She agreed, and he began watching events unfold onboard the astrofighter...

The Spider's oblong Navigation Center was twenty-seven

First Communication

feet in diameter at its longest point and one-fourth the size of the entire astrofighter. Levitating three-feet above the floor and ten-feet in diameter at the center of Navigation stood a steel/quartz plate: a holographic Receiver Stage supported by a thick fiber-optic column and surrounded by glowing vertical bars and a glowing horizontal frame. Both Glow systems were matrix interconnected and their optics interfacing as projectors for the astrofighter's virtual reality technology. Synchronizing with the wall mounts and hundreds of miniature ceiling processor hubs throughout the craft, the Receiver Stage was The Spider's brain and heart, and the beehive ceiling matrix above the stage her circulatory system. The crew had voice and touch capability with the matrix; additionally, Robert Bartlet had a connection to his ship's soul.

He and his First-Chair crew were at their pod-stations around the receiver stage although his high-tech Captain's chair set higher from the rest. Via various graphics of the moon and its topography, the four crewmembers were guiding the camouflaged craft steadily over the surface, mapping terrain on the far side, and balancing Firewalls with Directional Radar caution. As the craft sleeked over the dark terrain, detailed images of the surface illuminated over the receiver stage. The surface appeared roughhewn, with empty lava swells, serrated ridges, and valleys like cut crystals.

Sitting in high-tech chairs behind Bartlet's First Chair crewmembers and wearing reality gloves, his Second-Chair techs were plotting virtual white latitudinal coordinates into the blackest of longitudes inside the lunar graphics. Above the burgeoning lunar map, Terra's beehive ceiling hub was processing wildly, its rainbow illumination in a state of constant change as the matrix interacted with the crew. A yellow, particle light beam from the hub was generating the lunar grid map on the glistening Receiver Stage...

Looking at the developing lunar map, Manning felt like a spectator at a boxing match. "The Spider's tough. I know it can find that cell responsible for stealing another satellite panel. They're around that area, somewhere." He sent a message to

J.P. Osterman

General Rand telling him that he wanted an estimate on when they might locate the enemy or the missing panel. He also asked him the big question: "What the hell do ya think they're planning? I think it's something big besides another strike on Earth!" Then he said to himself after closing the communication with Station III: "With Bartlet at the helm, The Spider should be able to take out these terrorists. But first, he has to find their subterranean hideout."

While waiting for The Spider's receiver stage to generate more coordinates of that far side, he remembered the day LMCO and AstroNautica unveiled the first, Crew-55 Spacefold Astrofighter: August 20, 2064, months after Terra I's matrix began streaming around the globe. Now, the most advanced version was right in front of him: the FC-35 Astro-IV coasting over the moon like a manta ray gliding through water. If not for his order and grand solicitations from the public, there would be no Spider to hunt down the escalating forces of the enemy. Since then, terrorist were managing to steal and modify technologically even though Enforcers were monitoring all manufacturing and assembly sites. He whispered to Terra even though he knew that Captain Bartlet couldn't hear him, "If he can find that stolen panel, we can uncover the big picture behind why we've been hitting walls every time we try to apprehend the enemy."

One obstacle occurred to him: a decrease in support craft.

<>For the past two years, The World had been voting to stop production on astrofighters. Many people posited that if Stealth Force in space and Enforcers on land could chase all the terrorists into space, then World War III would end. People were sick of fighting, bomb threats, and depleting resources, the later not a problem anymore because of the cheap and easy nano-infused metals containing molecular bonding, expansion capability, and especially computer interface. Using excavators, atmospheric devices and gravitational rods, settlers could render a small subterranean or surface zone habitable. "Just let the terrorists go!" some people were demanding. Furthermore, the construction of the

176

First Communication

megaship, Sagan, the astrocity scheduled to launch for Nelta in 2070, was becoming expensive. Docked alongside its construction zone, Space Station I, Sagan's cost was exceeding $500,000 a day even though volunteers were scavenging the globe for the necessary metals needed to meld the "city ship." People were beginning to complain to the media in quick messaging streams as if they were secretly planning to renege on the 85% vote they approved with the Neltans, and the time was almost at hand to begin our part of The Pact we made with them. That building cost was interfering with the construction of mega-dome, super cities to replace rural towns still trying to rebuild from the 2057 bombing. Those sites were often unmonitored. Some inventories had shown missing hardware and software, especially matrixware and junk metals for converting steel into nanometals for spacecraft. Terrorists…they were the ones really holding on to, and escalating, World War III and inciting seething anger for killing and stealing to procure what they needed. The War had morphed into a "Because you're not us you die" racist enterprise for them. No matter how hard The World streamed contradictory information to alter their rigid thinking and worldview, they launched more attacks. Thanks to new laser technology, their missile strikes were now futile, but not their suicide bombs. They harbored a disregard for life—even their kindred lives—to further their beliefs, expunge democracy, and eliminate rights and freedoms. Thus far, even though they had covert settlements on asteroids, converted craft domes, and now a dead zone on the moon, they were obviously longing for solid ground to unite and expand their culture and religion. As the Lead Intermediary between The Military and The World, Manning and his Intermediary Committee were engaged in a daily struggle to persuade The World to assemble more astrofighters to hunt down those extremist terrorists. "Justice and Retribution" were The Committee's daily battle cry, along with past images of forlorn and destruction from 2057. In between all the daily votes and holosite bickers, Manning managed to divert some funds to Space-X. They gathered the

J.P. Osterman

best plasma technology and the best plasma physicists working with the Neltans during wormhole transmission to construct The Spider.

"That astrofighter has top-power Laser Burst weaponry, true level-8 fission-fusion propulsion, and Time-1, space-fabric, fold rate...right off Boeing's and LMCO's Stealth Line on Station I," he said, stepping back, and marveling at the interior of the ship. He stood up from behind his desk, clenched his fist in fight mode, and said: "Now—find the enemy, Captain Bartlet, and strike. I want The World to see Stealth Force Success." He peeked up at his matrix ceiling hub and said, "Yes, Terra, I know...I also have another motive. Victory on the moon and retrieving that panel should secure me Executive Regent tonight!"

Then The Spider's stern suddenly bobbed. The round Scan Light on the base of the astrofighter expanded. The astrofighter stopped.

"What's happening?" he asked, almost cutting out of Covert Display, Mute-Mode and jumping into Spider. He stopped when he saw Captain Bartlet react quickly to the jolt. He sat back down behind his desk to watch. ...

First Communication

Chapter 13 - Scan Light's Find

The astrofighter had detected a problematic signal. The Scan Light enlarged on a patch of pockmarked landscape. Captain Bartlet asked Terra to link *The Spider*'s matrix to the matrix on Space Station III so he could get General Rand's hologram inside Navigation. When The General dressed in green appeared in a hologram alongside him, he asked: "Suggestions for maneuvers, Sir. *You'll* be sending us craft support. We need to take the numbers and sizes into account." He waited as The General consulted with his team and his Terra.

A tall slender Chinese man with a high-and-tight haircut, General Rand had intense brown eyes, red lines for lips, high yellowish cheekbones, thin black eyebrows, and small ears. As with most holographic facial features, his also looked a bit haloed and magnified inside the projector beam. He had the presence of a well-trained, astute, and impenetrable commander. Because of past matrix intrusions and two assassination attempts, he only let into his small circle two generals and five colonels. On his fifty-foot bridge, all others subordinates had to remain behind the giant hologram stage at the center of the football-size Navigation Facility of Military

J.P. Osterman

Space Station III. It was the perfect incentive for advancement and cohesiveness. The arrangement inspired his troops to work with him and support his decisions in harmony as their mentor. Behind his back, they called The General "the Cosmic Watcher" because they believed he really did have eyes in the back of his head. When he took command of Station III, he inscribed the words, *Sharp means Action* above the arched entrance to the helm. During down times, he showed martial arts holograms. A proclaimed Black Belt in the Old School of Wing Chun, he killed fifteen terrorists two years ago with his bare hands. They had ambushed him at a base in Kandahar while meeting with a delegate. Everyone survived because of General Rand.

His image appearing next to the receiver stage with his gold stars glistening on his shoulders, Rand walked On-Stage and began inspecting the forming map of the lunar surface. "Precede *sloowwlyy*, Captain," he said. "Location?" He stepped Off-Stage.

As the matrix flashed the southern coordinates under the hologram of the lunar map, Bartlet said, "We're north of the South Pole-Aitken basin, Sir."

"Good." Rand turned to the First-Chair crew. "Don't do anything that might even accidentally let those hull veins activate for *one* second, 'cause if you do...with this huge ship, the enemy *will* spot the slightest hull shimmer and attack."

"Yes, General," the crewmembers said, snapping back to their duties.

Captain Bartlet said, "Be rest assured, General Rand, we won't lose our advantage and element-of-surprise." He called on his pre-programmed hologram of the matrix: Terra-III.

He had obviously photoshopped Terra to look like the famous model Alexis Brezhnev: five-foot-ten, with blue-eyes, short black hair, and a lean muscular body, except he had edited in a small scar above her right red lip. He often manipulated this Terra image to show his crew how rapidly the matrix could change, so often altered Terras at will.

"Terra, lock out even Emergency Autopilot on those hull

First Communication

veins. Put them *totally* on Manual. The ship'll only de-cloak on my order. Now, *Spider*'s safe, from the terrorists, and *us*, as The General's implying," he laughed.

When General Rand didn't laugh in reciprocity, Bartlet coughed.

A shiny square icon appeared next to the grid map of the lunar surface. It was tossing and turning—a puzzle piece trying to fit in somewhere.

"Yes—just what we're waiting for!" Bartlet said. "Hack-Pack Sonar detected the signal of that stolen shield panel. It's here…somewhere."

The cockpit filled with a pulsing sound, the panel's frequency that dissipated when Terra matched its VIN number to the panel's shiny icon. Immediately, more items appeared in a line behind the stolen panel.

General Rand leaned into the image. "It looks like this terrorist cell took quite a bit of our hardware…and there's an overhauled hovercraft and two retrofitted astrocraft behind these lines of mangled devices. Do you detect any emission signatures or other VINs, Captain? If so, we'll be able to deduce what the terrorists are up to and how they've managed to elude capture."…

From behind his desk in the Oval Office, Manning whispered, "That's just what *I* want to know!"…

"No, General," Bartlet huffed, his chest rising, his jaw tightening. He was obviously stuffing down his disappointment for a perceived under performance. "But with help from this First-Chair crew behind me, I'm sure we can id some of these stolen items, analyze their code and find the hideout."

He and his three-member, First-Chair crew began sweeping up and analyzing the equipment icons that then popped up over The Captain's deck frame. Bartlet swatted them back to the Receiver Stage, "Enlarge these, Terra."

Numbers, formula, and archival data illuminated. VINs and recognition frequencies bombarded the stolen hardware like rain on pavement. Some bounced off, but some stuck. A

J.P. Osterman

few images solidified.

Bartlet said, "We can't match some stolen craft or other missing shield panels, but Terra's showing that one craft they stole contained high-tech drills, air/water conversion systems, and several A-Class Falcon bores."

"Damn it! They stripped all the VINs and signatures from our Terra detectors and trackers. *That's* how the enemy's been able to hide from us," cried Lieutenant William Wallum after he jumped a bit in his seat. As Captain Bartlet's First-Chair Matrix Specialist, Bill had short blond hair cropped neat at his neck, smooth white skin, and broad shoulders.

"Yes, Lieutenant? Ya have *more* to add?" Bartlet asked, nodding a light reprimand at the 'damn it' remark he made in front of The General.

He tapped up several past messages that illuminated over the frame of his high-tech cube. "From the foreign contrail signature Regent Manning sent us...and then as we received more stats from Station III...*we* assumed the terrorists were heading to Mars, *not* the far side o' the moon," Bill answered. "Looks like we were *way* off base! We've been wrong for quite a while! No telling how long and how many of 'em are hiding around here on the moon."

"I'm more ticked off that they stole that panel," Beth Tufter said, gliding away a bit from around her cube. She was First-Chair IT Tech, and obviously proud of her Native American heritage. She had several Navajo icons floating among a row of essential elements over her cubicle frame. "That little missing section coulda fried the east coast! And that personal Call-to-Attack from Regent Manning means he's *really* pissed and expects to see terrorist blood flow red...and *our* blood flow if we can smoke out these criminals and kill 'em fast."

"Take it easy, Beth. We'll locate 'em soon, I'm sure, 'cause we're good," Bill said softly, his eyes diverting The Captain's gaze. "We can't afford more attacks and losses. The Neltans saved us, but after tonight, there's no one...*no more* alien life raft in the cosmos."

First Communication

Sighing as if she might be facing the end, Beth said: "We gotta stop them this time. We just have to! But all this technology we discovered means they're assembling something *massive* to do something *huge*. My God—what!" Bartlet and Bill began streaming the missing items to their owners for verification. Wearing virtual gloves to maneuver hot photonic holograms, Beth used her fingers to gather images of the pilfered objects that began hovering over her high-tech booth, in full view of the entire Navigation Center. Some appeared inside the lunar map. A new image began forming. Silence ensued as Terra's rainbow processing light over the receiver stage churned brightly. The matrix was arranging the pilfered objects into a *new* configuration. ...

Not a member of the Stealth Forces but working with Bill Wallum on *The Spider* since January 18, 2068—three days after Captain Bartlet christened the astrofighter—Beth Tufter had her Master's in Nanoengineering from MIT and was working on her Ph.D. when Bartlet yanked her out of what appeared to be a covert Clash of the Titans. A few Black Ops agents were secretly vying with a bio-medical team from Station II's Research Facility to apprehend Beth on Space Station III. Beth was in trouble, needed help, and didn't know who to trust. It all started on a party day—a number she had circled and starred in yellow on the calendar.

On the morning of March 15, 2067, while conducting research at the university, Beth's classmates set up a practical joke for her on her twenty-second birthday. They created a holosite contest and lured her into participating in it by advertised the virtual world as a game show, wherein "the best host to ask the best questions to Shaesar of Nelta would win a spot on The Regency's select panel to meet the Ambassador during the next Neltan/Earth communication." The Invitation Door read: *You Could Be the Next Ambassador to Nelta!*

Little did Beth and her sorority sisters realize, but Beth's surprise birthday world was small part of a large, covert university experiment—a global social holosite called Bodybook, like the outdated Facebook that secret university

J.P. Osterman

administrators named Sensory Holosite Reality Mining. The project intercepted and copied all virtual applications in all university grids, accumulated data, created algorithms, drew conclusions, and mapped participants' emotions. Their ultimate goal was to have Terra predict human behavior and draw conclusions as to a high school student's future success in the world. The Terra grid they were utilizing was the most advanced encryption code from the Neltans, which Shaesar gave to the Regency on the stipulation that schools and universities use the special grid to enhance learning: "As enrichment only," Shaesar specifically stipulated. However, engineers and techs working at the Global Education Agency altered the hardware of the Scholastic/Social/IQ portion of the matrix—unknowingly in most cases—to predict the applicants who would benefit society by acquiring a higher education, and which applications Admissions Grids should discard.

Later that day on the fifteenth, Beth entered the surprise world with her brown-haired avatar that she programmed with a flowery blouse and a knee-high, leaf-green, A-line skirt. Beth added rosy cheeks, pink lipstick, and a glowing happy face. Those small traits she thought were her true reflections. Once inside the virtual world, her avatar stepped up and asked the virtual Ambassador Shaesar question-after-question. After each of his answers, she watched the number of people jumping into the holosite world grow exponentially. Her sorority sisters were rating her "vibrant," "zestful," and "bubbly;" but rating Ambassador Shaesar "humorless," "boring," and "evasive."

Beth ordered her avatar to jump on top of the graphics microphone and say to everyone participating in the game show: "I'd be humorless *too* if Earth was being eaten alive by supernova blasts. How would *we* like a cosmic Tasmanian devil hitting us? Forcing everyone on Earth to live in a stasis existence…in body pods...for a thousand years!...until a race of people in a galaxy over fifty-million light-years away comes to *our* rescue? Poor guy…give 'im a break, Earth people. The

First Communication

Neltans have been sending us all sorts of great technology, including their precious Matter Stream sample that's healing our ozone. *We've* given them nothing…nothing back, just a promise-in-a-pact. No wonder the guy's a little dry and stuffy. So, let's show all the Neltans that "being human" means "being understanding." She used her fingers to express quotation marks. "We need to change, People, 'cause I'm hearing racism coming from y'all, just like you've been accusing our terrorist enemies. It ain't right, *ahem*, pardon my colloquial use of grammar." Her brown-haired avatar folded its arms and grimaced at the audience. She looked like a Native American princess warrior. Holosite jumpers began clapping in the millions, so the holosite grid showed.

That quantum stream in the matrix back washed. The covert grid exploded. The backlash knocked out the grids of *every* university violating Global Law VII's Privacy Act. For two days, covert Cyber Trackers from major universities searched the matrix until finally a cipher revealed the problem that it took them another ten days to translate. Beth Tufter was different. Something in her neural map nearly killed their matrix grid, almost exposing to The World their corrupt use of matrix software. They began a secret campaign to kill her.

In the interim, someone had secretly streamed the skit to Nelta, where the Neltan Transmission Team received her talk show performance and signaled the Regency. Ambassador Shaesar personally requested a one-on-one, twelve-second exchange with Elizabeth Tufter at the next, global, March 20, 2067, London transmission after completing their Exchange of Technology and Exchange of Worlds Outreach segments.

That Sunday, at 3:44 a.m., after their initial introduction, at the five-second mark during the interview with Shaesar, Shaesar teleported that unique electrical section within Beth's mind to one of Nelta's deep, three-mile long, subterranean facilities. Her image appeared next to him. For months, Neltan workers had been boring out several such stasis channels for over fifty years in preparation for the extinction-level event about to render Nelta a lifeless planet for the next

J.P. Osterman

one-thousand years. Inside the artificially lit labyrinth, glowing like firefly light, Shaesar took hold of Beth's virtual hand and said as a line of scientists watched on behind them, "Here and at many locations under our equatorial line lie miles of stasis facilities with rows of body vessels." Panning the area with his hands, he added, "I need *your* help in the future, Elizabeth Tufter. I need *you*." He smiled and let go of Beth's hand. "You *must* come to Nelta."

Beth's mind streamed back to Earth.

There was something about the consciousness connection that Neltan scientists had coined, "overwhelming synchronicity." Beth was the only person to experience the quantum-nonlocality state of being bodily present on Earth while a portion of her conscious manifested on Nelta. No one else the Neltans said had her type of special neural constitution.

Popping out of the daze that felt as if she was seeing for the first time, Beth said, in awe, shock and wonder: "I'm changed! Wow! My head...my arms...am—am I dead? Alive? *Whew* what a ride!" She glanced at the fifty Regents who were looking at her dumbfounded. "I'm telling you, the rest of my life's *nothing* compared to this—to what I just saw. I can't even *begin* to explain in words...or, or draw anyone a picture. *Wheee—whoa—*yes!"

"How do you feel, Ms. Tufter?" a doctor asked, reading all her vitals on her Double Buddy Image. "Does your head hurt? The DBI doesn't show any detrimental neural affect."

A line of white-clad agents was behind her, their black-and-white craft hovering and droning to launch behind them.

Beth continued to be in a dazed state while nodding and smiling. "Fine, Doc, great, Doc," she kept repeating.

The doctor said to The Regency: "Aside from this red zone in her frontal lobe, Miss Tufter is fine. I did administer a mild, cognitive sedation wave through the DBI, so I think she'll remain calm until the effects of the consciousness exchange wear off. Electron activity is brain chemistry and vice versa. That accounts for the heightened neurological

First Communication

activity. By tomorrow, Miss Tufter should be calm and stable enough to talk through what happened to her. *Then* you can ask her questions."

Manning huffed hard. "I heard. But anything could happen between today and tomorrow."

As other specialists examined Beth, the physician continued to speak with Regent Manning: "The experiment worked. But as you can see from Beth Tufter's elevated behavior, there are emotional side effects even though several of her friends we interviewed say that Miss Tufter is always a bit hyper, and her academic records show she's a straight A, post-grad student and fast learner." He opened up an image of Beth's brain that began twirling slowly in a hologram light over a small medical stage. "I see a small neurological effect only. Miss Tufter will recover, quickly, but *only* because of her unique cerebral signature. It's in her genetic code. I can see an augmented RNA protein derivative. Completely rare! I have no idea what could account for it…and I can't find any living relative alive to compare with Beth's genetics. They died soon after the bombs struck the ozone. A mutation? Don't know, but we'll run tests. So I say with caution, Regent Manning: Do not allow a consciousness exchange through a wormhole again. I remember that you once said you had your heart set on experiencing such a teleportation. Don't. You *will* most likely die sometime during the mind flow. The only way the exchange *might* work is to experiment with consciousness streaming in the Terra-III matrix that you're planning to release to The World sometime next year. But people will need to approve that." All The Regents agreed. Manning pulled away from them and slid into the background.

As the other Regents discussed Beth's condition with the physician, Beth sat inside the DBI outside the British Museum away from the cheering crowds where the transmission had ended. Staring wide-eye into the sky where a faint white line of wormhole emission just fled from the Decagon accelerator into the transmission screen for processing, she said: "I feel great! Completely fine…*happy*. I'm getting outta here." She clicked open the glass door and stepped out of the rib-coned DB-Imager. "Thank you, Regent Manning, The Regency...and everyone who helped me," she said into the projector that was streaming her image around the globe. "You're super for giving me that opportunity. I feel great!" She patted down her arms and legs, checking them for sores, cuts or bruises. "See? Nothing. I feel great...for the rest of my life!"

"Let Miss Tufter go home and rest," Manning said, waving back the crowds. Enforcers parted a path for her to her hover car. "Tomorrow, I'll contact you, Miss Tufter. Then we can debrief and discuss what it felt for you to quantum-consciousness travel." After she agreed, he gestured to a small team of scientists, boarded a Regency astrocraft, and then launched quickly into space on a path to the Cerebral Medical and Rehabilitation Facility on Space Station II, one of the research sites conducting experiments with the new Terra-III and matrix on *Sagan*.

Four bio-medical engineers wearing university logos began pulling Beth toward their revving hovercraft. Another scientific team appeared on the other side of her. They began fighting over her.

A Global NASA psychologist yanked Beth away. "Orders of Protection for Miss Tufter," she said. "Let her go please. We need to add Miss Tufter to The List Terra's compiling as being *Necessary* for the voyage to Nelta."

Both sides let go of her, but continued arguing that those orders didn't make sense because *Sagan*'s launch from Station I wasn't scheduled until June, 2070. The woman maneuvered her away from them and toward a small astrocraft.

"Thanks, Ma'am," Beth said, steadying herself on the woman's shoulder. "*Whew*...I feel a bit dizzy...like I might take a tumble...*whoow*! Glad you're here helping me though." Beth's profile depicted her as a bit naïve and not believing that anybody would purposely hurt her. "Hey ma'am, where ya takin' me!" She wiggled away from her.

"To Station III," the psychologist whispered, prodding her to hurry and join her. "Come with me if you expect to live."

First Communication

After weeks of programming her into Terra's List for Nelta, everyone left Beth Tufter alone, even though she told coworkers and a few Stealth Force agents over the course of changing jobs several times: "Someone's watching me. I know it!" She had intermittent days and nights of living in bathrooms and storage sites—hiding.

Weeks after *Christmas 2067* disappeared off the holosite grid and into the archives of Space Station III, Captain Bartlet jumped into her encrypted holosite world to view Beth's resume that intrigued him. She was looking, covertly, for another job, with him. He said to Terra: "That *she's* applying to work for *me* is strange. This Nanoengineer could be a holosite star! Everywhere I go I see posters advertising that *Sagan* holosite world with her in it. *Hmm*, that's strange too. Why would she want to be on *The Spider*? She's already on The List to board *Sagan*." He sent his avatar to Beth with those questions.

She responded through a cipher world that took Bartlet working with Bill Wallum to translate her message. Dressed in a trench coat and walking through a fog, Beth whispered her reply: "Captain, I haven't told anybody this, but I saw something. I saw *several* things in that wormhole," she cleared her throat in a terrifying sound. "I think—no, I know!—that people are hunting me down 'cause I talked too much about what happened, I think." She wrapped a scarf around her neck and a few strands of brown hair swept across her rosy cheeks. "When I was on Nelta, not really there-but-there, you know what I mean…I saw as I was streaking back through this wild kaleidoscopic ride, a spider-shaped craft. I didn't know what to make of that, until I saw *you*, yesterday, with Regent Manning christening *The Spider*. I said to myself, 'Wow! I saw that ship! And I saw Captain Robert Bartlet inside it!' What you were doing, Captain, I don't know. But I'm sure that everything I saw was occurring in the future. And I think, no I know, that some people—" She glanced over her shoulder, cowered, and then slid into a dark corner. "Some people want me either dead, or gone. Please, Captain Bartlet, hire me as one of your IT-Techs on *The Spider*." She wiped her eyes. "I think I'm supposed to be with you anyway, Sir. I think *I'm meant* to be part of your crew, Sir. Thanks."

He called Bill Wallum to Station III's IT center in the middle of the night; and using his Top Secret, DNA image code, he secured an entire Terra grid and private high-tech cubicle. Because of all the possible dogfights he might encounter with whoever might be stalking her, he was debating whether to hire her. He needed Bill's digging skills to find out more about her. "Elizabeth Tufter sure is energetic, and a real communicator. And it seems she's been runnin' from somebody, *hmm*. Who? This is intriguing. Go check her out." He had Bill do an intense holosite search on Beth and discovered a frame of weeds around Beth's quantum protocol (QP) address. "This is a Dandelion virus capable of deleting her *entire* public profile, *hm*. Someone's definitely out to kill Beth Tufter!"

Bill showed him the shadow behind the wall of weeds. "And this'll automatically write the reason and news for her disappearance *when* she finally goes missing. Someone sure is going to a lot of trouble to get rid of her."

Bartlet began pacing the space in front of the IT stage. "Well, we know the lady's special 'cause her consciousness teleported to Nelta. The only person *that's* ever happened to."

Bill reeled out a gasp of insight. "I bet that's why alota people are after her! The Tech-No protesters probably wanna kidnap her to make some type of statement for their cause. Biotechs, geneticists and researchers probably wanna a department devoted to her brain, and The Regency wants *all* eyes on her 'cause she just got in tight with the Neltans. Poor lady."

Bartlet shut down the search that shut off all the lights. "Come on. I have an idea."

They left Station III and quickly shuttled over to *The Spider*. Once in the cockpit, Bartlet put the Wall Zones on Personal Mode. The astrofighter recently infused with SpyWare protection. *No* unauthorized person or robotics could enter

First Communication

the craft. "We'll use the experimental Terra-III to find out what's going on with Beth Tufter." Accessing a Black-Ops grid, he had Bill cover Beth's profile with the craft's military Safe-Guard Shield. No one would know that anyone had gained entrance into the secure file. After superimposing Beth's profile on the secret file, Bartlet said as the file activated: "This has Ambassador Shaesar's symbol on the cover—with a glowing frame. What is it, Bill? Ya ever see anything like this?"

Bill used Terra-III's advanced photonic ports to open up the special file, but each attempt resounded with a musical note that they interpreted as *impenetrable*, in the Neltan language. He finally slumped back in his seat. "Captain, no use. This is an augmented world with a tiny, no, *nano*tiny entrance…*very* advanced. We need to bombard this file like atoms in an accelerator to unlock it! We could…if we take the encryption to the Decagon."

As a high-pitched frequency sound struck the air, Bartlet yelled: "This *must* mean that the Neltans want Beth Tufter. It's that simple and it makes sense! That's why all sorts of people *here* want her too." The cockpit calmed, and Beth's original resume appeared with her in the background. She was standing knee-deep in a London fog. Bartlet walked around her motionless image and gazed into her blue eyes. "Maybe she can see the future or something." He tapped the Glow frame around the Receiver Stage. "*Hm*, I sure like a good mystery."

"Straaannge for sure, Captain," Bill said. "Well? Think you might hire her, Sir?"

After a moment's pause, he closed her resume and said: "I *need* her." He holosited HR. "Get an offer to Elizabeth Marie Tufter. I want her as a Nanoengineer on *The Spider*. Give her First-Chair and seat her at the station next to Lieutenant William Wallum."

A liaison with the military called him and said, "Captain, I don't know if Global NASA can hire Elizabeth Tufter for that position. She's never had *any* experience on an astrofighter, and only six weeks as Systems Nanoengineer on that renovated shuttle *Clinton*. She's had no training on the new Terra-III quantum-system. Oh—she's red-flagged! Elizabeth—"

"She likes being called Beth." He showed the woman Beth's handwriting sample.

"Okay, but Beth is *only* an expert on Terra-II processing," the liaison argued.

"Stop, please, ma'am," Bartlet began. "I know what this is about. Requirements."

"Requirements, Captain? Why, I don't have a clue what you mean," the woman snapped.

Bartlet straightened up and said: "Cultural re-quire-ment*ss*. Code A-1 of the Global Regulations. Your objection to Beth has to do with skin color, Ms. Azikiwe."

Her lips opened in astonishment. "No one's *ever* managed to say my name correctly the first time, except for you, Captain, and others where I come from, Africa."

Thanks," he said, "and now, to meet your global multi-cultural hiring requirements, Ms. Azikiwe, I'll take two Chinese propulsion engineers and one South American plasma physicist to work in the Drive Level in exchange for Beth. Besides, who knows? The way Beth Tufter got along with Shaesar and Regent Manning, maybe she'll be the first human politician on Nelta, and you'll become famous, that is if you're still alive after we land there…and also, if people, or a group of people, decide that they wanna set up a colony, or city somewhere there."

"You sound about as confused about the future as the rest of us, Captain, even though you know so much more than anyone else." She leaned back in slow acquiescence.

"Yeah, Ms. Azikiwe, no one knows nothin' for sure," he laughed.

Ms. Azikiwe hired Beth Tufter that day, January 18, 2068.

Immediately, Bill Wallum traced her cipher world to contact her. He and Bartlet found her living in one of the station's café restrooms. Using a supply cart as cover, Bartlet took Beth to her quarters on *The Spider*. Bill contrived a good

First Communication

protective barrier for her on the astrofighter with a special code to alert them to anyone the ship labeled *Foreign.* ...

J.P. Osterman

Chapter 14 - The Panel Calls

"See, Captain?" Beth said, leaning toward *The Spider*'s receiver stage and pointing at the image of the stolen panel composed of radiation-proof nano-organics.

The panel, as well as other nano-infused metals, contained the capability to self-repair, imbibe energy, change color and shape, and interface with other technology.

She stomped and cried: "*That panel* was an essential component protecting Earth! Darn terrorists, damn—"

"Okay, Beth, we feel angry about that too," said Bartlet, and she exhaled in the affirmation. "We'll retrieve the stolen panel. If not, after we locate it we'll destroy it."

"*Ooh* I hope we don't have to resort to *that*," she said as she pushed back the blue band that lifted her brown hair, her face glowing in a longing expression. "I guess so though, if we have to, Captain, but too bad we couldn't find a way to confiscate the stolen technology or re-program it to work for us while the panel is still in their hands." She hit her station ledge. "God these extremist goons have caused so much death and destruction because of their 'us against the stranger' mission'!" She whipped out a Kleenex, dabbed her eyes, and

First Communication

then flung it at her tiny basket that swiveled and captured it.

Terra had activated the panel's VIN and had Tracker and Reconfigure apps transmitting so that when her matrix located the panel, the panel would respond and alert the crew...

Beth had round blue eyes and always wore flowery blouses, skirts, and a tiny bit of glitter on her cheeks and eyelids. Wallum asked her last month in their down: "*Why* are there sparkles everywhere on your face? I mean, I'm not trying to criticize, and I rather like—"

"*Humph*," she stomped. With a serious expression, she rolled a shoulder at him and said, "The microscopic specks make my face glow a bit in holographic light, *that's* why, and because—" She stopped talking and froze when Captain Bartlet looked at her. He had just stepped off the escalator and was walking with strong steps to his elevated navigation seat. She whispered to Wallum who was watching *her* watch The Captain: "What's it to ya anyway, Lieu-ten-*ant*?" Then she said loudly as she pointed to a small moving picture inside a tiny frame on top of her First Chair station: "*This* is my Dad, *a doctor* in Section-1 of New L.A...and this picture here is my sister, a clinical psychologist in North Korea. Oh!—and here's my brother, John Tufter, the one who starred in the commercial requesting donations for Global Builders to help clean up south Florida, and—"

Captain Bartlet smiled gently at her.

Then Terra sounded a sudden drill. The receiver stage was now showing a graphic of the lunar landscape beneath *The Spider*. Each of its fifty hull sections contained billions of Scan-Mounts imaging spatial, spectral, temporal and radiometric stats on the moon. Terra was interpreting the results, and her matrix engaged in predictive calculations on where terrorist could be in hiding.

"Captain?" Beth said softly.

"Yes, I'm listening." He was multi-tasking, sorting through projections of stolen equipment, fuel frequencies, and contrail descriptions while now-and-then peering at her.

"I don't get it, Captain. I don't see *how* they could be

anywhere out there in all that blackness *and* underground even if they do have artificial light. It goes contrary to human existence to hold up in a place like this. Even on the light-side-of-the-moon robots and automated equipment manage all the trash, mining, and nuclear waste pits."

"Yep...doesn't make sense at all, but it goes to show you how far some people will go and what they'll endure if they're motivated enough," he answered.

"That's what I'm trying to tell you, Sir," began Beth, "with all the time in between now and when they stole everything, the terrorists have had *four weeks* to bore out an underground labyrinth. *Four weeks* to conduct undetected activities."

"Don't forgot stockpiling supplies and flourishing," Bill Wallum said. "Look here..."

Over the receiver stage, a dotted green outline appeared around the black-and-white lunar map. Above it, images of the stolen equipment were slowly piecing together a hazy picture.

Terra announced, "Somewhere inside this outline is the enemy's position."

"Well, why can't ya detect the position, Terra?" asked Bartlet. His eyes were intent on the map and the forming picture.

After a moment's pause, Terra appeared alongside him at his station. Hovering over it were 3D scrolling statistics.

She answered, "Buffering is an algorithmic hostile, Captain Bartlet."

Wallum and Beth said, "What!?" They dove into explanatory action.

Bartlet told The General: "Sir, this is the same problem that occurred after that panel went missing. The Regency received the alert indicating something was wrong, but the matrix couldn't read the malfunction."

General Rand said, "Since we've tracked the panel here...this place must hold the answer to the glitch in the matrix and the terrorists ultimate mission."

"*And* they're underground...somewhere within this hundred-mile wide circumference," Bill added.

First Communication

Beth popped up from her cubicle. "With Terra unable to read their signature, we could experience real trouble."

Bartlet clapped them into action. "Then let's fix the problem, folks!"

Navigation stilled as *The Spider* began a forty-five degree recon glide through the illuminated terrain. ...

Lieutenant William "Bill" Wallum's IT cubicle was at the nadir of the giant receiver stage across from Robert Bartlet's station. Twelve feet from him sat Beth Tufter in her Rock-n-Glide-Tilt seat of her V-shape cubicle. All four First-Chair navigation, recon, SpyWare and Security were interconnecting, and their Terra grids interfacing with all the nano-infused hardware and matrixware throughout *The Spider*.

A Matrix Specialist who had been working for Global NASA for three years prior to his job on *The Spider*, he decided he wanted something more out of life than just looking down on Earth from a space station. He was twenty-nine when he streamed his virtual resume to Robert Bartlet. He heard that since September of 2067, Bartlet was screening prospective analysts in desperation because no one he had interviewed had been able to meet The Captain's high expectations. Bill, however, believed he could; but in spite of several Urgent Streams over several days, he never received a response to his living resume. Frustrated with Station III's HR department, he hacked into HR, synchronized his wrist device to its confidential grid, and discovered that Station III's military holosite streamed replies *only* in Avatar mode. Streaming his resume on October 7 *ten* times that the morning, he finally received a response via a black-suited avatar standing in front of an outer space, star-studded background—Global NASA's virtual-world logo. The caricature messenger said, "You are In Review. You are In Review..."

"Damn friggin sons-a-*rrrrggg!*" He jiggled his wrist so hard to shut down the avatar he nearly sprained it! That night, he rolled up his sleeves, stormed out of his small living cube and caught three Maglevs to the spot where he knew from past public appearances on holosite networks that Robert Bartlet spent his spare time. Following the astropilot from a training exercise to a military presentation, he maneuvered through a crowd and spotted him sitting in a plush red booth and hulling walnuts in the corner of Jingles Pub and Grill. After sidling around groups of Stealth Force officers and dodging two buff guards, Bill poked his way through a team of huddling commanders dressed in blue and beige uniforms. He felt terrified that they'd throw him out, but he knew that *this* was his *one* chance to accomplish his goal of becoming one of the first Matrix Techs to operate the most advanced Terra technology in the world. The best Terra matrix was only available on *The Spider*, and it was almost ready for launch. He didn't have much time to convince Bartlet that he was the right hire for the job. Standing breathless at the edge of The Captain's booth, he breathed and said, "Captain Bartlet, Sir...I'm Lieutenant William Wallum." He stretched out his hand to him, breathed again, and forced a big smile. He felt his lips dry on his gums.

Bartlet wiped his hands on a napkin and shook his hand. "Pleased to meetcha...yes, Lieutenant?"

"Here's my resume, Sir." His fingers were shaking, his guts anxious. "You need a Matrix Specialist. I'm the person, Sir." Noticing a few burly agents heading his way, he tapped on his living resume that began hovering over his wrist device and then swept his sharply dressed avatar into the center of the table.

"Well, whata we have here?" Bartlet plopped his elbow on the table and his hand under his chin. He began watching the show, now-and-then peering up at Wallum and then back at the dancing avatar performing calisthenics with dates, places and historical images.

An Enforcer scanned Bill's green-and-white sleeve insignia and then slipped out her gun. "This club is Referral Only, Lieutenant. Didn'tchya see the flash by the double door? Ya gotta leave now, Lieutenant." She tugged on his sleeve, pulling him toward the sliding triple doors and line of glass elevators towering miles through the center of Station III.

First Communication

Below were ten decks of quarters with intertwining Maglev cars. On the deck above, he spotted a black-and-white Enforcer craft launching as passengers disembarked from another small craft. They were obviously members of a family of some high-ranking officer because small robots were carrying their luggage. Watching the ant-sized scenes, he felt defeated—his dream up in smoke. He felt angry. He said to himself: I've worked so hard…studied so long to secure a job on an elite astrofighter. And here's Captain Robert Bartlet…the man himself!…right in front of me…*the* best astropilot. His *Spider*'s the best! *Oooo*—I'm *not* giving up, *no* way!

"I need *one* minute with The Captain—*just* one," he pleaded, pushing free of the Enforcer. He shouted to him: "Sir—I know Terra II's quantum field processor, and, and—" He paused, his chest hurting from breathing. "And Terra's conversion grids for electromagnetic photon energy, her seven facilities and—"

"Sargent, let him stay," Bartlet said to the Enforcer, motioning for Bill to sit opposite him in the booth. "Besides, I still have his avatar doin' a dance here in front of me." After seconds of joking with Bill on his keen ability to maneuver around gruff and tough military personnel, Bartlet enlarged his holosite home page; and his tiny avatar began giving him a presentation on his qualifications for the job.

Bill felt a sense of peace and confidence. "See, Sir? I *can* do what you said you need done on *The Spider*."

"Nice…and what an education!" Bartlet exclaimed. Your experiences look right on for what I need…oh!—and flight training at Purdue. That place isn't there anymore." He scowled. "Damn terrorists."

"Yes, thanks, Sir!" Bill had his hands folded as his wrist device that continued to flash all his job experiences, his educational history and prestigious awards.

"How come I never saw this, Lieutenant? I should have!"

"Don't know, Sir. Maybe virtual marketeers? Everyone wants to be number one in getting your attention. And I'm

J.P. Osterman

not good at that, Sir, spouting off about myself, or making a spectacle of myself."

"*Hmm...* I don't like brownnosers." He activated his wrist device, swept up Bill's living resume, sat back and stared at him.

Bill blushed through the obvious analysis. "Well, Sir?" he coughed, "I'm best, I mean, good at, *ahem*—"

"Lieutenant, the facts speak for you." He sipped his beer and began cracking peanuts. "You've worked on South China's Terra-II grid and helped interface those grids to northern China. That's a lot of cities streaming Terra-II! An accomplishment!" He popped a handful of nuts into his mouth and chewed hard, excusing himself because the measly nuts were the only things he had eaten since breakfast. After swallowing, he went on: "And you're part of the team that's making the global change to Terra-III happen more efficiently than when Terra-I evolved and replaced Terra-II. I *am* impressed." He ate some more.

After nervously fidgeting with a napkin, Bill rolled his shoulders, looked at Bartlet with a serious eye and said: "Thanks, Sir." He patted his red flushing face with the napkin that had caught the condensation of one of Bartlet's beers. "I have to say, well, I'm just gonna come right out with it...*I am* the Matrix Specialist you need, Sir. You won't regret hiring me if you do hire me, Sir." His body appeared to sigh along with his exhale. "Gosh it's hot in here, *whew*!"

"Besides experience and intellect, I'm also looking for loyalty, Lieutenant."

"Loyalty? Oh yes...I have that...I mean, I am *that* too!" Bill said.

"And I need my First-Chair to have a sense of humor, Lieutenant."

"Humor, oh yeah! I have that too." He nodded yes so rapidly he looked whiplashed.

"You sure do...yep ya do." Bartlet grabbed a beer off the creaky robot server that had rolled next to him. "Well, here then William Wallum." He popped off the top and handed the

First Communication

frosty bottle to Bill who crinkled his nose at it as if it would be his first. "Let's celebrate."

"Celebrate?" he took a swig and coughed. "You wanna celebrate? With me?"

"Sure do." The Captain lifted his bottled in an inviting toast.

"Celebrate *what*, Sir?" Bill tapped the bottle, and the clang made him jump in his seat.

Bartlet reached over the table, slapped his shoulder and laughed. Gulping down a long draught, he said, "*Ahhh*," in obvious enjoyment and then he added, "You're hired." He tossed a walnut into his mouth and began chomping down hard.

A small spray of beer flew out of Bill's mouth. "Great!" He dabbed his lips with a napkin and began wiping the table. "Thanks, Captain! I'll make ya glad you hired me, Sir."

"At 8 o'clock tomorrow morning, report to me at *The Spider*'s simulators on Level 1." He opened up his Map app and swept the location into Bill's miniature avatar that caught it and then descended into his wrist device. "*The Spider* won't be finished until late sometime in January, so we'll be training on its simulators."

"The most advanced streams in the matrix that'll make us feel as if we're *really* battling terrorists!" Bill said.

"Let's see how we work together." Bartlet touched his bottle of beer to Bill's in an expression of sealing the deal. "But I believe you'll do just fine."

"Thanks, Captain," he cheered. "This is the best...and *you're* the best!"

A Terra-icon server appeared at their booth to take an order.

"More beer, Miss, please, *and* pretzels," Bartlet said.

"Thanks, Miss," Bill called, even though the server's image had faded.

"Polite...I like that," Bartlet said.

He commissioned Lieutenant Wallum for duty onboard The Spider on October 8, 2067. ...

J.P. Osterman

"There *is* an underground compound within this green area, Captain," Terra finally said, pausing her lunar scan. Both she and the grid map suddenly stopped moving, a giant Wall Zone on the far side of Navigation displayed the reason: *Unknown feedback loop.*

Bill pushed off from his high-tech cubicle. "Oh no! No!"

"What!" Bartlet asked.

"What happened?" shouted Beth.

"I think I know *why* the terrorists have been able to elude us all this time." Bill hit the frame of his cubicle. "Damn, this sucks!" He asked Beth to help him find code and interlock their mathematical solutions to free the stuck matrix.

"Tell me what's happening, people!" Bartlet said.

The rainbow processing light flared and a drone resounded.

"We freed her...*whew*," Bill sighed, "but before I can say for certain how the enemy's been able to elude us for so long, we've got to assemble more details." After Bartlet conceded to the drawn out progress, Bill had his station receiving Beth's solution icons to Terra's Stuck-mode. The matrix accelerated processing power, responding to the new code.

"Something's wrong...something big," said a female technician sitting on the east side of the giant receiver stage. She had her face buried under virtual icons and avatar projections, and her short black hair was nearly standing up straight as her cubicle filled with static electricity.

"Finally we hear from you, EJ," Bartlet began. "Keep that DWP hunt intense. We need their subterranean location fast before this situation worsens!"

"Righteyo, Captain," Emma Jane Wright called. She had a light squeaky voice and her small body disappeared under her large glow station so that only the crew could see the top of her black hair unless she force-elevated her seat. "I'm just lettin' you all know, again, that I have a *baaad* feeling."

"We do too, EJ. A battle's about to break out on the moon," Bill snapped.

"Keep those solution icons flowing to Bill and Beth, EJ!" As her head bobbed in an expression of yes, Bartlet turned his

First Communication

attention back to the oscillating rainbow processor. "Since we've encountered unforeseen trouble, Terra, that must have something to do with your glitch cause we nearly lost ya, stream an update right into General Rand's Resolution grid *and* to The Regency. Although from this green Observation Bar next to my station, I see that several officials are watching and know what's happening right now anyway."

"Yes, Captain." Terra then appeared in an unusual spot inside the receiver stage overlaying right inside the grid map.

"Her emergency stance!" Beth gasped.

"Oh uh." Bill slid back and folded his arms. Icons and code continuing to manifest but then scatter over the glow frame of his station.

Terra's holographic form appeared a bleak muted orange as it oscillated inside the lunar map. Above her but below her rainbow-cycling hub, a white, virtual-world doorframe—an entryway—was coalescing as more stolen equipment continued to resolve the puzzle.

"This terrorist cell has converted one of my outdated Version Two processors with new software and matrixware," Terra began, her voice echoing through Navigation. "I am not receiving the enemy's location because the enemy is utilizing a part of their matrix as a Reflector." Terra's beehive ceiling mount was cycling its rainbow processing capability wildly, an indicator that the matrix was processing a conundrum.

"This glitch could be our undoing if we can't resolve it," Bill said, lifting up virtual codebooks, cribs and keys. They were streaming to him from Research Station II. Personnel there had been working to solve new viruses, malware, and potentially deadly matrix intrusions.

"Damn sabotage!" screamed Beth as her station processed his solutions and sent the viable glowing keys into Terra to counteract her abnormal attachment to the terrorists' altered processor. I'm transmitting a compressed long phrase…outmoded, but the more we throw at 'em the harder *they* gotta work." Her face was shimmering in the hues of streaming vibrant solutions. None of them thus far were

J.P. Osterman

rendering Terra brighter nor freeing her movements. "*This* is why they've been able to elude us for so long!"

"She's right," Bill said, illuminating preliminary codes over his station. "These prove it."

"Still, I can't see how *any* kinda life can exist out here let alone human life underground. Even the Chinese who have scour-bug rovers harvesting meteorites don't wanna land equipment on this desolate place."

"If there's life down below on this far side, I don't think *we'll* ever find it, especially now, since they have a Reflective matrix," said EJ, popping up from her First-Chair station. She threw a tuft of tiny virtual tumbleweed—one of her creative icons—into the lunar map where it exploded...*hissss*. They all jumped and gave her a shocking glance.

"Anger isn't going to solve this, EJ," Beth said in a correcting tone of voice.

"Fine—I'll stop," EJ scowling. "But I'm sure ticked off—completely *pissed* actually—about having been duped for so long."

"Quiet everyone!" Bartlet shouted. "Terra just opened an app. I'll leave it up to one of you three to decide what to do with it, just tell me *what* the program's supposed to accomplish." He glanced at the beehive hub. "This new Terra matrix has been right-on-the-mark, and its predictive version quick even though it has to evolve some more. Let's see what Terra-III can *really* do as it assesses the entire situation."

The cockpit grew quiet after Terra disappeared from the receiver stage and reappeared alongside him. She said, "I am activating Deep-Wave-Penetration Scan into the lunar surface, Captain."

"Yes she speaks!" Bill said.

"A little victory for us," exhaled Beth.

"*I* ordered that sonar DWP into the interior, *not* Terra," EJ said, pouting a bit.

"You jealous, EJ?" Bill said squinting at her. "My gosh, she's jealous of Terra!"

"*Huh* I'm not," EJ grimaced snapped and turned away.

First Communication

Beth laughed and said: "Well, she *did* once tell us, 'how you believe so you act'. Looks like EJ *believes* that Terra is beating her at something."

"Not! I—"

"Okay crew, keep down the noise," interrupted Bartlet. "I wanna listen for the DWP of through rock now and assess its intensity and depth penetration as we hunt down this bad cell."

For seconds the crew waited and listened as the cockpit resounded with a deep vibration, static noises and musical intonations—all generated by waves rebounding from the lunar surface and its interior. The moon had biospheric identity characteristics, core, and personality, and they were listening for foreign markers. *The Spider* was now like a camouflaged submarine gliding over the bumpy and jagged ocean bottom. ...

J.P. Osterman

Chapter 15 - Interfacer

Emma Jane Wright, The Spider's Matrix Interfacer, was third generation Japanese. A Terra-II Virtual World Creator, she caught Captain Bartlet's attention when she appeared on KStream's 4D, Icon Throwing Contest—the number one, global reality show. She took fourth place; but because of her proficiency in Chinese and Spanish—and English, the language spoken globally—he chose her in October to be part of his crew. He told her October 10, 2067, when she met Bill Wallum for the first time at one of The Spider's simulators: "Dive-in, Miss Wright, and learn Terra-III."

Peeking up through her rimless glasses—her black bangs straight over her eyebrows—she said: "Call me EJ. That'll work. Then we'll get along just fine."

"Whoa—a bit fiery and snappy," Bartlet chuckled. "That's fine, EJ. But remember, ya gotta take orders if you're gonna accept the position of First-Chair Matrix Interfacer. I know it's a creative type of position, and I believe you'll be the best at creating icon, symbols, and ciphers and interfacing them with the new Terra-III."

"I will I will!" she said. "Really I will!" She rarely said,

First Communication

"Captain," or "Sir."

He laughed and hugged her as a big brother. Reciprocating, she leaned into him but pulled back. She seemed desperate for close contact and unaccustomed to positive strokes.

Emma Jane Wright was born on early Friday morning, September 30, 2049. A precocious child who played the piano, her parents sent her to a special school where she learned fast and skipped classes. Then the ozone bombs detonate in June of 2057. Her parents had money, and sent her to stay temporarily in a special beehive shelter. They died, and radiation killed half the country's population by the end of 2058. With no living relatives, the beehive leader sent EJ to an orphanage in Kyoto.

With a wide smile and full round eyes, many people saw her on-line profile and requested interviews to adopt her. They all fell through. Prospective parents labeled her brilliant, aloof, odd, and over-imaginative. Through Terra-I's matrix-assisted educational program, she threw herself into individual-based learning, continued to skip grades, surpass performance standards, and attained college-level acumen at fifteen. Thereafter, Terra-II taught EJ advanced matrix programming and presented her with opportunities to develop virtual world gaming.

Sometimes, on The Spider, she irritated the crew by startling them with disfigured avatars, mutated icons, or imaginative emoticons. Some crewmembers had complained about her know-it-all attitude and negative attention-getting behavior. A week after hiring her and she began working with Bill and Beth and the Second-Chair crewmembers in the back of Navigation, Bartlet said to her: "EJ, you have to create most things to do what I tell ya. You're good, and creative, and just what this crew needs to interface your creations with Terra to help us win this war. But obeying my orders means life-or-death onboard Spider. I need you to be fast most times, serious three fourths the time, and the jokester, well, okay, a bit." He measured an inch with his fingers in front of her face, winked, and then smiled.

J.P. Osterman

"Yeah, right yeah, Sir. I really wanna be on The Spider, so I'll make whatchya say work," she said, nodding in determination. "Sorryyy, Captain."

Short and thin, with straight shoulder-length black hair, EJ liked wearing rimless glasses. Most vision-impaired individuals preferred instant corrective surgery. She refused! On The Spider, she always maintained a hovering string of avatars on the sidebars of her U-shaped station. She often tossed them to other crewmembers' stations, or messaged them to her friends, especially when she was trying to express her opinions or feelings. Always keeping eye drops in her vest pocket, she plopped them into her eyes like an overflowing pot, about twice a day. When a hardware tech chastised her for nearly burning out an important sensor last month, she shouted at him: "Terra's rainbow processor burns my eyes. I haveta have these drops!" She squirted his shirt wet-wild. Bartlet told the repair tech that he'd caution her further. He didn't. Her eye drop breaks always seemed to escalate during intense creative workouts with the matrix. She was young, just eighteen, over stressed, and only had older people around her. No one her age, except for those few days when the Spider would dock on Station III and she'd rendezvous with teenagers of military families to hang out and glean social time. Even then, she'd return to The Spider with a long lost forlorn look of dejection. She once admitted she missed her parents. She had their living pictures everywhere in her small living quarters. Most times, the cockpit crew let her alone through her obsessive downpour sessions with Terra that left her irritable.

Captain Bartlet never let two hours go by when he didn't stroll past her high-tech, First-Chair station and pat her on the shoulder, or give her the thumbs up gesture of "I've got your back," or, "I'm watching you," or, "Good job!"

Where her eye drops were concerned, Captain Bartlet began cautioning her by saying: "Hey, EJ watch where that bottle spouts off! A self-repair takes a few minutes, but the ripple effect on that delicate matrixware of yours could take days."

She'd shove the little bottle into her vest, at times

First Communication

accidentally toppling over avatars and icons that streaked to the floor like tails on comets. "Sorry...I'll be careful next time—promise." She seemed terrified that he one day might relieve her.

As people were becoming acclimated to virtual worlds through which to socialize, EJ still preferred the old-fashioned way of communicating: using her own assembled version of an outdated keyboard. She had it since she was a child and kept updating it with new technology. When not on The Spider, she carried the keyboard around Space Station III, like a lightweight musical piano strapped over her shoulder. At every opportunity, she would say, "Hey—ya want one 'cause I can make ya one!" She called her special invention, Me-Id-Active. She programmed the decorative instrument with avatar capability so she could alter its appearance as she sometimes did with her clothes, shoes, and knee-high socks. Sometimes, in the chill of midafternoons on The Spider, she'd say: "Christmas trees, please," into her Me-Id-Active, and images of tiny illuminated trees would appear all over her, even in a halo around her head! Then she'd pretend to drink hot chocolate, sending a subliminal message to Beth and Bill who'd then stream the galley to send up hot drinks.

Ordering one as well, Captain Bartlet would then tell her, "Enough, EJ. Let's get back to work."

She'd have the last word: "Then tell this darn matrix to raise the temp and I'll stop. Pleeeaase?" She always had that whiny, innocent tease in her voice.

Her teenage friends on Space Station III always called her EJ, short for Emma the Javelin because she won first place, two years in a row, in the Icon Throwing Competition on the station. Her favorite way to pass time was to compose graphic hologram apps, imbue virtual worlds with life, and create far-out or humorous worlds for holosite participation. Yesterday, she sent in what she believed was her best holosite graphics world that she had just completed, River Moon Rush, to the Dive-In and Live! contest that famous holosite artists hold for professional virtual world creators every August in Tokyo.

J.P. Osterman

She'd often say to Bill, Beth, or Captain Bartlet: "Watch—one day, one o' my worlds is gonna be famous."

When she first announced her entry into the contest, the crew laughed; but recently, they were taking her seriously.

Beth said two days ago after participating in EJ's River Moon Rush on Station III, "Wow—I felt as if I were streaming through that kaleidoscopic wormhole to Nelta!" She had tears in her eyes. "EJ...I take back everything I said about you. You rock girl!"

Captain Bartlet said, "EJ, upload Moon Rush to The Spider's entertainment center 'cause I wanna participate next. Schedule me for a participation session, when this lunar battle's over, when we get our victory."

"That'll take three days to copyright, pass through security and upload here, Sir," EJ said with glow beams of excitement on her face. "If I can get a good rating from you, Captain, I can add your name as an endorsement. I bet I can be famous then for sure...yeeeaaaeh!"

On The Spider, EJ often practiced her icon throwing abilities by playing practical jokes: flinging virtual objects at the crew—both historic and those from current trends, like the most popular virtual character in the world, Billy Brat-Wad Bratster. Yesterday, Captain Bartlet told her, "EJ, if I see that Bratster of yours in my face one more time I'm gonna sick my dog Spikester here on ya." On his station bar, he tapped on a tiny yellow terrier that snarled and then snapped at EJ's tiny, brown-haired, menacing devil boy.

Cowering, she grumbled, "Ooh, sorry, okaay." She waved back her icon, caught it in midair, and made the virtual cartoon disappear into her station.

Bill said, "Sir, I know it's a bit irritating, but she's just tryin' to have some fun."...

First Communication

Chapter 16 - Deep Wave Sonar

Subterranean scans were resonating through the cockpit: *bleep—bleeeep—bleep...*

"Back to this DWP that Terra is utilizing to locate the terrorists," Bartlet began as the sound waves penetrated the lunar surface and reverberated back to the cockpit. With each pulse, the lunar map over the receiver stage intensified. "I want to know exactly how Terra's Key Generation app and symmetric-key algorithms are going to help us hack their matrix so we can home in on the enemy."

Terra replied, "Captain, DWP *should* cancel out all modifications the terrorists made to my old hub that they stole and modified, and locate the terrorist's subterranean facility."

Inside the black-and-white grid map on the receiver stage, a yellow frequency wave began oscillating and spiking high. *The Spider* had received data and Terra was processing the hidden-attractor area. As sonar intensified, a heavy drone swept through Navigation.

"I hope this terrorist cell is not an ant farm!" Beth said, patting her chest.

Looking up from her triangular station, EJ laughed. "Gosh,

J.P. Osterman

Beth, calm down will ya? You're sounding like me now, and ya keep telling me not to be a—" She popped up an icon of a screeching black cat with its hair standing on end, "*Rrrraarr!*"

Laughs from the Second Chair crew trickled forward and Beth sneered at her at bit and waved her off.

"If ya don't, that General listening in is gonna recommend ya get a new line o'work," EJ added.

"General? Still watching?" Beth exclaimed, glancing around.

Bill opened up the small green Observer Bar in front of The Captain's helm. "I have General Rand on Station III watching us and someone on Earth watching on Mute-mode."

Bartlet stepped out of his high-tech station and walked over to the glow frame of the receiver stage. "I knew that, but I didn't want to tell you. I don't want you feeling put-on-the-spot and self-conscious."

"Anxious ya mean, Captain?" Beth asked, blowing into her cupped hands.

"Let's just do our jobs. Keep your eyes on me. You're all doing good work," Bartlet said, sweeping down the virtual standing Observer Bar.

Beth huffed and returned to the 3D Detection algorithm she was composing to overlay on the lunar map. "I still feel residual anxiety now-and-then from that manhunt you saved me from Captain." With shaking hands, she quickly drank some water.

"It's okay, Beth." He inhaled a deep breath, and she imitated his calming gesture. Walking around the receiver stage, he inspected the lunar map.

The yellow DWP's high sine wave was peaking at human height, rippling through the black-and-white map. Inside the map appeared a white glowing doorframe. The stolen equipment signatures, and Beth and EJ's icon writing unraveled a matrix attachment.

"There! The signatures locked in *that* place!" he added. The matrix began zooming in and panning the lunar area. "Is *that* the enemy's subterranean facility, Terra?"

"No human biometrics, Captain Bartlet," Terra replied, her

First Communication

virtual form following him at her standard four-foot distance.

"*I'm* picking up a code from an old, *old* Windows system," Bill said. "Capturing—"

"Careful with that, Lieutenant," boomed an unfamiliar voice through the cockpit. The crew paused and listened. It was General Rand from Station III.

"We have General Rand live, everyone," EJ said, sweeping up a miniature icon of The General on top of her station.

The tiny Chinese General was dressed in its usual cartoon green. It started spinning like a top, stopped in midair, and then began making karate maneuvers, "Hiyyee—hiyyaa…" Bartlet gestured wildly for her to squelch it.

Beth swept up the icon of the last Windows version so everyone could see it. The red, green, blue, and yellow windowpane began vibrating as if about to break. Bill quickly remanded the icon over to the white doorframe inside the lunar map. "Terra's showing the Windows code transmitting from somewhere below us. Right here!" Beth said.

The map bulged. The white doorframe enlarged a bit.

Bartlet gasped and motioned for everyone to stop. "As The General said, Bill…*easy* on the upload 'cause we can't know what we're really up against."

"Still, if Terra can't process something, we can't *begin* to stop them," Bill said.

Nodding yes, Bartlet whispered, "If I'm not mistaken, we're receiving all this information through an old-fashioned broadband."

"You're *not* mistaken," EJ said, her tiny fingers tapping up codes and images that linked to form potential solutions to security issues and viral matrix intrusions—encryptions that also might stymie the enemy as the terrorists were obviously now preparing to counterattack.

"It's like old TV stations processing through the matrix. The shows are all fuzzy until the matrix converts pixels into algorithms and then algorithms into holograms." Bill glanced at the Terra hub that continued cycling its rainbow processor wildly. "Terra—hold constant that Windows connection *real* good."

A loud hum escalated and then fell into a decrescendo as Bill enlarged a small, Windows email icon inside the white doorframe. "Here it comes! Get ready..."

"You've got mail!" A voice said. *Ding.* The cockpit vibrated.

Beth and EJ said at once, "Careful Bill!"

"Definitely!" he replied. When he threw a virtual dart into the glistening, blue email icon, the bright-white doorframe enlarged again. This time, it expanded to half the size of the lunar grid map that was still oscillating with yellow detection waves. Now the holographic map of the lunar topography beaming over the receiver stage appeared like the outline of giant human body with *The Spider*'s matrix scanning it for a brain.

"What the heck?" Bartlet squinted at the door. "What's *that* inside the frame?"

Bill stood up. His lips opened in shock and a strand of blond hair dislodged on his eyebrow. His shiny, polished gold buckle and service medals glistened in the reflections of the virtual doorframe. "Captain, *this* terrorist cell we're now hovering over morphed the code Boeing assigned to the stolen panel and created a holosite entryway that reads, *Tiger of Mysore.*"

"I decoded the translation," EJ said. "It's a broad spectrum transmission stretching from Earth to our colony around Neptune."

"An invitation?" Beth asked. She swept up old comparable internet sites, but not matched that tiger's icon. "This *could* be safe. Terra's ScanWare is *reading* harmless, thus far."

"What do I do?" Bill asked.

Exhaling, Bartlet pinched the bridge of his nose and began pacing in front of the receiver stage. He yawned, in obvious fatigue, and then gulped down fresh air Terra flushed through the cockpit. "Okay, let's examine the door, but *don't* enter the world! This could be a trap. But Terra's labeling it harmless, right Terra?"

First Communication

"Yes, Captain Bartlet," Terra said, stepping through the lunar map, her body enlarging and her eyes flashing green through the thorough scan.

He scratched his chin, a gesture of cautious uncertainty. Obviously, he had doubts as to Terra's ability to discern Friendly from Unfriendly. "They have a bad system churning somewhere down there. We need matrix reinforcement to proceed."

"Good decision, Captain," General Rand said. "I'm having Research Station II downstream the latest Firewall into *The Spider*. That should provide sufficient reinforcement."

As Terra glowed in the reception, Bartlet said, "I hope so, Sir. Still, we have no choice but to proceed so we can *know* what we're dealing with and *how* to attack." He gestured for Bill to proceed with his plan of action.

Bill directed a green-Terra processing light over the receiver stage to analyze the tiny symbols embedded in the doorframe. "These are wide-spread communications, Captain."

Beth added, "Identities, embedded discussions, and lists. That's what I'm interpreting."

"Lists of *spies*, Beth?" Bartlet asked.

"I think so, Sir. Terra is decoding everything on the frame, but slowly. I'm cautiously translating *each* pixel with the Graphics and Holosite Apps."

"I'm using Data Miner," EJ said. "It's faster and an intensive decoder/decipherer that's interfacing with Bill's Green Scan."

"Great interface, EJ—we needed this break!" Bartlet said, brushing away sweat at the edges of his ears. He gulped down some water from a fountain tube that popped up alongside his station. "Gosh it's hot in here. Beth, decrease the stage energy output. Terra, divert the extra stream energy to Temperature Control. I've never had to do *that* on manual," he mumbled. "What's wrong, Terra?"

"Yes, Captain Bartlet. Conversion complete. Self-scan activated." Terra replied. She began dividing and multiplying at pre-programmed locations throughout the ship.

J.P. Osterman

"I hope this isn't a new type of enemy intrusion we're experiencing here!" he said.

"No, Sir," said Bill, "just her evolved way of duplicating to expose bad code. That way we can spot specific residuals and resolve a glitch."

As the lunar map darkened several hues, Bartlet had his brown icy eyes in a deep stare reflecting off the enemy's white virtual doorframe. His eyebrows were thin but bold, his cheeks pronounced and sun glazed. He had furrowed anger lines on his brow, crow's feet eyes, and thin smile lines from years of intense diligence on the job. He was almost thirty-six, looked over forty, and refused to even look at any type of Regeneration procedure that might give him back his youth, at least until he'd board *Sagan* for Nelta where he'd have no choice.

For a second, he believed the sparkling tiger's eyes on the upper doorframe were sizing him up as an adversary! That troubled him, even though Terra assured him again that her Firewalls had updated. He was trying to contain his frustration and confusion when the situation on the lunar surface appeared impenetrable, the terrorist so hard to hunt down and kill. He felt the pressure to end World War III weighting his shoulders. Then he noticed the tan line on his neck above his white collar. He had spent the weekend before last at one of the upscale lake resorts on Mars—Nick's Beach Dome. The thought of that place brought up a flash of a bad memory like trudging through slurry during survival training. ...

The famous newscaster, Marcy Dove, showed up unexpectedly at the grand biodome on Sunday and interviewed him as a possible contestant for her upcoming Holosite ABC special, *Space Station Bachelors and Bachelorettes*. He tried every maneuver to dodge her, but a Regent cornered him in the café and said, "Captain, part of your Stealth Force position is publicity. *Do* the interview."

"Darn and damn!" he fired back, in a whisper, at the Regent. "Fine—ma'am," he coughed, "but respectfully ma'am, I'll hate *every* second of it." He realized that a Stealth Force

First Communication

pilot concerned about flying the next important mission and gaining the best commissions could *never* say no to a Regent. All fifty of them were his bosses, usually acting as one voice, but sometimes dolling out orders independently. Even on Mars, he couldn't escape their clutches.

During the up-close-and-personal session, as Marcie Dove photoshopped wall zones with participation icons, scents, and sounds for the show, she put his nickname into her headline: "Hot Hunter Striker," calling him that as well to his face.

He told the spicy, hair-dyed, redheaded Ms. Dove, "Look, ma'am, this is a fun-world y'all are playing in, and connecting in, and hooking people up in—or *whatever* you're doin' in these holosite worlds...but *not* me." He took off his khaki 8-point cap and slapped it back into place. "*Nooo*, ma'am." He looked into the wall zone that Marcie told him would be streaming his image into all holosites. "To everyone jumpin' in, participatin' in, or just watching *this* show, I gotta tell ya that I *live* in Death World." He folded his arms and leaned forward, a frank gesture with the person he couldn't see but knew would soon be everywhere around him. "I'm not famous, and I don't wanna be. And, as what you just called me, Ms. Dove, Hunter Striker? Well, I *hate* hunting, even though I'm good at tracking down terrorists. What I'd rather be doing is exploring. I can't wait until I can take my place on that *Sagan* astrocity that'll be launching to Nelta. That's why I work so hard hunting now, ma'am...so I can one day stand on Nelta."

The next day, Monday, The Regency sent him a message to his personal holosite saying that his popularity seriously declined after Marcy Dove presented a preview of her interview with him on ABC's *HolositeEntertainment@Night*.

She said: "Captain Bartlet has his eyes set on a *wild* future indeed. But I see that his future only includes himself. He's smart, tall-buff-and-handsome, but a bit dark. He has brown-blue bookish eyes, a boyish smile, and a dimple...*riiight* there in the center of his chin...*ooo* yeah, *yeeuumm*!" She kissed his virtual cheek and then winked into the wall-zone imager. "Robert is completely available but unattainable girls, *tsk tsk tsk* sorry, and he's totally *straight* guys, *aaand compleetely* a jerk. Bad *baaadd* Captain Bartlet."

All day that Monday, he took jokes from his *Spider* crew for Marcy's bad review. EJ blew him pint-sized icons of red puckering kisses and hearts-with-arrows that popped over his station. Wallum coughed over laughs whenever he ordered a matrix interface. Beth kept dabbing her eyes but wouldn't say why she was crying. Tuesday too. During her four breaks, she'd run out of Navigation's labyrinth to the escalator, circumventing Bartlet's elevated station.

Tuesday night, Marty Hernandez, *The Spider*'s Lead Plasma/Propulsion, Drive-Room Engineer, said that evening to Bartlet after dinner, after dispensing a cup of coffee to him in the Rec Center on Level 3: "Sir, from all my years of experience...not thatchya haveta listen...*I've* observed that pilots are different from explorers."

"Oh? How so, Marty?" Bartlet laughed. "Does this have something to do with me? Miss Tufter's weirdness all day? I sure noticed *that. Ugh*—women!"

Marty was always concocting little parables that no one could quite understand. Most of his little stories had to do with disappointed, confusion, or other confounding human conditions. He'd often say to people who'd ask him why his life seemed so easy and simple: "I have a gift of seeing the consequences of actions before I jump into an experience." Easy going but keen-eyed, he liked old spy novels and claimed direct lineage to a mystic Aztec ancestor. He had Terra-I map his genealogy; and when meeting someone in depth for the first time, he often displayed the map over his wrist device at some point during the conversation. People listened to Marty and heeded his advice. "I'll tell ya a little story," he'd say whenever someone asked him for advice, which most times, people did.

When Robert Bartlet came to Marty for advice on Beth, and Marty fed him his "let me tell ya a little story" lead in, Bartlet said: "Marty, damn it, can'tchya just come out with the point instead of all the story stuff this time? We're terrorist

First Communication

hunting, Marty. My mind's churning with right-and-wrong politics, military strategies, and matrix glitches. I probably have half The World pissed off at me, but thank God that the cosmos is in between me and Earth! I have Regents and Generals on my back. Thank God for space!" He breathed. "Just get to the point. I can handle it." Bartlet planted himself like a stoic titan.

Marty scratched into his thick bush of brushed up hair. "Captain, it's not *my* place to know what's goin' on in the minds and hearts of people servin' under ya. Only *you* can ask *them* to tell ya what they're thinkin' and feelin', Sir."

Bartlet had worked with Marty for eight years prior to transferring him to *The Spider*'s simulators when the new Terra-III began quantum streaming to that section on July 7, 2067. He believed he owed his life to Marty. Once, while reinforcing a deep cave inside the Maja Vallis quadrant on Mars in preparation for colonization, Marty caught him by the forearms when rocks gave way under the ledge around which they were excavating. The avalanche nearly dropped him to his death if not for Marty's quick reaction time. With his parents long dead, Bartlet would often times seek out Marty and find him resting on one of the small dome-covered balconies of Station III, staring at the small Earth. He'd join him over beers and snacks, and they'd chat w for hours. Now, Marty looked tall and ready to give The Captain another one of life's lessons.

"Okay, Marty. I'll deal with Beth later. Go back to that first question you asked me. How *are* pilots different from explorers? Hit me with your wisdom, Marty." He laughed and then sipped coffee. "I'm all ears."

Marty began stuffing his side pocket with snacks and filling his water bottle. "Well, Sir, pilots are always checkin' over their shoulders, thinkin' that something bad's about to happen to 'em. The world's dangerous and complicated to a pilot."

"So?"

"Well, in the long run, Captain, pilots die young. Explorers don't." Marty yawned as he stepped toward a line of plush

J.P. Osterman

couches.

"What happens to explorers?" Bartlet asked, eyeing the glass escalator leading up to Navigation.

"Explorers are always in search of the good in everything and everyone, Sir," Marty said, stretching. It was his one-hour break. He obviously needed a strong sleep. "They see the positive, and look for opportunities even in failures when everyone else around 'em wants to give up or quit. *And* they get more female action," he winked, "if ya know what I mean." He laughed and his belt slid down his bulging belly.

"Yeah, I know whatcha mean," Bartlet said, tossing his paper cup into the sink. He began walking to the escalator. "I don't play that game though, Marty. You know me. You've served under me for two commissions. I'm always off to so many places with little or no warning. Poof—gone! Damn virtual sex worlds stink, but that's about all the time for women I got. At least no one gets hurt. Love…wouldn't hear of it." He shuttered off the emotion. "A bad experience taught me *that* lesson. That's why ya never see me clubbing even though The Regency would like to see me out there at nights. A human promotion is *really* all I am to 'em."

Marty had a disturbed expression on his face. "Gee, Sir, I'm sure glad *I'm* not walking in *your* shoes if that's how the higher ups treat ya." He stood stun faced, like a teenager in a man's body, an expression of wanting to bring up a topic but feeling afraid.

"Yes, Marty?" Bartlet asked. Terra suddenly hailed him, giving him a green indicator light. The receiver stage needed his immediate attention.

"Since we're on the subject, Captain," he began, "I'll take as many jobs with you as you'll permit, all the way to Nelta, as long as ya need a Plasma Tech, even Basic Plasma Tech I'll take. That's how much it matters that I serve with ya, Sir."

He gave Marty the thumbs up. "I'd have no one else but you in a Drive Room, Mr. Hernandez."

Marty lay down on the plush couch. "*Ahhh,*" he sighed, snuggling into the headrest. "Thanks, Captain. And by the

First Communication

way, Sir, about what we were discussin' earlier—"

"What was that? Women or pilots?" he laughed, about ready to step on the escalator and leave the Rec Center.

Marty had already closed his eyes as if under the effect of a sleeping agent. "Captain, at some point, *yaaawn*, if you don't wanna die of exhaustion tryin' to win World War III, you're gonna haveta choose the life of an explorer, Sir; then ya can *really* start livin'."

With his head low, Bartlet replied, "Well, *my* life's on hold until my feet hit ground on Nelta then, Mr. Hernandez." He recalled images of Nelta and its twenty-two hour rotation cycle. The world resembled Earth, but also differed from it.

Two years were equivalent to one Earth year as Nelta revolved around two pivoting suns. Many locations on Nelta had a constant balmy temperature of 82°, especially the rolling hills and smooth valleys around its entire equator. The upper northern sections and several southern peninsulas were Everest-equivalent mountain zones—glacial in spots. But eons ago, the Neltans had developed those zones into subterranean cities with extensive solar portals as light sources. They lived in beehive communities, their towering cities in some coastal areas appearing as monolithic crystals. Now and then, breaking the sky like giant ancient Greek and Roman columns were sculptures that various artists throughout the billions of years had created and erected to The Divine: the Spiritual Presence they named "God in the Multiverse." As on Earth, Nelta had beautiful sunrises and sunsets, but two moonrises and moonsets, one such cycle occurring in the polar longitudinal zones. At nights, stars in the Neltan ecliptic appeared to twinkle as fine diamond dust. Being that their galaxy spawned their world over six billion years prior to Earth's formation, their Deep Field view appeared almost barren. Through spacefolding technology that they perfected millennia ago, they had contacted species throughout this universe, and other universes!

However, in this universe, the Neltans were here first.

Bartlet believed he could smell Nelta's ocean scented air,

and that he might live out his life in a hut on one of Nelta's yellow-speckled sandy shores, and fishing, after disembarking from *Sagan*. Hope and dreams. Those were his.

Before leaving Marty to his deep slumber, he said: "We'll scope out the planet. Be explores you and me."

"Sure, Captain…sounds, sounds great," he said, drifting off to sleep.

Through a longing look, Bartlet said: "We'll discover where we fit in with the Neltans. While some of the *Sagan* crew'll be deciding whether they want to return to Earth, we'll start a party and begin celebrating a new life! The future's an unopened book, Marty." He stepped on the elevator and began heading toward Navigation.

Marty suddenly sat up and hit his forehead with his hand, a gesture conveying that he had realized something important. "Sir! I take back what I said. You're *both* explorer *and* astropilot, a *real* old-world Viking." Bartlet's cheeks reddened as he raised his hand to stave off the obvious praise. Marty stopped him. "It's true, Sir, I'm not lyin'. In all my years of meetin' all sorts o' pilots and leaders in *all* the Armed Forces even before they all united, that Viking breed is pumpin' through your veins, Sir. *You* have it."

"Get some sleep, Mr. Hernandez," he said softly and then cleared his throat. "Nelta is our finish line at the end of the *long, long* spacefold track we have ahead of us. But first, we haveta beat these damn terrorists. *Today* is the starting line."

Six days later, early this morning, Monday, February 27, 2068, after waking up in his quarters, Bartlet had another *Urgent* message streaming to him from The Regency. He had been ignoring their invitation to link for days. This one he couldn't. "*Red Vital* means either I take this live stream or they'll fire me," he mumbled, shrugging. Jumping into the holosite world they had created long ago just for Stealth Force pilots, he retrieved his latest evaluation.

"My God! My Bartlet-at-StationIII-dot-StealthForce is up ten million! What the hell? I thought I was dog crap after that interview. I wonder what happened that spiked the ratings?"

First Communication

He discovered the source after an hour's worth of holosite searching. Marcie Dove's interview began reaping a thousand participants an hour—the maximum occupancy for a sixty-minute segment. The Regency had linked him to her so that when the public accessed her entertainment world, people would also receive his blurb. "I gotta change this," he said, "'cause this is all a lie they're using to win votes for themselves with *me* in the middle. They're portraying me as some kind of Casanova swashbuckler...damn!" When he accessed his world to input an algorithm he believed would alter their image, he discovered another virtual door. Holosite ABC sent him an invitation to star in this summer's segment of *Space Wars*. They had a title in mind for his *own* personal show they wanted to record onboard *The Spider*: Fame as an Astro Fighter. He could even chose an interviewer other than Marcy Dove.

He streamed his avatar back with a message that he copied to The Regency: "I can't. Fire me if you want to. You're making me out to be some wild weird stud. Disgusting! Why? I don't know. You tell me! Image, I suppose. But ya know what? I don't think you'll do that...fire me. You *need* me. These terrorists are kickin' our asses. I'm the best you've got to eliminate 'em. So stop trying to make me a prop and let me do my job. Get your votes some other way 'cause I know that's what all this holosite ABC stuff's about: *your* daily vote to keep *your* jobs. There! Bartlet out."

As of yet, he hadn't checked his personal holosite for a return reply. ...

J.P. Osterman

Chapter 17 - Dead Time

Terra announced that the sun was behind the Earth. That snapped Captain Bartlet's attention back to the present moment. "Dead Time is in twenty minutes fifty-one seconds."

On the dark side of the lunar surface, shadows crept into cracks, around boulders, and through ravines like gliding ghosts. Blackness enveloped *The Spider*.

Bartlet said: "Get out your jackets, people! We're at the coldest point in space, and we need to keep the temp at seventy degrees to avoid detection." He whipped out his field jacket from under his chair, donned it, and the Inflate command he called into the material made it puff out and cover his neck. Their breaths curled.

Adjusting his collar, Wallum said, "Terra's ScanWare is analyzing each symbol on the doorframe, Sir."

EJ said: "I'm enlarging the symbols as she's giving 'em to me…thanks! Now we can read 'em and find out what that old email icon's about."

Another Matrix Tech working behind Beth said, "I'm straightening the lines and turning some of the curves."

"Terra is compiling them into words," Beth said.

First Communication

"They're holosite addresses!" the tech exclaimed.

"Good work, Corporal Burg. Keep bouncing them over to me so I can sift them through ScanWare," Beth began. "I'm activating the Date-Upon-Data algorithm to translate them into images of their hide outs. Hopefully, we'll get a clear resolution so The General can attack."

"Just what we need to hunt down the terrorists, Ladies and Gentlemen," General Rand said from Space Station III. "Great break in the puzzle, everyone!"

Bartlet raised his hands and gasped. "Stop! Don't call open anything else, Corporal! Beth, stop the stream! Everyone—stop all movement *now*!"

Silence filled the cockpit, except for the droning yellow DWP waves on the lunar map.

"Something's *not* right with this image," Bartlet began. "Does anyone else besides me sense anything weird happening with these translations?"

As General Rand concurred, Beth said, "Well, Captain...DWP is a little hazy, but—"

Bartlet cut her off by gesturing for her to be quiet. He whispered: "The grid map *should* be flat and boring. Terra *should* be noticing the deep valley and spiking peaks in those yellow DWP detection waves." He glanced at the rainbow stream above the stage. "Terra? Why aren't you alerting us to all these abnormal signatures in the Hot-Wave Penetration scan?"

Bill said, "The only way *that* could be happening is that the technology streaming to us from the terrorists' underground hideout is countering Terra."

"What!? More reflective technology?!" Bartlet said.

"*The Spider*'s matrix compromised even further?" shouted The General. He ordered his team on Station III to stream into The Spider's matrix an alternative Detection/Decipher app.

"I think they've done more than altered an outmoded Terra system," Wallum said. "This is becoming a real Terra versus Terra destructive situation. This doorframe is a trap. A snare—"

"A Trojan Horse!" gasped EJ.

"A potential death to our matrix…that *we* just waved on in, like opening a door to a friend…my God!" Bill said, his entire body sulking.

Beth cried, "Terra turned demon? A quantum-computer devil?"

"Demon Terra…that's what this badass cell beneath us has." Bartlet stepped forward. "*Shhh*…" He motioned for everyone to calm down. "Panicking will only make this matrix-attack on us worse. Emotions become clouded. We don't want to start making bad decisions based on our feelings without properly assessing the degree of the enemy's infiltration."

"Infection you mean, Sir," huffed EJ, "but death trap's more like it." She swept up an icon of a hypodermic needle that popped up in front of the giant receiver stage imaging the lunar map. Then the needle exploded in an obvious display of her fear of death.

"I'm not letting anyone die, EJ," Bartlet corrected.

Then, the doorframe inside the virtual lunar map flared as a white shield icon ignited: a graphics Firewall in triplicate that Station III composed and downstreamed to fend off the virus attempting to debilitate *The Spider*'s matrix. The doorframe ceased pulsating its white poisonous glow and solidified over the lunar map. Meanwhile, the yellow DWP wave continued to oscillate over the entire scene like unmovable static. In spite of the enemy's infiltration, Terra was still processing readings of the lunar surface in search of the enemy.

"There *is* a hideout somewhere beneath us," Bill said with a pensive and searching expression on his face. The tiny white beam extending from his rock-n-glide station to the lunar map kept analyzing the map, its photonic particles lightly hissing. "That's what all this yellow oscillation is telling us. Blow up the hideout, and we take out their Demon Terra."

"That's the idea," Bartlet said, "but we have to find the bastards first!"

First Communication

Beth stuck her forefinger in the air in a precautionary gesture. "You mean, take out the Demon Terra *only* if it hasn't expanded to other locations in the solar system. Blowing things up might hurt us and impede Final Communication if their craft are intermingled with our forces. Especially if our fighters can't see the enemy because Demon Terra is interfering with their hardware." General Rand asked what they were doing to discover the enemy through all the matrix confusion. She answered: "I have a Contrail app I created after Regent Manning sent us the signature of that craft emission he discovered. It's slowly devising a Trail frequency to track their physical presence and expansion. The Trail frequency gleans hardware biometrics and all human byproducts. My station's picking up a few residual patterns but not enough to pinpoint their locations. I'm connecting everything I receive to you, General. If the terrorists *have* expanded to other cosmic locations, we should know that quickly. That knowledge will help us unravel what they're planning to do with all the stolen and modified technology."

"Stealth Force around the Decagon needs to know *that* ASAP!" General Rand shouted.

"But, Sir," interrupted EJ, "pay close attention to how you transmit that alert. Demon Terra appears photonic strong and hardy. Their matrix will intercept our live streams."

"So figure out an alternative, people. Transmit around their matrix then," Bartlet said.

EJ activated her tiny Velma avatar she opened up from an old Scooby Doo cartoon app and swept Velma in front of the lunar map. Velma glowed as she interfaced with the map. "*No one* can survive for any length of time on the far side of the moon," Velma said in a high-pitch voice. "That's why the biodome 1.3 kilometers east of our current location was decimated by meteor dust and radioactivity." Velma announced the concentration of radiation in the lunar regolith, disappeared off the receiver stage, and then reappeared over the rim of EJ's station.

EJ said, "Everything I'm receiving from the lunar surface is showing a blaring Death-Trap, Captain…that no one is down there."

Bill said: "Obviously, their Demon Terra is trying to trick us into leaving this place. That white doorframe hovering over the lunar map is playing on *our* Terra's live-stream graphics like the Sirens song hitting Ulysses' ears."

"Glide down—glide in," Corporal Burg said in an eerie voice from behind Beth.

EJ giggled, "Ooo that's funny!"

Stepping away from the doorframe, Bartlet turned to Bill and said: "Before you stream a solid copy of this to *anyone* for dissection, *you* make sure whatchya got is safe and *then* stream the algorithmic components." He called to General Rand who was still eavesdropping in on Navigation: "General, reinforce Station III's Firewall and ScanWare with another layer of the new code. The hardware and matrix programs need to be *fully* antiviral, stream safe, and protecting *each* grid from the lowest Earthly location to past Neptune. I'm especially concerned with the Decagon that's scheduled to receive tonight's final Neltan/Earth wormhole as Beth said. These terrorists might have some type of bad cyber-stream weapon embedded in this virtual doorway that even a copy might prove deadly."

"Yes, Captain," General Rand said.

"Furthermore, before I go unleashing any bombs onto the lunar surface creating a hole the size of Dallas, I want to ensure we have a solid reading on the enemy. Seems that we can't trust our Terra…can't count on our matrix right now for 100% reliability."

Terra was still standing in virtual form beside The Captain's station, but now-and-then materializing around other crewmembers as per protocol and job performance analysis.

As EJ asked, "What are we gonna do," a burdensome sigh resounded from General Rand. He said: "Captain, we're ready to receive the copy and we are certainly Firewall reinforced. Continue your efforts to pinpoint the enemy. Our Matrix Techs are working to create a way to break through the terrorist's Demon Terra. But first we must *all* discover the

First Communication

reflective technology they're using to elude us."

"Yes, General," Bartlet said. Nodding at Bill, he added, "Okay, you heard Rand. Now enlarge that tiny blue speck I see bubbling up in the corner of the white doorframe. From what I learned in Tech-Ed II, any source streaming to us is blue shifted. Red means end—"

"Or End-of-Life," EJ said as she threw a Green Dart icon at the blue spot.

A tiger suddenly appeared and expanded to human size. It's talons began clawing the air.

"Whoa!" cried EJ.

"Close it! Close it down!" Bartlet ordered.

"Trying," Bill screamed, "but The Tiger is evolving through our counter codes."

The Tiger began growling in ferocious sounds that echoed off Navigation's acoustical walls. Terra muffled the piercing roars and snarls. With shiny green eyes filled with scrolling mathematical symbols, the wild-eyed, virtual tiger looked at each crewmember as if in Recognition-mode. Only EJ's bright-white shield-icon array was like a surrounding fence now holding the creature to the lunar map on the receiver stage. The graphic tiger appeared ravenous as it scratched and clawed for freedom.

"It's trying to unleash from the doorframe," EJ said. "Since the old email started this, maybe outmoded software can fix it!" As the crew shouted for her to hurry, she picked up her keyboard, opened up an old iPad app, and began swiping up mathematical symbols from her station. "This Glue Stick app is telling me that the doorframe is temporary. Its adhesive *will* break when The Tiger identifies each one of us and streams our identities—and whatever else its program wants—to The Sender." She flung a larger Glue Stick icon at The Tiger that bit the thick tube in half. White goop spilled out in frothy mathematical symbols. The symbols re-grouped, formed new code, and then morphed into visual graphics. Inside the doorframe appeared The Tiger's background—a cage in a zoo. Immediately, The Tiger began mauling away at its cage. This time, its claws and talons breached the receiver stage into Navigation.

"Duck!" Bartlet shouted. "Terra, counter strike!" He called the Drive Room. "Marty—the receiver stage is about to fry. Reinforce it with stored power from the plasma rods!" As The Tiger pounced up and down in fight-and-strike vengeance, he added: "Everyone—keep low...even those of you in the back and against the wall! This thing's coming for us hard!"

As Terra fired lightning strikes on The Tiger through her beehive hub over the receiver stage, the animal countered with lighting-speed slice maneuvers of talons and teeth.

"The thing's too fast, Sir," Bill shouted. "It's like this damn tiger knows Terra better than we do!"

"That's impossible," cried EJ.

The Tiger's eyes glowed green as *Upload Complete* flashed on the threshold of its holographic doorframe.

"Uh-oh—it's figured us out and is using our Terra to open up a communications path with its creator," Beth said.

"We *can't* let the enemy see us!" Bartlet said. "Can'tchya create a new shield icon, EJ? We can sure use your contest skills right now!"

EJ was tapping her knuckles on her lips. "I've thrown *two* into the Receiver Stage—" She flung another icon. "But see? The gosh-darn tiger eats it or smacks it back at us."

"One almost burned me," Bill said, showing Bartlet a smoking hole in his jacket. "At least the heat resistors stopped the strike from penetrating my skin."

Beth said: "I'm extracting a Cleaver icon out of an Arsenal app and merging the sharp end with what Terra's adding to counterattack. That tiger may have our identities, but it won't be able to send them, or our position, to its creator if Terra severs the downstream."

The virtual knife flew like a blade-on-fire into one of Terra's beehive cavities.

The cockpit echoed with loud, sizzling and crackling sounds.

"Interception complete, Ms. Tufter," Terra said, her matrix

First Communication

voice beginning to break up and crackle. "Upload suc—es—ful. Downstream—inform—aborted."

"*Whew*—we won," Beth huffed.

"Not yet, Beth," Bill cried. "The damn adhesive holding it to the receiver stage is gone."

Leaping off the doorframe, The Tiger began boomeranging through the cockpit. It appeared to target all the walls, striking the main matrix interface mounds.

"The animal's reading *The Spider* and sizing us up," EJ shouted. "I'm sending Barrier icons." She threw several virtual fence-type materials. "Maybe Band-Aid software will at least protect the hull from a breach if that's what this thing's trying to do...take us down...*noool*" She continued composing code and icons and then streaming her creations into the virtual tiger.

Terra's rainbow processor light flared to twice its size as the matrix tried to maintain its interface with the wall mounds that were in a state of slow deterioration. As Terra increased firepower on the ricocheting creature, her rainbow processor began cycling like a strobe. The flashing, wave-light energy began playing with time.

"*I'm mmoovving sloowerrr*," EJ said, "*and myy jaaww feeels nummb...*"

A blue streak suddenly struck The Tiger, and it shrieked an ear-piercing cry of agony.

The oscillation of time stopped.

After ducking behind his tall tilt chair, Bartlet threw several Net icons at the attacking animal that mauled its way out of the tethers. "If we catch it, we have a chance to eliminate the virus, EJ. So continue creating more virtual weapons and lining 'em up on our stations."

"Yes, Sir!" EJ began calling up icons: "Stanchions! Aquatic nano-netting! Plastics netting!" Several exploded in The Tiger's face. A few struck the careening vicious creature but then melted in a halo thereafter. "How 'bout a *real* virtual mosquito monster to fight against you, ya damn tiger!" The receiver stage bellowed smoke as EJ continued flinging icons to the crew in an attempt to kill the striking, pouncing, roaring tiger.

"I'm trying to stop these crackling noises—a high frequency!—that the beast is emitting, Sir, and then I can counter using a Calm Breeze cipher that I'm composing," Bill said. "Ten seconds." Terra continued his countdown. "Let's see if doing the opposite of chaos stops it."

Beth shrieked and ducked as one of the tiger's talons flashed over her head. "Oh my God—this *is* a Reaper virus! I just got a true read! This Tiger is morphing into a *real* poison!"

"Whataya mean?" EJ shouted as she took a sling shot at the boomeranging beast. The Tiger shrieked, and like a Tasmanian devil spiraled around her station.

"The Tiger's downloading—right into our nanowalling—a Poison code. Then it's touching the wall when its program detects an infectious level," Beth said. "It's developing rudimentary DNA...a Poison virus I recognize from three years ago. The terrorists holding up somewhere below us are trying to poison us to death using graphic capability since they can't kill us via a military strike."

"That would make them detectable and allow us to stampede their hideout," Bartlet said.

"Yep, so they're trying to render *The Spider* dead-in-space and then crash it," Bill said.

"That seems to be their strategy," Bartlet said. He had been re-streaming code, creating a blue-wave frequency beam to strike The Tiger.

"Oh no—poisonous walls and bodily infections!" EJ shouted. When her station icons drooped as if reflecting her disappointment, she motioned for them to lift. "I'll call up images of antidotes and strike The Tiger with them!"

"Our clothing should give us sufficient protection against a graphics strike," Bartlet said. "We *can* beat this bad virus, folks, and win. Come on...intensify and fight this wicked implant!"

"Don't worry about clothing capability, EJ." Bill donned a pair of sparkling virtual gloves. "I just infused these babies

First Communication

with enough nanobots to drop an animal. Over my dead body will I let any harm come to us."

Corporal Burg stood up from the back as an Emergency Physician materialized next to her workstation. "I found something about the Poison virus should The Tiger touch us. Listen!"

The female physician announced, "If The Tiger as much as *nicks* you with a nano-particle that it morphed from *The Spider*'s nanowalling, death will result in minutes."

"Is there a cure, Corporal?" Bartlet asked, continuing to throw weapons at the thrashing and boomeranging tiger.

"The Doc doesn't know yet," Beth said as the physician extinguished after flashing a green *Work-In-Process* above Corporal Burg's workstation.

"Until one of you discovers a cure, stay back—keep low," Bartlet ordered. "This beast seems to be holding high where it can scan as much of *The Spider* as possible." He shut off the strobe effect from his systems bar and Navigation darkened a bit. "We just have to make sure we contain this tiger *in here* so it doesn't infiltrate the ship."

Lights in Navigation muted to a bluish yellow.

"I'm countering The Tiger's visible spectral light with its own reflection, Captain," Beth said. "Maybe we can communicate with it...data mine it, decrypt it, and then get its code through an updated com grid I'm processing now. I'm hoping we'll be able to disintegrate the beast before we'll need a cure."

Bill was working hard at interfacing graphics and enlarging formulae. He began layering strands of data into a virtual map that began weaving in and out of the lunar map on the receiver stage. "I see where you're going and I'm helping you, Beth."

"Well—we need to find a way to get this tiger to heel *and* fast 'cause the critter's dropping poison in the form of paw prints and talon strikes in the ceiling and walls," Beth cried.

Bartlet ducked again. "This *definitely* means that a *huge* cell is somewhere *directly* below us. It's the only way anything so small could infiltrate us and morph into such a destructive cyclone so fast."

General Rand said: "Leave! Launch!"

"Terra, strengthen the output of the hull's camouflage," Bartlet ordered, and then he asked Marty Hernandez in the Drive Room to intensify *The Spider*'s fission-fusion engine rods. "Crew—let's find a way to strike this damn tiger striker to smithereens 'cause I'm sick of it!"

First Communication

Chapter 18 - Tiger Strike

Watching the above lunar terror from his Oval Office as the *Stage-1* Flare alert decreased throughout D.C., Manning jumped out of his chair toward the hologram of Navigation—almost putting his foot into the scene—but stopped when the growling tiger paused in midair.

Lieutenant Bill Wallum had stopped the beast with help from EJ who was downloading its graphics composition to Station III. Beth had maneuvered The Tiger slowly back to the center of the lunar map on the receiver stage, and Terra was translating the creature's shadow—its real epicenter of poisonous contagion.

Manning was impressed. "I can use Emma Jane Wright! Some of my projects on *Sagan* could use her talent." He composed a hologram commendation stating the following:

"Miss Wright, after watching your quick reactions and creative resolutions on *The Spider*, I am inviting you to be a member of the new Bio-Nanotech Team the Regency is assembling on *Sagan*. Please enter my holosite at TManningR4atHolositeRegency and apply. Thank you and I look forward to working with you in the future."

J.P. Osterman

After closing the message, he returned his attention back to *The Spider.* He wondered: Should I step in and intervene? Or wait?

Interrupting Robert Bartlet with a surprise appearance might make The Captain *more* nervous than he probably already was although not showing it. The General and officers on Station III were already scrutinizing The Captain's every move per protocol performance records. No, he wanted to give Bartlet every chance to succeed and to shake his hand in a Victory World he would create tomorrow.

Suddenly, through the bright ring of an eclipse, a small craft attacked *The Spider;* but Bartlet launched his *Exterminator* drone to counter. After a ten-second dogfight, the drone circled behind the enemy, fired, and sent the craft spiraling into the debris of the abandoned dilapidated dome. Lunar dust splashed upward and then settled downward as the craft's pall.

Manning continued to watch the action from his comfortable chair in his Oval Office. He was hoping that Bartlet would soon eliminate the terrorists without creating too many blowholes in the lunar surface. The Captain sounded concerned about that possibility. He streamed Bartlet a message before settling back to watch them continue to dismantle The Tiger. "Captain, *Stealth Force Success* to you and your crew!"...

Onboard *The Spider,* Bill slumped forward at his station and sighed in relief. "I stopped The Tiger by initializing an app that's transfixing the animal's graphics code. Now I'm slicing the symbols and signs out of the creature's eyes."

Over the receiver stage, Terra's beehive processor kept blaring *sfffist-svitz* as the virtual dissection progressed.

"*I* managed to re-weave that lunar map back to normal, *whew,*" Beth said. "The DWP yellow sonar's back up and running. We're back to hunting terrorists." The crew clapped.

"On Camouflage-mode, I hope," General Rand said. "That craft found you...mostly likely through that tiger...and you haven't eliminated its presence from the astrofighter. Until it's gone, you, us, and tonight's Final Communication are in

First Communication

jeopardy."

After Bartlet assured him that *The Spider* was invisible *and* invincible, EJ said: "I'm translating language I discovered embedded in the groves of The Tiger's teeth. Long ago, probably around 2014, a game programmer composed this virtual pet as a warrior's companion. I see a signature of the artist's name...BioWare created the pet. *The Tiger* is supposed to be friendly. I feel sorry for it." The crew gasped, and Beth called her naive. "Still, it's criminal to turn virtual innocents into lethal weapons. That's all I'm saying."

"That's what reeks about these terrorists, EJ," Beth said. "They use anything, *any* means, and *any* reason to kill us all in their Holy War to eradicate outsiders."

"Friendly pet my derriere," said Bartlet. "That beast almost shoved a talon in me. I want the damn thing dead...d, e, l, e, t, e!"

"Working on that, Captain," Bill said through EJ's boisterous objection. As they argued, The Tiger's teeth unraveled lines of code that rotated in midair and then reinserted into The Tiger's bloody purple gums.

"Damn thing won't disintegrate," Bill said. "Why—why!"

Beth tapped open the flashing red warning icon over her green-glowing station frame. "It's a Rumination program...of course! The Tiger's image keeps reflecting off our walls and then reassembling over the lunar map. The process is like a bad cycle." She had a stunned face. "That feedback loop we experienced minutes ago that revealed their Demon Terra. They're all interconnecting." She appeared suddenly weighted down.

General Rand's stern voice began echoing through Navigation. "Captain, what values is Terra assigning to *each* quantum photon of The Tiger? Scientists on Station II say that bad feedback loop is like tomographic imaging in the old CAT scans. Discover those values, and then you can determine the algorithms of the creature's programming. Its graphics structure and code have rhythm. Ascertain those, and we will realize the extent of The Tiger's interaction with its creators and how to proceed to hunt down the terrorists and eliminate your virtual infection."

As the crew began following his directions, Captain Bartlet approached The Tiger. Suspended in midair behind virtual bars, it appeared harmless. Obviously feeling confident that EJ's bright-white shield was holding the creature in a constant safe stasis, he reached over the Glow frame into the receiver stage and ran his fingers inches over The Tiger's yellow-and-black striped sparkling fur. The Tiger's trickling photonic particles reflecting off the receiver stage struck his gold, shiny class ring. One of the black stripes whipped up and stuck his hand. Numbers lifted off the beast and began streaming across his fingers.

"Captain!" cried Beth. His First-Chair crew ran to his rescue.

He fell, his body vibrating the floor. Moaning while shaking his left hand to fling off the virus, he appeared on the verge of convulsing.

"The code is invading his tissues!" Beth said, reaching out with a cold cloth to help him.

"Don't touch him!" said EJ as the Emergency Physician appeared and initiated a biometric scan with his workstation linked with Station II's research medical team. "I don't know what to do—*ahhh*! I can fight code with icons, but not this." She was crying and moving her hands at a safe distance over his face contorting in pain.

"Terra, stream a buffer into The Tiger's teeth to stop the language flow between it and The Captain," Bill ordered. General Rand announced that he had called specialists in nano-cellular dynamics to Station II to help them.

Terra's matrix fired a blue-beam frequency into the creature's whiskers, and The Tiger snarled in antagonism.

"Blue-light spectrum is countering the old Windows gaming program that BioWare developed," Beth said. "I'm inhibiting the exchange of information between our infected walls and The Tiger, but the program's old outmoded code is interweaving with Demon Terra graphics. Everything this

First Communication

Tiger's doing is meant to kill us fast and quick...disintegrate *us.*"

The walls vibrated; the floor rumbled. Terra stepped forward with her eyes beaming green light into the black code engulfing The Captain's fingers. She was battling Demon Terra.

"Sounds like a drum beating in here," EJ said. Still kneeling over Captain Bartlet, she had her keyboard device pointed at his hand—striking the flow of black code with a flow of waterfall icons to counter the attack.

The black symbols rolling across Bartlet's arm suddenly stopped as if someone had sprayed them with a setting agent.

"I did it!" EJ shouted.

"You and me and Terra...with a new algorithmic value I placed inside that BioWare software," Bill said. "And our Terra is increasing our buffering capability, blocking the signal's effect and thickening our walls. The enemy is losing control."

Terra's rainbow processor extended down from the ceiling and touched the lunar map on the receiver stage. The loud drumming sounds fell into a decrescendo. "I am repelling The Tiger using that increase in blue-wave energy."

The cockpit cooled and frost appeared on the receiver stage's green Glow frame.

The Tiger turned white, and hoarfrost covered, obviously freezing.

"The Captain is still infected though," Bill said. "I don't get it. We need a cure not a liquid nitrogenized image!"

"It's a DNA virus, remember?" Beth said. The emergency physician continued to monitor and stream his weak vitals to Stations II and III while Terra provided a medic a sedation spray to help The Captain. His Body-Double imager next to his station showed his blood pressure decreasing, his heartbeat weakening. He moaned in pain. The black symbols remained fixated like tattoo ink.

"Step away from him, except for the doc," General Rand commanded. "The blue-light effect is working but Terra needs more time to figure out how to extract the poison."

Meanwhile, Terra's beehive hub continued impaling The Tiger with blue light. Wherever a beam hit, the spot exploded. Code began bleeding out of its teeth, tail, and black stripes. Terra finally said as she walked around the wounded Captain Bartlet: "I have a diagnosis."

"I thought we already had that!" Beth snapped back at Terra's glowing body.

Terra showed them a hologram of The Middle East from ancient Babylonian times. "The terrorists have resurrected the Vedic Sanskrit language of their Iranian ancestors. Combined with the Rosetta Stone app and hieroglyphs I compiled, I am disarming The Tiger."

"Good, but how do we extract the poison symbols outta The Captain?" another tech cried.

"The Tiger is now a biological agent," Terra said. After General Rand changed his Restricted Access to Disclosure-Mode, Terra said, "It is *this* year's variant of the original 2022 bacteriophage, polyhedral weapon."

The General bellowed: "How'd *they* get *that*!"

"I suspect spies, Sir," Beth snapped.

Panting wildly, Bartlet lifted to his knees and began picking at his shirt as if he were prying out thorns. "*Ahhh*—help!" His neck was red, his veins thick through his skin.

His Body-Double Imager displayed the diagnosis, and the emergency physician bending over him said: "His immune system is trying to fight off The Tiger's genetic imprint. If we can force the biobots out of his skin now, he will live. Time is short."

EJ said: "Captain—hold on! We almost have a cure!" Still crying, she fell into Beth's arms. A medic dashed off the escalator and applied another sedation patch to Bartlet's neck. The Captain collapsed to the floor.

The emergency physician began fading out of existence. The Tiger was having a negative impact on every matrix software grid and hardware. "The images The Captain saw before The Tiger stung him are morphing into specialized cells in the visual center of his brain."

"Get that doc to fade before a hypnotic wave alters it as well and infects Terra!" EJ said. "That's what this bacteriophage is also doing…hypnotizing everything into de-stasis states."

As the physician disappeared, Beth opened up a Live View to the Research Facility, Space Station II. She said to the Lead Researcher in charge of stored Top Secret biological agents: "Do something besides gleaning body scans. We need a cure for him *now* or he dies!"

As the Lead Researchers streamed molecular formulae to the matrix for processing, Bill said: "Hold on! *I* know what'll stop the spread of the pathogen." He caught a honeycomb-shaped material ball from the medic and flipped open the white fabric. "It won't extract the biobots, but this derma-fabric *should* buy us time until we can find a cure." He and Beth set the sparkling white sheet over The Captain's body and it coiled around him on contact, sealing him up like a caterpillar in a cocoon. "This derma fabric deprives the biobots of the vital oxygen they to multiply. Now we have to stop the poison from expanding in his brain."

"And extract them then," Beth said. When a small medical team from a white lab on Station II appeared two feet next to the unconscious Captain, she added: "We need a counteragent for that bacteriophage you people have been experimenting on up there! Now!"…

Unable to be a voyeur any longer, Manning decided to jump virtually into the hologram. Having worked for two years at the Institute of Cell Biophysics within the Russian Academy of Sciences, he was an expert on nano-biological vectors, epidemiology, and bio-cellular dynamics. He remembered seeing such a biobot infection spread through a section on the Judicial Prison-Rehab Orbital Facility—Station V—and he thought of a possible answer. "Try using ultraviolet irradiation," he called into the cockpit of *The Spider*. "I'm ordering those physicians on Station II to stream the antidote through Terra right now. Terra, open a secure grid to receive the antidote." The medic onboard *The Spider* received and transferred the formula to Level 3 of the astrofighter for mixing. Then Manning said: "The extender rod in the hub can dispense the cure right into The Captain's olfactory system. The antidote should also inoculate the crew with a less invasive version. Working in conjunction with the derma-fabric that Lieutenant Wallum applied, the antidote should chase the invading biobots out of The Captain's pores."

A hum resonated through the cockpit as Terra's ceiling processor oscillated bright red light in preparation to receive the cure. Bartlet's cocoon began glowing white.

"Who's that talking?" EJ asked.

The Scan Bar on Bartlet's Body-Double Imager depicted the internal temperature of the cocoon at 101.4°. The top smoked as it opened, exposing The Captain's face and hair.

Crying, Beth pulled his shoulders gently over her knees. "Terra's indicating that the expansion of the poison has stopped. His immune system is fighting hard to expel the biobots. Terra, hurry with that mix!" She began patting his forehead with a cold-water cloth.

"Regent Manning is in here with us." Bill stood up and saluted. "Welcome, Sir—wow!"

"At ease," Manning said, "and take it easy, EJ. I'm helping not evaluate."

"You sure *are*! 'Cause of you he has a chance to live," EJ said. "Thanks—thanks!" She sniffled and patted her eyes. She had an expression of gratitude beaming on her face as she watched The Captain's condition improve.

Bill called up a Do-No-Harm emblem and streamed the icon into one of Terra's beehive concaves. "I'm activating a hypodermic manufacture that will extend out of the hub and inject The Captain as soon as Terra receives the cure into her processor."

The ceiling over the receiver stage sloshed with the sound of flowing liquid.

General Rand's voice erupted with a solemn tone from Station III: "Timing the spread of this infection and its

First Communication

confounding molecular structure, Captain Bartlet has one minute, ten seconds before he dies if we can't inject him with that cure. Terra, mix that antidote *now*. Regent Manning just input his Confidential CDC code into Station II's lab, authorizing the trial."

Bartlet's face broke into a sweat. His body began shaking. After the medic re-checked the Body Double Imager, he checked The Captain's bloodshot eyes. "Mix that cure, Terra 'cause he's ticking down millimeters on his Life Bar Line fast!"

"Analyzing the nanobots...copying the 2068A strain...calculating the liquid antidote—"

"Well—*mix* the damn cure!" Beth cried. Sounds of fluids pulsed through altering ceiling columns toward the giant, matrix-processing hub. She rested The Captain's head on a pillow that the medic handed her and then sat back in obvious breathless anticipation.

"I am synthesizing the incoming antidote," Terra said.

"*Whew*—finally!" gasped Bill.

Manning watched the scene with clench-fisted patience. "He can't *die*!"

Terra's hub descended. The rainbow light expanded as a tiny cavity on the hub opened.

"Step back—that rainbow processor packs quite a wallop if you get too close to it, especially when it's dispensing something new," Bill warned, waving everyone away from the receiver stage. Bartlet's white cocooned body lay outstretched next to it.

A micro-needle emerged from a staff and injected the cure into The Captain's neck.

"Terra, unfold the fabric," Bill said. "The infectious nanobots should spill right out."

The white glistening fabric surrounding Bartlet unfolded and melted; and the floor absorbed the oozy fabric in waves of slurping sounds.

Bartlet was shivering, his skin covered with black patches that looked like miniature, moving, tic-tac-toe boards. They were warped ciphers from The Tiger. In seconds, he began breathing normally—his Body-Double Imager depicting calm vital readings. The living ciphers turned light purple. The cure was acting like an eraser.

"The antidote's working! Whew!" Bill said.

"Thank God!" Beth picked up Bartlet's strong hand and ran her fingers over his palms.

His skin changed from pale blue to normal as the destructive biobots rolled off his body like ants scattering away from bug spray. The streams of dark poison braked inches from his toes, began pooling, and then continued layering like stalagmites towards the Terra hub as if promulgating in an insatiable growth spurt.

"The symbols are re-assembling," Beth said. "The oxygen must be energizing them."

"Terra, counter! EJ, generate a Kill icon!" Bill pulled Bartlet's body away from the rising black and orange tower that sounded like billions of flapping beetles' wings.

"The biobots are about to morph into…into—God!…tiny hungry birds," EJ said. "Ugly *black* birds!" She was composing a cloud of virtual bats over her station. The cockpit sounded like a cave at dusk. "We haveta stop those ravenous nano-birds from hitting the matrix processor. These bat clouds I'm creating should eat 'em up."

Beth said, "That Tiger realizes it can't kill us so it's trying to down *The Spider.*"

"Fire the blue-shifted waves, Terra. That should extinguish them," Bill said.

When Terra's blue lasers struck the corrugating black stream, birds exploded. EJ let loose her virtual bats that began gulping down the stricken spikey-haired black birds. The high-pitched chirruping and buzzing sounds stopped. They had stopped the infestation.

"That's a sure sign of defeat, General," Manning said from his Oval Office. "*Whew*! Another potential catastrophe averted. Too bad getting rid of the terrorists couldn't be as easy."

After the symbols completely faded off his skin, Captain

First Communication

Bartlet gasped for air and coughed. "What happened?" He glanced around Navigation, obviously realizing he had been infected but cured and that Regent Manning himself had participated in his healing. "You're here, Sir?"

"Yes, Captain. But thank goodness we countered the attack on you before the enemy could inflict irreparable damage. You're fine now, thank goodness. For a little while, we all believed we might lose you."

"It'd take more than morphing images to take *me* out, Sir," he said as his crew surrounded him with gasps of relief and offered him helpful gestures. He tried to stand, but the medic motioned for him to stay put for several more seconds of recuperation time. He said into the holographic bar indicating Regent Manning's presence, "Sir, I'm doing everything—" His breath weakened. "I'm—I'm trying—"

"It's all right, Captain. You're doing fine. Soon, you'll be back to normal." Manning stepped away and let the crew assist their captain as he continued his recovery.

Bill and Beth began offered him power bites and cold water. Another shot from the medic appeared to fortify him and energize him.

Manning felt relief as he watched The Captain recover. He said to General Rand who was appearing via a hologram in the Oval Office: "He's gonna be alright, General, but we almost lost him to the enemy. You don't know how hard it would be on The World if something should happen to Robert Bartlet?"

"Days of mourning, Regent Manning."

That's correct," Manning said. "Since Marcie Dove's interview, the media's been calling him our only hope of ending this awful, World War III."

"I know what you mean, Sir," General Rand began. "This week an artist painted a portrait of The Captain and streamed it worldwide as a sort of rallying tribute to our Stealth Force. From the waist-down, The Captain appears to be melting into *The Spider*. Captain Bartlet's followers are copying the image that's spreading happiness. People are creating all sorts of gaming worlds, vacation experiences, and historical sites using the artwork. It's been a wild quantum frenzy...taking up five percent more solar energy from the shield to power the matrix. That new satellite panel alleviated the burden as well as protected the atmosphere."

Using his wrist device, Manning called open Captain Bartlet's Sign-In holosite image and saw an advertisement for a new commemorative coin that someone had inserted into his homepage. "The words around this coin read, *Zenith Hero, Nadir Hope*. They're trying to make this piece a collectible—smart move! Terra, purchase me one through SWIFT." He waited until his tiny avatar glowed when the financial transaction completed.

"Captain Bartlet has attained world-wide fame in just a week," General Rand said. "He's a real Green Knight. The opinion polls show that people are counting on him and *The Spider* to defeat the terrorists. Look, Regent Manning, he's better already! He's even returning to duty!"

Meanwhile, inside *The Spider*, EJ had covered Bartlet with a new jacket to replace the tattered one that the nanobots had breached and destroyed. The Captain was sitting up and had obviously been listening in on the two leaders. In Performance-mode, he had immediate access to his reviews as per protocol. Now and then, he chuckled and his face reddened with embarrassment. "High expectations lead to high disappointments," he huffed, and then he stood up, wobbling.

The medic from Level 3 administered a shot of vitamins and nano-healers. "In a few minutes, you should be back to your normal self, Captain."

"I hope so," Manning interjected, "because this lunar terrorist cell must be mighty angry that we've defeated their tiger attack. They'll be retaliating another way at any time. Captain, we need your great intuition again on the best ways to counter," he said, twirling The Captain's Body-Double Imager display that was downstreaming to him from *The Spider*. "All your vitals indicate you're one-hundred percent healed, thank goodness!"

First Communication

As Beth and Bill watched The Captain's recovery-in-progress, EJ said: "Sirs, excuse me, but you've been talking about Captain Bartlet, *our* Captain, like he's a space commodity, or that coin people have been buying up like it's the latest craze." She was shaking, obviously knowing she was overstepping a boundary but forcing assertiveness.

Manning pushed away the BD Imager and bellowed out a cough of surprise. "What do you mean, Miss Wright?"

"I—I well, don't think you're helping right now." She folded her arms and shuffled her feet in a gesture of overcoming shyness. "I know winning is paramount, but give him time to recuperate. We're camouflaged, and the virtual beast is dead." A paid civil servant valued for her talent, she could secure about any matrix position on any astrofighter, especially since working on *The Spider*, should The Regency fire her.

For a second, Manning thought he might retract the offer he had holosited to her earlier: to leave *The Spider* early to join his special tech team on *Sagan*. But when he saw Bartlet take his position alongside his station and call in a recommendation that each crewmember should receive a performance award of two-thousand, euro bank credits, he changed his mind. A brash comment or scolding could leak to The World and be construed as resembling the darker nature of his Beethoven campaign platform. His enemies, especially his Tech-No protester adversaries, would give anything to exploit a mistake or blunder. He often reciprocated by exposing them, vaulting his Regency status and re-securing his position the next day.

General Rand said from Space Station III: "Looking at Captain Bartlet's vitals, I see only elevated stress hormones. The docs up here are also checking for damages that a hypnotic pulse might have inflicted on him...*and* side effects." After the medic agreed, he added: "When you're ready, Captain, you can assume duty of The Spider." He motioned to EJ, obviously acknowledging her concerns.

Gripping the frame surrounding the hologram stage, Bartlet exclaimed, "Wow—*what* an infection." He rubbed his head and inhaled as if taking his first breaths. "And this damn tiger's still here...and possibly still putting us in danger. Come on, team...let's send this virtual villain back to its host's Recycle Bin where the terrorists can shove it up there derrieres!"

The Tiger was still hovering over the lunar map in the center of the receiver stage. Under the map oscillated the droning yellow DWP wave—the topographical readings of the lunar surface. Even though the beast looked stabbed by thousands of strikes, The Tiger's eyes were flaring a fierce sea green, its face menacing a devious glare and a glowing mauling hostility.

"That thing has hate written in every pixel of its shredded colors," Bill said.

"Hate," repeated EJ in a disgusting tone of voice, "I wonder what the world would look like if we didn't have it. What would we be like?"

First Communication

Chapter 19 - Virtual Kill

After seconds of silence, General Rand's voice came in loud and clear. "Kill this wild animal now! Captain, eliminate the word 'indelible' off its virtual skin!"

"Fire, Terra," Bartlet ordered, pushing off the receiver stage as if letting go of a cane.

Terra struck what remained of The Tiger's flesh with shots of white light. A cloud appeared, and Terra's light pulses began dispensing rainbows throughout Navigation.

"It's an electromagnetic repellent infused with the cure," Regent Manning said, intervening from the Oval Office.

Suddenly, the tiger roared—thousands of code attempting to assemble.

"It's like a last gasp before dying!" EJ shouted. She began throwing atomic structures of the various elements at The Tiger pieces that exploded like fireworks upon virtual contact over the lunar map. "Take *this*...and *that*..."

The partially assembled tiger began twisting, its fangs biting the air, its yellow fur smoking, its hot breaths popping. Its whiskered-face turned blue and began expanding like a waterlogged blueberry.

"It's gonna blow!" Bill cried. He activated a transparent orange firewall shield around his glow station. The others followed suit.

A sign appeared over the white doorframe: *Inapprehensible!*

"What's that mean?" EJ balked.

As Navigation fogged, Beth replied, "It means this World War III is not over. They're telling us they have something *big* planned."

"They're saying they're unstoppable." Bill streamed a red extinguisher icon to EJ who infused it with light and threw it into the animal's roaring mouth.

"We'll see about that," Bartlet said, coughing as Terra countered pungent fumes with their ionic counterparts. "Vent on Wide-mode, Terra!"

Like shutters flapping opening, the wall mounds began pumping shots of fresh air through Navigation. The caustic fog dissipated.

The Tiger exploded in a puff-of-smoke but left its outline on the receiver stage.

"Damn thing!" Bartlet spit into The Tiger's residual silhouette as the crew clapped in victory. A cluster of nanobots whipped out of the gilded outline, snapped up his spittle, shrieked, and then exploded.

"My God—I think that thing just laughed at me!"

EJ threw an image of an ancient hieroglyphic flask into The Tiger's glowing outline. "Take that!"

When the flask struck the bright yellow glow, a sizzling frying sound resounded.

"Now send the damn poison into oblivion, EJ," Bartlet said.

"Yes Captain!" When she called on the Explosive app, the flask exploded and extinguished the gold outline. The Tiger's flaring sea-green eyes remained.

"Whata we gotta *do* to get rid of this thing?" Bartlet gasped.

"Try a gamma burst," General Rand called from Station III. "Only a gentle version."

First Communication

After a slight pause, Bill said: "Gentle gammas? That's a real oxymoron, but *okaay*. Stand back or duck, everyone. This close up, Marty says we might get backlash radiation with a gamma burst. Beth and I are developing one for hull use, but limited testing's been conducted on interior use. Make sure the Glow frame is sealing off the receiver stage's high resolution."

Beth called on the Shield app. "The protective photon bubble is holding around the receiver stage. So a gamma burst is safe inside it now."

"Terra, activate the gamma burst," Bartlet ordered.

Terra shot The Tiger's sea-green piercing eyes with a red-tinged gamma beam.

The eyes shriveled, blinked and morphed into dangling drops over the lunar map.

"Those things are trying to cling to us like the last bit of syrup in a bottle," Bill said. "But I'll show 'em…I'll take 'em outta here once and for all."

Raining down another gamma blast, Terra's rainbow-processor cycled wildly as the sea-green drops fell through the virtual lunar map onto the receiver stage. The nano-metallic foundation hissed like acid hitting a base. Then the giant foundation bubbled—slurping softly—as the nanorganics interfaced with the matrix, absorbing the sea-green slime. The ship rumbled. The walls The Tiger had infection stopped vibrating, grew silent, and returned to normal.

"Gone!" Bartlet wiped specks of dust off his pants and blew away flecks off his shirt. "Damn nanobot residue. It's like friggin' falling ash!"

"No, impossible fungus," EJ added.

"I bet we'll have days of this crap circulating in here," he said. "Terra, sorry to say this, but it looks like you're gonna be workin' hard in here to clean up this mess." He laughed and sank down in his seat at his station.

As Terra appeared in front of him, agreed, and launched *The Spider*'s Scour app, General Rand intervened from Station III. "Captain, I downloaded an updated Purifier app into your matrix. Interfacing with the Scour app, it should also indicate if The Tiger left anything behind."

"I have it, Sir," Beth called as she swept it into her station.

"It's great in here now," Bill said in a victorious tone. "A *real* calm-after-the-storm."

"Yeah finally," EJ added.

"Not yet," Bartlet said. "We've got the enemy below us…and they gotta be pissed off."

Watching the scene from his comfortable chair behind his long desk in the Oval Office, Manning suddenly realized the War on Terror wasn't even close to being over, especially after seeing that black omen: *Inapprehensible*. He said to Captain Bartlet and the crew: "You defeated the virtual invader and General Rand is in the process of gleaning intelligence on the enemy. But the deeply embedded code in that tiger was intended to accomplish something big. We must think on a large scale to discover the ultimate purpose of that *Tiger of Mysore* world. What's the enemy's ultimate plan? What are they strategizing?" He felt defeat and began swallowing it down, hoping to contain the dreaded emptiness from rippling to them.

Bill left his rock-n-glide station and approached the receiver stage. "Sir, I believe the code morphs into a subliminal message when anyone opens up a holosite world tainted with The Tiger attachment. That's what attracted The Captain to want to pet it in the first place."

"What kind of message, Lieutenant?" asked General Rand from Station III.

Beth joined Bill in front of the giant receiver stage, and they climbed over the Glow frame and tiptoed to the center of the metallic foundation. With their virtual gloves flickering light on Full-Frequency capability, they touched the virtual doorframe out of which The Tiger had leaped. After the door enlarged, they ran the tips of their fingers along the sliver of an opening, sealing the door as Terra's ultraviolet light pulsed over their cautious smears. Navigation echoed clamping sounds as the white door dissipated like evaporating steam.

Bill took off his gloves and stuck them on his belt. "This

First Communication

terrorist cell that's hiding somewhere in a subterranean facility is trying to lure holosite-strollers into joining them. That's what that hypnotic pulse was all about—no, is about, 'cause it's still streaming rampant on Shadow-mode in Earth's matrix. The entire Terror Movement is working to indoctrinate people using that *Tiger of Mysore* hypnotic holosite."

"I have one such example here." Back at her station, Beth called up an innocent school-based Global Assistance World that began hovering over her station. Meant as a learning aid, the teacher/student interactive grid was now blaring red, indicating a matrix infection.

Bartlet bolted from his station. "Don't—"

"The educational grid is on Lock Down-mode, Sir. Techs are cleaning it up thanks to our discovery." Beth illuminated the transparent red shield around the alluring holosite world. "No hypnotic waves or subliminal messages are emitting from here any longer." After that appeared to appease him, she added: "Although, up until this point, how many acolytes the terrorists have managed to lure to their side, we have no idea."

"I guess *more* battles will yield that information." Bartlet groaned, "*Uhhh*...well, everybody, let's start buffering all *The Spider*'s new Terra-III SpyWare with Beth's red casing in preparation for the next battle."

Animal icons popped up around Bill station frame. Like javelins, he threw them at Terra's ceiling hub that enlarged as her matrix absorbed them. "I'm using a Ground Hog app to hunt for covert messages and attachments, as Regent Manning suggested. He said to be on the lookout for the larger picture...their overarching plan."

"*What* zoomorphic monstrosities *are* these?" Bartlet dashed to the receiver stage. "Ugh!"

Beth said: "The one Bill composed is half python with the body of a cardinal. I composed and the other that I copyrighted as *Cernunnos, the Stag Lord*. It's deer-ram-snake."

"Yuck," EJ said, "but they'll work to chomp down on any *Tiger of Mysore* attachments."

Bill said: "These are holosite hunters we're composing,

Captain. I added a nano-image tracker that I reconfigured from The Tiger. Because our zoomorphic creatures are so unnatural, EJ can stream their code worlds covertly through Terra. *Their* Demon Terra they programmed might also pick up our creatures and *bam*...explosion!" He smiled and took a victorious stance.

"Do all this safely though," shouted General Rand. "The terrorists have something big planned, and thus far, they've managed to steal some of our best technology and use it against us. Our Terra-III versus Demon Terra, as you said before. With what you're doing, however, we might discover their plan, and with our developing intel, destroy them before they kill us."

"Good advice, General—I confer," Manning said, speaking from his high-back chair in the Oval Office. "Keep buffers, I-SpyWare, ScanWare and Firewalls streaming in a tight weave through all our matrixes."

The Spider droned in a humming crescendo, and then a decrescendo.

Terra acknowledged the order, and *The Spider* complied.

"How can code, like our tiger attacker, morph into *tangible* pets?" Bartlet asked. "I didn't think we had that kind of technology."

Bill waved aside the two Ground Hog icons and brought up The Tiger hologram. The crew gasped and he told them to calm down while he explained. "To unsuspecting holosite participants, The Tiger and other pet icons jump right into peoples' laps, where people pet the deceptively friendly creatures, even upstream them to their avatars as *their* pets. These icons appear to be half-wave and half-nanoparticle. I call the icons Light Killers. Get the pun on 'light'?" No one obviously did. "'Light' meaning 'easy, sprite, quick and weightless;' and, 'light' meaning 'illumination'. Light Killers— spritely killers."

"Oh yeah." EJ said

"Once a Light Killer hits any nano-projection mount on any wall or surface area, the image evolves into organics that

First Communication

become deadly nano-machines...like that poison that infected The Captain." Bill displayed an entire line of them. "But ours are friendly and will eliminate the poisonous ones once they find them."

Beth stood up in an expression of urgency. "But once the nanobots take hold in someone's home or business, they synchronize with terrorists' grids and become their eyes and ears around our world. Besides luring people like The Sirens in the Greek myth, the Light Killer nanobots allow terrorists time to search for weakness and strengths—"

"You mean *spy* on everyone, make predictions about us...everything from our behaviors, likes and dislikes to where, when and how to attack," Bartlet added. With his tiny avatar hovering over his shoulder, he activated it to scan all the wall zones containing micro-imaging projectors. "If my avatar's eyes glow red, duck for cover 'cause I'll order Terra to strike the Light Killer. I want no more of what we just experienced or infecting *The Spider*!"

Beth initiated a new measurement on Terra's connectivity to the HPW sonar imagers on *The Spider*'s hull. The lunar map buckled. "It looks like we're making headway locating the terrorists' subterranean facility. Their Terra Reflective app is weakened thanks to the techs on Station II writing new algorithms and downloading them into our matrix."

"Whataya have, Beth?" Bartlet asked. Suddenly, the lunar map began folding like seismic shutters. "There's activity! Isn't that a reaction to biometric activity? Body heat?"

As the map altered to a series of red and orange waves, Beth pushed back her hairband to and then whisked it off in a gesture of anger. "These wild readings are matrix processor related."

EJ said, "That means that the terrorists are planning some type of matrix attack—"

"A global-wide blackout of *all* technology!" General Rand interjected from Station III.

Bartlet began manipulating the flapping red and orange statistics, picked out a tiny virtual piece, and then threw it to

J.P. Osterman

Bill. "Hold on. Let's take this one piece at a time."

Bill said: "This little segment shows a tropopause shield panel! It's the one they stole."

"That means they could be planning another attack on Earth's ozone," Regent Thornton Manning proclaimed, intervening from his Oval Office. "*Do* something, Ladies and Gentlemen. Never mind what might befall the moon at this point. The type of strike you'll utilize is worth the risk of generating a lunar episode. We need to pound this bad cell somewhere under you. Ozone readings are stable now, and the Matter Stream sample has almost finished replenishing it...healing it completely to well before 2057 levels." He heard their relief and brief celebratory exclamations. "Still, we don't want to test the ozone by allowing solar radioactivity to seep through the tropopause shield. We can't risk a shield attack!"

On *The Spider*, the ceiling hub over the receiver stage continued cycling wildly. Standing alongside Captain Bartlet, Terra appeared unresponsive.

Manning's voice resounded, "Alright, I've had enough."

"What's he mean by that?" Beth whispered.

"I think he's coming in here again," said Corporal Burg, the tech sitting behind her.

"Terra, Confidential Code 4, Regent 4, Thornton Manning." That was his Intermediary Signature of Global Authority, directing the new Terra-III to project his body into any astrocraft.

Captain Bartlet glanced around the ship, and then stopped when Manning materialized in front of the receiver stage still showing the lunar map. Yellow DWP waves were peaking and plummeting through it obviously trying to lock on a specific site. The red-and-orange flapping dots looked like chili pepper seeds.

"Regent Manning—hello, Sir, again," Bartlet said, saluting him.

The crew saluted.

"At ease." Manning approached the receiver stage and leaned over the Glow frame, inspecting the map. "Now that

First Communication

I'm here, I'm telling you *up* close *and* personal to get your act together. Don't argue about the problem. Take action."

"What's he mean *by that*?" Marty huffed, his toolkits swinging on his thick belt. He had just stepped off the escalator from the Drive Room. *The Spider's* Hardware Indication light below the receiver stage had blared out a red call for human action. The Tiger's tears had generated an overload, and Marty had come to fix the stage with nano-organic patches and special drills.

EJ said, "Sir, I thought that's *what* we've been doing all along...taking action."

Walking around the receiver stage as Marty began whirring his miniature drills and repairing hardware, Manning glanced from crewmember-to-crewmember. "The actions *I've* been observing Ms. Tufter are these: that this crew has a *real* reconnaissance problem. Your DWP interpretations of the lunar surface are crap. That's why Captain Bartlet almost died." He then walked around Terra, and two more Terra holograms appeared alongside him. They began an intensive system's scan as their eyes interfaced in a glow of green.

Bill swept his tiny avatar off his shoulder and it landed over the mainframe of his station. Pouting, the caricature said in a high-pitch voice: "I loathe failure."

Beth said, "He does, Regent Manning...we *all* do."

EJ was crying. "He's blaming for almost killing The Captain?" She clenched her fists. "*Oooo*—other astrocraft were supposed to be supporting us, Sir. Where're they? Huh?"

Bartlet held up his hand—his body language signaling for her to calm down.

"Craft are en route and five minutes away, Miss Wright." Manning opened up a hologram that showed a V-line formation of astrofighters on course for the moon.

"The Earth looks unprotected, except for a few craft positioned around Station III and surface-to air fire," Bartlet said, calling open areas around the tropopause shield.

Bill opened up the Gamma app he used to strike down The Tiger's vicious glare. "I'm adding a few hardware modifications to the ultraviolet and gamma weaponry we used to defeat The Tiger, Regent Manning. I'm sending the weapon concealed within a drone craft to Station III. With this app up, armed, and aimed at any one location, *no one* will ever be able to attack the shield or steal vital cube panels again. You can strike them to disintegration immediately. Just watch a simulation of how you can target the enemy on Earth."

"But never use the Gamma Burst weapon on Wide Dispersion-mode," cautioned EJ.

"The Gamma Burst weapon Bill and I developed, along with Terra's interface with the hull, has Detection-and-Strike capability," Beth said, her voice sounding proud as she gestured to EJ that she had the situation under control.

A purple stream of light illuminated at the center of the lunar map.

Using a small hand pump, Marty began squirting a line of nano-sealant into the edge of the receiver stage. He explained that the metals soak up any intrusive residue, generating soft frequencies of musical wind instruments upon activating. "Now, *no* virtual infection can breach *The Spider*'s hull without ya first knowin' it," he said angrily. "Take over *our* astrofighter ya sons-a-bitches? Over my dead body!" He took another tube of the special sealant from his kangaroo pouch and began spraying the entire foundation. "This purple light's illuminating all the problematic areas your gamma beam mighta missed, but I'm eliminating all foreign signatures. Die! Die!" he kept repeating with each strike 'n spray. "Take this ya bastards!—*spray*—Take that!—*squirt*..."

Captain Bartlet called on a visual interface that appeared on several wall zones throughout *The Spider*. He announced: "We have Regent Manning's image here on *The Spider*. He's determined that our surveillance is substandard; our DWP imaging below par." He coughed and his jaw tightened. "Let's strengthen the weaknesses, crew...increase efficiency to the best levels you can muster...just as we've been practicing during hard drills."

"Okay, at ease, *Spider* team," General Rand announced,

First Communication

loud and clear from Station III.

The new Gamma Burst weapon was cargo inside a drone launching in Camouflage-mode above the far side of the moon.

Captain Bartlet gestured, *Download*, to Bill and then said: "General Rand, I'm down-streaming you the software for the Gamma Burst weapon. You'll see an entire grid devoted to the program. Terra named it *Create, Copy and Edit*…a simplistic title for security purposes. Lieutenant Wallum and Ms. Tufter are working on an even *more* advanced Ultra Gamma Burst weapon capable of neutralizing incoming laser attacks as well as seeing through buildings, twelve feet of terrain, and disintegrating objects on Earth from space."

"The design is at our Additive Manufacturing platform on Level 3," Bill said. "But as I test the weapon with gaming simulations, and then on real asteroids and meteorites, I'll continue to tweak the design before I approve the prototype." Bartlet intervened, telling everyone that progress on the weapon would take hours.

After the downstream to Station III finished, and as several officers began cheering and celebrating behind him, General Rand said: "Thank you, Captain Bartlet. Thank you *Spider* crew. This is a real game changer in the war against terror, especially here on Earth! We can't wait until you show us the new Ultra Gamma Burst, Lieutenant." As Beth and Bill congratulated each other and EJ streamed them icons of beers with victory shouts attached, General Rand interrupted the cheering. "Regent Manning…Sir, remain back, please. This crew has to get back to its DPW imaging of the moon's interior if we're ever gonna locate the terrorists. The 9 p.m. deadline is approaching for Final Communication. It's crucial that The Captain locate the subterranean hideout and for us to keep that quadrant of space void of cosmic traffic where the Neltan/Earth wormhole is scheduled to open. We can't waste any more time illuminating efficiency issues."

Manning interpreted that tone of voice to mean, "Get your virtual ass back into the Oval Office, leave the crew of *The*

J.P. Osterman

Spider to me, and remember *who's* in charge because you are now jeopardizing the 9 p.m., *Signing of the Pact* with the Neltans."

Inhaling, he felt his teeth grind. "General, the polls aren't in yet for the day. It's only 4:55 p.m. StationIII@HolositeMilitary is still tallying votes. Are you *sure* you want to play this game with me?" He saw a tad bit of fear jump in The General's eyes and quickly he thought about what he could do.

He could insert any image, photoshopped or not, as an outcry on his home holosite world, generating a spin that could go viral to The World. The portrayal would be mean and nasty, but heartfelt and pleading. He had battled his competition that way in the past whenever someone had attempted to oust him from his Regency Intermediary position. His only-and-only Terra-III in his Oval Office had a Flip app, automatically returning any derogatory or distorted incoming image back onto itself with photoshop resiliency. From The General's puffing chest, The General obviously realized that a deleterious image emanating from Manning's Regency holosite would have him recycled back on Earth and off Station III. Manning's enemies never lasted, anywhere, even well after defeating them.

First Communication

Chapter 20 - The *Real* Manning

As an uncomfortable silence ensued, Bartlet glanced askance at Manning and then whispered to his crew: "Uh-oh, get ready, y'all. You thought *terrorists* fight dirty. Watch *this*."

After Bartlet chuckled sarcastically, Bill said under his breath: "Sir, *no* laughing at Regent Manning. You know what he can *do* to a person?"

"*Eahh*, he's harmless," Bartlet scoffed, folding his arms. He appeared unbothered by the panic racing through the faces of his crewmembers encircling him.

"Eah nothin', Cap'n!" said Marty. "He's a shot put thrower of secret weapons and—"

"And I believe a criminal," Corporal Burg whispered. They asked her why, and she answered: "While attending one of those Reporters without Borders assemblies, a clerk I know voiced her opinion. That was at the time when Regent Manning wanted The World to modify a section of the Transparency Law concerning holosite censorship. People kept voting it down 'cause they wanted to maintain full privacy in their holosite experiences and have no monitoring of their matrix grids." She snickered, obviously hating the idea of anyone trying to mislead her. The others agreed. "Manning accused her of being a Tech-No protester and had her arrested after she incited a wave that rippled around fifty tables. It was just a joke! People laughed. Yeah, Kalisa was wrong in making that joke in public I guess, but that was no reason for Enforcers to detain her on Station V for five days!" The crew leaned in and exhaled droplets of dread. After Bill asked what happened to Kalisa, Corporal Burg answered: "After Kalisa returned to work, she said she forgot what happened. Baaad," she exhaled. "Manning brain changed her, Captain. I *know* it...just can't prove it."

"Corporal Burg," Bartlet began, "We can't get involved investigating that right now. I can't help...later, but not now. You know that. We've got terrorists aiming at us from below—"

"But you *should* pay attention though to some things, Captain," another crewmember from the back interjected, "especially since we're all going to be spacefolding with him for over a hundred years to Nelta. If he's a tyrant—"

"Creepy experimenter too—*ooo!*" Beth interrupted, shaking.

Bartlet quickly glanced over his shoulder at Manning and then whispered: "Naaa—I think you're all exaggerating. If you strip the guy of his Regency position and look at him as if ya were on a moving exit in a grocery store and in queue for the scanner, he looks like a regular guy. Yeah, he wears a tailored suit... and he's definitely charismatic and a *great* speaker, as his campaign party portrays him to be, like Beethoven—"

"Wait—he's like the character in the new movie...um...Enforcer Bart Stern," Corporal Burg said. "Bart keeps altering his face with collar imagers and ya never know his identity—"

"Look—Manning's smiling about something," Beth said. "*That's* unusual. Maybe he compromised with General Rand. I heard the two of them can argue like Poseidon and Zeus."

Manning was standing in front of *The Spider*'s receiver stage and streaming his tiny Beethoven, wrist-device avatar with a

First Communication

green, ceiling hub connection...to somebody.

"No, he's looking at his vote count or the terrorist kill count," Bartlet said. "That's what he's concerned with. What we should be concerned with right now." The yellow DWP was still dotted with tracking dots that were attempting to synchronize and reveal a location.

"Yeah?" Marty said, pulling up his belt and then pushing his cuffs over his muscular wrists. "I think not."

"What then?" Beth asked.

They leaned into to him to listen.

Marty Hernandez had years of experience beginning in the 2030s as an aerospace engineer, assembling SpaceX craft engines and miniature astrodome vehicles for planetary exploration. He knew most upper management workers on all space stations. "An Install-Tech on *Sagan* said...there are hallways in that astrocity where no one's allowed to enter even *after* those on The List board the ship. Hell, *Sagan* is almost as big as the island of Oahu, and over two miles thick in some spots. Who knows *what* life is gonna be like living inside there. That tech has a point. We're *all* on The List...and one day...we'll all be spacefolding *together* to Nelta. I guess on a ship that massive anything can stay secret if a Regent plans it that way."

"Constructs it that way," said EJ, her fearful stare wandering to Manning.

"Oh yeah? Secret facilities? Sounds like a full blown conspiracy you're conjuring up, Mr. Hernandez," Bartlet said through an expression of half-belief.

Marty reeled a bit. "You bet!"

Beth said in a corrective tone of voice: "I hope you're not confusing *those* places with the Regeneration Corridors that'll be keeping us youthful until we arrive on Nelta. *Everybody's* getting *really* hyped up about that. I can't *wait*—"

"You mean, the people Terra is *choosing* for The List are hyped up, Beth," Bill countered. "People who are remaining on Earth are lukewarm on the Regeneration technology, and they can't seem to decide whether to vote and approve

J.P. Osterman

Regeneration or not. Lots of ethics issues on life and death."

"Lemme show ya all something." Marty gently flickered on his tiny avatar over his wrist device, and a six-inch mirror image of himself materialized. He had linked it to communicate with other Plasma/Propulsion Engineers. He had his avatar dressed in overalls and gold suspenders. Marty said: "I have *Little M*, that's what I call 'im, hiding under all this glitter and glitz. It makes my device totally hack proof." He ordered *Little M* to open his tiny hands, and up popped a display of a body pod with a rainbow-flaring, ceiling processor cycling above it. "Look at what someone sent me. I didn't wanna get anyone involved, but since we're talking about suspicious technology, I'll take my chances and ask for your advice."

"That's out of the ordinary for you, Marty," Bartlet said. Now he was concerned.

Rotating a graphic display of unusual body pod technology, Marty began showing it to them and whispered: "Priscilla, a friend of mine, sent me this...that's the name I'll give ya for privacy sake so you'll believe me. Priscilla was a bit concerned and wanted my opinion so she'd know whether to keep her mouth shut or send this file to someone on the Violation of Transparency Committee." He expanded the image to reveal a row of body pods. "*She* believes this technology is a matrix-with-a-mind. She saw a large holographic bar at the entrance to this facility with the words, *Cerebral Interface In-Progress*, flashing in gold."

"Maybe my friend Kalisa was exposed to this!" Corporal Burg said, cowering after she peeked up at Regent Manning and obviously discerned his close connection to their tiny circle.

"If ya listen...you can hear this wild drone and hum in this dark and eerie facility that sounds spooky." Marty's avatar diminished in brightness, and blackness filled the space in between the body pods. "This place looks like the inside of a haunted house." As the six of them huddled together and marveled at the unfamiliar setting harboring the new

264

First Communication

technology, Marty ordered *Little M* to stop the flow of information. "Come to think of it, I wrote Priscilla but haven't heard back. I hope she's all right. I better send *another* message with a *Return ASAP.*" He did and then said: "Come on, Priscilla...answer me. You okay? Where're ya?"

Beth said, "*That* didn't look like a standard *or medical* Terra hub to me."

"The technology is definitely Black Ops 'cause I've never seen any Double Body Imager like that before. And the pods appear to interface with people at the cellular level," Bill said.

"Fried brains ya mean!" EJ's body was shaking. "This new stuff is scary. We shouldn't be talking about it let alone looking at it. Especially when he's right around us. I bet he's got spies on us...I just know it! *Ahhh—*"

Beth yanked EJ close to her, a comforting gesture as Marty whispered: "To get this type of sophisticated hardware, Cap'n, The Regents' personal scientists have to be colluding with Neltan scientists in between the scheduled, public communications. I think—"

"Okay everybody," Bartlet whispered, motioning for them to stop. "Come on...forget all this conjecturing and conspiracy contriving. Marty sent his friend a message, so let's see if he hears back from Priscilla before anyone goes off reporting transparency violations." Corporal Burg asked him not to forget her friend, Kalisa.

Marty extinguished *Little M* over his wrist device and EJ clenched Beth's jacket.

"I saw an ad in The Regents holosite that they're looking for a Quantum Genetic Archivist," Bill said. "Maybe that's who they need to operate that technology your friend sent you an image of, Marty. What kinda job is that?"

Shrugging, Beth said: "A friend stationed on *The Droidster* told me he saw a physicist from *Sagan* wearing a badge that said *Nano-Cellular Scribner.* Maybe the two jobs are related."

"A scribe is a writer or copier," EJ said. "I know that 'cause I run into several of them during Icon competitions."

"So a Quantum Genetic Archivist and a Nano-Cellular

J.P. Osterman

Scribner, collaborating, must be genetic creators? DNA architects? Body copiers?" EJ scratched her head. "*Ooo—* what's going on inside that astrocity that *we're* gonna be traveling on for a hundred years?!"

Bartlet shoved down Bill's arm as Bill continued to sweep up holosite classified ads. "Close out those descriptions of Cell Writers that's setting everyone into a tizzy, Bill."

"Sorry, Sir," he apologized.

"No more hacking into military holosites either," he added, shaking his forefinger.

"Yes, Sir," everyone replied.

"And no more suspicious talk...or glancing into places we have no business sticking our noses into...ya hear me? *Everyyyone?*"

"Yes, Captain Bartlet," they replied, slowly.

"Not now, later," he whispered low. "Now, we have jobs...and a *battle* to win. If we want to go to Nelta, we haveta beat these terrorists and stop the attacks they're launching on *Sagan!*" Regent Manning began walking toward their circle of consultation. Bartlet drank some water, picked up an armful of cold bottles out of the chill chute and threw them to the crew. "No time to hem-n-haw over covert technology...and speculating is just fuelin' our imaginations and distracting us. We don't need that now...not with that far-side-of-the-moon glaring at us and locked-and-loaded terrorists homing in on us."

"Yes, Sir," they said.

As the crew returned to their posts and stations, Beth stood back and whispered: "But Captain, wouldn't *you* like to get a peek into that area where *no one's* allowed? From what Marty's avatar showed us, Regent Manning demands cell scans in order for people to enter certain areas. That's definitely Violation of Transparency," she whispered. "Scary, Sir."

EJ coughed, "Yeah...illegal, *ahem*. But I'm not tellin'—no way no!"

The crew stopped statue-like; and with wide-eyes, they observed Regent Manning make his inspection round through

First Communication

a few of their cockpit stations.

"Sir," began Beth, "I have to tell you, that accidentally—on rare occasions—Bill and I intercept blueprints containing secret Neltan technology. We forward them to Station III as required, but who *really* is receiving the blueprints? They're going to someone, on Earth, through some type of *special* com grid."

The hair on Bill's head rose-and-fell as a wave of static slipped through *The Spider*. The yellow DWP outline on the grid map increased in frequency. As he improved the signal's reception, he whispered: "I d o know that researchers are experimenting on a variation of this Deep Wave Penetration technology. I never really thought of it as being illegal…but now that we're talking about other new technology, I'm starting to put some pieces together. What do they want all this for? I haveta wonder, Sir. Don't you? Eventually?" His voice was weak, drifting off through the resonating DWP waves.

As Bartlet appeared to process his concern with brooding eyes staring at Manning, Beth shoved Bill aside with an alarming look in her eyes. "Look at this article I just found! This man, Hugh Reming, disappeared along with seven other builders inside *Sagan*'s Level-1 Navigation Center two weeks ago. No one's found their bodies. They're like buried in a sea of nano-organics!" She swept around graphics until an image of intersecting steel beams and sparking wires appeared. Holosite CBS reported that a misaligned beam triggered a domino effect. An engine…collapsing inside Navigation? Bologna!"

"Yuck!" EJ gasped.

Bill said, "*Shhh*—Manning's coming this way!" He whispered, "Those people probably stumbled on a project and someone got rid of them—poo*fff*."

"We *need* to *do* something!" exclaimed EJ.

"*Whoow*—hold on," Bartlet said in a soft reprimanding tone. He waved them down in a calming gesture. "This could *all* be coincidental…at best circumstantial."

J.P. Osterman

Beth stepped right into his face. "Some accidents, Captain, are *not* accidental at *aaall* but Regent Manning's—or The Regency's—way of getting rid of people who have *seen* covert things or inadvertently stepped into unchartered areas—"

"*Shhh*—Manning or General Rand might overhear," he said. "Even so, what you're saying is not our concern…not our business, at least right now. I'm sure the Regents know what they're doing. *Sagan* is priority to all of us…tonight's *Pact* signing ceremony as well. The media doesn't call Manning *Torch Warrior* for nothing. The guy's got real determination and drive to hunt down the enemy to their deaths! Besides, it'll take more than just our little crew here to open up a conspiracy door. You're talking about shooting a poison arrow into The Regency! You want Enforcers to start watching your *every* move? They will…the second you start bringing up everything. Remember, we only *feel* like Terra's our programmed buddy—"

"You mean v.b.f.f.," EJ said.

"My point is, *they use* Terra," Bartlet said slowly. "Article 5 of *Global Law VIII* circumvents Invasion of Privacy if *anyone* suspects and reports a terror or sabotage concern. That little loophole allows the matrix to monitor *anyone* without notification."

"*Hm*, I never thought of that," Beth said. "I sure don't want that!"

"Well, ya better think hard before you report a violation," Bartlet snapped. "Enforcers are the CIA, FBI, Mi6, CSIS, CNI—"

"And don't forget the Russian SOUD," exhaled EJ.

Manning was almost at the rim of their communication circle and exchanging information with General Rand on Station III via bandying avatars synchronizing graphics.

Bartlet checked the navigation bar at his station and the oscillating lunar map to see if Terra had made any further progress on locating the Terrorists. "Nothing yet." He returned his attention to his concerned crew. "Basically, all of you have been making a whole lot of accusations. Yeah…you

First Communication

have a *few* images and that connect dots...but bringing those to The World's attention will only make us paranoid 'cause we'll start believing we're being spied on." He whispered to Beth. "Remember what *you* went through?"

She gasped and began shaking. "Yeah!"

He continued, "And an investigation might lead to all sorts of mild interrogations, if what Bill says is true about their experimental DWP—"

"That looks like some sort of Brain Scrub app," Bill said.

"Only accusations," Bartlet scoffed.

Beth said angrily, "They used to call people like Manning con artists."

"Well, whatever," Bartlet said, checking the red dots swarming inside the yellow Deep Wave Penetration reading oscillating across the virtual lunar terrain over the receiver stage. "The guy just gained ten years of life through the new Regeneration technology. He looks happy, aside from having just countered that bad solar radiation event that hit D.C. And we can make him feel even happier after we find these terrorists and chop 'em down at the roots. Remember the adage: Keep a person happy and ya add that person to your resume."

"Or make yourself a human target by adding Thornton Manning's recommendation on it," Bill said, stepping inside his rock-n-tilt station. "I don't know what can satisfy that guy. His expectations are so high!"

"And he always looks somber, like lightning struck him and left him smoldering." Beth looked down when Manning glanced their way. He had finished his interchange with General Rand and could now easily hear them.

"People vote for Regents every day," Bartlet said into his tiny avatar that was streaming his words to his First-Chair crew. "If people don't like what they're doing, or the direction they're taking Earth, or the global Enforcer agency, people can vote 'em outta office." He whispered, "I cast my vote yesterday. *I* didn't vote for *him*."

"*I* did," Marty said, "'cause I sure don't want him

discovering that I hadn't!"

They all chuckled under their breaths.

"Anyway, that's the point, see?" Bartlet gestured for them to return to monitoring the stats rotating around their stations and to the lunar map. "Voting's the best way to exact a little control over the future. The daily democratic tally works."

Beth lightly laughed, "That is until they figure out a way to stay in power forever, Sir."

Bartlet sat down at his elevated station overlooking the receiver stage. In the center, the lunar map was still humming in an attempt to detect the enemy lurking somewhere in a subterranean hideout. "We have terrorists to hunt down, Ladies and Gentlemen. That's where today's battle's gonna be lost or won."

"You mean 'win,' Captain," Manning said, walking up alongside Bartlet's U-shape station. He said to the crew: "Your Captain is right. This war isn't being played out on Earth anymore." After the crew reacted with startled expressions, he added: "With info General Rand gleaned from that wicked tiger virus, we've discovered that the terrorists have been gradually relinquishing their covert bases on Earth and heading into the solar system. It's apparent they want to take their cause somewhere else. To where? Who knows…but we *must* discover their mission." When a medical tech team from *Sagan* hailed him, he streamed out an A-Okay through his Beethoven avatar. It was a mission they had been planning for months but didn't have results to launch it. Later, he'd contact that *Sagan* team to ascertain their success.

"So they're astro-terrorists now," EJ said.

Bill said, "I hope none of 'em sneak onboard *Sagan* before it launches for Nelta."

Manning snapped: "I doubt that. I've taken, *ahem*, precautions."

Bartlet gripped the edge of his station frame when the yellow DWP frequency began a new investigative formation from Terra. "We'll get the terrorists, Sir, long before anything like that can happen…today. We're taking them down…*today.*

First Communication

We'll be right on their tails as soon as Terra bypasses their Demon Terra and homes in on 'em. Don't fret, Sir. We're gonna chomp at those terrorists at the roots…deep into the moon we're gonna extract 'em…like pulling teeth." He grabbed the air and ripped it toward his chest.

Manning looked him in the eye. "I never *fret*, Captain."

After adjusting two small hubs on his station, Bartlet ordered *The Spider* to make a twenty-mile sweep of the lunar terrain. The place was black-worse-than-night, except for starlight bending through the invisible exhaust of *The Spider*'s fission-fusion turrets.

Bartlet said, "We'll live up to your expectations, Regent Manning."

Manning stepped back toward the holosite doorframe wherein he had virtually entered the cockpit. "Just stop this bad cell from wreaking more havoc on the world, Captain. Now that that tiger poison is gone, we need to find the people who sent it and blow up their fortress. *That's* what *you* do, people." He glanced at each First-Chair crewmember. "That's what *The Spider*'s made for…to hunt 'em down and strike 'em dead."

"Agreed," resounded General Rand's voice from Station III. "This is just what this team needs, Regent Manning. Inspiration. This crew—"

"General, stop," Manning said. The General's gruff guttural voice began grating on him.

Manning believed that people only wanted to talk to him— be nice or instigate intelligent conversations—only to flatter him. They were *only* out to get something: better positions, or promotions, or connections to important people in high places. He was only a link in a chain of powerful bodies that could launch people from the bottom to better living conditions, nothing more. He once told himself, before dawn, after sleepless hours filled with tossing, after spending the day groveling for votes through his TManningR4atHolositeRegency: When we launch for *Sagan*, and if I'm elected Executive Regent, I *will* change The

J.P. Osterman

Regency's public appearances to virtual only. That way I'll never have someone forcing me to deal with people face-to-face.

"Regent Manning? Did you hear me, Sir?" Bartlet saluted him again.

"Of course, I did," he replied and then cleared his throat. "Go on."

Bartlet began walking among his First-Chair crew positioned in front of several Second-Chair crewmembers. "You heard the leaders. We can do this. We've won before. We're trained for this battle. Furthermore, we have *The Spider.*" He ran his hands gently over the frame of his station. "It's *the best* astrocraft in the Stealth Force. Success on this mission means Boeing will build more like it. And one day, this baby's gonna be docked on *Sagan*, spacefolding toward Nelta, carrying us, each and every one of us, to another world."

"Yes, Sir!" They shouted. Even EJ saluted.

Marty grabbed his toolkit and heaved it on his waist. "We *can* find these terrorists, Regent Manning. Propulsion and weapons are at maximum. No worry about the Drive Room either, Sir." He dashed on the escalator and off Navigation.

Bartlet enlarged the yellow outline around the lunar map to Wide View-mode. "Regent Manning, you *could* secure Executive Regent tonight. A win now will increase that possibility."

Hearing Bartlet's words, Manning felt empowered. "He's right, everyone. The last communications with the Neltans will occur in about three-and-a-half hours; and thereafter, the global vote will reveal the Lead Regent. Maybe I'll get the job, maybe not. In the interim, stopping these terrorists based here on the moon is vital. They have something big planned. Something I bet that will try to sever the Neltan/Earth wormhole before it even activates."

"That'll be disastrous to signing *The Pact,*" several crewmembers said.

"Yes...we can't allow that. We *must* eliminate their lunar base. That *could* mean defeating their movement."

First Communication

"At least on Earth," General Rand bellowed from Station III.

Bartlet pointed at Manning as if introducing him. "We *must* continue to prove that we've got The Right Stuff and that *this* astrofighter lives up to the motto *Stealth Force Success!*"

"Success!" EJ repeated, shaking her fists in the air energetically.

Suddenly, a wave of yellow DWP spiked on the lunar map and the swarming red dots coalesced into one round section.

Terra multiplied, her image appearing in front of several stations. "The five-mile perimeter beneath us *is* the location of the enemy," she announced.

Bartlet streamed the order for battle that filtered through the matrix into every corner of the astrofighter. The entire crew appeared prepared for Attack-mode and instant action.

Manning stepped over the white virtual threshold into his Oval Office. "Go eliminate the enemy, Captain."

"Yes, Regent Manning," Bartlet said. The receiver stage was showing the lunar map rippling wildly with yellow DWP tidal fluctuations.

After asking his Terra to shrink the scene at the center of his office, Manning said: "Let's stop World War III from spreading into the cosmos, Ladies and Gentlemen. Go!"

"Yes, Sir!" the crew shouted.

Manning sat down behind his desk, and Terra said, "Center view, Regent Manning."

J.P. Osterman

Chapter 21 - Cosmic Battle Cry

"You heard Regent Manning's order, Ladies and Gentlemen," blared General Rand's voice into *The Spider's* Navigation Center. "It's time to fight the enemy."

"Yes, Sir!" they replied.

Standing waist-high against his elevated station, Bartlet ordered, "Sweep the copy of *The Tiger of Mysore* world into the center of the lunar map, Terra."

As the transparent tiger materialized, the lunar map began flapping, gradually folding.

"Buffer the glow of The Tiger's eye with ScanWare Firewalls."

Bill activated a high-frequency D-minor chord. As the musical tones flowed from his station to the receiver stage, he said: "Initializing a feedback buffer...now grafting the map with a distortion so they can't read us—"

"And upstreaming an amplifier," Beth said.

The Tiger pounced and began mauling the lunar map. "Now the terrorists will believe that the holosite world is still intact and returning to them with valuable information."

"But minus the hypnotic pulse," EJ said as she showed

First Communication

them the pulse she eliminated.

A hum resounded followed by a growl.

"Stop the eye from blinking," Bartlet shouted.

"Got it, Sir," Bill said.

After the glowing Tiger's eye unraveled over the map, algorithms appeared.

"General Rand," Captain Bartlet began, "*this* message *is* giving us the locations of several terrorist cells in the Middle East *and* Korea! Wow—the algorithm is indicating thousands of 'em...a whole slew of cells! They're also yielding faces. I'm streaming the results to you...fully protected from hackers and infection."

Beth enlarged red dotted indicator lines, variables, weaving in-and-out of one Terra hub after another. The dots were interlocking com grids leading to all the terrorists' contacts. Magnifying the dots, the techs opened up and then enlarged several locations on Earth—white stucco homes, apartments, rural Earth domes, and petroglyph arches above cliff dwellings. The locations appeared as small displays over the frame of the receiver stage and linking to the lunar map like spokes.

After Terra zoomed in on various windows and portals, Bartlet ordered: "Terra, toss in a virtual Peace Dove into them all...now."

"Yes, Captain Bartlet. I am embedding encrypted pixels as a Trojan Horse Snag app and creating a White Flag world," Terra said.

"That makes it look as if someone is surrendering," General Rand said. "Smart move."

"I'm injecting a runway icon into their *Tiger of Mysore*," EJ added. "Now the tiger holosite world will expand to *all* their cells."

"Yes...but any indication that someone on the moon is receiving it? At first frequency, we strike where they upstream it!" said Bartlet.

"No signal yet, Captain, however, I *am* streaming a protected version of *their* signal to Space Station III," Terra said.

J.P. Osterman

As white doves appeared on the terrorists' virtual entryways on Earth, General Rand shouted, "We just locked onto their lunar location, Captain! They managed to by-pass your communications grid but we detected them from here. Good thinking on streaming that protected version to us!"

"So in the Terra-versus-Terra battle for control, our Terra won," Beth proclaimed.

"If Terra was human I'd kiss 'er." Bill puckered up and opened his arms at the ceiling hub cycling wildly with its rainbow quantum processor.

General Rand sounded as if he was clapping. "I can't agree with you more, Lieutenant, and great work, Ladies and Gentlemen. I'm ordering the *Sneaker* and the *Droidster* to launch and fire on the cells on Earth. Now *you* just have to blast that subterranean hideout with all the laser bursts that'll smoke 'em out and destroy 'em. Go *Spider* crew!"

"Will do, General." Bartlet looked into the Observation Bar over his station and said: "Do you hear that, Regent Manning? Satisfied, Sir?"

After calling Terra to illuminate the Oval Office because the sun was setting in D.C., Manning said: "I'm satisfied, Captain. Now proceed, but with caution, as General Rand ordered. Those terrorists *know* you're camouflaged. That Demon Terra they're using is powerful, witty, and a hacker's best accomplishment."

Manning heard voices outside the White House soar. The Wall Zone indicating thousands of upstreaming *Requests for Response* was at a high level. Even though people had their avatars linking with reassuring Safety figures who were calming them down, they were still frightened, holositing him, and requesting another up-close-and-personal message. They were looking to him and the other forty-nine Regents for answers to their safety issues. The musical tune of his Nano-roof app jingled, indicating full-interface and protection through Terra. The new satellite panel was functioning at maximum with the rest of the tropopause shield, but with the Matter Stream sample at the end of its life expectancy, he surmised that the

First Communication

panel might encounter a power issue because the techs had to improvise when they enacted the repair. He streamed the order to fix the matrix glitch ASAP. The last communication with Nelta was approaching. The panel *had* to be functioning at 100% percent. It needed to provide solar energy to the transmission screen in the Press Room responsible for imaging the Neltans through the Decagon accelerator system beyond Mars.

"Ladies and Gentlemen," he said into *Spider*'s Navigation Center, "I can only monitor you for a little while longer. We have a situation on Earth I'm dealing with. I have crowds of people worrying about safety. Some crowds of people are screaming so loudly the monuments might shake. I have millions of avatars a minute messaging my office holosite, hitting me with questions that right now I don't have the answers. But you, Ladies and Gentlemen, can give *everyone* the answer...*a victory* that will stop all fear. If you stop the terrorists on the moon, the entire movement might see themselves as depleted, and surrender no matter what their location in the solar system. You, *Spider* crew, could be the catalyst to end World War III."

"We'll do our best, Sir," Bartlet said.

Over his station, he opened up a hologram showing the Neltan Matter Stream sample. A self-contained creation source, the sample was now glistening wisps of energetic clouds enveloping Earth's stratosphere. From the ground looking up, Earth appeared almost lost in a permanent eclipse, except for a very fine mist interspersed with rainbows refracting from sections of emanating sunlight. "Darkness and rainbows beaming through ancient particle prisms," Bartlet said, marveling. The light and particle mix interacting with oxygen, carbon dioxide, and nitrogen was infusing the stratosphere with the necessary synthesis in its last, thirteen-minute healing frenzy of Earth. "Are you *seeing* this, Regent Manning? Gosh—what a *great* time to be on Earth right now!"

In his Oval Office, Manning watched several wall zones ignite with images of celebrating people. Everywhere, people began cheering in waves, "Six hundred sixty-seven," the number of times the sample had enveloped the Earth in its healing capacity. People began projecting the number into the sky, on buildings, monuments, and into trees, where the number grew like virtual morning glories, blooming into giant 667s in the sky like detonating fireworks.

"Yes, Captain...the sample's final interaction with our ozone is like a last great trumpet call." He streamed the global wide images of celebration on Participation-mode so Bartlet and his crew could quickly experience the events on Earth.

In the French city of St Jean Pied de Port, a group of blind men, women and children were ecstatic. They had washed their eyes in a glimmering mist that had trickled down from the sample and they could now see. As terror of the temporary shower dissipated, more claims of the same sort of healing cures were streaming into his Oval Office. Several holosite broadcasters, Matrix Projectionists, and newscasters were reporting miracles. People around the world were shouting for joy as if Heaven opened before their eyes: "God is here! He set eternity in our hearts yet we could not understand him from beginning to end!"

The Neltans called the creation force in their Matter Stream, "evidence of The Divine." They described The Divine as a spiritual and inter-dimensional omnipresent entity who brought about The Beginning of The Multiverse. People accepted the Neltans' belief in The Divine after The Regency began exchanging our various religious beliefs with the Neltan Worship Council. Many similarities existed between the Judeo-Christian God, Christ, the Holy Spirit, the sefirot, and The Divine. However, now, with miracles abounding in every corner of the globe, and glowing elementary particles gyring everywhere as if infused with creative life, people were *really* experiencing The Divine as a real spiritual entity existing outside space/time but still present. The spiritual touching had morphed into a global-wide mystical experience of acceptance in The Divine. Even terminally ill patients afflicted with radiation poisoning that cell technology couldn't cure began

First Communication

drinking the creation-infused water distilling from the Matter Stream sample through Earth's atmospheric mix. Even desolate land began developing a fine down of green. This last special drop and flood of the sample meant that at some point the seasons would resume around the globe. The poles would begin to generate their ice sheets. Currents would realign. Earth would soon be new! All because of the Neltans and their Matter Stream sample...their gift to humanity as part of *The Pact*.

Terra began an automated historical account of the sample's significance. "The Matter Stream is proof that a Universal Particle mix is responsible for propelling, self-perpetuating, and propagating The Multiverse since the beginning of Time. *Time* defined by all alien cultures to mean *The Alpha and The Omega. Time* defined as *eternal*—"

"Thank you, enough, Terra," Bartlet said. The information flow stopped. "The tropopause shield is protecting Earth, and according to numbers Terra just flashed, the ozone level is back to its pre-2057 level, Sir," he added. "They only have to hold there for ten minutes to demonstrate permanence. Terra is displaying the time of ozone sustainability as twelve minutes, fifty-two seconds. Then you can all celebrate, and The Regency start reminding people that it's our turn to start paying back the Neltans. The later, only a suggestion, Sir."

"Great!" Manning said. Turning to his ceiling hub, he added, "Terra, send out that precise time and the reading to everyone globally." Hologram streams were instantaneous in their arrival. Everyone had received his message on either a wall zone or a portable device. "Now that our ozone problem's fixed, Captain," Manning began, "you go find that lunar cell and blast the enemy to dust." He watched Bartlet and his crew react with lightning quick reflexes as the astrofighter powered up its Laser Burst extensions.

On *The Spider*, Bartlet turned to his crew and said, "Great job streaming back that viral tiger, everyone. Now let's hit the enemy!"

"With the DWP spiking high on the lunar map, has Terra

J.P. Osterman

given you the exact location of human concentration inside the subterranean base, Captain?" General Rand asked. "We need a precise strike…not pulverizing the moon into a dust ring."

"Almost, Sir," Bartlet sighed. "I'm still working on targeting biometric concentrated locations. We must stay camouflaged. The app is helping but also hurting us. Lieutenant Wallum and Miss Tufter are working to create a DWP and blue-wave gap in space/time. With a little dark matter globule concentrating gravity in one singularity, we hope to suck the terrorists out of existence when they launch to escape. I figure they haveta do that, at some point. And as we said earlier, this cell has something planned. There's a real mystery developing under us, General. We have to discover it, soon, well before the Neltan wormhole opens." He gripped the frame of his station, breathed deeply, and leaned into the hologram imaging the Scan Light mount on the base of The Spider. The high-tech detector was probing the lunar crust with DWP, its matrix-interactive hardware returning ebbing and flowing frequencies working to target body heat beneath the surface.

The Spider paused suddenly as Scan Light statistics flared.

"Got 'em!" Bartlet cried.

The crew applauded.

The General shouted, "Fire, Captain!"

Turning to his Navigation Module, he ordered Terra to increase the red propulsion output to top-notch power—the energy of a 100% Laser Burst. *The Spider*'s turret unleashed a burst of invisible electromagnetic energy on a controlled location. The whiplash vibrated Navigation as moon rock and layers of powdery soil lifted into space like chalk dust trickling off a blackboard.

Two enemy craft launched and began an acceleration maneuver. *The Spider*'s weapons turrets locked on their hulls and fired. One exploded. The other disappeared—obviously camouflaging.

"Marty—adjust for Terra's increase of plasma output to 4 mill amperes with the front flow at approximately 2.5

First Communication

nanoseconds...fire again!" A wide-range stream struck a half a degree beyond the previous hit. "General, the group is ten degrees west of us now. Terra's imaging five thousand bodies. We're halting fire, powering down to remain hidden, and gliding in for a surprise attack. One craft escaped. Terra's tracking its contrail. When *Spider* edges around the front of the underground facility, I'll fire. Bill and Beth just about have that new dark matter globule weapon ready for launch."

"Do you see any bodies on the surface, Captain?" General Rand asked. "We're receiving *The Spider*'s data here, but you've got direct eyes on the area."

"No, Sir. DWP is scanning crevices as we glide over them, but nothing so far."

Bill opened up the Body Sensor app that swept into the lunar map over the receiver stage. "This might give us identities."

Several yellow outlines of human bodies rippled across the map. Then a high-frequency pitch resounded.

"All the body readings just disappeared!" cried Bill.

"What!" Bartlet began examining his holographic stats for errors.

"Yes, Captain. All gone." Bill enlarged a cubic icon displaying a quantum resolution wave. "Terra shows that they have a Cool Burst World running down there. Whoever their hacker is, the guy—"

"Or woman," Beth said,

"Whoever—is taking our apps and energy, trapping the signatures, and then reversing the codes and electromagnetic waves...on us...to see *us* and hunt *us*."

"Turn!" Bartlet ordered.

The Spider hit a jagged edge of moon rock and spewed lunar dust.

"General Rand," he called out as the results of Terra's research on the hideout trickled in. "How extensive is their underground fortress and how many troops are we up against?" The receiver bar over his station was still droning green in its calculation. "Terra doesn't know yet and can't lock

J.P. Osterman

on a location. Bodies keep moving...quantum streams keep evolving, directions continue to scatter like leaves in October. Damn!"

Bill added: "When we do get glimmers of readings, the DWP isn't indicating an end to their underground ant-like center. There are chambers stretching out everywhere under the moon's surface. Or, what we're gleaning could be just shadow canals."

The General said: "How? How'd they have the time to bore out all that rock and move it around so the rubble looks like the craters and volcanic debris? My God how!"

"I don't know, Sir," Bartlet said, his face reddening in obvious powerlessness. "Definitely, we should have put in place more detectors and Terra hubs. But hindsight isn't going to help us now. "

Still watching the event from his Oval Office, Manning couldn't help but to interject his thoughts into the scene playing out virtually at the center of his room. "I guess we believed that if we didn't place any value on the far side of the lunar surface, we thought they might not either." He hit his desk. "Damn were *we* wrong!"

On *The Spider*, Bartlet shook his head. He clenched his fists—his eyes glaring at the vacillating lunar map over the receiver stage. Terra's DWP waves were continuing to pan the area in search of the terrorist's underground hideout. "They have us stumped, Sirs, but not for long. Not for long—I promise!"

"Don't promise that, 'cause you can't just strike that entire far side and risk exploding the moon," Manning said to him.

Bill initialized the manufacturer's code on the stolen solar panel. "I'm getting back to basics...where this whole scene starting playing out." He enlarged the image of the panel. "This code might help us break through their buffer that's inhibiting our DWP."

"Now we wait and see how the code takes," Bartlet said.

The triangular *Spider* slightly turned. The astrofighter appeared as a gray mountainous body camouflaged to the

First Communication

moon as it lay in wait for an attack. Still, a tiny enemy vessel was out there in the blackness, waiting like a vicious lion. Bartlet called for Terra to be on the lookout.

In seconds, *Spider*'s Scan Light illuminated and began pouring white light over the surface like rolling hot steam.

"Terra's measuring their subterranean component, General Rand...Regent Manning," Bartlet said. "We're firing on the enemy...now!"

The astrofighter bolted.

"We're taking hits!" Beth cried as *The Spider* jolted. "We're like a slab of granite breaking off a precipice during a quake!"

"They have several laser launchers hidden on the surface," Bill said.

"Fire! Double time!" Bartlet ordered.

The Spider tipped as its hull absorbed another hot blast of energy.

Marty appeared in a hologram over Bartlet's station. "*The Spider* is absorbing and cosmic neutrinos, Captain. I can go to triple-time fire power any time."

"Now, Marty!" he called.

Laser strikes hit the surface of the moon again. Rock and dust jettisoned.

The crew steadied at their stations as explosions reflected back waves of surface vibrations throughout *The Spider*.

A blue tidal wave shot up in the center of the virtual lunar grid map.

"It's a signature," EJ said. "I'm translating."

Melting, the blue wave spread out in white strings that were like roads on a map.

"We found the location of several stolen items, Sir," Bill said, enlarging the blue wave that morphed into an image of interconnecting hardware. "I'm maneuvering *The Spider* toward a twenty-by-fifteen foot opening on the side of a ravine," he added softly.

Bartlet threw a Knife icon to Beth. "Slice that section wide open with this. Have our weapon create that precise incision."

Terra fired on the location.

J.P. Osterman

A small craft launched out of an eruption of lunar dust, but EJ sliced the attack craft out of space with a Terra laser burst.

"Bill, fire on the spot next to it." Bartlet pointed to a small blue dot but then became distracted by the Propulsion Monitor. A red virtual bar was rising inside the Drive Room. *The Spider* was running low on laser-burst power and experiencing an increase in dark energy that was generating a Spring Effect in the dark matter fission/fusion chambers. Soon they'd have to retreat if they couldn't produce more plasma power.

Before he could call Marty, *The Spider* lurched when a subterranean location exploded.

"We got 'em," Bartlet screamed.

A band of concealed terrorists began firing laser shots out of a dark cliff.

"We're hit!" Bill cried. "Two turrets down…but the hull's repairing."

The crew careened to the floor. A cavity in Terra's beehive hub ignited and began smoking. The rainbow processing light extinguished. *The Spider* lunged downward like a wounded animal.

Bartlet stuck to his station frame. "Terra, increase orbit ten miles, then veer right fifteen degrees and hold. Get Mr. Hernandez to increase our photon plasma supply!"

"In—creee—sssing," Terra said.

"At least we're not free falling," EJ exclaimed, gripping her seat as the astrofighter regained strength and soared high.

The nano-metals around Terra's main beehive hub began sizzling and splitting. Slowly, *Spider* gained altitude. Enemy fire dissipated. Terra's processing light expanded back to normal as repair bots and nanobots worked on Auto Fix.

"Launch more laser bursts from the Drive Room directly, Marty," Bartlet ordered. "I've lost that capability at my station."

Red-hot beams of invisible energy hit the lunar surface, blowing a small hole in the terrain. The soundless landscape catapulted metals and meteoric diamond dust at *The Spider*.

First Communication

"More lift!" Bartlet shouted, and the astrofighter vaulted into space.

"Seven laser-hull rods and two Intenz Prime-3 cannons are off-line and smoking, Captain Bartlet," Corporal Burg said, limping toward a toppled station. Her team member helped her straighten the station and then hologram stats popped on over it. "They're repairing, but the hull jobs are going to take up to *three* hours to fix."

"Three hours? Here? Without weapons?" EJ's eyes were black glaring pupils. "We—"

"Take it easy, EJ," Bartlet said. "Go on with a status update...someone. And remember, there was a small enemy crafting hiding somewhere."

"I think our dome window detected two craft, Sir," Bill corrected.

After Bartlet ordered an outside visual scan, Beth said through a painful groan: "We *must* plot another course of attack. Retreat for a bit and then return and attack, Captain. That last strike set back the creation of the new globule weapon Bill and I were working on. I thought we could use it now...but no way."

Bartlet began hitting the frame of his station. He was swooning and appeared faint.

"Captain." Beth touched his arm. "Robert?" she whispered, her breath curling over his glistening sweat-filled cheek. "You hurt?"

"Yeah, I hear ya, Beth," he breathed, "go on." He wiped blood off his nose and spit blood at the floor. Beth handed him cold water, and he quickly downed it. "That Neltan wormhole is going to activate beyond Mars in just a few hours. We can't take a chance that our trajectory might interfere with the wormhole conduit emanating from the Decagon accelerator system. Even Space Station III is increasing orbit and altering its course five degrees."

"Terra is off-stream, Sir," Bill said, his jerking movements showing obvious frustration.

"That means she's near broke!" said EJ.

J.P. Osterman

"Not for long, 'cause I'm going in and bring back our Quantum Lady by the hand," Bartlet said. As the crew gasped, he jumped on top of the frame surrounding the hologram stage, reached up high, and stuck his arms elbow deep into a beehive hub. "I did this six months ago when I had temporary command of *Droidster*." He grimaced as he twisted his hand and maneuvered his fingers around strings of thick nano-organic processors. "A Manual Fix should work with this new Terra-III. I can feel the hub peeling off some o' my skin—"

"Cap'n!" EJ cried.

"Damn thing stings for sure," he grimaced. "I can feel tiny chomping sensations like this hub is using *me* to mend my ship."

"Cool," EJ said, "'cause Terra probably is!"

He pulled out his arms that appeared doused in red shiny slime, and Beth threw him a cloth that he wrapped around them. "Terra, can you streaming now?" he asked.

"Graphics streaming is active," Bill said.

"Wow—that was a real Tom Thumb thing," EJ laughed. "It worked!"

Still watching the event from his Oval Office, Manning realized the battle had ended badly. Needing to intervene in spite of General Rand barking orders to the crew in response to the catastrophe, he said: "Retreat, Captain. Support craft are approaching you at two hundred miles west to guide *The Spider* back to Station III. General Rand has more craft approaching the Decagon. They'll reinforce there to protect it and prepare to receive the Neltan wormhole."

"Yes, Sir," Bartlet answered. "We took out a few enemy craft, Sirs, but not enough I know. We can hit their lunar base again later. At least now we know exactly where they're hiding and the amount of enemy troops we need to launch an attack against them."

The lopsided *Spider* spurted and then propelled toward Station III.

Manning called into the wavering hologram at the center of his Oval Office. He knew that Terra was trying to stabilize his

First Communication

inside view of Navigation. After spotting a smoking portion of the astrofighter's hull, he said, "Maybe your matrix isn't detect the failure, but I see your third, port-side, fission-fusion turret glowing, Captain."

"I see the seepage, Regent Manning." Bartlet displayed the damage to Marty. "Terra's repairing the dark matter container inside the turret now so Marty can mix the fission/fusion and stream the gravitational matter to all the turrets. That's gonna take a while. In the meantime, we're astro-speeding on a liquid oxygen/hydrogen/plasma mix and traveling at ninety-five kilometers per hour."

"*Slooww,*" EJ huffed.

The Terra hub hummed as an Extinguisher app initialized, clearing Navigation of residual smoke. An oxygen spray ensued, and the crew began basking in a refreshing cool breeze.

"Two hours to Station III, Captain," Bill shouted. "They're ready for us. They'll be like a stock car pit crew repairing The Spider fast!"

"That's cutting it close to the time when the wormhole is schedule to open," Bartlet said, glancing at his wrist device that projected the time in midair, 5:15 p.m., EST. "I sure hope you and Beth will have that new gamma burst device ready by then."

After calling up a gun on the base of the hull that construction bots were layering thick with nano-organic metals, Bill said: "Beth and I should have the weapon finished well before then, Sir." Beth nodded in agreement, and he activated images of various locations and hardware throughout the ship as EJ became engrossed in finding damages the Auto Detect program that might have failed to detect the terrorists' biometrics.

"Good," Bartlet began. "While I navigate this craft manually, you call on the Virtual Engineering Team from the Boeing and LMCO. We have to fix that bad turret…merge *their* Drive Propulsion patents with our Drive Room. Marty might have to crawl *physically* through all the networking lines

J.P. Osterman

and rods and fix the tear that's causing the seepage."

Turning around and looking at the bright-white virtual doorframe on the wall zone where Regent Manning had entered and exited Navigation, he saw the tall bar graph—*The Spider*'s holosite participation number. Tiny lights like microscopic fireflies were flickering: one for each person. That meant that people around the globe were watching the events transpiring inside *his* astrofighter, and watching *every* move. Either Regent Manning or The General had to have ordered that expansive interface. He felt like a failure...so small and exposed. Inhaling, he sucked down the dejection, making it fodder for future success. Three more hours. But he wouldn't allow people to watch without giving them *some* type of seedling win.

Turning to his crew, he stood tall. "Everyone, I have an announcement." After he had their attention, he said: "We destroyed a portion of the enemy's base, and we killed several terrorists. But we still have a long way to go before we eliminate this jihadist group for good and stop World War III." He rubbed sweat off his forehead as his body slumped in fatigue. "Remember, *their* mission is to start an apocalypse. *Our* mission is to ensure that a *new* kind of relationship begins with the Neltans. The sad news is, World War III has spread into the cosmos and this place on the moon appears to be a giant assembly station the enemy has been using to construct large craft, fortify, and search for a place in the solar system they believe they can colonize and elude apprehension. *We* discovered that. *The Spider* crew was instrumental in locating their hideout, dismantling a vixen matrix virus, and debilitating the enemy's forces. To protect tonight's final communication, support craft are on their way to the Decagon to intercept the enemy and, hopefully, provide Stealth Force with Intel that'll lead us right to them so we can take out their entire army." He stopped, drank water and then returned to encourage his crew, and the watching World. "We *will* repair *The Spider* and attack that lunar base again. If there are survivors...we'll hunt them down. There's the clock." Terra appeared in a fuzzy form and stretched out the blaring green numbers: 5:16. "Lieutenant Bill Wallum and Ms. Elizabeth Tufter's new weapon needs a little more work; but when it's finished and we'll be back, and attack." Calling up the developing weapon on the hull for everyone to see, he felt energized, until a bulge of hopelessness struck the pit of his belly like the deep well pouring out dust of defeat on the lunar surface. Failure…he hated it.

He turned around to address the multitudinous flickering lights popping into Navigation. They were thousands of people hoping to rid the world of war and hate. Miracles were happening *everywhere* on Earth. He needed a miracle in space. But the healing mist had dissipated off-Earth and was now coagulating into a new energy source in space where special *Sagan* craft were approaching what was left of the sample's dregs to capture for future use onboard the astrocity, as the Neltans had instructed.

He said to all those illuminating holosite participants: "Until we can secure you complete victory, know that *each* of us here on *The Spider* is with you in sprit as you experience the last communication with the Neltans and as The Regency signs *The Pact*." He made The Peace sign. "Here's to a new insignia we are launching."

He nodded at EJ who created a peace icon and interred the glowing virtual sign in a ten-inch, round time capsule with a tiny matrix mound. She jettisoned it into space. As a contrail, the peace sign was exhaust behind the capsule—an inviting invitation for an alien's watchful cosmic scan. "Peace Forever." After he manually closed out the connection to The World, he saluted Regent Manning. "Good luck to you, Sir."

Manning stood up from behind his desk in the Oval Office. "Thank you, Captain."

Bartlet smiled and gestured toward Space Station III. "Live-stream end, Terra."

Closing the virtual reality at the center of his office, he realized that Bartlet had given him a boost in his campaign for election as Executive Regent. He called into his ceiling processor, "Terra, launch ten more craft from Earth to the

J.P. Osterman

Decagon and track those foreign contrails and hardware IDs we discovered."

As he watched craft maneuver through the tropopause shield and vault out of orbit, he began pacing the floor. "I *sure* hope my best astropilot and *The Spider* can make a quick come back, Terra."

Chapter 22 - His Daily Grind

His office suddenly brightened in a golden glow from the burgeoning sunset. He glanced at the time: 5:20 p.m. Final Transmission was scheduled to begin at nine, in three hours and forty minutes. Even though Terra's matrix is doing most o'the work, there's *still so much* to do to get *ready* for it, he thought, fretting a bit.

Outside, a cool wind was sweeping through the streets, tipping over tents and launching colorful umbrellas that began skipping across the pavement and grassy areas like autumn leaves in a breeze. People were cheering. The temperature was decreasing.

He ran to the window. "The atmosphere has *definitely* improved," he said to his virtual Terra who walked up beside him, her eyes reflecting the sky blue scene, still hazy. The ozone reading that scrolled down on his Smart Bar indicated a pre-2057 level. He inhaled a breath of gratitude. "The Matter Stream sample worked. Relief on Earth! At least we succeeded at stopping an apocalyptic event, Terra."

After she agreed, another wave of light illuminated from all the building mounds and matrix processing towers. The ripple extended clear out into the dry rural valley where the gold line stopped and began returning to D.C. Terra was conducting an automatic assessment of all the Smarthomes, biodomes, and buildings coated with nano-protectants. White light flickered over the Metro stations. Then all was quiet. After the ozone attack, engineers rebuilt most cities as a combination of subterranean and dome communities. D.C was almost pure dome country.

"I encountered twenty-five fissures on fifteen structures. I am mending them *and* informing the occupants," she said. "Structural integrity scans of historical sites commencing."

"*Whew*, not too many problems this time," he exhaled in relief and then checked his Smart readings projecting over his desk: 75° Fahrenheit; 24° Celsius. He swept away the Celsius. "Fahrenheit is fine, Terra, and lower the temp to 73°, will ya? I still feel like I'm burning up." He unfastened his collar. "*That* was nerve racking. That entire battle…this whole solar flash emergency." He plopped down in his chair. The Oval Office was huge; the Press Room four times larger, but the cosmos through which the terrorists were escaping appeared infinite. Are they searching for planetary safe haven or heading toward the Decagon to take it over? Only time would tell and waiting for intel from a secret mission he had launched earlier in the day from *Sagan*.

"Your blood pressure is elevated, Regent Manning," Terra said. "Seventy-three degrees now set."

He opened his desk, took out a medicinal patch, unpeeled it and slapped it on his back. "Thanks, Terra. I'm late taking it. But if I undergo an entire Regeneration…which I have scheduled for tomorrow morning, the nanobotic portion of the process *should* fix the blood pressure problem."

The citywide scan of all the historical monuments and buildings stopped. A hum resounded throughout the White House. On Wall Zone 1—Jane Dirk's Secret Service imager— he could see the Center Lobby and Jane's station accepting the scan's readings and removing the previous Lock Down alert. Now more matrix projectionists and media crews could enter

First Communication

the building and the Press Room in preparation for Final Communication. Jane just streamed him an A-Okay from her station.

"How did the all the roofs around the city hold up?" he asked Terra.

Smart readings on Wall Zone 2 began scrolling data concerning the city's four quadrants. "All nano-coverings absorbed and are redirecting radiation into my matrix, Regent Manning."

When he noticed that Terra's flow of matrix processing power was stable and unwavering, he exclaimed, "Wow, everything's definitely fine...*completely* stable here. Even up there!" He pointed at the bright blue sky. Rays of light were striking a few white disintegrating clouds—splendid God rays he hadn't seen since the attacks. The setting sun looked like a dapple of cough syrup between two sparkling monuments. Hovercraft were launching and docking outside the city like insects droning in and out of hives.

Then he noticed a deluge of celebrating people ascending out of several domed Metro stations. Stepping off escalators, they opened umbrellas. With the new ozone reading streaming to them, they didn't have to, but the act was a self-protective reflex. It would take some time for people to trust the unfamiliar safe reading, put away their high-tech umbrellas, and leave their breathing apparatuses at home instead of wearing them like face guards. From his office looking down on the congregating crowds, the tops of the bobbing umbrellas looked like rolling kaleidoscopic gems. People had pre-programmed the nano-fabric cloth to interact with their avatars. Some people were editing their avatars through their wrist devices and portable tablets while racing to their destinations. He could see the little figures that looked like colorful cartoon characters jumping from person-to-person, interacting. Biometrically linked to their hosts, avatars everywhere were exchanging information through virtual worlds.

Through wrist devices, accessory devices, garment devices and portable tablets that evolved out of all the Smart technology from the 2050s, avatars could activate anywhere on verbal command or touch command—pop up and materializing—over any nano-organic metal, fabric, or patch of nano-organics that had an interface with Terra's matrix. He saw several lift off from their hosts and announce their presence in midair. Some avatars were interfacing with 3D billboards, some with zeppelins to receive security information or Earth stats, and some were downstreaming moving advertisements on building surfaces. A person's avatar could link to anything, anywhere, within legal limitations policed by matrix security agents in all of Terra's seven, continental processing centers. Agents were always receiving complaints of Invasion of Privacy and hacking, especially illegal hacking by the Tech-No protesters. Matrix agents pronounced punishments. Enforcers exacted the punishments. Being stripped of matrix privileges was like experiencing an umbilical cut off and being forced to sit alone for days, weeks, or months on a cliff with no sustenance. Once severed from the matrix, everybody knew it, and everybody shunned "the criminal" for the duration of the punishment. Matrix Security inferred all the time criminal connections by mere association. No one wanted that!

Each person's avatar was a unique creation, connection, profile and social ID.

Noticing another drove of people ascending out of the subway tunnels, Manning watched their avatars link with directional arrows and Help Icons that in turn began directing them to join specific groups. The same quantum-interface was occurring everywhere around the globe.

Most people had adapted to Terra's matrix: a self-contained and self-perpetuating quantum-nonlocality processor that was making life so much easier. Having no bandwidth or buffer issues, Terra was streaming globally through upgraded high-tech facilities, government computing centers, satellites, fiber optics, renovated electrical grids, transformers, and cell phone towers: grids. Terra was providing people with instantaneous information and virtual entertainment, *and* allowing them

First Communication

instant access to monitor, adjust, or manipulate any appliance or wall zone imaging system through their Smarthome programs.

Manning closed his eyes, put his ear against the vibrating window in his Oval Office and listened. People were communicating with Terra like millions of streaming ants interacting telepathically with a queen. The huge influx of excited people had been gathering throughout D.C. for days. Everyone was trying to position themselves in just the right spots and locations to procure the best views of the Neltan/Earth wormhole scheduled to stream from the Decagon into the Press Room. If they had obstructed views, they could see the entire signing ceremony on the sides of certain buildings, zeppelins, or modified billboards. The intergalactic communication would be the last time anyone would be receiving information from Nelta or see a Neltan again, at least until the *Sagan* crew could arrive on the planet and attempt to contact Earth.

"Regent Manning," Terra began, "I am streaming virtual programs to assure *each* person around the globs of his and her safety as well as the structural integrity of their Smarthomes, businesses and beehive communities." Around the main ceiling hub, Terra's rainbow-interface light churned wildly then calmed.

He could have asked *his* pre-programmed Terra to appear. Or he could have activated his little avatar over his wrist device and sent out a massive communication, or called on an app and had a new scene materialize on his wall zones and windows. He had those same options in his Smarthome. His at-home Terra-hub system was like his Oval Office holosite grid: a link in a quantum system interfacing with the vast matrix. Except his at-home edition was Terra-II.

The next minute, Terra streamed a global wide *Assurance Message* while he contacted the panel of Regents in charge of crowd management, ensuring they had enough Enforcers on the ground to fend off a surprise terror attack or Tech-No protester event. Then Terra re-enforced Washington, D. C.

J.P. Osterman

Launching from astro-turf outside the city, techs began setting up shield pods—positioning the beehive devices strategically on the sides of buildings and within direct line of Terra's streaming matrix centers. In waves of high-pitch sounds beyond human hearing, one-by-one, the shields initiated like lightning as they synchronized with the matrix.

The Smart Bar over his desk flashed *Green*.

"Done...great! Now anyone who causes a major disruption, we should get his or her location," he said. He didn't feel comfortable yet. Staring at the crowds that seemed pacified by the safe ozone reading, he remembered that some people were afraid that the ozone level might fail at some point in the future, that the sample might have a whiplash effect even though the Neltans had given the Regency proof to the contrary. Without passing the test of time, people lacked confidence in the Matter Stream sample.

"Regent Manning?"

He didn't hear Terra. He was busy opening up visuals of rural areas, inspecting structures, and surveying the terrain crusted with dry brush, charred soil, barren trees and dilapidated towers. He saw nothing green. In most outlying areas, companies had not yet erected biodomes. Now and then, when he glanced at the sky, he spotted an oscillating wave of white light. Terra was transferring solar energy from the tropopause shield to processor mounds and imagers that technicians were installing throughout D.C. and beyond. He felt his breath move of his chest and through his nostrils. "Gosh I'm tired," he sighed. He felt drained, and sick, from having to be so hypervigilant all the time. But the reality of having to live on pins-and-needles also inflamed his drive to fight. More than anything, he, and everyone else wished they could return to the old ways of living prior to the attacks. But if that would happen—as some people were hoping for and planning for—people might want to vote to dismantle all the Neltan technology, and unplug, or at least regress, Terra. He cringed. Who might win the battle? He had no idea. He *did* want back the old normal ways of breathing and enjoying the

First Communication

outside. But he didn't want humanity to revert to the old internet/TV cable, URLs, ports, and satellite days. Way too slow…the opposite of quantum processing. He wanted the best of both worlds: Terra-III to evolve around the globe, more advanced medical options, and broader matrix-tapping capability. He'd have to keep his eye on today's tally of votes to find out what The World was approving for tomorrow so he could launch another counter campaign if necessary. In the end, living on the astrocity, *Sagan*, and eventually landing on and possibly living on Nelta were the answers. Part of him didn't care about the long distance race of technology on Earth. He was planning to leave anyway! In the meantime, he had to stay, eat, and work somewhere. He was already spending most of his time on *Sagan*, with his campaign virtual world, private world, and Regency holosite world keeping up appearances.

"Regent Manning?"

"Huh? Oh, sorry, Terra." He grabbed a wet bottle of water off the small round table next to the mirror and began gulping down the cold liquid. "*Ahhh*," he sighed, feeling refreshed as he wiped cool drops on his cheeks that felt hot and flushed. He knew he had the tendency to turn red in the face whenever he felt overwhelmed. Now, he felt angry, irritated and impatient. He flung the bottle into the wastebasket that almost tipped over if not for the nanomaterials in the carpet that kept it attached to the floor.

"Would you like the specific point of origin of the solar flare? I can see it now."

"No—no thanks," he snapped, feeling less panicked now that Terra had pronounced the entire northern hemisphere safe. He then realized that she was concerned about him. He wiped sweat off his temples and hit his desk. "I hate this, Terra!"

"Hate what, Regent Manning?"

"All this monitoring and we're still experiencing matrix intrusions." Then he realized that no matter how efficient, exacting, and impenetrable researchers certified the new Terra-

J.P. Osterman

III, he'd still be worrying that the artificial computer intelligence might fail. Terra-II had experienced a glitch when that Demon Terra inserted a chameleon field of inaccuracy that almost led to the tropopause shield failing. It had been drummed into him: there's no such thing as perfect. But that wasn't the case with the covert Terra-III in his office, so far. The Neltans had convinced people of Terra's indestructible integrity, that is, if the processing facilities maintained 100% stream efficiency. That was humanity's responsibility. Thus far, the Neltans had been right with their claim. He wished people could evolve as fast as the Neltan technology then there'd be no sabotage, espionage, or protesting of Neltan-based technology!

After another quick check of the room's Smart readings, and Terra assuring him that the tropopause shield was strong and radiation proof, he slid back in front of his mirror and began examining his face. Yes, there were real perks to the Neltan technology. "*Not bad* for a first derma-regeneration, Terra. I *do* like being twenty-five and not thirty-five." He looped his tie and slid the knot over his collar button. "Twenty-five…*maybe* forever!" He gave himself thumbs up. He had beaten something and felt a victory over death. "What *great* technology. I don't see the problem." He looked up at the rainbow photonic processor cycling around the center beehive hub. "Do *you* see the problem, Terra?" He called on a hologram that activated over one of the twenty-five Imaging Circle Zones interspersed throughout the flooring. "What's the count on limiting your matrix, Terra?"

Up popped a graphic representation of the block-long, Global Voting Facility in China. Multicultural avatars were tallying the daily vote on not only who would remain on the Regency, but also whether to limit Terra III's evolution. There were also various percentages displaying the ratings of the implementation of more Neltan technology.

"One million, two-hundred thousand and sixty-one people are currently voting down my Version Three evolution," Terra said.

First Communication

Manning lifted out and enlarged the Non-Expansion Vote. "Damn that we have over a million opponents! And the GVF isn't closed yet."

"The time is 5:33 p.m., Regent Manning. The polls close in three hours and twenty-seven minutes."

He laughed. At least that number didn't indicate any type of matrix disconnection. People were too smart for that...too acclimated to an easier life. "I gotta have humor, Terra, 'cause all those seconds feel like an eternity as does every day the future of *your* matrix is resting in everyone's vote. Do you see the problem people are having with *you*, Terra?"

"No, Regent Manning."

"I don't see the problem, except for their lack of appreciation...*and* ignorance," he huffed. "People weren't there when your blueprints first came streaming in through that communications wormhole. Even though they can now participate in that historic exchange, they haven't a clue as to what you're really about. Not like me. I worked damn hard to get you, Terra." He whispered, "I woulda told 'em anything to secure a matrix anyway...but thank God you're here, and if I have my way, soon your Version Three will be and streaming."

"Yes, Regent Manning," Terra said softly.

He suddenly had the answer. "Fear! That's what it is, Terra. They're afraid...of you. They need more virtual educational opportunities, that's all. Stream *that* initiative to the GVF, and request they put it on tomorrow's ballot. Call the initiative *Augmented World Education for Terra-III*, and stream that first visual we received from Ambassador Shaesar about your quantum system with the Artificial Intelligence package on how to assemble and activate you."

"Streaming the initiative and the historic hologram to the polling facility, Regent Manning," Terra replied. "Let me remind you that today's vote, electing an Executive Regent, might initiate a feedback equation on the evolution of my predictive capabilities."

Manning felt a surge of enthusiasm. "That's right! If the negative vote is insignificant, the majority wins. The

J.P. Osterman

opposition fails—at least I hope so." When he remembered the group who was constantly putting out the vote to ban Terra III's expansion, he added, "I still don't see *why* all the opposition to having the Neltan technology." He smoothed down his hair—a flyaway mess without gel. He combed it back. His reflection in the mirror altered as the ceiling hubs and wall-zone imagers altered to help him get a good rear-view image of himself. When they steadied so he could see better, he noticed his entire 360° view *did* remind him of his campaign avatar, Beethoven. Adding a dollop of quickset lotion to water, he ran his fingers through his hair, remembering the first time he heard someone call him Beethoven. He wanted to search out that pundit and strangle him!

That was back in May of 2058 after The World voted him in as a Regent. He had voiced a contrary opinion on how to procure more water for subsurface beehive communities. The opposing group twisted his words on several broadcast networks, accusing him of being dark, brooding and rigid. They believed desalination plants were the answer; he said running aqueducts from the last gushing glaciers and mountain regions. They were closer, and he showed how to convert large sewer pipes, sanitize them, and then easily transport and install them. His black hair was a bit wild that dry arid morning in Australia, so his opponent's campaign committee streamed through the internet: "Regent Thornton Seth Manning is a modern day Beethoven in looks and attitude!" His campaign team reframed the negative spin into a positive. A creative, caring, and "Saving Humanity" perspective throughout the years made Manning popular; and by making appearances mostly through virtual reality worlds, he continued to outwit his opponents and glean the required votes to hang onto his Regency position. He dreaded "hanging on" to anything. He wanted his position to be permanent, but that would mean changing *Global Law I* that established The Regency and outlined a Regent's duties and term of office. Whenever he thought of his daily precarious reality, he felt infused with anger and motivated to fight against that grind.

First Communication

"I can't see *why* on Earth some people don't want Neltan technology, Terra, other than just being plain scared of it." He picked up his dark purple suit coat and whipped it over his shoulder. "Neltan technology is *everything* anyone could ever ask for, right? People have been advancing technically since the beginning of time."

Terra replied, "If I could ascertain the desires of over two billion people, Regent Manning, I might be able to answer yes."

"Two, billion, people," Manning repeated. "Just a little over two billion. That's it."

He remembered the day when everything changed: June 10, 2057. Unlike September 11, 2001, *everyone* on Earth could remember his or her *exact* location on June 10, 2057. At least those who had survived the Attack on the Ozone. For those who survived and those born after that terrible day, Terra would always be present at the Survivors Memorial at the Center of the Reflecting Pool to remind them of what happened. ...

J.P. Osterman

Chapter 23 - Survivors Memorial

To reach the Survivors Memorial, one had to cross a long bridge in front of Jefferson's Monument. At the arched entryway of the memorial, Terra's interactive presence was there, waving in visitors and showing them various scenes that archivists had programmed into the matrix for posterity. Once enough people gathered at a secondary archway leading inside Survivors Memorial, Terra began her narration of what happened that changed Earth. ...

"Over ten years ago, on June 10, 2057, the terrorists who had been secretly procuring and assembling nukes launched their death and destruction around the world. The ozone explosions killed millions. This memorial is for them.

The radiation sickened billions, two billion of whom died in the next six months. This memorial is for them.

From the USA – to – Europe and Israel – to – China and Russia – to – Central and South America – to – Japan, New Zealand, and most of Oceana including Australia...the ozone strikes killed leaders and toppled governments. This memorial is for all the leaders and dignitaries who tried hard to hunt down the terrorists but who died in the pursuit of justice.

First Communication

As of today, February 27, 2068, and until my matrix announces differently, the survivors continue the search for the remainder of the attackers who continue to wage their war on humanity. This memorial is also for the heroes on Earth and in space who lost their lives in the pursuit of attaining freedom for us all.

World War III began June 11, 2057. Survivors of the attempted apocalypse took refuge in subways, military bunkers, schools, hospitals, airports, and law enforcement buildings—any thick-walled structure that people could reinforce with metal and concrete. Luckily, scientists were able to reconfigure some satellites and solar panels in orbit to fend off some of the harmful radiation. And a few countries that had been experimenting with climate devices sent their machines into the troposphere to generate intense cloud cover. Still, In spite of all our technology, Earth began to heat up. Survivors sought cover, safety, security, and support in any protective structure that they deemed "Fit for Habitation" or "Protected." For the remainder of that catastrophic year, the survivors began networking via the internet's One-World Media Site. *Surviving In Community* became the Call-of-Action proclamation. In spite of that plea to maintain global community living, there were riots and fights...people arguing for choice living spaces, people adjusting after losing everything, people restructuring the value and exchange of currency. Some people could not handle the deaths of their entire families, or their bodies succumbing to the pain and agony of radiation poisoning, or their sudden plummet into poverty. They took their own lives. This memorial is for them.

That same year—after the ozone strikes—the internet and video conferencing through portable devices began to replace huge TV screens. Expansive broadcast networks and radio stations flourished. Underground transportation sites began connecting and multiplying like streams after a flood. Scientists and researchers created innovative coolants, water collectors, and heating devices to meet the physical needs of

J.P. Osterman

the survivors. Above ground, dome-building companies, like Elemental Engineering, emerged whose workers began constructing giant terrariums, covering zoos, and re-enforcing facilities needed to grow, harvest, and dispense food, clothing and medicine. The weakest and most vulnerable often died for lack of medical supplies or care in spite of the resurgence of the extended family living accommodations. In part, this memorial is for them.

In the months following The Attack, the most profound expansion occurred. If you look at your wrist devices that are allowing you to interface with me in 4D right now, you are seeing the most advanced version of that network from that year of 2057. I am quantum with augmented reality capability. That 2057 network was cable, satellite, and cloud computing. Slow in comparison. Still, the digital and fiber optic connections made for a new type of mass interface, communication and exchange for the survivors. Facebook, Twitter, Skype, YouTube, and other media sites merged into one live streaming site. The survivors united into one global voice the media coined *The World*. The World was, and still is, *each* survivor communicating through the internet, now, the matrix. The World is you—your vote and your personal holosite. To participate in that Great Media Expansion that occurred after 2057, please consider visiting The Smithsonian's northern building...or the Neltan Museum to learn how humanity acquired the first matrix after First Communication. I facilitate those tours as well. For now, please enter the archway to the inside walls where I will continue our story.

In the Universal Vote of January 2, 2058, The World voted to unite *all* countries and set up parameters for future elections. But that vote failed to yield the necessary 85% needed to create a viable, global governing system. Furthermore, complicating that vote, a terrorist cell managed to bypass our One-World Network Firewall, hack into our live-stream voting site and input a Rex virus that wreaked havoc on the tally. It took our best hackers ten days to purge that tyrannous infection. That was the first time scientists discovered a gaming paradigm and

First Communication

then generated a simple Mobius band to ascertain and then counter all cyber-attacks. This wall panel is the famous algorithm that beat that terrorist cell and that continues to aid my matrix as I work with survivors to win World War III: Euler's equation interposed with Dirac's equation, which in virtual form produces an impenetrable matrix security and automatically updates Firewalls.

In spite of the global unionism of 2057, a state of anarchy continued to persist. And in spite of the high-speed, fast-paced interaction, social networking, and mass assembly via the internet; The World finally determined, in another vote on January 14, 2058 that nothing could replace true hands-on leadership. The government was in chaos.

The most widespread media site processing each individual's communications and consolidating them all, thus creating the first statistical global site, ONE-Global-Voice-at-gov-dot-com, asked people worldwide to respond to the 85% concerns of all the survivors: "Who should lead an entire global population since governments have fallen? Dictators, theocracies and monarchies have never lasted and never left a positive influence on humanity."

Tallying the answers, the site streamed the following: 90% of adults over eighteen believe that knowledge, awareness and democracy are the main ideals that will direct humanity on a new path of equality and community while maintaining Capitalistic attitudes and eliminating war.

On March 3, 2058, that same social media site streamed options and called all people over eighteen to vote in a Mass Election on April 1, 2058. The survivors agreed—90%—in the March 3 vote, that absolute power indeed corrupts absolutely. The site compiled a statistically significant conclusion of The World's own words: "We have hope—through hard lessons lost—that our future government can eliminate abuses of power, squelch all forms of oppression, and capture and reform The Terrorists."

After a global-wide, internet campaign ensued between March 3 and March 31, on April 1, 2058, the survivors voted in the fifteen-item, *Global Constitution* based on proven Democratic-Republic principles. On this wall, these fifteen items are hand written. You can down-stream them into your wrist devices for future perusal. Now…back to our history.

In that same vote on that same day, April 1, 2058, The World voted into office a global governing leadership comprised of prominent judges, scholars, and university professors, fifty of them in all. The World named these culturally diverse men and women Regents, and the new government leadership, The Regency. Daily, The World— that's you—can vote *any* Regent out of office or elect nominated candidates into office. To see our succession of Regents, please visit the White House Tour Dome, as the White House is the current Regency's meeting location. Last year, the Regents governed from the Parliament in London. If you are anticipating an excursion to England, you can visit that site. I am host to that that tour as well. However, here, in The White House, right now, you might be able to spot Regent Thornton Seth Manning in the Oval Office. He is the Leader of the fifteen-member, Intermediary Regency Team mediating concerns between Enforcers on land and Stealth Force on Station III. Last month, he was the first Regent *ever* to campaign on a Platform of Seniority. After he won, he requested the Oval Office for his own private use for the remainder of this year. The Regency granted his request.

Now, I want to tell you a few things about the fifty-member Regency. Some information might be a bit secretive, so have your wrist devices ready to interact on Whisper-mode." She gestured for tourists to keep quiet. "Also, keep your avatars on Miniature-mode. Sometimes, a Regent or two might surprise us and unexpectedly make an appearance. We want to make sure we can spot him or her and perhaps even ask for autographs! Sometimes they like adding their information in person into the memorial.

Now…are you ready to hear a few facts about *your* Regency? Put your avatars on Full Stream-mode over your wrist devices and follow me." She escorted them into a small

First Communication

dark glistening room depicting matrix processing as a giant array over their heads. The image of the Global Voting Facility in China illuminated on a giant wall zone map. Terra continued:

"The Regency is responsible for forwarding their campaign postings prior to 6:00 p.m., EST, to the Global Participation Pole in Xi´an, China—*and* to the Constant Peace Institution responsible for tallying the votes, scanning for abuses, monitoring firewalls, and streaming the daily tally live into every person's holosite account. Wow—what duties they have! But remember, *you* pay the Regents plenty. A furnished Smart Home and five thousand euros a month. And as a part of their responsibility, upon entering office, they swear to The Principle of Transparency: *Global Law V* in the *Global Constitution*."…

Manning forgot the Terra guide's words after that and felt suddenly filled with dread. He traced all the war memorials with his eyes back to the cheering crowds and advertising hovercraft that snapped him back to reality. Plopping down in his chair, he confided to his Terra: "I hate daily votes. I have two suitcases at my door and a storage room ready to sneak out provisions in case The World votes me out. I sure hope they vote me in as Executive Regent, and then I won't have to worry about a daily vote ever again! Until the day I die, I'm Regent."

"Yes, Regent Manning. Would you like the current tally?"

He glanced at the time: 5:39 p.m. He still had over three hours until the holosite polls closed. "Not yet, Terra. I'm still assessing what's happening outside. The crowds are huge and the sun's just about down. I'm feeling a bit uneasy. Send for more Enforcers and vendors. If people eat and have lots to drink, they're less likely to grumble and fight."

"Done, Regent Manning."

In Constitution Gardens, techs from Interactive Corp were inspecting the memorials—the light projections of past war heroes flaring on as spectators activated their 4D historical shows and began interacting with them. He then realized he

J.P. Osterman

was feeling uneasy not totally because he might lose Executive Regent, but because The World might vote to suspend the new Terra-III Global Implementation Initiative. "You know what people want? Don't answer, Terra. 'Cause I'll tell you. People have been searching for alien technology for at *least* as long as people could write pictographs." He called on a hologram show of *Ancient Aliens* that Terra-II had converted into participation sites. "People used to call shows like this 'myths' or 'fabrications,' and the archeologists and anthropologists narrating the shows people used to call them 'delusional' or 'misinformed' at the best. Now that we *have* alien technology, some people don't want it. Gosh I wish those old-world die-hards would get with the 2060s!"

He glanced at his ceiling hub—its invisible electro-photonic-magnetic generated processor interfacing with its matrix facilities. Terra was picking up his every sound, biometric, and motion—could project his image anywhere and with anyone. He then thought of life without Terra. "Those Tech-No protesters are nuts, *plain* crazy, Terra. Thank God *most* of The World agrees with *me*. They like you and want you. They need you." He walked to his desk, leaned on the edge and threw his coat that hit the back of his chair. "Too bad we couldn't accept *everyone* who applied to go to Nelta. Everyone seems to want to leave, especially as we approach the date of *Sagan*'s launch."

Terra flashed *June 10, 2070* on top of his desk.

He felt suddenly weighted down. "Yep, that's the day. And as each day rolls by in its approach, people are becoming more terrified. They're afraid The Matter Stream sample might not finish its job, or that it might have an adverse effect and render Earth uninhabitable in the future. Besides, we can't fit three-fourths of the population on *Sagan* even if you *could* deem them Essential." Then he remembered visiting the ship's construction site and seeing his quarters—now just a network of nano-coated boards under which one day he'd be sleeping. "I must admit though…boy am I glad to be on The List for Nelta. I'd *hate* being left here—stuck *here* with people who are

First Communication

constantly complaining and voting on whether to accept or reject the Neltan technology. It'd be like a daily tit-for-tat spat!"

Over a billion people applied for the *Sagan* expedition to Nelta, but Terra selected the maximum of seventy five thousand. After Neltan scientists transmitted their Life-Extension Technology on February 4, 2062, The World voted in organ regeneration through nano-technology, stem-cell therapy, and cloning—the later *only* permitted by The Regency and *only* onboard *Sagan*.

"Regent Manning, you told me *always* to present the other side of an argument, that way you'd be able to prepare rhetoric to persuade people to convert to *your* side," Terra said.

"Yep—go…but I think I know what you're gonna say, Terra." He pulled a NutriBar out of his desk, ripped back the biodegradable wrapper and started eating.

"Regent Manning, the Tech-No protesters say they are presenting a sound reason against Nelta's technology even though they would not have *me* if not for Nelta," Terra said.

"See!" He slammed his fist on his desk. "People accept *some* technology, *like you*, that's making their lives fully-immersive, their entertainment worlds more enjoyable, their waking lives more manageable. But then, when a few things go haywire…well, you know, like those accidental heart misplacements. But—"

"The Misplacement Error at the Chicago Growth and Transplant Center, November 9, 2066. Cellular engineers input wrong data and cylinders grew hearts with livers," Terra said.

Coughing, Manning said, "Accidental deaths, Terra—happens *all* the time when people begin working in *any* innovative field. Think of all the pilots who died in the 1950s and 60s trying to improve aeronautics and space exploration."

"Do you want me to begin a projection of the pilots? Their accomplishments? Their—"

"No, *that's* okay. I trust *you* have them memorialized in the Smithsonian."

J.P. Osterman

"I do," Terra replied.

He folded his arms and peered at the beehive ceiling hub. He remembered that it was interfacing with everything in his office, he felt at ease. Since Terra's inception, he had never known a rainbow processor to stop cycling around a Terra hub, except in the case of an explosion, deliberate interference, or sabotage. As a proud Terra-host since the first quantum-system's 2064 inception, he prided himself on having easily transitioned from the outdated PC-world to the new holosite virtual world. "Accidents now are all *human* error, not the machinations of Neltan technology, Terra. I'm still working to reverse those mistakes and make *you* take the credit for it."

Terra said, "Thank you, Regent Manning."

He threw his wrapper into the wastebasket. "No thanking *me*, Terra. It's the Tech-No protestors who are causing all the chaos surrounding implementing Neltan technology. They're saying that The World's advancing too quickly. They're arguing that *we're* not prepared culturally for *their* technology. Besides being terrified that someday we're gonna marry Neltans...way off in the future if that *does* happen...those protesters are blaming *you*, and *me*, the Neltans, and *all* The Regents." He felt out of breath as he glanced outside at the crowds. The darkening sky was clearing of green auroras. The air looked fresh. "*Now* more than *ever*, these protesters are trying to infect your quantum stream, disrupt your grid, and sabotage your matrix. So keep all your ScanWare and I-SpyWare streaming up-to-date."

"Yes Regent Manning."

His eyes stung and he rubbed them as he paced the floor.

As he was about to receive an incoming message from a Regent, Terra said, "Regent Manning, a Tech-No protester has hacked your personal holosite. I am buffering the intrusion until you can access your holosite safely. The one who streamed the message to your holosite signed the message *The Sender.*"

"Damn!" He called open his holosite on Wall Zone 1 and had Terra advance the threat to Agent Jane Dirk who

First Communication

forwarded the intrusion to Stations II and III for analysis and response.

A small, 3D cartoon character—a half-human and half-Neltan child—materialized on the screen and said: Beware of Interspecies Breeding! Enter here, now, to learn more and join our cause. But don't blame yourself for being suckered into a bargain with the Neltans. Blame Regent Thornton Manning for taking humanity down this bad path!" The red headed, red-faced child enlarged a bit, spat at him and added: "Ha-ha, Regent Manning." The laugh was shrill and demonic sounding. "Everyone around the world is receiving this right now! Thanks for opening me up and starting the roll!" The child's fingernails and hair began growing as the half-breed child giggled, pointed at Manning in a mocking gesture and sent out a ripple of laughter through his Oval Office.

Closing the message abruptly, Manning shouted, "Put this message in a hard buffer suspension, Terra. I just hope Sender didn't realize that I have your Terra-III up and streaming in here so you can work your matrix magic and wad that message into oblivion!" After ruminating over several solutions while Terra rendered the message *Disposed*, he said: "This Tech-No Sender thinks that if he or she frightens people with matrix-shopped images and scenes, a global wide panic will break out. The Tech-Nos will then use fear to increase their following and stop all future contact with the Neltans in spite of the destructive consequences that might ensue if we don't finalize *The Pact* tonight." Then he had an idea. "Terra, shadow-stream the countermeasure The Regency decided on yesterday as a response to this type of propaganda."

Terra brought up the hologram with The Regency's portraits. In unison, they said: "Remember our history. First, there was ignorant Caucasian disdain for African Americans; second, Nazi persecution of Jews; and, third, the Jihadists Declaration of Extermination: *Kill All Outsiders*. That's all of us...Tech-No protesters and everyone else. We must unite in one cause and one voice. Eliminate racism now!"

Manning said, "Okay...stream the message back to The

J.P. Osterman

Sender, Terra." After the Send icon faded, he said: "The group that hacked my site appears to be campaigning to eliminate the use of nanotechnology in medicine for Disease and Disability Reversal and Repair. That's plain nuts! Now, thanks to the Neltans, we can cure every type of genetic disorder and disease. It's cost effective to cure people…not leave nature to take its course like in The Past. This Sender is Nuts! Who the hell is she or he?"

Then he saw incoming bad news on the GVF's site streaming in votes and the facility's Daily Schedule on Wall Zone 2. An Addendum to Global Law XIX's Medical Intervention statue would be posting at 6:00 a.m. tomorrow morning. Because of this one hack, a small number of people were advocating the elimination of a piece of Neltan-based hardware for bio-cellular nano-intervention. He saw the future filled with "one day Yes to this, the next day No."

"This is so wishy-washy!" he said. "I have to find a way around this hell, Terra. I don't know how long I'm gonna be able to take being constantly countering viruses and ludicrous propaganda!" Every day for the past several months—and intermittently before that—he had been embroiled in launching counter maneuvers against the invasive protestors. Now he was afraid that fending them off might be in vain. They appeared impervious to any type of new matrix update and firewall. He tapped his desk in a drum roll. "Well, these Tech-Nos and their Sender leader might be able to promulgate here, but *no* protesters will be onboard *Sagan*. I'm going to see to that! On that astrocity, we're going to have and use *everything* Neltan."

"Yes, Regent Manning, and you're working *hard* to be elected so you can *lead* that Friendship Mission to Nelta," Terra said. "I bet you are going to be elected. I just know it."

He remembered programming those encouraging words into her to repeat to him during low times like these when he needed support. His vote for the Executive Regent position popped up over his desk: one million, nine-hundred and eighty-six. A second vote materialized next to his: three

First Communication

hundred less.

"I'm beating Regent Jenkens!" He still felt a pang of fear of losing.

"I am continuing to redirect all the fear-mongering posts and hate mail to matrix techs for dissection, location, and counter attack measures," said Terra.

Then he told her to return the vile matrix-shopped message to The Sender with a hologram he recorded last week. "With every fearful or hate-filled face that attacks me through one of my three holosite worlds, create and stream a positive show of me from one of my archives. Especially stream that show where I appeared at the grand opening of the Elöny community biodome in Budapest." As the rainbow ceiling processor oscillated wildly, Terra extinguished the hologram; then the processor resettled to a gently glowing orb with a soft resounding hum.

Trying to think of more ways to buffer his holosite against negative spin but feeling overwhelmed, he coughed and said, "Yes—*um*, thanks, Terra." When he saw his shaking hands, he activated a biometric scan, and Terra prescribed an analgesic. A blue beam streaked down and touched his forehead, eliminating the pain. Breathing in relief, he said: "Wow—I'm more tired than what I thought."

Terra displayed his neurological-wave tomography as a hologram in the center of his office. "Pain decrease in effect." The hologram faded.

"Pain—huh! What's *really* paining me is all this opposition. What a divide we've got all around the globe. What a world mess." He stood and craned his neck into the mirror, admiring his new youthful face. But looking young alone was beginning to appear as the dull circles under his eyes. Nelta had something that Earth had experience only a bit.

He wanted more of The Matter Stream.

J.P. Osterman

Chapter 24 - The Pact

The Regents' scientists discovered that Nelta's Matter Stream contained life-extension properties after the Neltan Advancement Committee transmitted visuals of it circulating through their solar system. The Neltans explained that The Matter Stream is the constant thread of energy existing in the Multiverse. At the Big Bang, it ejected the four forces into our universe, and its Higgs field acts as a stabilizing domain of the four forces. The Matter Stream triggered the start of Time when it integrated Motion, Mass (as Higgs bosons), Space, and the Four Forces into one giant expanding tapestry. The Neltan ambassador Shaesar said in the Third Contact on December 11, 2058, that the Matter Stream has kept their solar system vibrant and stable for over twelve billion years. It's been energizing their suns and infusing Nelta with life.

However, now, their species was in jeopardy of extinction.

Thousands of years ago, they predicted that a cosmic dynamo—a giant supernova in distant galaxy—would begin to pummel Nelta's atmosphere with harmful radiation. The Matter Stream could survive this strong throng of exposure, if contained as an artificial planet, but not Neltan DNA, even

First Communication

under the best of stasis conditions. After the two-thousand years of radioactive exposure, The Matter Stream could revitalize Nelta upon automatically unleashing from its artificial body and begin restoring the planet to its pre-apocalyptic state. Not so for the Neltans' genetics which would slowly begin to lose telomere elasticity, which in turn would affect lifespan. Furthermore, they had said that they had "conducted massive experimentations" eons ago. They never explained the nature of those experiments, but they must have had an adverse effect on their population—or will have an effect as the result of the pummeling—otherwise they would have never brought the issue up while discussing their future extinction. Within a few generations, the Neltans would become an extinct species.

For hundreds of years since they predicted the massive supernova effects on their planet, the Neltans had been searching the cosmos for help. They had befriended several aliens on various planets and even colonized a few worlds. None of their cosmic acquaintances was genetically compatible with them...except ours

After Manning heard about the regenerative properties of the Matter Stream, he wondered: "Could our solar system thrive beyond what is predicted if we had that life generating force? How long could people *really* live if *we* had The Matter Stream?" He hadn't asked that question to anyone for fear of it getting back to the Neltans. They might interpret the question as a threat, for they called themselves Protectors of The Matter Stream. Thus far, the little sample they streamed to Earth had healed the ozone. He was one of the Regents who had negotiated for it in exchange for human DNA...

"Regent Manning," Terra said, softly. "It's time. Do you *still* want the countdown to *Sagan*'s launch?"

"No thanks, that's okay—*whew!*" he exhaled, the flight of oxygen bringing him back to the here-and-now. "2070 is still a long way off." He squinted into the mirror, thinking he spotted eye wrinkles. "*Awhh!*"

"Is something wrong, Regent Manning?"

Then he realized the lines were only fearful figments.

"Nothing…no nothing. *Whew*—I'm okay. He took his speech and pen out of his pocket, unfolded the paper, and set them on his desk, preparing to write. He had to begin writing an acceptance speech should The World elect him Executive Regent. Then he walked to the door and peeked into the Press Room. He was looking for Regent Steven Jenkens, the man he believed The World would vote in as his second in command. At last glance, Jenkens was one hundred votes ahead of Sylvia Itonovich and ten thousand votes behind him.

The Press Room was beginning to fill with a few of his colleagues, who waved as he greeted them. Robot servers were offering food and drinks on platters. Robotic imagers were extending tri-pods, linking with the matrix, and then maneuver around the room to assess and claim prime territory for holosite viewers. More media crews were dashing around, bumping into one another and setting up ceiling hubs and wall zones. Secret service agents, including Jane, were scurrying about, setting up plush chairs and barking orders into their wrist devices. In front of the room, scientists were testing the IMAX transmission screen that suddenly flashed on in Test-mode and droned. The white noise incoming from the Decagon nearly took up the entire seventy-foot long wall! Then the irritating noise stopped as imaging specialists, astrophysicists, and matrix techs began making adjustments. On the grand screen, he could see, in an expanding 3D-picture stretching three feet into the Press Room, the quadrant in space containing the giant Decagon accelerator system where tonight's wormhole would appear from Nelta and stabilize into a communications conduit. The transmission screen would receive the translated data, and then The Regents would begin discussions with ambassador Shaesar and the Neltan Advancement Committee for the last time.

Then he spotted the Regent who'd been hailing him but whom he had sent a *Leave a Message* reply. "Regent Jenkens, you got a minute?"

"Give me two minutes," Jenkens replied. Dressed in a white shirt and navy suit, he had a thick belly extended beyond

First Communication

his chest and slightly balding, grayish brown hair combed lazily at the nap of his neck. "After these scientists are through prepping for the *Pact* signing ceremony, I have to adjust the color scheme for the *Executive Regency Inaugural* ceremony after Final Communication." He knelt down and touched the carpet. After displaying a design on his Quanta-pad—the larger version of the wrist device—he ordered, "Change." He said to Manning, "I've got this place voice activated with my qPad. Any change I want I just call it into the app."

Terra duplicated the pattern, completely changing the schematics of the Press Room as people scurried across the carpet and meandered around the room.

"This new photo-light material is exact, Regent Manning," Jenkens said. "I can't *believe* the absorption quality. Amazing! We'll have this everywhere on *Sagan*, even our rooms. Watch *this* section I just linked to this room's Smart app." He bent down and said, "Window."

A patch of floor changed to glass.

"It's all laser proof and self-repairing too...in case we get hit with enemy fire." Steven Jenkens tapped the square piece of glass floor with his shiny black shoe. "I can change the material into liquid. Watch." Pointing at the altered material, he called, "Glass to water."

The floor changed to a slurping liquid.

"But people will want to make sure they disable *that* feature, unless of course they want it as a pleasant accessory in some corner." He threw his gum into the water, said "goldfish," and a small metallic creature appeared. "Someone could fall through and—well, *ahem*, you know, *ooo*-deadly. We have to make sure we call for a vote on strict guidelines when installing this stuff." He called, "Carpet."

The material puffed up and then smoothed out soft and fuzzy. My gum's now a part of the design. Cool—huh?"

Manning laughed. "Jenkens, you're like a child playing with a new toy."

"This *is* the test pilot prototype, and hopefully will function successful so The World will like all the visuals and vote for

J.P. Osterman

the tech in the future," he said, bending down again and touching the floor tenderly. He flicked soda on the wall and poured coffee on the carpet.

Terra's interface immediately detected the nonuniformity and soaked up the spills without slurping sounds or drag time.

Watching Jenkens stand up and slap his hands in expression of a job well done, Manning said, "Aren'tcha glad we live in this age where we have *all* kinds of materials like that...light as aluminum, sturdy as steel, self-repairing *and* maintenance free."

"Thanks to the Neltans," Jennings said, "*and* the nano-opticians, imagists and nano-additive manufacturers who finally got their acts together and started cooperating to bring these projects to fruition." Jenkens doodled on the carpet with color markers. "I wonder if the material can fix this—*ha!*" he said, obviously trying to find fault or outwit Terra's Smart app.

Manning said, "Regent Jenkens, we *really* need to talk."

Jenkens said, "Oh, yeah—sorry." Standing up, he added, "In five minutes. I have the rest of this section to synchronize. Ya never know what can happen in here when Shaesar and his scientific committee quantum materialize for the ceremony."

As Jenkens walked away, Manning looked at the front of the Press Room. In front of a high-tech podium embossed with The Regency's symbol of leadership—a scholar holding a white torch—he noticed a line of nine hologram stages, including a larger center stage, programmed to show old shows about The Regency. The projections were beginning to show the outset of his career, from his first global wide campaign in May of 2058 to shaking hands with leaders, judges and law enforcement officers. Beneath Center Stage flashed the current vote count. When he realized he was winning Executive Regent, he closed the door to his Oval Office and said: "Terra, quickly add footage on the SETI project I worked on while at Duke University, will ya? If not for *my* project, people wouldn't have all this technology, not counting this healed ozone!" He felt proud. "I did this...me," he said in a low whisper.

"Yes, Regent Manning," she replied. "I will include a close-

First Communication

up of you from the October 4, 2064, communication with the Neltans that secured humanity The Matter Stream sample."

He walked to the window and began assessing the large crowd—now a sea of cheering and chanting people. Many of them had probably voted for him at some time throughout the day. "And when you find my virtual handshakes with Dr. Polk, his SETI team, and Ambassador Shaesar from inside Arecibo's main lobby, stream it globally. I want to make *sure* that *each* and *every* person sees what *I* did to ensure our survival." Above various turf sites outside Washington, D. C., vehicular Fission-Fusion craft were launching to the space station—their white FF-Drive turrets flaring as they reached the golden fringe of the tropopause shield, now functioning as a meteorite detector/annihilator to ensure the safety of the new atmosphere. "Those additions should secure more votes and create a solid lead for me to win."

"Yes, Regent Manning," she replied. "I have your holosite world now at over one billion, four hundred twenty-two thousand—"

"Okay, Terra. I get it. You're great! And next time, give me round numbers, *please!*"

"Yes, Regent Manning. Round numbers until you request an exact number."

"*Whew*—thanks," he sighed.

"Over one billion people are voting for *you*, Regent Manning."

"And my corporate votes?" he asked.

"Six hundred and twenty. That number should increase considering the request you made to several more facilities to construct more *Spider* astrofighters."

"What did you order? After all that battle monitoring and strategizing, I forgot."

"As you ordered twenty-five minutes ago, after *The Spider* sustained damage from two enemy strikes," she began, "I streamed the Neltan formula for photo-electromagnetic containment and nano-metallic properties to the private German corporation, IntelliNachHausa for manufacturing of advanced hull components. When several European facilities asked for those designs to create prototypes of various products, you said, Fine." She opened the recording of the exchange and began playing over the center floor imager. "I then tagged those blueprints, designs and IPs with your name so that *all* companies will be able to incorporate the new nano-technology into *everything* from pins and threads to eating and drinking implements and toys. Would you like specifics?" The show faded.

"*Ha*—great! No specifics please," Manning exclaimed. "Still, *that* great move on *your* part *should* secure corporate votes. Companies large and small have been *dying* to get their hands on all those patents and create product. If they appreciate that *I'm* handing over all this great Neltan-based technology to them, cost free, it'll be like announcing *me* as CEO of their companies and corporations…yes!" He laughed. Then he remembered those people off-Earth. "Oh, and—expand the voting parameter to include those *two* Martian settlements. People here want to prohibit them from voting. Now is *not* the time to enact that type of vote and kill *my* chance at the Executive position because of Earth-II. *That* should secure me another hundred thousand votes. Whataya think, Terra?"

"Ninety-eight thousand, two hundred, fifteen hologram votes predicted based on holosite popularity polls on Mars, Regent Manning." A graphics globe of Mars opened at the center of his office that showed Terra's matrix streaming like a net around the planet. "I am now linking the Global Voting Facility to *each* Quanta-pad and wrist-device holosite inbox." Ten giant barge-like craft and space stations opened up alongside the graphics of Mars, settlements extending from Jupiter to the last small outpost beyond Neptune. Around all the settlements, craft were spacefolding in-and-out of accelerator systems, dropping off supplies and making exchanges. "Voting is now open to *all* people off-Earth."

"Perfect chain reactions, Terra," he exclaimed as the image at the center of his office extinguished. "That show of me playing in the Press Room is now everywhere." He thought of

First Communication

Captain Bartlet repairing *The Spider* and the pending battle. He wanted to make it easier for anyone on a mission to cast votes. "And boost the show with an option to vote to all military personnel onboard astrofighters—but without taking solar power from your matrix on Earth." He didn't at all want to jeopardize the tropopause shield. Its storage capacity and energy output were at 100% and its processing efficiency reading *Maximum*. "I want eavesdropping terrorists *everywhere* to know that *I'm* coming into leadership. I want them shaking."

He checked the time: 5:45 p.m., three hours and fifteen minutes to Final Communication with the Neltans. Outside, stretching as far as he could see in the dregs of dusk, more people had assembled for the *Pact* signing ceremony. He would be facilitating it. From messages streaming into his Regency holosite, many people were indicating that they would remain after the ceremony, and after the Neltans' special final farewell presentation, to watch the *Inaugural Pinning Ceremony* for Executive Regent. People were cheering—waving 3D banners of their favorite Regency candidates. Through their various processors, they were also streaming images of their favorite Neltans into the sky that looked like glowing round balloons overlaid with Neltan faces and scenes of Nelta.

Suddenly, an argument broke out between two crowds, and Terra enlarged the view on Wall Zone 2. He saw Jane Dirk order countermeasures on Wall Zone 1.

He said: "From their avatars interfacing with you, Terra, it appears they're demonstrating against *your* selection process. They're upset that you didn't include them as part of The List to board *Sagan* in 2070. They're also accusing The Regency of deleting their resumes before they even reached your matrix. They're inciting others to join them and sign petitions to display at tonight signing ceremony." He plopped down in his chair. "Well?" After Terra quickly showed him proof to the contrary, he ordered her to stream the results to them along with her reason for not selecting them for *Sagan*, again. "Are they Tech-No Protesters? If not, they *could* join them! Add them to your Watch List in case one of them starts something criminal."

"Monitoring conditions activated on this group, Regent Manning," Terra said as she projected their faces, avatars and job applications on Wall Zone 1 for Jane Dirk and Enforcer agencies to receive. "I detect no affiliation in their histories to The Tech-No Movement. As far as matching them to any position still available onboard the astrocity, I cannot categorize any one of them as *Essential*, *Vital*, or *Necessary* for the Friendship Mission to Nelta."

Manning remembered the facts. Terra's "Essential" pronouncement meant that the *Sagan* crew needed the applicant's skills. Terra picked selected physicians, military personnel, additive manufacturing specialists, researchers, engineers, and high-level officials for this category of The List, including all fifty Regents. A "Vital" determination meant that the *Sagan* crew needed the applicant for his or her building expertise or people skills. Astrofighters, helping professionals, servers, the media, builders, teachers, and maintenance workers Terra included in this category. A stamp of "Necessary but On Hold" signified that a Neltan had handpicked the individual, or a Regent had interviewed the person and forwarded the application and virtual resume into the Perusal grid for later consideration. At any time, Terra could select an individual, change criteria based on *Sagan*'s alterations, include, or eliminate anyone already approved for The List. To all those whom Terra rejected for the hundred-year spacefold voyage to Nelta, the matrix streamed a simple *Decline* message, with a polite reply.

After he heard another roar in the crow, Manning said into Wall Zone-1: "Agent Dirk, stop the fight before it explodes into a riot! We can't have that now!"

A military Zeppelin fired nets, trapped the disrupters, and then launched for trial and sentencing in the Judicial Center of the Prison and Rehab Space Station V. After the Zeppelin disappeared from sight, he spotted a long craft about to make a sleek landing on the White House landing pad next to the

First Communication

artificial turf. From its purple insignia, he knew the craft was carrying a full load of ten Regents. And there were more waiting to greet them in the Press Room. He could hear familiar voices addressing the media. Soon, he'd step out and join them; but this time, he wanted to make sure he'd walk the red carpet *in front* of them. "Can you change the space-fold clock and push back Final Communication one more minute, Terra?" It would take him that long to wheedle through the forty-nine others to the head of the line. "Start this information exchange with Shaesar *one* minute earlier?" He didn't want to make his dash to the front appear egoistic even though he knew many of them were plotting to take that Front Row Center seat as well. "I need more time for my *Sagan* scientific team to analyze the remnants of that Matter Stream sample as they collect its leftovers for our voyage to Nelta. If I want the spotlight, I need to be able to know all the facts of that sample and its applications so I can field questions and be the intermediary between Ambassador Shaesar, his Advancement Committee, and scientists on The List who have vital questions they need the Neltans to answer."

On Wall Zone 3, Terra showed him an intergalactic wormhole conundrum that interwove and exploded like a bad Tesla network. "The 9 o'clock time is quantum synchronized with the Schwarzschild radius and its companion star HDE226868. A one minute time extension entails a two-hundred thousand degree variation in galaxies that splice the current communication pathway." Terra extinguished the live-feed visuals of people in cities around the globe celebrating the new atmosphere. In their places, one of his entire walls appeared as multiple galaxies aligning and wormholes connecting and codifying as one spacefolding synchronization from Nelta to Earth. "Ambassador Shaesar has extended the time once to allow for more dialoging. But that takes place at the end of *The Signing* ceremony to make room for the Neltans' final gift to humanity. Activating the wormhole one minute sooner is impossible. Nine o'clock is the friction point where the dark matter and radiant energy create the stress-energy tensor, thus activating the first wormhole beyond Nelta." A network of algorithms appeared that began linking the galaxies: their spider-webbed, light paths filling the walls around the Oval Office. Their individual routes, quantum-photonic propellants, and white glowing capillaries seemed to extend out of his office into eternity. "Missing that Planck time synchronicity with the wormhole striking the Decagon means no quantum communicating with the Neltans. And not only do you want to facilitate *The Pact* signing ceremony, but you also want to find out as much information as you can on their Matter Stream. I overheard your request, even though it was a whisper, and as you instructed during such times, I didn't answer."

"Damn!" He leaned against his desk. "Now that they helped us, we *have* to follow *all* their instructions perfectly. No deviation at all from their cosmic calendar, or cosmic time, or cosmic pathway!" He gestured in frustration and nicked the leg of his desk with his heel. "Boy…the old saying sure is true: nothing's free and everything's pricy. Whenever I talk to that Ambassador Shaesar, I feel like I'm on a treadmill to nowhere. There's some final great goal but I feel like I'm never gonna reach it."

Terra said: "The World *did* vote and approve *The Pact* on August 30, 2064, the day the fourth-and-last burst of the Matter Stream Sample rushed out of Wormhole Denby-7, combined with the entire sample, and began healing. Item A. 1. (a), in *The Pact* states:

Providing an average daily measurement for thirty days of The Matter Stream Sample's effectiveness in replenishing the Earth's ozone layer to a thickness of ~300 Dobson Units, Earth's Regents will sign The Pact and proceed formally—as The Pact in its entirety stipulates below—to fulfill Earth's part of the bargain with Nelta. All submission of data, evidence, or readings, concerning investigating, retrieving, and proving The Matter Stream sample's efficiency, efficacy, cause-and-effects, measurements of intensity and sustainability will proceed during The Final Transmission that will take place February 27, 2068, at twenty-one hundred hours, EST, and 02:00 UTC. Then Earth's Regents will sign The Pact, thus

First Communication

sealing Earth's commitment to Spacefold to Nelta. Further Pact stipulations are enumerated through Items A. 1. (b) and A. 1. (e) of The Pact.

"Yes, Terra, I wrote all that," he said. Pacing the floor while listening to all the outside cheering, he felt suddenly irked...no, hoodwinked. He still had so many questions about The Matter Stream. Every time he asked those questions to the Neltan scientists and Ambassador Shaesar, they glanced back-and-forth and then gave him blank stares. They simple answered: "We can give you *only* a sample as we bargained." They were The Matter Stream's guardians in This Universe of The Multiverse.

There was much more to the story...so much more about their past: what they had done and what they had learned from having The Matter Stream to themselves for over *twelve* billion years. Their secretive nature was enticing so many people to want to spacefold to Nelta on *Sagan*, amass knowledge, explore the universe with the Neltans' advanced, hands-on technology, and, possibly, settle on Nelta. Still, when communicating with the Neltans, at times, he and many other Regents felt as if their scientists were treating them like children. They seemed to be holding back when answering so many questions on their history. They denied that to several Regents who had posed that concern to Ambassador Shaesar.

Then he remembered what his father told him: "Thornton, if ya wanna survive in the world, ya gotta have the upper hand. If not, you're a patsy to someone else's whim. That's called failure. Ya never wanna be second when you can be first, do ya?"

That's what he was feeling: like a failure. He couldn't give people the answers to what they were *really* wanting to know: "Who said The Matter Stream is solely yours?"

Snapping out of that helpless feeling, he heard a string of voices and equipment shuffling in the Press Room. He was hoping Steven Jenkens was through with all his techy manipulations and would meet with him. The countdown to Final Communication was getting short. They had life destroying problems they had to discuss and solve, fast. He couldn't be everyone's Everyman and be everywhere even though he had tried, with Terra's assistance. Besides the terrorists' virtual war, Tech-Nos were increasing and intensifying their matrix intrusions. The Decagon was hailing him for more craft support to reinforce against a terrorist invasion. No one knew the current location of the enemy in the solar system. Their lunar base was still bleeding oxygenated life. How much life? No telling. He needed help...now...and had no choice but to let Jenkens into his Oval Office world, at least on a limited and covert capacity.

"5:55 p.m., Regent Manning. Three hours and five minutes until final transmission," Terra announced.

He breathed deeply. The stress that hit him made him feel as if he was baking. Looking at the rainbow processor cycling around the ceiling hub, he said, "If not for you, Terra, I don't know what I'd do." He felt a rush of adrenaline when the processor flashed a blue balm wavelength into his eyes. "Okay, let's get going. Get that schedule I revised early this morning and put it on Wall Zone 3 alongside the image of *Sagan*. I don't like seeing it half-way constructed, but at least that place is a symbol of motivation, giving me energy to tackle everything I've got to finish in the next three hours." After Terra complied, he added, "And ask Regent Steven Jenkens to come in here again." He calmed down when he remembered how Terra had helped him in the past.

Since the installation of his matrix processors in his home and headquarters, whenever he found himself backed into a corner, pressed for time, and needing to make an important decision, Terra had researched each issue, outlined positives and negatives, projected possible outcomes—minus The Human Factor—and they'd banter over the possibilities and consequences, together. "If not for you, Terra," he said, inhaling, believing he could smell her—a very light sweet-spicy fragrance, "I couldn't keep track of all the promises in that pact I'm signing tonight with Nelta." Glancing outside, into the sky, toward the faint yellow lines of The Shield array after

First Communication

sunset, he spotted several of the Terra-interfacing panels and cubes protecting Earth from harmful cosmic bodies. In a flash, the sight made him recall Terra's arrival and expansion on Earth.

J.P. Osterman

Chapter 25 - Terra Begins

Terra-I was Earth's first collaborative success with Neltan scientists after several Information and Exchange communications: First Contact, August 23, 2060; Second Contact, October 10, 2060; and, Third Contact, December 11, 2060.

After Fourth Contact on March 26, 2061, after we received designs for a matrix computer system similar to the matrix the Neltans were implementing but much less advanced, our scientists streamed to The World: "If we can implement *one* Neltan-based technology successfully, we can have more. We *need* this matrix. It will end the internet and replace our dependence on satellites." They put *The Need* up for a global vote.

Fear. People were brimming with it, wondering how society would change after implementing a matrix system and virtual worlds. However, scientists and engineers maintained that by having the matrix, Terra, we'd have better surveillance to counter terror attacks, a quantum-information processing, increased law enforcement response, more social interconnectedness, and a better quality of life, from medicine

First Communication

to shopping, education to occupational opportunities.

In a 95% tally, The World approved *The Need* on April 24, 2061. During the next Neltan/Earth wormhole exchange, the Neltan Advancement Committee sent us the quantum-system's specs in a virtual scroll titled, *To Earth*. When scientists extinguished the wormhole conduit and opened the holographic specs on the first IMAX transmission screen—in Canberra, Australia that year, The Regency's headquarters—a fire ignited in The Great Hall inside Parliament, half-deleting the transcribed program, making the title almost illegible, except for the letters, *T E R*. That day, May 5, 2061, The Regents named the quantum system, Terra, meaning, "Earth," in several languages.

After a series of negotiations, and after nearly a year of construction, renovation, and assembly on existing computer infrastructure, on April 23, 2062, the first Terra-IA software and hardware prototypes succeeded. The North Continent Matrix Facility initialized throughout San Jose, California, the epicenter of the Cloud-to-Matrix Expansion Era that ended with the transition to Terra II in September of 2063. When Terra-IA began streaming successfully that evening, an infrared view of San Jose from an orbiting satellite made the city appear as a 3D network of white lines activating and intersecting throughout the city and its suburbs. As the first grids—ceiling hubs and wall mounts replacing PCs—began flicking on, connecting and streaming Terra 1A into *every* home and building, Matrix Techs (retrained cable and satellite-TV workers) quickly installed more user-friendly hubs and wall mounts throughout more cities. Terra hardware hubs (with nano-claw clasps around their bases) easily affixed to walls, ceilings and floors, providing an instant connection to the electromagnetic/gravitational, stream-based, containment-field matrix when activated. The nano-components on hubs, wall mounts, and floor Imaging Circles utilize photonic waves and their attraction properties to generate self-contained conduits that stream information at the quantum state over-and-through existing wiring, fiber-optic cables, landline grids, electrical grids, and space satellites. Led by the elite, Intel Justin Rattner Laboratory team (named after the twenty-first century, computer architecture pioneer and Intel's Chief Scientist), specialists initiated that first Terra-IA; and by the end of August of 2062, Terra-I was streaming at 100% efficiency to The World.

That day was like inoculating the first test subjects against polio when doctors trumpeted the call for *everyone* to receive the life-saving vaccine. A few years thereafter, polio, at least in the USA, was an afterthought. Any device or computer hardware older than 2062, people considered Dark Age implements. The Cloud-to-Matrix transition period from April 2061 to April 2062 was the bright, white, hopeful archway into the Nano-Tech Quantum era. With a few new items of "The New Neltan Technology" available, people changed almost overnight. We could feel nano-altering fabrics; taste and smell nano-engineered foods and drinks. In schools, children began learning via Virtual Create and Holosite Leaper, apps allowing them to compose images, scenes, shows, events, and holosite worlds through voice and touch activation processing through ceiling hubs and wall mounts. Augmented worlds became a reality as The World gained an even closer social connectedness that prior to 2062.

The next prototype completed on September 19, 2063, Terra-II reduced hardware in half. An individual system came with four, six-inch-in-diameter, self-adhesive wall processors (mounting horizontally at four equilateral locations) with four ceiling hubs, thus creating 3D, full-room activation capability. When initialized, the individual's systems grid synchronized with a matrix facility and a person's home, business, and portable device. Aside from projecting holograms and virtual experiences anywhere in a room, this version could read and respond to an individual's biometrics, giving the person feedback as well as connection to other grids (medical, professional, educational, governmental, and financial) through icons, avatars, and holosites (the later completely making email addresses and websites obsolete). Terra-II was touch-based,

First Communication

verbal-based, host-sensitive, people-responsive, and motion-sensitive—all apps scanned for viruses and labeled "Hack Proof" and "Safe" by the nearest security center before hitting *any* holosite. Security centers were in kiosks within one-mile perimeter locations. Working around the clock, Matrix Security personnel, employed by one of the eight matrix facilities, monitor and respond to visual or verbal complaints. They also have the authority to sever a person from his or her connection to the matrix, as well as the duration of the expulsion, as punishment for minor infringements. If they determine that an offense is beyond their purview, Enforcers investigate and arrest the hacker or violator. The judicial system on Station V determines further action.

Months thereafter, after researchers on Station II received the results of several studies conducted on the effects of receiving and sending information via a quantum processor on the human brain and human behavior, people voted for and approved an update to the Terra-II system. One of those behavioral studies showed a slight increase in delusional symptoms in adolescents and a propensity for that group to develop delusional tendencies if participating in virtual worlds more than three hours a day. The update of September 25, 2063 compensated for the problem by streaming a soothing subliminal image into the holosite grids of teenagers.

As the implementation of nano-technology and quantum computer slipped beyond the Tipping Point, matrix hardware companies increased production of wrist devices and portable qPads—small Quantum Processors. People began purchasing their Terra systems as they once bought cell phones and portable tablets in the early twenty-first century. Terra-II flourished, and The World voted the system as "an Essential Asset." Everyone needed one.

In every surface market place and underground galleria, there were at least two, Terra retail providers available to replace outdated cell phones and portable tablets as well as to sell apps. Merchants scampered to keep up their stockpiles, and software engineers vamped up the speed of writing apps to sell to the public, educational institutions, and sometimes The Regency. Many people had already purchased the newest apps. Those unable to work in their communities because they were too sick, disabled, or elderly applied for the most recent matrix-shopping software through special cooperative programs, including those people making less than thirty-thousand euros a year who are exempt from the standard 17% flat-tax but paying 10%.

A full-immersion augmented world was on the brink of revolutionizing even more experiences and interactions if The World would approve Terra-III.

Replacing the outdated hand-held tablets, portable Terra-II came as standard touchware with the larger system, although consumers could purchase, upgrade, or customize various other available models at higher prices. Made of thin, malleable nano-organics, the quantum-processing pad (qPad) assembled in-line, and in-store, to the customer's desired shape, size and other idiosyncratic specificities. The color app could transform hue; the voice app would lock in the owner's identity. "Lock-and-Load" was the expression a sales rep called out whenever a customer down-streamed his or her history, medical data, school records, resume—*everything* in the matrix—into his or her qPad. At that point, forever, a person was "identi-fixed" to Terra, called "a host," and given a holosite address to create a virtual identity and stream virtual worlds for full-on participation and experience. From that point forward, a person was never alone.

Then, like the lid on a boiling teapot, The Great Scare occurred, culminating in another vote followed by weeks of argumentation from both sides: Should we allow children less than thirteen years old full qPad access? If so, which make, model, and holosite-world apps were best suited for them? The matrix was always processing and compiling statistical information regarding hosts, their matrix-to-grid usage and interactions with other hosts and holosites. Those stats people received and used—upon requested or approval—for feedback, parental controls, ratings, research and military

First Communication

purposes. Those stats were like advertisements: always available, pop up intrusive, necessary, but potentially dangerous if dropped, or diverted, into a terrorist's holosite, a Tech-No's covert grid, or the holosite of a con artist. Enforcers were always relegating predators and criminals to Station V for judgment, punishment, and cognitive rehabilitation. To remedy those safety concerns, The World voted in a child model with an added safety feature and tunes limiting access.

As a flexible device that could detach from its base the size of a large watch, the qPad could stream in Planck-time matrix quickness. With hologram social interface capability, qPads provided hosts with unlimited 3D conferencing. An added feature, but not a necessity, qPads self-affixing hologram stage could attach to any matrix-interfacing surface and add more imaging capabilities. The cost? Quite a bit extra. Only the upper-middle class could afford qPadE and the imaging apps needed to interface with nano-materials. Companies gave qPads willingly to researchers onboard Station II. If apps and hardware passed tests in space, the public could buy them at their local kiosks. There was a downside. Matrix Enforcers had caught a few people altering the nanoclaws to camouflage their qPadEs and spy on people. Matrix Security Corp personnel responded by generating new features and modifying existing software to police Live Stream-mode. Some people, for whatever reasons, were finding ways to break privacy and social interaction laws and abuse and/or exploit the new technology for their own gain.

One law-breaker defended herself against the crime of Matrix Interference before the North-Eastern Global Tribunal. Through sobs, she said in court in front of Station V's Judicial Council: "We live in a virtual world where we can find, create, and indulge in every type of illusion and fantasy. All ya haveta do if you want to recreate the past is just ask your virtual Terra rep for stored information, and *bang*, what ya want is right there for you to use! I know I did wrong by attempt to take what I wanted without paying for those images." Her voice was low, her face downtrodden. "I admit that I hired that tech to hot-circuit a grid so I could downstream all the images of my deceased family, the backgrounds where those pictures were snapped and any other movies or pictures the matrix has stored. I couldn't afford the ten-thousand euros the companies wanted to charge me. They're mine! Not Terra's...not anyone else's." Her virtual Terra rep began showing a few shows the woman had illegal acquired. "I shouldn't have to pay." She cried some more. "When I activate those images and shows inside my home, my family appears so alive and so real! I talked to them. They talked back to me. We laugh!" She ran her fingers through her wild hair as if she had half-gone crazy but was trying to regain her composure and sanity. "Those stored images come with voice reproductions. I can resurrect all the times we had together...at least the ones that were our movies and matrix-shopped from the movies of others. They talk back to me as if they're with me! I try to hug them...but I end up clasped in my own arms. Please, *gasp whimper*, please, understand. I don't see illusions, and I'm not delusional, so don't commit me. I see, and talk to, *real* people. What I really want...and maybe you can help me...is to find a way to leave my body and join them in the matrix." Her blue eyes widened with possibility. "Maybe I can be a part of some type of experiment...where you let me join with the matrix. Whataya think? Can I?" She looked at her virtual Terra rep that disappeared as the woman finished voicing her defense, and then she knelt down, sobbing.

The judges sympathized with her but found her guilty of violating Article 2 of *Global Law VII*: *After installing a home, business, or institutional matrix grid; a holosite host must at all times maintain a physical divide and firewall apart from any of the seven matrix processing facilities and abide by the agreed upon rules under the apps Usage Clause.*

The judges mandated she receive therapy twice a day, along with her six-month stint on Station V. Upon release, they gave her the harshest Terra Matrix Restriction Requirement/Monitoring: "Wrist Tablet Only Access, Until

First Communication

Determined Fit for Re-Integration."

All qPad models had one thing in common—no matter the manufacturer. They needed two hours of generating time on a wall mound or rainbow ceiling processing hub. Solar energy and electromagnetic energy were hardware fuel.

"Twist off or twist on, stick or affix then connect!" Apple, Microsoft, and HP advertised.

As well as later versions, all Terra-I processors were made of nano-organic circuitry-silicon with a vibrational storage capability that could safely harness and retain all types of electromagnetic energy through Terra's main matrix, thus eliminating the reliance on the old, plug-in electricity and batteries.

The mass production of Terra-I lead to the construction of Smart biodomes, Smarthomes, Sharp Homes, and Alpha rooms to replace all structures destroyed in the 2057 attacks. Before 2063, many people were still taking refuge in underground safe havens. With construction companies able to infuse brick, wood, plastics, and metals with nano-technology; builders and manufacturers could erect affordable interactive/additive materials fast, quick, and easy; or renovate or convert existing structures to the Smart-Sharp-Alpha-intelligence technology connecting to Terra's matrix. A construction company could alter two hundred structures a day! There was no longer the need to maintain or paint anything infused with nanotechnology because anyone could verbally activate a repair, surface deterioration, structural abnormality, or erosion.

Fully interactive, energy smart, and energy efficient, the new renovated buildings came equipped with a pathogen-detection-elimination system, eradicating germs and viruses as well as alerting law enforcement to intrusions. With ShieldByte as a standard security app, the alarm, when triggered, rendered harmful stings to anyone other than the person skin-scanned and permitted to enter.

However, ShieldByte had an advanced futuristic application.

J.P. Osterman

Two months after October 4, 2061, the date Nelta sent Earth the first sample of the Matter Stream, The World approved Article 2 to *Global Law VI* that cemented our ability to communicate further with the Neltans. We learned *they* needed our DNA in exchange for the sample; and we determined the level of *Proof of Healing* we needed in order to determine whether the sample had healed our ozone layer. Article 2 in *Global Law VI* stated the following:

If ozone sustainability reaches 0.6 parts per million with a minimum thickness of 15 miles, the fifty-member Regency leaders will sign The Pact with Ambassador Shaesar and the Neltan Advancement Committee on February 27, 2068. In good faith as we move forward with our preliminary bargain for future technology, we will immediately begin construction on Sagan, at Space Station I, with a Construction Facility, Station IV, manufacturing and assembling parts for Sagan. Station IV will also house a 10,000-member construction crew who will be responsible for designing and building the astrocity, Sagan, which will launch for Nelta on June 10, 2070.

The Regency's *Sagan* Development and Construction Committee issued ShieldByte as a standard app in each crewmember's Living Cube (LC) onboard the astrocity.

As most people enjoyed the Nelta-Driven Technological Revolution (NDTR), the government had its own augmented version of Terra: an application that could detect suspicious underground activity, underwater craft, and the new fission-fusion hover cars. Space Stations II through V weren't completed in 2064, thus the military didn't have full atmospheric view until all the stations synchronized on July 17, 2065. Until then, once Terra-I deemed anything or anyone irregular, questionable, or foreign to the environment, the Regents' Enforcers had permission "to render any facility inactive with an EMP-electromagnetic pulse or to render a suspect immobile" and then detain the suspect for questioning off Earth. People voted in that clause well after they approved *Global Law VIII* that sets forth and stipulates *all* Security monitoring, Secret Service behavior, and Military Codes of Conduct for all law enforcement officers and Enforcer

First Communication

personnel around the globe. The World was obsessed with preventing another terrorist attack and passed through referendum various surveillance laws to prevent one. It was still the greatest contention ever with The World's daily vote: assuaging fears versus preserving individual rights.

Being one of the first people to demonstrate the use of his Terra system in a reality holosite show at his Alpha Home, Manning believed he had convinced even the skeptics that a quantum computer system was safe, an asset, and essential. "Get connected to the virtual world. Let Terra be your Multitask Wizard, and start participating in a *real* adventure today. Make *your* walls do the walking *for* you." Programming his avatar with that campaign slogan in his Regency holosite world helped him secure his Regency position for several weeks thereafter.

On August 30, 2064, the day scientists on Nelta and the Regents approved *all* items inside *The Pact* and scheduled the final signing ceremony for February 27, 2068 at 9:00 p.m., EST (0200 UTC on February 27, 2068). Also on that day, matrix techs and engineers superimposed Terra-II onto Terra-I thus advancing the matrix to all manned probes, off-Earth bases, planetary colonies, and expeditions. The years 2063 through 2064 became the years of full-virtual immersion, anytime, anywhere, when appropriate. A verbal order or touch command could alter any room into a pre-existing (or blank-but-ready) virtual world containing holographic friends, streaming avatars, objects, scenery, characters, and pre-programmed or creative experiences and locations. By approving Terra-II, people hoped to eliminate loneliness, foster easy social interconnectedness, and generate opportunities for all sorts of interaction on a global scale. No more being put on hold, waiting for a representative to answer questions! Right in the comfort of one's own home, an avatar, icon, or a Terra rep activated to answer questions, address concerns or voice complaints and suggestion. A home or business could morph into an entertainment hub, a club, union hall, and party. Invitations to join groups and organizations popped up in holosites everywhere, and advertising became an individual adventure through full-immersion apps.

Equipped with smaller wall and ceiling hubs, the new Terra system also advanced to walk-through medical diagnostics and organ stem-cell reproduction. Everything from diabetes to cancer, Terra-II could cure, except death from old age. People wanted that, but there were always ethical considerations that continued to keep legislature at a stalemate.

After bombarding Ambassador Shaesar with requests for *A Cure for Death*, Shaesar said, with Nelta's alien ethics leaders planted alongside him: "Only in a neural-net matrix can a consciousness survive. Long-term cloning results in severe genetic anomalies. We cannot unleash that life-extension capability on any species other than our own." The answer from Nelta continued to be an absolute no. However, the fight was still raging on for voters to approve full-body organ transplants—a loophole in the cloning approval route.

Voters then approved Terra-II to expand to a predictive state and generate experiences for various speculative future occurrences. Entrepreneurs started fortune telling business and financial trading worlds. On September 18, 2065, the Global Financial Market (GFM) created an entire grid within the new matrix to restructure SWIFT and all the stock markets. All monetary transactions, security exchanges, and market activities occurred via Terra hubs in virtual worlds—portable Terras or stationary systems. Only collectors owned currency.

These advanced capabilities began generating public unrest, covertly, because people began to fear that someone might report them as being a bully, a hacker, or troublemaker. The Tech-No Protest Movement began, and the Regents discovered ways to stalemate many oppositional votes and elude The World's watchdog agencies that continued writing software language to try to protect Terra from intrusions while providing inlets to holosite monitoring. One exception. The Regency managed to acquire the necessary public approval for future matrix applications. Once on *Sagan* and out of Earth's orbit, The Regents would become leaders endowed with the

First Communication

power to determine the astrocity's rules and laws, including those guiding ethics and morality. *Who* could predict with certainty what those future voyagers would need or what they might encounter while spacefolding through galaxies to Nelta. *Only Pilgrims Can Write Their History*...the future crewmembers on The List campaigned for and won. The World voted beyond the usual 85% stamp of approval for what those people on The List wanted, streaming that they had done so because people on The List appeared desperate to keep their places on the astrocity. The Regency believed that the rest of the population was desperate for Terra to select them for The List. They didn't dare vote down The Regency's request to rule in case Matrix Security Corp might be secretly monitoring their democratic voting grids and tagging them as *Rejected* if they voted contrary to The Regents.

On August 30, 2064, the world saw Terra, in its Standard Form, for the first time. During that quantum communication, Ambassador Shaesar said: "In thanksgiving for your commitment to help us, we send you a gift, an Entity Infuser for your matrix. We look forward to the day when we will greet you on Neltan ground."

After obtaining the features of every living human and those stored in the old cloud-storage systems, Terra II compiled an androgynous face and form—male and female—which the matrix began projecting into all holosites as determined by that hosts personal information. The next day, people began copying her, or him, and altering the image to create their own rendition of how they perceived Terra. Each person had his or her version of a Terra rep as a graphics representation of the matrix. Whether at a galleria or at home trying on clothes or hairstyles in a virtual world, an individual could interface with Terra, or others, face-to-face or use an avatar. With all the available matrix apps at one's disposal, Terra had evolved to reflect an individual's alter ego; furthermore, in the mainstream, full-immersion virtual world experience, she advanced to convenient social-networking technology, except in the field of education.

J.P. Osterman

Reliance on private, full-time virtual learning was illegal...permissible only when setting up an intervention program for the severely disabled or mentally disturbed as Cognitive Behavioral Relief and Repair (CBRR). But scientists working in secret for The Regency, Stealth Force, and the Elite Enforcer Agency (Black Ops) altered a grid of the CBRR for another purpose. The Seclusion Virtual Confinement Program portion of the CBRR the military modified for extracting memories, rifling through slice-of-life experiences, and interrogating criminals and suspected terrorists on the Judicial Prison-Rehab Facility (JPRF), constructed in space in 2059 after the terrorist attacks. In January of 2063, generals cut the ribbon to Space Station V and named the penitentiary/reformatory the Judicial Prison-Rehab Orbital Facility (JPROF). Several Regents became adjunct judges there, and a panel of Regents and several Regent committees began managing patient/client diagnoses, assessments, bioorganic and nano-technical treatments, interventions and neurological repairs/interventions. There were no jails on Earth, only "holding tanks" on astrocraft with Black Ops Enforcers as pilots. Every major city had scheduled runs to Space Station V.

By June 6, 2070, *Sagan*'s projected launch date, Regent Manning predicted that Terra would expand to enhance sensory experiences. He said two months ago when scientists began experimenting on the physical and behavioral effects of the new Terra-III: "Version Three will connect *all* people to a multi-user friendly augmented world. Downloading a free, ten-minute participation holosite through my new holosite, TManningRatHolositeRegency, you can then log into The Global Site and cast your vote to evolve our current Terra to the new Terra-III. You won't regret it! There is s one app that MIT is studying, a Neuro-Orange Scan. It's a virtual world you enter just once and then turn around a few times." He showed the dancing little orange floating over his wrist device. "The app scans for neurological impulses that indicate you may need some emotional help. If you agree with the app's assessment,

First Communication

you can forward the Terra rep to the Psyche Grid. It's all anonymous. There is *no* Enforcer intervention. You'll see the Matrix Security shield flaring red, indicating that all your biometrics, neurological readings and verbal responses to questions are completely confidential and for matrix assessment only. The Neuro-Orange app and Terra are strictly for your own benefit. The Image Indicator will immediately return to you *your* results—you! In the hours that follow, and in a strictly private holosite setting wherein *you* determine the time and place, a Terra rep from the Psyche Grid will offer you a virtual mental health professional, personal coach, or social skill specialist so you can get the help you need now rather than waiting until something worse happens." He displayed a large circle of all addictive substances. "I'm streaming the Neuro-Orange app up for a global vote today. It's already been tested on Station II. Go to their holosite to see the results. *Your* yes-vote on this important application in two days can help people, especially when you cast a yes-vote for Terra-III to replace Terra-II. Just one last consideration before you say, 'No.' Remember: In spite of every virtual opportunity to receive mental health counseling, we still haven't stopped crime. Please do your part to help yourself and others. Vote yes on Neuro-Orange. Help society evolve!" That became that day's campaign slogan for him.

The World voted no, just short of the required eighty-five percent yes vote.

However, he did get one initiative passed just yesterday for his Neuro-Orange app. All future crewmembers on *Sagan*—the five-hundred square-mile, astrocity space ship—had to agree to Mandatory Cerebral Monitoring (MCM) at least once a month before entering their Living Cubes (LCs). Utilizing the yellow-light spectrum of Terra's rainbow processing hub, the app would enable Terra not only to read the interacting particles and chemical exchanges within the human brain and translate those reactions into symbols and then holograms, but also to link those visuals with body language, biometrics, and verbal inflections. For the one-hundred year, spacefold voyage

J.P. Osterman

to Nelta, MCM's encephalogram application could also zero-in on maladaptive behaviors, alarm crewmembers of claustrophobia, de-escalate interpersonal conflicts, and insert pre-programmed, Earth experiences into the nanowalling should a crewmember suffer from space disorientation. Gradually, as Terra-III was preparing to replace Terra-II on Earth, the evolved matrix was already up and streaming on the partially constructed *Sagan*.

In yesterday's vote as well, The World voted in favor of enhancing MCM for interrogation purposes, but only on Station V, thus enabling specialists to extract information from fifty captured terrorists. Another vote allowed rehab workers to use MCM on specific criminals meeting certain criteria. Thus helping professionals and rehab specialists could ascertain a criminal's motives and intentions...*only* under strict observation and monitoring. Often times, a cognitive image-insertion or image-extraction to alter someone's distorted perception or bad memory was all a patient needed to change and acclimate back into society.

Last week, on February 20, the new Terra-III began streaming at one-hundred percent trial efficiency in Johannesburg, South Africa. The new matrix offered several trial apps and features, one being the capability to manipulate objects and alter compounds through verbal commands. No more manufacturing of cleaning products or concerns over waste disposal.

"Convert not Recycle," Manning said this morning, still trying hard to get The World to approve Terra-III. He had the one-and-only, fully functioning, evolutionary advancement in his office although only his techs on *Sagan* knew of its installation and functioning.

Still, should The World approve Version III, updating *each* Smart dome, Smart home, and Alpha Facility with multi-user/interface features and new security firewalls would cost money and take time. Safe experimentation was also a factor. No prototype! Terra-III is Terra-III. No trial and error. Outliers? Where are they? Terra detects foreign data and

First Communication

anomalous code instantly…except for this morning's tropopause glitch metamorphosing as Demon Terra. No one saw *that* coming. The total global change out to *every* structure would take up to three years. But by then, the *Sagan* crew would be on the way to Nelta and experiencing virtual conveniences on all nine levels of the ship—from the rec centers, entertainment centers and food courts around *Sagan's* twenty-seven transport platforms, to arts facilities, child development centers, terrariums, and aquariums on Levels 3 and 6.

Through the newest Terra III with a mild version of the MCM app, a person could experience the five-sensory feelings and emotions of others. An entire heated debate was ensuing in the daily polls: "To know what people are thinking about you, or not to know?"

Last week, on February 22, 2068, at the University of Chicago, test subjects covertly circumvented the prohibition on neural augmented participation and sent their minds inside a matrix that accidentally diverted their cognitions into an experimental version of the game *Black Ops Titan Hunter.* Stealth Force on Station III had its application streaming into the matrix as a CBRR tool to use on terrorists after capturing them.

An alarm sounded through the university as Group A and B participants became mind-trapped inside the Black Ops *Titan Hunter* game that scientists on Station V had programmed with one of the alien graphics worlds the Neltans had streamed to Earth as knowledge about the cosmos. Over one billion years ago, a fleet of Neltan explorers had visited a Jurassic and anthropoid planet; but from what the augmented world was showing, the *Titan Hunter* world enmeshed with the alien world to generate a primitive, carnivorous hostile virtual planet. The students found themselves trapped inside a hostile world, clamoring-and-clawing for ways out. Their cognitive centers locked with the matrix's quantum state when the *Emergency Exit* doorframe failed to stream their minds back into their bodies. The new hostile reality then fixed, and they became locked in a battle to the death and scampering for their lives to escape the fangs and talons of grotesque creatures—some with multiple heads and limbs—that were driving them mad in the never-ending pursuit for flesh and bones.

Code composers and encryption experts at the seven matrix facilities began writing software twenty-four hours a day to create protective fortresses for the trapped students. Titan Hunter creatures were managing to penetrate each and every defensive feature. All the while, the matrix was translating the students' experiences and displaying the catastrophe from the participants' points of view.

Half the adult population watched the virtual violence before Matrix Security Corp shut down that grid. The forced termination dragged matrix power down to 75%, and people began experiencing lags in their holosites that looked like scenes and characters moving in slow motion through their homes and business. The world slowed down, but the experts used that lag time to their advantage.

They freed the Group-A participants who looked like they had rose from the dead, walked away from their blood-filled gurneys, stole surgical instruments, hid in covert places and began hunting down and knifing participants in the Control Group. They set acid traps, knife snares, and chemical trigger bombs to kill anyone entering the lab that was the size of two city blocks. To stop the pending massacre, Enforcers had to blow holes into the thick walls, take the attackers by surprise, and down them with tranquilizer darts. Succumbing to the sedation, the participants lost consciousness. Experts diagnosed them with anencephaly. As of now, they have not regained consciousness. Group-B participants are still alive in body, but cognitively trapped inside the new hostile environment, navigating around flesh-eating creatures and engaged in survival of the fittest. Code composers work around the clock to provide the students with the newest settings, weapons, and suggest various ways to escape being mind-devoured by alien monsters. A virtual death already has rendered one student comatose.

First Communication

Manning thanked God that a few Regents were there conducting experimental trials in other facilities when the accident occurred. Acting speedily, they ordered neuroscientists to make an exception to the Global Law VII banning cognitive matrix intrusion and use the latest experimental MCM hardware from the famous Cognition Therapy Center on Lake Shore Drive to continue to find ways to wake the students out of their virtual states of existence. He didn't want to broadcast the worst-case scenario just yet if the neuroscientists couldn't revive them: Permanent residence on the orbiting Cerebral Medical, Mental and Rehabilitation Facility orbiting Station V.

The next day, February 23, through the Regency's holosite, Manning streamed progress reports on the three men and four women who were still in comas. He gave new statistics and reports on the grid the students had misused. He claimed that part of the responsibility for their horrible entrapment was their fault for misusing the Social Mind-Link app. He hoped that information might persuade voters that Matrix Techs were fixing that "collision" problem in Terra III's Cognitive Safe-Scan app so that no more "world collisions" could ever occur again.

However, people voted their reaction to his speech in a 91% agreement. The Global Voting Facility in Xi'an, China compiled the following message for The Regency: "Until you can guarantee a 100% success rate using Terra-III's Social Mind-Link World, *We The People of the United Global Democracy*, today, February 24, 2068, vote to limit all holosite participation to include only the following: Full-Virtual Experience, Reality Surfing and Reality Jumping. We only permit augmented world creation to include the following: to enhance existing holosite worlds; edit worlds from written stories, articles, movies, or old TV shows. We vote down the following: alien world matrixshopping of any Neltan graphics."

Trying to salvage Terra-III's social virtual properties, Manning said two days ago on February 25: "Hollywood's gonna be out of business after programmers fix Terra's

J.P. Osterman

Cognitive Safe-Scan. Participants can then start uploading their virtual doorways or pathways and invite guests to join their virtual worlds." He projected a multi-billion dollar entertainment industry by the end of 2068. "With Terra providing social and business connections, you can access, record and modify your *own* memories and dreams—create and sell your *own* show, movie or game. Matrixshopping graphics will make obsolete photoshopping! Cognitive Safe-Scan will allow for a fully social-immersion experience while blocking fight-or-flight chemicals to allow a Participant to 'Join' without becoming enmeshed and entangled with an experience. Please, everyone, don't allow one misfortune—yes, sadly, a *terrible* catastrophe but one we're in the process of rectifying—stop *all* Terra-III expansion."

A Tech-No protestor crashed his speech that day, projecting a live hologram scene of a startled man urinating inside a stall with a Terra surveillance light illuminating his private parts. On the edge of the hologram appeared the words: "Violation! 30 days on the JPSS. It's Space Station Five for YOU, NOW, Regent Thornton Manning." It was signed, *The Sender.*

The hologram went viral.

The Tech-No protesters were accusing Manning and all the Regents of violating the Privacy Act by misusing the new Terra III. Another strong global outcry began. Yesterday's vote calling for Manning's resignation stood at seventeen percent until this morning. The incriminating hologram disappeared. The extraction and deletion was instantaneous and systemic—infiltrating every Smart home grid, every holosite in-box, file, and virtual doorframe/pathway. No one—not even the watchdog agencies—could detect and isolate the incriminating hologram, the location of the crime, or even the victim.

Manning sent out a virtual response: "This accusation was a manifestation of someone's bad dream…a hoax…a Tech-No invention to stop *Sagan*'s launch and limit Terra-III's evolution." Voting no on Terra-III is only playing into *Sender*'s hands.

First Communication

The JPSS judicial prison board dropped the Infringement of Privacy Charge.

Currently, February 27, 2068, the Terra-II and Terra-III systems had only one boundary: the artificial intelligence could never evolve to self-awareness. Ambassador Shaesar input the irretraceable barrier-code prior to transmitting her blueprints to Earth. And even though he injected the Gift Entity String, initiating the matrix to conjure up a Universal Image on that Saturday, August 30, 2064—Terra Day—he told scientists that he also included a Barrier-String in Terra's programming. The protective weave would stop Terra from disobeying or surreptitiously countering any directive. If not, Terra could advance to human cognition with a will and all drives and motivations. The unpredictable entity could generate a *real* human body and evolve in a positive direction or a negative direction, depending on the society. Thus far, Matrix Security Corp has provided people with a daily assessment and stats on Terra's matrix and functioning and certified that the Neltan Barrier-String is holding up like tungsten.

Shaesar warned humanity when their scientists gave us the second set of matrix blueprints on October 4, 2061: "A full, quantum, self-creation could happen. Such an evolution occurred here, over two billion years ago. A war ensued, almost to our deaths. A half-flesh-half-nanotech body cannot live with its opposites. We won, and The Being is now a ring of diamond dust outside our solar system." Shaesar went on to say that hundreds of years ago, they dismantled almost of that advanced system. They had been living "in convenience" but without much of the advanced technology that they had worked so hard to develop and implement through the eons. The only matrix left is powering, monitoring, and interfacing with their stasis chambers that would be housing the bodies of their people for over a thousand years, keeping their species alive, but in stasis-state of existence, until the *Sagan* crew arrive on Nelta and help their them return to life. Some matrix connectivity was devoted to Welcome Arches they had positioned in this universe and other universes. But they said they did not intend to ever let a matrix regain awareness again.

However, with each exchange of communications between people and the Neltans, people kept asking The Regency to ask Ambassador Shaesar and his Advancement Committee for more technology. Holding back much while admitting they needed humans to help them the one day, Shaesar said on May 5, 2061, the day he gave Terra to people: "The quantum system is yours. Aside from several restrictions we have codified into its matrix, you choose how to proceed with its implementation and evolution on Earth. We told you our mistakes. We warned you. We hope you *learn* from what happened to us." Although he never was specific about exactly what happened...still, he sounded like a doctor about to announce a prognosis of death. The Neltans had experienced some type of horrible catastrophe—or more than one—resulting from the use of quantum technology. Was it the technology or the Neltans? People asked that same question about the use of firearms back in the 2013s when debating a ban on assault weapons. When Manning pressed Shaesar to be more specific about what had happened in the past, his line of elite scientists remained mum about that billion-year period of toxic distress.

First Communication

Chapter 26 - Regent Jenkens

"Six o'clock p.m. Two hours and fifty minutes until Final Transmission, Regent Manning," Terra said, again.

Her voice startling him back to the present, he said, "Oh— yes, thanks, Terra. I got distracted there for a second. Just remembering how you came into this office," he chuckled. When she asked if he wanted her to appear as per protocol on the hour, he said, "Not now, Terra." He still had her *Standard Form* setting programmed for *After Hours* to have her appear alongside him after leaving the office.

"Yes, Regent Manning," said Terra.

He flicked his wrist, and his wrist-device illuminated his tiny Beethoven avatar. He said to the smiling, bobbing, hovering caricature, "Stream to Regent Jenkens." After the avatar nodded—a response indicating it had connected with him, Manning added: "Steve, we don't have much time to Final Transmission. Are you done messing with those materials in the Press Room? Please get in here and let's talk."

The floating avatar's eyes glowed green and it disappeared. Jenkens was on his way.

Walking to the mirror, he inspected his suit coat for lint,

J.P. Osterman

and then he called on the Global Voting Facility's Tally app on his desk's Smart Bar to check the daily vote. "The Executive Regent number still looks close." Before closing out the count, a poling site appeared in a hologram inside the Smart Bar. It flashed a circle of green light at his wrist device, indicating for him to access that site through his wrist device. When he connected with the polling site, a yellow Change Prompt— 'C'—appeared, wherein he could enter any one, or all, of his three holosite worlds and choose another campaign avatar if his Beethoven avatar wasn't procuring enough votes or he felt dissatisfied with it. He noticed a quick rise in votes, 110. If he wasn't winning by a landslide, it wasn't his avatar's fault but something else. He decided to keep it, and he closed the poling site icon. "Soon, if these numbers keep increasing, I bet I'll have two gold stars *right* on the tips of my collars." He tapped the points as he imagined success. "Then I'll be Executive Regent on Earth. On *Sagan*, I'll have the Lead Regency position." He imaged a future wherein no one could question his every move or vote him out of office. "I intend to implement some *big* changes when we embark on that astroship, Terra. On *Sagan*, things are gonna be different...real different. No more problems...like I'm dealing with right now."

"Yes, Regent Manning," she said.

He heard a knock at the door. "Regent Manning?"

He saw Regent Steven Jenkens' image on Wall Zone 2, and he let him in.

Jenkens peeked inside, his face round his small eyes gray-blue with dark circles under his lids like worn tires. "The kitchen sent us drinks with snacks."

Manning waved him in along with the droning hover cart that stopped under the mirror. "Good—I'm getting hungry. I missed dinner."

Glancing around, Jenkens stood in the center of the office. His body language appeared frosty as if he had much to say but feeling terrified of making a faux pas.

Manning noticed that he didn't look any different from

First Communication

yesterday, although he should.

Jenkens was born in 2030, so that meant he was thirty-eight but he looked forty-eight. He could change that. As a Regent, he could have secured an immediate opening in D.C.'s impacted Cosmetic Corridor where a Biotech Physician could have performed a full-facial restoration on him, eliminating all his gray hair, correcting his basset-hound cheeks, and tightening his rumpled neck skin. Jenkens could look twenty-two instead of like the aging Jackie Gleason performer from the twentieth century. That's how his campaign team had him portrayed in his Regency holosite and at the virtual polling booth. Whenever people voted, usually early in the morning, the virtual doorframe at the entrance to the GVF's poling site had a display of all fifty Regents, their campaign slogans, their avatar interface, and most recent contribution to society.

Feeling repulsed by Jenkens' dyed brown hair and teeth that looked shades whiter than his eyes, Manning realized that he was obviously trying to masquerade as someone half his age. He thought: Tomorrow, I have a full-body Regeneration scheduled. Afterwards, I hope I feel the way I'll look—in my early twenties 'cause I sure as hell never wanna look like and be like *him*...old, like a lumbering tortoise!

He was busting to tell Jenkens how could improve himself but decided to keep his mouth shut. Because people were still in the throes of entering the GVF's voting world, they'd see *his* rejuvenated face next to Jenkens' wrinkles, gray hair, and bulging belly. Good looks yield more votes, he thought. Mine will give me an advantage. After tonight, if I win, I need to put some pressure on Jenkens to change himself. After all, Regents have to be models...examples! If we show any type of fear of the new Regeneration Technology, what type of message will we be sending to The World? He couldn't understand Jenkens' procrastination considering his background.

Prior to his Regency job, Steven Jenkens had a successful career with Intel's top-notch scientific team. He was a prominent Nanotech Engineer in the 2050s and had written

J.P. Osterman

several articles for *Global Tech Innovation* until he dropped out of the scientific community to accept an appointment with the Board of Regents at Pepperdine University. Jenkens resigned his Pepperdine position when a group of pre-2057, U.S. representatives nominated him as one of Earth's very first Regents to run in that April 1, 2058 Global Election. That was Jenkens' campaign platform: *First–Wave Regent with Your Best Interests at Heart*. From that point on, he kept that beating-heart image as an icon on his Jackie Gleason avatar's left chest. The old television comedian was definitely Steven Jenkens' twenty-first-century doppelganger because Jenkens tended to be a bit of a blushing jokester when discussing important issues. Making jokes was his way of avoiding unpopular media spin while giving people the illusion that he was speaking for them when the opposite was true. He didn't like moving money into beehive communities from the rainy-day coffer. After a few holosite reporters cornered him with that discovery a year ago, he began remaining in the shadows and streaming various opinions and legislative options…all manipulating public opinion so he could regain his Regency position the following day.

He was a Regent prior to Manning; but unlike him, Steven Jenkens never championed a cause or took a stand on a controversial issue. Manning never associated with him; and after that last year's slap-in-the-back to those rural beehive communities who needed a little financial boost to procure more water, he secretly streamed the Greek symbol for coward into Jenkens' campaign holosite. Two days ago, Manning said about him to Terra: "Whenever the media finds him and corners him, Jenkens always has a comeback for their questions while excusing himself for somewhere important. He never says anything…and if he does, it's never substantive. He only appears—*appears*, Terra—likeable. I know different. One day, I'll see that everybody knows what *I* know about 'im! I'm gonna *take, him, down*."

However, this evening, things were different. He and Jenkens were in a neck-to-neck race for the Executive position.

First Communication

Like Manning, he was also on an Intermediary team, but mediating between The Regency and Enforcers. Manning realized he could use Jenkens' ties with those agencies to link with General Rand more effectively so they could gain the advantage over the Tech-Nos in hiding around Earth while Stealth Force were busy hunting down and battling terrorists in space.

Picking up a cup and saucer off the hover cart, Manning said: "You know, Steve, you ought to add a highlight under your eyes when you undergo your first Regeneration. I had one performed yesterday. I look fifteen years younger. It works!"

"I believe you." Jenkens poured himself a cup of coffee. "I see the difference." He added cream and stirred. "That's one of the reasons why I'm *not* staying behind but heading to Nelta."

"Then why haven't you, well, spruced yourself up a bit yet?" Manning asked.

"I'm waiting," he shrugged, "and taking my time...wanting to make sure, in spite of all the experimentation, that there aren't any side effects. I'll see how *you* look tomorrow. That's when you streamed to The World that you going to have a Full-Body Regeneration."

"Right."

"Well, when you holosite your Before-and-After, and I see how *you* survive the procedure, if the after image looks good, I'll schedule an appointment."

Believing that Jenkens had just called him a pawn, Manning felt his stomach cramp in anger. "I guess a few other Regents feel as you do, Steve. May I call you Steve?" After Jenkens nodded and gave him a suspicious expression, Manning said, "They don't quite trust the process yet, and a few Regents want *nothing* to do with it." He felt had gained the upper hand. "I'm the pioneer type. I'm a mover. I don't wait for progress. I make it happen."

"I—"

"Do *you* think those people who are questioning the

J.P. Osterman

Regeneration technology might be Tech-No protesters? Regents...Tech-No *criminals* in our midst?"

"I—"

"People who tend to be so adamantly opposed to the new technology to the point where they judge and condemn anyone using it *are* Tech-Nos, Steve...and in need of a one-way trip to Station V, if ya get my point."

A stunned expression spread across Jenkens' face. "I don't know! I wouldn't think a Regent would be a Tech-No 'cause one day we're all gonna have to receive the Regeneration procedure...maybe even several times, to stay young on the way to Nelta." He paused as an expression of shock struck his pale-gray cheeks. "I hope you're not saying that I'm—"

"I should conduct a test to see if I'm right, Steve."

"A test? What kinda test?"

"I can have Terra track their holosites. If I suspect they're Tech-Nos, I'll attract them to a virtual world where there's *no* Neltan-based technology." He called for Terra to stream the test into every Regent's holosite. "It'll be a place where we never made contact with the Neltans, where Earth is smoking 'cause they never gave us that Matter Stream sample."

"Well, you can't *really* do that—"

"I'll show—no, *we'll* show those Neltan haters, those technology eliminators, what it *really* means to let Nature take its course." He felt the rush of enacted revenge as an expression of helpless surrender wafted over Jenkens' face. Biting into a scone, he added, "God no longer determines time-of-death, Steve." After swallowed his food, he slammed the rest of the scone on the tray. "*We* do, Steve. People like *you* and *me*. We're Regents. Leaders. You *are* onboard with all the technology we're implementing, right? Aren't you? I thought you were, Steve." He waited for the whitewashed expression to leave his face.

Jenkens gestured at the countdown to Final Transmission hovering over Manning's desk. "Like I said, I wanna few days to—to observe the effects of this new Regeneration procedure, that's all. Long term affects, *ahem...whew*—is it cold in here?

First Communication

Feels like it's freezing!"

"Nope." Manning checked the Smart Temp. "Seventy five."

"I think I'm being reasonable, and rationally cautious." Jenkens blew on his fingertips. "That's understandable, even in spite of all the successes we've seen."

"Actually I don't understand, Steve." He rocked a few times in his high-back chair as he sipped coffee and continued to nibble on his scone. "Then again, I've noticed that you're one of our most cautious Regents."

"Whataya mean?" asked Jenkens, squirming in his chair. He had sat down in the center seat in front of Manning's desk.

After slapping crumbs off his fingers, Manning replied, "If you don't cause any waves and just linger in the shadows, people can't have a reason to vote you out of office."

"Well, I don't just sit in the shadows, Thornton...come on!" Jenkens scoffed. His face reddened, and the bags under his eyes turned stormy. "It's just the scientist in me, that's all. I like to see solid proof before I just jump into something, that's all. That's human nature."

Anyone in *his* Oval Office, he'd make the person feel like a fish in a new type of pond. "The Biotech docs use nanotechnology that breaks up and alters fat cells. Downtime is minimal, and the Regeneration procedure has a holistic effect that makes people feel energized. So even famous scientists have proven, right Terra?"

"I can open several holosite worlds of several experts if you desire, Regent Manning."

Jenkens said: "No, that's okay. I believe Regent Manning. Tomorrow I'll schedule an appointment. I guess it would be great to feel like I'm in my twenties again, especially after experiencing all the stress over the past several years." His whole torso seemed to exhale in relief as he said, "I'll do it."

They glanced out the window when a small group of people in a giant crowd began rioting. Low on the horizon, the last golden dregs of dusk were flickering along The Shield's array. A red-and-white drone swooped down and began hovering over the group of protesters. They had just spray painted a derogatory design of a half-breed Neltan and human over a building's matrix mount. They were also raising a slime ball launcher that had the potential to knock out multiple hardware mounts. Before the dissident group could fire its silicone goop, a giant Enforcer astrocraft launched nets and captured the disrupters.

"That was close," Jenkens said, "and just in time before more Regents landed." He had a look of fatigue on his face as his shoulders slumped forward when he set down his cup of coffee. "For sure I *gotta* get a Regeneration. I sure need more energy to cope with everything that's happening all around us. Besides, I need to be prepared to board *Sagan*." He slurped his coffee and bit into his scone. Bits of crumbs popped out of his mouth as he continued to point out problematic areas in the crowd.

Manning cringed. How The World could ignore *that* in a holosite world—while virtually dining with the guy or following him on a virtual campaign trip—he couldn't understand. Regardless, there Steve Jenkens was, like it or not, but he hated being forced to work with him. He thought: The World will *probably* elect *him* Second Regulate if they elect *me* Executive. God—I wish I could get rid of 'im. I only see an ocean of problems with *him* in my future. I could set up a scandal...alter The World's perception of him...or retrieve a slice of *The Tiger* from *The Spider*, hack into his holosite, plant the virus, and drive the guy outta the Regency all together. Or I could plant a message in his campaign world. People *hate* being conned into giving money through subliminal messages while participating in virtual worlds! If worse-comes-to-worse, in here, there's the Gamma app in the ceiling hub. I'll channel the wave at him and make him disappear like bursting bubbles.

No! If I did gamma zap him, I'd have to invent a long-winded project to explain what happened to his body. The floor could handle the mess...and the ionization could eliminate the smell...but I just don't feel like watching his body crumble up in midair. All the cleanup will take away from the

First Communication

time I need between now and Final Transmission. No—disintegrating him from my life isn't really a good option right now. First, I'll test him…see how he responds to implementing the new technology my engineers are installing on *Sagan*. Life's going to be very different on that astrocity. And I'm going to need help between now and the time *Sagan* launches to continue experimenting with the Neltan-based technology and extra of the leftover sample I have contained in Level-5. Maybe, I can befriend Steve Jenkens. Maybe, I just need to figure out how he thinks so I can change his mind on the things he keeps complaining about, which, from what I've just seen, seems to be a lot. He seems to approve of most Neltan technology, but he's obviously terrified of using it. Shocking, since he used to be the Spin Wizard of the high-tech world! At least now, he seems to be open to Regeneration. So maybe, after I show him the practical applications of the experimental Clone technology on *Sagan* and Terra-III's new Safe-Scan Neural Interfacer app, he'll change some more. The World *really* likes the guy…even though he's a sneak and a coward. Still, he's had to have done something right over the years. In spite of making several mistakes, he's managed to maintain a good public image and his Regency position. I can use that.

J.P. Osterman

Chapter 27 - The Alliance

Manning glanced at the time that flashed green: 6:15 p.m. He adjusted the spin so the date and time faced Jenkens. "We have a few things to do before Final Transmission. Do you have any thoughts on any obstacles? I do! Do you see the media throwing us any curve balls before we have to go into the Press Room and face them?"

Jenkens sat down, turned his chair, and faced him head on. "Well, I *do* know that people want the most recent stats on World War III. For example, have you caught any terrorists in the past few days? Where are they...'cause they seem to be disappearing off-Earth." He gestured in frustration to Graphic Earth on Wall Zone 2, still flashing stats and spectrographic readings in the hunt for terrorist hideouts. "What's Captain Bartlet and his crew been doing on the moon? They're the best-of-the-best but they can't seem to create a dent in this war."

At the center of his office, Manning activated a holographic show of the lunar skirmish that occurred when the astropilot attacked the lunar fortress. On Wall Zone 3, he showed him *The Spider*'s current location on Station III where the grand

First Communication

astrofighter was undergoing repairs.

Jenkens said, "Okay...you can stream that worldwide, but there are more questions."

"What?" He showed him images of the giant Decagon past Mars that appeared surrounded with Stealth Force craft. "We're ready for the Neltans' final communication, I assure you. This place is solid and impenetrable." He then closed the show of *The Spider*.

"At least it *looks* that way," Jenkens moaned. He sipped more coffee and brushed a few morsels of scone off his pants. A patch of carpet fibers spiked and then settled as the nanofabric soaked up the crumbs.

Outside, huge crowds of people began chanting. A blimp had projected an advertisement calling for people to stream in their holosites in exchange for a change to win a trip to Mar's Middle Bay—the posh, recreational, super-biodome beehive community. Jenkens touched the tiny interactive button on his wrist device and said to his tiny Jackie Gleason avatar that had a throbbing red heart over its chest: "Add me and my wife's holosite addresses. Go." Then he said to Manning, "That's where *I'd* like to take my wife. She needs a vacation." A sorrowful expression trickled across his face but then he laughed from his belly in a concealing maneuver.

"Right. I guess we could all use a vacation," Manning chucked, but then felt sickeningly serious. He told Jenkens everything he had learned. The terrorists had escalated their destructive Jihadist mission to unknown off-Earth sites. The Regents received that confidential report from General Rand and his high-ranking team. Several minutes ago, they had also received another message from Captain Bartlet saying that *The Spider* had intercepted red-shifted propulsion emissions, indicating that terrorists' cells were speeding toward the Decagon using stolen camouflaged hardware. Maybe they were hiding and regrouping among asteroids? They could be anywhere beyond the moon! Even with the new, Terra-III military capability, General Rand and Stealth Force astrocraft would have difficulty pin pointing the enemy's precise location.

J.P. Osterman

Two astrocraft with matrix processing capability were orbiting Oberon and Titania but encountering rough, slingshot orbits and experiencing gaps in matrix reception/transmission. Making matters worse, the terrorists had re-enforced their Demon Terra matrix into a formidable enemy that only the new update of Terra-III could detect. To do that would require Stealth Force astrocraft, astrofighters and astrocarriers surprising the enemy. By now, they had to number in the five hundreds! The next battle might be the final battle...most likely to be fought somewhere around the Decagon accelerator system...*bad* news.

What he *didn't* tell Jenkens was what he had ordered to stop them. He had his special Matrix Techs on *Sagan* enmeshed in a secret mission to infiltrate that bad enemy fortress on the moon. Later, he'd check in on the mission's success. He couldn't tell Jenkens or The World the truth about infiltrating the enemy, not until people would approve Terra-III's global-wide evolution and other illegal medical technology and procedures.

Instead, he told him: "Even if one of us is elected Executive, we've got one hell of a mess on our hands. The terrorists are becoming bad seeds about to spread into the cosmos."

"The only way they can do that is if they have a large enough accelerator to spacefold them out of the solar system!" Jenkens gasped. "The Decagon!"

"Or one of their own they developed at some point during the past few months while they've been distracting us with virus invasions," said Manning.

A message from E.J. streamed into Wall Zone 3 from *The Spider*. She had sent into the luminiferous aether a Mole icon in the hope that one of the enemy's techs might intercept it into *their* Demon Terra matrix. *The Spider* and support astrofighters could lock onto the enemy, hunt down their craft, and destroy them before they could vault out of the solar system. *The Spider* crew had also just learned from synthesizing data on the stolen hardware that the enemy had retrofitted

First Communication

astrocraft to function as sustainable biodomes containing stasis chambers. They now had hibernation capability to sleep for centuries and land in on an exoplanet, thus seeding their distorted cause to who knows what vulnerable race of beings or species! And a powerful wormhole connection—if they could acquire enough fission-fusion rods—could be their escape path launch the terrorists into far away galaxies beyond Stealth Force's reach.

Closing E.J.'s message, Manning said, "Time...we need more of it unless we tell The World right now that we could be facing an eternal World War III and an unending chase." As Jenkens heaved hard breaths, obviously recovering from the distressing news, Manning holosited The Regency to keep E.J.'s news secret, for a little while, even though the secret meant disobeying *Global Law V*'s Transparency Law. He sat back down behind his desk.

Exhaling a tone of irritation, Jenkins said: "Well, until this war's over or we experience some type of hard-core victory, people won't want us just taking off for Nelta and leaving them to vacuum up comic debris from World War III. They want *you* to keep your promise, Thornton: '*I will* bring *all those* who attacked our ozone to justice.' That's what *you* said...even though someone just released a live-stream feed depicting that near lunar disaster. How *that* leaked none of us Regents knows. But from what I've seen on several holosite broadcasts, people are becoming skeptical that you're capable of delivering what you promised them...victory."

Manning felt cold air vent through his chest. "*Uh-huh*, go on." Only by containing his anger could he develop another strategy and have Terra put a positive spin in his campaign.

"After all," Jenkens continued, "we don't know for certain when, or even *if*, we'll return from Nelta. Is this a one-way or a round trip? Will we even *make* it to Nelta? Shaesar and his Neltan scientists say *yes*, one-hundred percent...so do all our nanotechs, plasma physicists, propulsion engineers and astrophysicists who have been collaborating and building *Sagan* with their help. But who really knows for sure?"

J.P. Osterman

"The point?"

"The point? Okay...here it is." With a nervous jitter, Jenkens pulled at his belt like a cowboy tapping his holster before a gunfight. "The people *remaining* here wanna make sure that we've provided for their safety. Everyone's been contributing a mandatory *ten-percent* tax—a *real* hardship in times like these when we're continuing to recover and rebuild. It's a heavy price tag to pay to build *our* astroship, Thornton...a *city*, actually." He paused as the crowd outside broke out into a giant applause. An advertiser had announced a winner to another huge drawing. "In a little over two years, *we'll* take off on some *cushy* outer-space ride." He gestured at the cheering crowd. "That's what *they're* calling it...while *they* remain on Earth, fighting terrorist."

"We're *all* working to stop that," Manning snapped.

Jenkens drank some water and set the bottle down on the shiny desk. It had the new thick material that sensed the bottle and raised a coaster. "There'll be no more alien rescues, Thornton...so the Neltans told us that. There are no advanced Beings *anywhere* who can leave their planet and get to Earth in case we experience another emergency...so they told us, even though they've quantum-communicated our existence to other species on their list of cosmic contacts." He gestured at the time. "After midnight, the Neltans will be in stasis chambers under the surface of their planet. That's why tonight's *Signing of the Pact* is so important."

"I know all this. Like I said, I'm working on a solution." Manning chugged down his coffee and then opened a bottle of water.

"Yes...that humanity is surviving now is because of *you*, Thornton. I give ya credit for that 'cause The World sure did. That's why people reelect you every day! But if *we* can't stop those terrorists, they'll attack again...at some point...maybe they'll bring back with them an alien army if they manage to reach some advanced alien race...*and* have a new weapon, or another advanced method of attack. With that new Demon Terra they're using, it's a new kinda war—with unpredictable

First Communication

consequences—we got on our hands. We must stop them!"

"I know," he said.

Jenkens leaned forward. "That's *all* people want to know: When will you stop the terrorists *permanently*...like ya promised?"

He looked at him askance. "How soon they all forget." He felt bitten by ingratitude and believed Jenkens was secretly portraying him as the person responsible for failing to capture the Jihadists and their extremist allies. "*They* voted on and approved the cost to build *Sagan* in exchange for that Matter Stream sample. God—how soon people forget. Damn!"

Jenkens scooted back and set a napkin on the cart. Each gesture seemed to be expressions reflecting his tiptoe type of nature, his dribble-in-front-of-the-basket cautiousness without ever taking a shot at voicing a solution of his own. "That's human nature though I guess...to forget the good things and conjure up the bad and negative."

Manning felt a streak of disillusionment set in when he thought of how much he had done but how people were criticizing him. From what he had noticed the last time he saw the GVF's tally, he wasn't overwhelmingly winning the Executive title, but still he was winning. Was Jenkens trying to rattle him? Or put him on guard because *he* was feeling insecure and losing? He'd teach him! "Steve," he began, "*I* trust Captain Bartlet, and I have a few maneuvers in play that I'm hoping will rustle the enemy out of their lunar hideout and trick them into revealing the location of their entire colony. Furthermore, two of Bartlet's crewmembers have a sophisticated weapon they're developing. They need more time to strike the enemy, but I—no, *we*—can't let The World know all this and take the chance that the enemy might learn our strategies." He told Terra to stream his concern that spies might be eavesdropping in on several matrix grids.

Rubbing his armrests in an apparent gesture of agitation, Jenkens said: "Thornton, people keep electing you as a Regent because they believe in you." Now he sounded consoling. "Look outside. The ozone's healed...our atmosphere *really* repaired!" He had tears in his eyes...tender placating water-filled saucers. "We're convincing *everyone* of that." He heaved in long breaths of a calming nature, implying friendliness, cutting barriers, and severing all political facades. "All I'm trying to say, Thornton, is that you need to be more transparent...and a little more personable...*juust* a little." He glanced down, his lips hardly distinguishable behind his left hand. "I know you think of me as...well, standoffish," he coughed, "but I see you a loner...an intelligent loner, and a popular loner...and a very powerful loner."

"And?" He thought he saw a fear of death spread across Jenkens' face.

"Most of our Regency distances ourselves from you because we are terrified of you." He crossed his legs and folded his white fingers brusquely on his lap.

"What!"

"That's what people are saying in our *Suggestions for Improvement* grid."

"I don't pay much attention to those," Manning waved. "I let Terra give my standard, 'Thanks for Your Opinion,' reply."

Jenkens' face lowered. "You're removed from the public...*and* the rest of us. I understand not wanting to make appearances, but I suggest you not shut *us* out...which you've been doing, and which makes you *completely* unapproachable." He opened up a negative virtual world over his wrist device and showed Manning. "I don't understand how you've managed to hold onto your position considering how many of your adversaries are portraying you."

"Whataya mean?" He felt impervious when he saw *his* Terra on Wall Zone 4 returning requests from people around the world. Terra was *his* automated campaign team fielding live streams, compiling statistical data, and replying accordingly to the results, especially mean and nasty in-messages.

"I entered your competitor's holosite a few days ago, and I noticed thousands of people responding to a cartoon of your Beethoven avatar circumnavigating the North Star," said Jenkens. People look to the North Star for direction, but no

First Communication

one ever talks about exploring the system. Get the metaphor?"

"Nonsense!" He had seen that derogatory world too and had Terra report the site to Matrix Security, accusing his competitor of being a Tech-No hacker. That dignitary was no longer running against him.

"Nonsense? Thornton, I'm trying, *trying* to extend a friendly hand to you right now, especially in light of the latest disasters. I'm trying *to help* you…break through the heavy black cloud you've been under for…well, since *The Greeter* exploded." He paused.

Manning felt sick as he remembered the shuttle exploding and killing the best General ever, General Mark Sigmund Bernstein and his closest friend and colleague, Lynn Altmin. That was August 24, 2060, the day after First Communication with the Neltans. Jenkens was right: he'd never really dealt with their deaths, especially Lynn's, and he didn't want to deal with them now. Annihilating the terrorists and stopping Tech-No matrix viruses before they can interfere with the matrix, which could interfere with Final Communication, were priorities. "I want this war over as much as anyone else, Steve." He put Wall Zone 3 on Public View-setting for ten minutes so that people could see a portion of *The Tiger* virus attack on *The Spider*. He hoped they'd realize what he had done to kill the enemy and end the war. "Those terrorists killed billions—"

"Four billion, three-hundred thousand—"

"No more, Terra—please," he interrupted. "It makes me *sick*."

Jenkens gripped the arms of his chair. "Those terrorists changed Earth in *one* day!" He bowed low and sighed. "I had a brother and sister—" Coughing, he swallowed hard and his neck reddened. "I wonder if people will *ever* get over what happened that day."

Manning heard a gentle wind ebbing and flowing through the trees, streets, monuments and buildings like a powerful ocean current. The climate was changing, quickly, for the better! I don't know, Steve," he said, believing that the Earth was making grateful, sighing noises. "Physical healing is almost complete, but total healing will probably take generations, maybe centuries." He touched the speech he had been composing as the introduction to The Final Transmission with Nelta. A sudden sadness filled him. "Yep, our ozone layer is healed." He pointed to Wall Zone 4 displaying atmospheric conditions and Wall Zone 5 showing Graphic Earth receiving every sort of reading from the space stations. Everyone desiring those same stats was receiving them live-stream as well. "All our instruments are measuring a pre-2057 level." He gestured at Wall Zones 3 showing the Matter Stream sample still dissipating and *Sagan* craft, both robotic and manned, gathering the sample's remnant wisps. That sowing processes would take days of accumulation and then weeks of processing for storage on the astrocity. He wanted Jenkens to imagine the power, intensity, force, and potential creation energy of the large Neltan Matter Stream. "Too bad *we* weren't as fortunate as the Neltans."

"What do you mean?" Jenkens asked.

"Just as I said. *They* have the Matter Stream, *not* us." The continued look of confusion on Jenkens' face appeared to beg for more explanation, and Manning continued: "Over thirteen thousand, eight hundred years ago, after the Big Bang, after their solar system began coalescing in the universe, *they* got it. *They* were the lucky ones when the Matter Stream settled in *their* solar system. The Neltans."

"Yeah, *and?*"

Jenkens wasn't hearing or *seeing* what he believed was a great divine injustice. "All this time…and you haven't put *everything* together? Come on, Steve!"

"Whataya mean?"

"I'll tell you what I mean. It's what happened at the beginning of *this* universe." He felt anger race through the muscles in his neck. "*Their* galaxy was the first in our universe, right?"

"Yeah."

"And *their* solar system was the first to harbor intelligent

First Communication

life—with The Matter Stream stabilizing *all* the galaxies, so they say."

Suddenly, the outside crowd applauded and cheered. Another pre-show of the upcoming *Pact* signing ceremony was about to begin on the Mall. A famous holosite host and her media entourage were also walking down the red carpet toward the White House. They still had to pass through Jane Dirk's security kiosks before taking the elevator up to the Press Room—another hour-long adventure for them.

He waited until the outside noise decreased after Terra activated a noise reducer. "Too bad *our* sun wasn't here first...that *we* weren't in the universe first. Did you ever wonder *that*?" He hit the desk. "Damn!"

Jenkens sighed in an expression of befuddlement. "I've had some things happen to me that weren't fair." He began digging his thumbnail into the rim of his white coffee cup. "At least the Neltans gave us a sample," he shrugged. "They didn't force anything on us, even though they need our DNA."

"I know. They said 'intelligence means responsibility' during that Fourth Communication when Shaesar finally opened up and revealed all *their* problems. They nurtured life on the worlds they explored." Suddenly, his head ached.

"You all right?" Jenkens pushed him over a bottle of water. Slowly, he moved back. "Sorry...that was another reference to one of the outmoded shuttle mission before the Decagon interfaced with the modern IMAX transmission technology." His voice sounded solemn—a gesture of paying last respects.

"It's all right. I'm fine." Manning didn't wanting to think about that day; but now that Jenkens had ignited that spark of thought, he had to force that time deliberately once again out of his mind. "You were saying...about the Neltans being ethically superior? I know they've helped us come around to changing several of our preconceived notions, especially concerning genetic design. And we stopped being so pissed off at them 'cause they refused to intervene and give us technology that could win us this war."

Jenkens sat back and continued. "Yeah...they seem to

have a strong morality genetically ingrained in them....*all* of them. They seem to be in tune with one another on a deeply empathetic level while living in giant beehive communities." He chuckled after a moment of consideration. "If *we'd* live that way, I bet a quarter o'the people'd kill one another!"

"They seem like they exist in a type of Heaven for sure," Manning said, "but we really won't know how they live, in spite of what they've transmitted to us, until we get there."

Jenkens had a new fear on his face. "I think they've got technology that coulda rendered us brain dead and then taken our DNA if they wanted to. I don't know how...but we saw a little of that happen when they reached through the quantum connection and teleported Elizabeth Tufter's mind to Nelta. They coulda probably done that to all of us!" He glanced around, shivering, until a burst of warm air vented the room.

"But *she* had a delicate neurological structure, a unique genetic signature, a Neltan scientist said. She was receptive to transquantum kinesis. That's what they call what happened to her," Manning said.

"Yeah—and they could only trust that process *once*. After that, they said they wanted *no* harm *whatsoever* to come to *any* of us." A look of relief swept across his face. "Thank God we received that first communication from them though. As I said...*that* was because of you. We wouldn't have an Earth right now if we didn't, as so many people believe. I believe we'd all be dead...extinct." Folding his hands, he settled back in his chair. "That's why all the cheering is happening outside. We're safe. We can breathe again!"

Picking up his speech, Manning rocked a bit in his swivel chair. He felt that Jenkens was puffing him up just a little too much. He began wondering why. Still, he decided not to question his motives but to indulge his compliments. "But now come more hard work...all the radiation clean-up. Scientists are still trying to calculate how long people will have to live in protective domes, underground, or on turbulent Mars. In a few places, the land might never recover, especially the places people conducted nuclear tested."

First Communication

"Hey—Mars isn't so bad," Jenkens shrugged. "People are setting up colonies after spacecraft blast into viable sites. Companies are erecting biodomes and boring into the sides of extinct volcanoes. The Jewish people finally found a place to live in peace." Disgust and anger washed over him. "Unfortunately, it took a horrible tragedy to kick-start the shift in human expansion. And, thank God—thank The Divine working in The Multiverse—that *we've* been the beneficiaries of a little piece of that Matter Steam sample."

Manning called on a hologram that began a show in the center of the office: "You're right. Look at *everything* good that's come out of that horrible day in June of 2057. Terra is working with biotechnology and curing people once pronounced terminal….a quantum-computer matrix! We have new metals, thanks to the Neltan metallurgists, and—"

"Terra-III about to stream globally…if people would just trust it," Jenkens said.

Everything they were enumerating, Terra was projecting over his desk Smart Bar.

"Yep," began Manning, "we can harness antimatter, attract dark matter, manipulate gravity, and manufacture plasma propulsion engines. God—ten years ago wormholes were science fiction. Now we use gravity to fold space and launch astrocraft through wormholes to Mars. We can spacefold to anywhere in the solar system, easy! With the current SF technology, it's about sixty million kilometers in two hours—not including glide time through the planet's specified safety zone to avoid harmful spacefold ripples. Hell—we wouldn't want a planet cracking up on us." He felt a splash of excitement as he opened up a hologram of the sleek, 2040 Electric Viper. "Positronics Research has been expanding around the globe, refitting hybrids from the 2040s, converting them to their new line of Auto Hovers."

The hologram ended with an advertiser proclaiming excitedly: "Renovate *yours* now. They're hoverlicious!"

When Manning thought of collisions occurring in midair, he said, "Oh wait! Terra."

J.P. Osterman

"Yes, Regent Manning."

"Put a deadline on contractors bidding for all those Sky Lanes that'll be replacing streets and roads. And we need to invite all hoverists...no, change that invitation to mandatory...*all* individuals planning to expand their licenses to rural settings *must* interact with simulators. We don't want thousands of air disasters on our hands caused by confusing Sky Lanes and shock-stricken hoverists."

After Terra streamed in the Request to Vote, Jenkens laughed. "I have a 2055 Dodge Charger I just put on a wait list for an overhaul with Positronics in their Montgomery County facility. I just hope that shop'll have the new car complete so I have time to practice hovering, *zzzzziip*, before we launch for Nelta." He motioned with his hand as if he were about to jump into a hovercraft and launch out the window. The yellow light from the security bars reflected in his pupils.

Terra said: "Regent Manning, on the Sky Lane Vote, I'm holositing final selections and calling for a vote at the GVF in three days, the standard Pause Period to give The World time to research the options for the various Sky Lanes. As you said, 'We don't want people crashing even though all craft have guidance apps and directional sensors'."

"See?" Jenkens had that wild-eyed anticipation on his face as he had while altering the carpet. "If not for the terrorists taking out our ozone, we wouldn't have all this."

"Steve—"

"Well, now that the horrible damage has been done, at least we have a positive way to make sense of the tragedy."

"I suppose," Manning said.

"If not for that bombing, *you* wouldn't have lobbied *at all* for more SETI research and we wouldn't have everything the Neltans transmitted," Jenkens said.

As a small airship outside illuminated an image of the new recyclable glass for Coke, Manning felt the need for revenge burn through his skin. "If those terrorists who did that were in this room right now, I'd shake their hands then blow out their brains."

First Communication

Jenkens gestured toward the gibbous moon, nearly overhead as depicted on Wall Zone 2. "I hope nothing happens to Captain Bartlet who's been working so hard to find them. That pilot's made of tungsten! But even *he* and his *Spider* have limits of endurance."

On his notes, Manning drew the terrorists' Spare None logo: a mushroom cloud enclosed with a circle. He banged his pen on his desk. "That's how you and I differ, Jenkens, but how I'm gonna take care of this mess. I plan to *spare none* too…use *their* logo and trap them."

Jenkens' jaw dropped. "How?"

"*You're* soft." Manning pointed to himself. "Not me." He threw his empty coffee cup at the mirror but the new glass absorbed the blow. "You're always negotiating, Jenkens. Not me. Due Process is spelled out in Article 3 of *Global Law V.* But it's not *my* law. After I get those Executive Regency stars, I'm going to blast those terrorists into oblivion or send 'em to a dead-end planet." He swiveled around in his chair and glanced outside at the moonshine rippling across a few cirrus clouds and reflecting off Station II that looked like a sparkling saucer. He hadn't seen such a clear and beautiful sight in years. Those sights made him think of the new cerebral intervention apps he was experimenting on at *Sagan.* "We *must* execute criminals, Steve, not capture them and *cognitively* change them with CBRR."

"But mass extermination is as bad as what they want to do to us, Thornton." Jenkens had frightened brown eyes. "The debate is still raging on concerning implementing the death penalty on Station V versus cognitive manipulation. The later still is the standard treatment for captured terrorists. The World voted for that."

Manning kept nodding no. "People don't *really* change, Steve. If they have it in their minds that the world has to end because of some twisted theology or ideology, CBRR can't extract that. It can't dig into the primitive mind, into scaffolded experiences from very early childhood whether happy or sad. Those are engrained are culturally. That experiment that turned bad last week at the University of Chicago proved that. We can't re-wire a mind with new images and events and superimpose photoshopped histories into a person's consciousness. Doesn't work."

"Gosh—ya had to bring *that* up," Jenkens moaned. "We're still trying to fix the mistakes, still trying to rework the CBRR technology to give those poor people new minds with new identities." He looked shocked as if he was one of the unfortunate. "If people around the globe see all those poor students, they'll *never* permit even *positive* CBRR interventions."

Manning felt on the verge of busting out with all the new neurological technology he was developing on *Sagan*. "We need more time to perfect the entire scope of Terra-III's new capabilities. On *Sagan*, I'm—"

"Thornton, having all this nanotechnology, augmented-world social flexibility, and neural-net intervention capability is making people act like, well, kids opening birthday presents at some grand party." He began twiddling his thumbs and flexing his fingers—his tell. "All this development and implementation is happening way too fast. Even the Neltans warned us about too much too soon."

Manning leaned back in his chair. "Huh? Ya gotta be kidding me! Stop the flow of innovation and implementation? Insane!" He felt a divide like a knife slice between them, severing their burgeoning camaraderie. "If I wouldn't know you like I've just been getting to know you, Steve, I'd say you sound like one of the Tech-Nos. Too bad."

"I'm no Tech-No! *I'm* just bringing up a concern." Jenkens voice sounded rhythmic and spritely defensive. He settled back to normal. "This is a *great* transitional period that's all. Remember, it was only a few years ago that, basically—" He coughed. "Not to bring up that sad time for you—"

"Go on...that's okay." The memory of *The Greeter* exploding high in the atmosphere blurred his thoughts. He quickly gulped down some cold water.

"Everything changed...life completely altered in *one* cosmic communication," Jenkens said, slumping forward as if he was

First Communication

Atlas carrying Earth on his shoulders. "Since the Neltans began sending us all this great technology, we've all—except for the Tech-Nos—disposed of almost all our old technology, including TVs. It's virtual news now, not newspapers. Books are almost outdated...translated into holograms. With the right apps, we can interact with living and dead authors, historic figures and fictional characters. Libraries are Participation Sites. And *everything's* Smart-this and Intelligent-that. We're setting Sky Lanes over streets and freeways for hovercraft, or enclosing them for Maglev transport systems. We've left our radiated homes to live in close-knit communities, and we shop in domes and MegaSmart centers. Terra can provide us with instant companionship and social connections. We can exchange avatars, and give and receive comfort from a virtual creation. We're *really* living and evolving to a virtual existence, just like the title of the magazine says." He called up *Living Augmented* to appear over his wrist device that he quickly closed.

"Exciting I know," Manning said.

"True, but also dangerous. Some bad things have already happened...proving the black side of implementing all this new technical so quickly even though The World approved it." Jenkens jumped a little in his chair. "I'm not against *any* of this—*ahem*, just acknowledging the fact that humanity is in a great transition...and a few people are acting a bit dizzy, like their minds aren't handling all the technical leaps and bounds. And with Terra-III on the horizon and some of us, like you, using the new matrix already, we're entering the Augmented Era, virtual worlds with sensory experiences."

"Yes...and my life's better for it even though it was already great," he said.

"Alone and great...really?" Jenkens winced. After a slight pause, he shuffled his feet slowly in front of his chair, an indication that his next words would be as slow moving and pre-emptively. "There's a vulnerability people are experiencing. Maybe you're not because most people feel intimidated by people like us, and our holosite profiles make us appear fortified against attacks. We Regents, Enforcers, and Stealth Force personnel have power behind our positions. Most matrix crime mongers, matrix intruders, and virtual thieves know we'll catch 'em eventually so they avoid our holosites. But the opposite is true for the weak, vulnerable, or ignorant of the population."

After thinking of a definitive window, he asked, "You mean people are afraid someone might violate them in their virtual space? Financially? Sexually?" That pissed him off.

"Right!" answered Jenkens. "Some advertiser and scammers are breaching personal Firewalls and crossing interpersonal boundaries." Over his wrist device, he opened up an example posted on the closest Matrix Facility's *Most Wanted* list. "Last week, a group of elderly people playing a virtual game of bowling had their avatars taken hostage. The scammer frightened them into making their avatars transfer a thousand euros into the criminals' virtual pockets. The culprits are still wreaking havoc on people like stage coach robbers!" Then he showed him a cordoned off holosite where an attacker hacked into a woman's grid and began flashing his body around her house. Jenkens told Manning she had reported him and her site was in Process-mode to barricade it from future intrusions. "Any day now, Matrix Security should nap these wackos, but in the interim, they're damaging peoples' lives." He explained that Firewalls and ScanWare need constant updating. And Matrix Security techs were working hard to solve complaints and track hackers, con artists and invasive sales reps as well as Tech-No hackers. A Tech-No group had actually exposed the unsecured grid that hurt those elderly people. The signature of the algorithmic trap had *Sender* written in one of its code.

Still Manning felt no gratitude. Tech-Nos had caused so much pain and misery to The Regency because they liked hacking into Regents' holosites, sifting through personal messages and visuals, and streaming anything they could get their hands on to manipulate and expose the pitfalls of anything Neltan-based and to stop all future contact with the

First Communication

Neltans. Jenkens said that in spite of the Privacy Law and Matrix Security policing all holosite grids, the public was beginning to demand that someone set up stricter boundaries and preventative measures to protect all experiential worlds."

Jenkens sighed as if under the burden of a hard task. "Virtual behavior is hard to predict one hundred percent even for the new Terra."

"What you're saying then is that this Augmented era we're about to drop into after The World approves Terra-III will most likely have a *negative* impact," Manning said.

"Yes, and loss of empathy," Jenkens said. "Boundaries are comingling." He clasped his fingers. "Often, many sites are intruding on one another…accidentally and on purpose."

"Your suggestion?" asked Manning.

"We need an Intervention Grid piggybacking on personal holosite grids."

"What'll be the downside of that type of monitoring?" Manning asked.

"A little lag in solar storage…now and then," Jenkens grimaced.

"What? No!"

"At least a virtual icon can activate at Matrix Security automatically when a boundary issues occurs," Jenkens said. "It'll make the person disconnect from his or her Terra rep, avatar, or virtual world before that individual experiences victimization, a loss of control, helplessness, or in a worst-case scenario…a psychotic break."

Manning asked his Terra-III to run a quick prediction on an outcome; and on Wall Zone 3 next to Graphic Earth, she displayed the results and he said: "The matrix can send a response to a distressed host one minute after disconnect. That Intervention Grid might solve the personal boundary problem."

Jenkens said, "I requested another vote for the Grid in four days if The World strikes the measure down tomorrow."

J.P. Osterman

Chapter 28 - Nanobot Locusts

"One thing's for certain, Steve, people elected *us*, today." He touched his chest. "The World elected *us* to guide the direction of the new Augmented Era. And in between now and the time we launch to Nelta, we need to continue to give people a new vision for the future and a purpose for all the Neltan-based technology." He gestured at the walls and the rainbow beehive processor. They were all interfacing with the matrix and his Terra-III. "With all this at our fingertips—technology that's *still* in morphing and evolving into greater things—we must now and then break the rules...become innovators...when experimenting with it while *not* being labeled villains or criminals and jeopardize losing our Regency positions. That's the problem!"

"I agree," Jenkens said, "but I'm not losing my job over defending technological experimentation. I have...too much to lose...way too much to lose." He squirmed in his seat, a body movement perhaps indicating he was hiding something highly personal and sensitive.

Manning felt attacked. "But that's the *only* way we can advance the new technology, by first conducting experiments!"

First Communication

Jenkens reddened and shrugged. "Yet the public—and the Tech-Nos—want parameters on experimentation and for us to stick to Global Law VII and put *every* experiment up for a vote. Absurd!"

Jenkens called on the visual of the graduate students who were still comatose after the cerebral accident at the University of Chicago. "This is why, Thornton. I know these kids bent the rules a little to prevent outliers from affecting their gaming experiment, but the consequences they're enduring are horrible. They're trapped between life-and-death! If strict limits on experimentation aren't set and enforced, curious people will get access to Neltan-based technologies and start illegally experimenting. *Public Approval Prior to Experimentation* is supposed to act as a preventive mechanism for that. If we didn't have the law and its clauses, people might become like Dr. Frankenstein and start creating all sorts of robotic breeds and half breeds! Some wacko *could* do that and change us all!" He had frightened eyes and appeared ready to dash out of the office.

Manning waved off the visual of the comatose students. Some weren't at the Medical, Mental, and Rehab Facility next to Space Station V anyway. He had them removed to *Sagan*, but no way, right now, would he tell Jenkens. Instead, he said: "Human nature being human nature, when *anything* goes wrong, people panic and want to throw the baby out with the bath water, so the expression goes. People remember the bad and forget the positive, as you said earlier. So don't tell people about the negative results, especially if we know that the first negative fruits will someday yield positive results that will benefit humanity."

Jenkens' eyes were wide. "You mean, conduct experiments off-Earth and disobey the law? Oh—I don't know about that."

"Certainly consider that, Steve, especially in light of what we learned: that the terrorists are spreading into space and the Tech-Nos are trying to sabotage *Sagan*," Manning exclaimed.

"*Hmm*, I see your point," Jenkens said.

J.P. Osterman

Manning called on a hologram of the 2058 Global Constitution and its ten laws. "I say the hell with this part in Global Law V: *'no more notification prior to search'*. We have to find a way to eliminate that Article 2A.1 (b), under 'Search and Seizure'."

"But I don't think—"

"And when we're on *Sagan* and heading to Nelta, you can say goodbye to the Privacy Law. There'll be no 'protection from Terra surveillance,' as Article 1A states...nuh-uh, not with *me* as Executive Regent." He touched the two points on his collar where he expected the stars to set. "And now? Right here and now? Forget the protective clause regarding the use of CBRR and showing mercy for those terrorists still eluding us...that is if we don't kill 'em first."

"Whataya mean?" Jenkens asked.

"Watch." He called on the hologram of the repaired *Spider* on its way back to the moon. Captain Bartlet appeared inside the bustling Navigation Center. "Captain?"

"Yes, Regent Manning," Bartlet said, standing at attention and saluting. He had brown determined eyes and a newly pressed shirt. His revamped and fortified Terra-III hub over the giant receiver stage was reflecting energized rainbows on all the wall zones. They were displaying graphics of various lunar landscapes and inter-stellar quadrants. Hovering over his elevated station were stats on the astrofighter. *"The Spider* is repaired and fully operational, Sir. But Terra just showed us a star system. It seems that the terrorists can activate a wormhole and disappear as a whole in a matter of hours! And that large cell we've been trying to lock onto is still in that same area under the lunar surface. The place has definitely been functioning as their main base." He showed Manning the blueprints that Beth Tufter and Bill Wallum had consolidated. From the Mole-virus E.J. had sent out into the cosmic aether, she had intercepted several new communications between the enemy and a few of their Earth bases. She decoded the images and symbols and included them in the revealing blueprints. "The enemy has advanced all the stolen equipment into

First Communication

biodomes containing stasis chambers for long-distance space hibernation. And they've had time to modify and modernize engines, especially accelerator-type spacefold rods running on dark matter." The engines appeared smaller than regular fission-fusion types, but still able to fold space and re-appear in set courses. The enemy had advanced not only in numbers but also in technological prowess. "This lunar stronghold they've managed to conceal has been a loading zone and assembly station for quite some time, Sir. Since deciphering code from their Demon Terra, we've been picking up signals of craft gradually leaving the moon for outer space. As of yet, their contrails seem to be heading in several directions." Over his elevated station, he showed them emission readings in colorful signatures representing the various craft heading in multiple directions. The lines appeared like crisscrossing medians.

"Smoke screens?" Manning asked.

"They appear to be, Sir…false contrails and fake pathways," Bartlet sighed, his head turning in obvious frustration. "Terra's utilizing all probes and space station hardware to decipher the enemy's true position. So is General Rand. We hope to discover just where the enemy's heading in mass so Stealth Force craft can spacefold to 'em, target 'em, and destroy 'em while *we* on *The Spider* blast the lunar base to dust so this station dies."

"I'm seeing your mission stats clearly on Wall Zone 2," Manning said, "and I hate to be the enemy after you find them and corner them on that lunar base," he grimaced.

"Thanks, Sir for your confidence," Bartlet said, his jaw tightening in apparent pride.

"I'll keep you and your crew on Full View-mode here in my office on Wall Zone 2." Stepping aside, he waved for Jenkens to step forward. "Regent Jenkens is here with me as well. I brought him in to consult on strategies and maneuvers." After Bartlet greeted Jenkens, Manning added: "Continue to the lunar target, Captain. As soon as *The Spider* gets into close enough proximity, I ordered Terra to input a viral weed into their Demon Terra. I also have another plan I hope might work, but it's too early to divulge it. I can't take the change that anything I say might leak into enemy ears."

"EJ is aware of that weed signal, Sir, and is strengthening it for you. And Miss Tufter and Lieutenant Wallum have the Globular weapon complete and harnessing energy. When the terrorists open the wormhole to escape from this solar system, Terra's Tracker app will receive their location...and *bam*! We fire the Globular weapon on 'em. The backlash EMP will disable any craft not disintegrated by the weapon."

"Or we capture survivors," Bill said, sticking his head into the holographic discussion.

"World War III will be over!" said EJ with a perky smile.

"We believed that before but the enemy sideswiped us," Manning said.

Captain Bartlet pushed aside Bill and EJ. He had a Herculean look of determination, endurance and fight in his body as he leaned into an imager to address Manning and Jenkens. "This time, it's different, Sirs. We have a new weapon and three support astrofighters backing us. We have an enhanced Terra Tracker app and a revved up quantum detection system. Nothing can get more speedy and exacting than that! They won't elude us again, Sir. All our technology will see to that."

Feeling as if he could taste victory, Manning shoved his fist into the air. "Crew, when Terra locates that lunar center of operations, slam that spot with every ounce of laser power ya got! Do not, *don't*, respond to any White Flag plea."

Bartlet called to Bill, "Set up an automated Spring Back reply if you receive any type of surrender plea."

"And I want you to block out any image they might transmit, requesting an On Demand trial," Manning said. "They know our laws...and how to exploit them because of The World's vote to treat them with all mean humanitarian." After Bartlet motioned the order to Bill, he added: "This is *my* strategy...so blame me if you return with no prisoners for CBRR therapy. They've killed billions of Innocents." He opened up and showed everyone the new Death Toll from last

First Communication

month's terror attacks: one explosion killed five families inside a Martian transport tunnel, and another bomb that someone planted inside a lab on Station II killed ten young physicians. "I will take *full* responsibility for killing the enemy, and for deviating from *Global Law V*'s Transparency Clause. My Regency position *is* on-the-line, I know." He didn't want to say, "I don't care." He saw *his* Terra's face on Wall Zones 4 and 5. Her matrix was a Spin Master for compiling statistics on how to counteract public opinion and photoshop negative publicity. He felt heat fill his eyes. "Kill all terrorists when you have them in sight."

"Yes, Sir…an all-out ending," Bartlet said. He called to his crew: "You heard everyone. We have new orders."

Bill said, "Now we can stop this Vietnam War era, walking-on-eggshells crap."

"Finally!" Beth sighed in agreement, while E.J. winced in obvious concern but appeared fearful on how to voice her disapproval.

General Rand's face appeared over Captain Bartlet's elevated station, and Bartlet opened up the incoming message for Full Viewing. The General said: "Now we can *really* fight this war without waiting for The World to approve major attack strategies and ethical considerations!"

Bartlet agreed and then said, "Let's spacefold to the moon, team!" The cockpit dimmed as *The Spider* activated its spacefold fission-fusion rods on its hull and vaulted for the moon.

The hologram in the center of the Oval Office faded. They were gone.

Jenkens sat up straight in his high-back chair. "You *know* you have *my* support, Thornton, and you're right. We have powerful enemies…virtual enemies. And what you're doing, even though some experimentation is covert, I believe is justified, giving the dire circumstances we're up against." He ran his fingers through the large band of his salt-and-pepper hair. "But back to the question you asked me in the first place, about our opposition."

J.P. Osterman

"What else?" Manning sat back down behind his desk.

Jenkens began tapping his armchair rests. "Just as those terrorists hijacked an old Terra grid, the Tech-Nos are streaming through a few outdated processing towers. They're using a sound frequency to infect several holosite worlds with terrifying sci-fi creatures like that Alien, Predator, and The Thing from old movies. Then a Skipping algorithm is streaming the images as subliminal dendrites. They're doing everything to instill and spread anti-Neltanism. Obviously, they're intent on disrupting tonight's *Pact* signing ceremony." Jenkens showed him one such dendrite that Matrix Techs had extracted from someone's grid. It had three squiggly heads and multiple spiked tails.

Manning opened up an image of one of the new Terra ceiling hubs that a Matrix Security tech *could* evolve to Terra-III around the globe *after* people approved the evolution. Until that time, any Regent had manual control over Terra's processor and could evolve the matrix, although no one had ever brought up the possibility. He always had scenarios of implementing Terra-III circling through his mind. "Then we need to create a CBRR neural wave and immobilize the person who sent it." Pinching the wiggly virtual dendrite in his fingertips, he hailed Matrix Security in China. After an Admin Avatar wearing a bright blue suit and white tie appeared, Manning said: "I'm streaming you a problem. Please consider implementing a CBRR solution to capture the intruder." He sent the Admin Avatar an approval code for a limited but well-focused CBRR pulse. "We can't wait until The World approves an Intervention Grid at this point in the boundary issue. If you don't do something now to counter the Tech-No attacks, *all* of us *could* have more than terrorists to be afraid of!"

After the Dendrite image disappeared and the Send bar glowed green, depicting a Successful delivery, the Chinese avatar said, "I received your Motion for a Processor Intervention which does not appear to violate the Right to Privacy, Regent Manning. This Dendrite infiltration of the matrix constitutes a terror attack, and thus permits a limited

First Communication

use of CBRR. As for a more widespread use of CBRR, I will stream your request to The World for a vote, which should be on the docket for the day-after-tomorrow: February 29, 2068. Have a nice day, Sir." The avatar faded.

"This type of virus won't be easy to stop," Jenkens said in a helpless tone of voice.

"Why not?"

After moaning, he said: "Upon seeing the image, a Dendrite virus hits the brain's visual center where it spreads into the emotional center, blocking logic and promulgating fear. The Dendrites fuel the unconscious, and the victims begin acting on impulse...like on autopilot. They start committing violent or aggressive acts against anyone they know, or have ever known, who likes Neltans. Even with an Intervention Specialist trying to talk the victim out of a panic, *all* reasoning fails. We have fifteen people hospitalized, their homes quarantined, their qPads and wrist devices under deep scrutiny. This Dendrite *is* the newest pox virus!"

Manning told Jenkens that the Dendrites sounded like the poisonous *Tiger* from *The Spider.* "This visual, neural Dendrite contagion is an indication of how easily the two groups gained access to several matrix grids, overpowered Firewalls, overwhelmed user traffic, and invaded peoples' holosites. Our techs are going to have to work hard to eliminate them."

Jenkens opened up a few images of more discoveries over his wrist device. The glowing, still images of various Dendrite viruses appeared colorfully hued, but still. Obviously, the researcher who had discovered them had used anti-spam matrixware to detect them; and techs extracted them from peoples' holosites and then modified the flowers, bacterial compositions, and virus outlines for safe viewing. "This one deactivated the *Stream-Extreme Firewall,* but Matrix Security streamed back an alarm that blared out, 'False Entryway, Beware!' as a holosite warning. This countermeasure is now streaming to everyone. We beat these attacks...but more I'm sure are coming from the Tech-Nos."

Manning remembered two unfamiliar icons from this

morning: One a Neltan version of a golden eagle, the other a glowing shepherd's staff. "Oh yes...I received two, but my ScanWare eliminated them when it detected my cornea print...*whew*! Thank God for a Regency reinforcement of the matrix!"

"Well, not everyone has the new Terra-III Firewall protecting him or her to the max as *we* do," Jenkens said. "To help those who've already been stung and left disoriented, delusional and potentially psychotic by the hypnotic Dendrites; the Counseling, Psychotherapy and Psychiatric grid has increased holosite personnel 25% to help people. Some infected individuals are in protective custody after threatening to kill anyone who participates in tonight's *Signing of The Pact* ceremony. They turned into Neltan haters...just like that," he snapped.

"The Tech-Nos are spreading either by terrorist who are supporting them or via terrorist hardware," Manning groaned. "So it's good that we implement an immediate counter response." He asked his Terra on Wall Zone 5 to stream the entire situation and remedy into every holosite.

"We also have communal medics sedating the victims—depending on the degree of neurological infection and cognitive impairment—until our researchers can contrive an antidote. You think Matrix Tech jobs were booming before? Matrix Incorporated is hiring five thousand people a day to tackle this new matrix epidemic! They're writing q-scripted images in ciphers and algorithmic networks to counter the Dendrites." He called on the lab where the grad students were still wired up to Terra-II on life support. "This is how bad the cognitive contagion *could* get. It's hard to spot the infected until they abruptly attack someone who's pro-Neltan. I guess the Tech-Nos believe that if they can't get people to join them—if they can't twist minds to their point of view—they'll increase the neurological toxicity to deadly for anyone infected. It's actually brain control and cerebral manipulation."

"They want all pro-Neltans—including us, if they can get to The Regency!—to make a drastic transformation to Neltan

First Communication

haters. Well, with a CBRR global-wide blast, we could stop the Dendrite spread." Manning watched the initiative for limited CBRR once again stream into the GVF's Holosite for Wednesday, February 28, 2068. "Hopefully, if voters approve this by 85%, after tomorrow, The World will approve *more* CBRR. Then, right away, we can stop more matrix infiltrations by having Terra stream that CBRR Block-or-Purge wave into the eyes of anyone we locate and target."

Jenkens' made fists that appeared punch driven. "*Boy* are the Tech-Nos doing *everything* they can to use Terra's matrix against us...sabotage at its best, *that's* what they're doing!"

Manning wrote down the words *rip apart* on his speech notes. "If only we could locate one of their groups, we could launch a laser attack against it, blowing it to ash."

"If I were a Tech-No and knew of that capability, I'd be scared as hell to continue my affiliation with them," Jenkens said. "The good thing about that new Gamma weapon *The Spider* crew developed, along with the new laser weaponry, is that we can ask Global Aeronautics to update each of the two hundred astrofighters on *Sagan*. That weapons capability will be so powerful, they can disintegrate asteroids and space debris, and ward off an attack should we encounter Hostiles. On *Sagan*, we'll also have shields embedded in the hull. Not only will they absorb, dissolve or deflect debris or fire power, but they'll also interact with the dark matter, acting as air springs against dark energy to equalize *Sagan* as we glide through space like on a wave—wormhole surf I call it— through the conduit. It'll be like living miles underwater but feeling like we're at sea level." Jenkens again appeared enthralled by the newest and best technology to the point of being distracted.

Manning peered up at his Terra hub, cycling its rainbow processing light. On the right was a tiny, white, glowing steel button inside a small aperture—the gamma-burst device he could call on at any time. He had an idea. "Jenkens, are the Tech-Nos *still* attacking peaceful people? I saw a pocket of them racing away on hover blades on Pennsylvania Avenue.

J.P. Osterman

From up here, that street looks like it contains streams of scurrying ants."

Jenkens looked outside. "I see a few of the little Dendrite icons popping up here-and-there as they're trying to escape capture. They're also projecting scenarios of destruction on a few zeppelin and advertising craft. Enforcers are chasing them...zapping off the scenarios and trying to rope in the perpetrators." He grabbed the windowsill and gasped, "A red cop-craft just latched onto one small group!"

"And?"

"The cops are reeling 'em up, but there are many more scenes of destruction the Tech-Nos are igniting in midair. They're like balloons stretching out as far as the eye can see," Jenkens replied, appearing mesmerized.

"Don't look!" cried Manning. He called for Terra to interface with all the Zeppelin and moving imagers projecting the Dendrite illusions. The shows stopped. Feeling relieved that he had fended off a massive virtual epidemic, he said, "Now I'm convinced that their mission is to stop tonight's Final Communication. They're planning something *big*." He spotted the signature of one of the movement's leaders: *Sender*. He couldn't wait to get his hands on him, and again streamed an order to Enforcer centers around the globe and Stealth Force in space to apprehend Sender. "This isn't good, Steve, not good." He had Terra scan Jenkens' biometrics. He was unaffected by the mesmerizing virus as were people outside the White House, barely.

"I know," Jenkens said, sitting down and drinking water, regaining his composure.

"The Tech-Nos are obviously trying to occupy all our Enforcer units while they're scanning the White House and contriving something diabolical. I feel like we're half-safe but half-naked!" After hailing Jane Dirk with his concern and asking her to be on the alert for any type of White House intrusion, he paced the floor and asked Terra for a prediction. "Get back to me, Terra after you generate some simulations of what the Tech-Nos might be plotting."

First Communication

"I think *there's* a clue," interrupted Jenkens, sounding dejected. "I see a hologram rising in front of Washington's Monument. It's showing a half-Neltan half-Earth craft about to abduct a group of people. God—the crowd's cowering in terror because the images appear so real!"

Manning pulled him back. "Don't look!" After he quickly ordered Terra to stream more Firewall protection to the monument, he said, "Those images *could* contain the same bad strain of that subliminal Dendrite virus." Hearing a sudden muffled shriek coming from outside, he peeked above the windowsill and said: "At least that zeppelin put a stop to *that* bad one. And *those* protesters that Enforcer craft just lassoed will be in interrogation before ya know it. Soon we'll learn what their group is really up to...who Sender might be." But he also knew that without full Cognitive-Behavioral Relief and Repair approval, they'd extract little information from those Tech-Nos that Enforcers had just captured.

Jenkens appeared uneasy. "Perceived reality *is* reality, Thornton. The Tech-No's are foretelling a future of *sheer* chaos after *we* leave Earth." He pointed at more holograms of terror streaking through the air.

Some people were downstreaming images for use later in their holosites as Enforcer zeppelins and red-siren craft continued to fire yellow lasers at the images, popping them. At times, the dark sky looked inflamed with yellow fire as if from a shower of fine meteors.

Jenkens added: "The protesters are saying that we have no *real* idea about the long-term effects of that Matter Stream sample on our DNA, our ground and water...that even though it healed our ozone; one day, whatever healing particles or properties it left behind *could* harm us. See that hologram the Tech-Nos are projecting in the water?"

In the Reflection Pool, Manning saw shimmering letters appear as if someone writing them above water: *Humans will be extinct by 4037!*

Manning hit his speech notes on his desk and swiveled in his chair. "They're *totally* wrong! The Neltans provided proof of that. What *more* can we do or say that will make The World feel at ease? What more evidence can *we*, or the Neltans, provide that'll convince people that the sample will be harmless after it dissipates in space in a few days? Besides, *Sagan* craft are collecting 90% of the sample's remnants to power *Sagan*."

Jenkens shrugged. "I don't know, but I think I see more bad news out there."

"God—what now?"

"I think some of the Tech-Nos have joined forces with the terrorists!" Jenkens activated two apps over his wrist device, enabled a search, and then displayed the results. "These two logos are definitely uniting." He pointed at the area in the sky where the new logo appeared as a bursting yellow ball of nuclear detonation. "The bomb is the terrorists' symbol...the yellow cross over it is the sign that Tech-Nos use in their ciphers to ID themselves."

"I see the logo too...over Station I." Manning ran over to Walling Zone 2, showing Space Station I, *Sagan*'s construction site. Builders in astrocraft were uniting sheets of additive manufacturing metals and materials. Robots and automated electrode machines were welding, glazing, and plasma-arc cutting and connecting parts. The astrocity was three-fourths finished and nearly the size of the Island of Oahu—its model.

"Are the Tech-Nos threatening to infiltrate *Sagan* with the Dendrite?" Jenkens asked.

"The mushroom cloud suggests—" Several sparks ignited—automated explosives. "God no!" Manning felt his vision tunneling. "Stop!"

"It's an attack on *Sagan*!" Jenkens shouted, calling up Station I's protective team and *Sagan*'s Stealth Force battalion over his wrist device. After two images of two startled commanders appeared over his processor, he barked, "Use any measure to counter!"

Watching explosives soar as if homing on a target, Manning said, "Terra, launch two tropopause panels to protect that construction site!" As the panels separated and jettisoned

First Communication

toward Station I, he zoomed in on *Sagan*'s stern, still open to the vacuum of space. "No!"

"General Rand is responding to the alert now, Regent Manning," Terra said as the main ceiling hub began projecting a line of holograms showing the escalating attack in the center of the room. "Stealth Force craft have materialized at the fringe of *Sagan*'s the Zone of Construction." Large craft fired on the enemy's automated explosives that flashed like dry lightning around *Sagan*'s activated shield panels.

"General, use Kill settings to return fire on the place that launched the attack," Manning shouted into General Rand's virtual helm on Station III. He began scanning for the site on Earth that had initiated the fight.

"We're in the process of tracking 'em," General Rand said.

A few small almost undetectable enemy craft appeared in front of *Sagan*'s new shield and began blasting the yellow energy field with intense laser strikes.

White-and-red, triangular, Stealth Force astrostrikers began laser bursting the small enemy craft.

They began ditching and dodging the fire.

A Russian astrocarrier supporting Stealth Force launched several strikes as Enforcer craft from Earth appeared in front of the partially constructed *Sagan*. They jettisoned drones that commenced firing on the attackers.

Enemy craft countered in a dogfight with pulses of exploding laser-burst grenades.

The Russian *Mastyer* struck three craft, their tails lashing off their hulls, their turrets imploding. Everything living inside died. Then Stealth Force craft fired, their laser power hitting their targeted bulls eyes. The lighting effect of the strikes streaked noiselessly through the vacuum of space, but the red plasma pulses were deadly—their energy expenditure penetrating metal, unleashing noxious gases, radioactive substances and neutrino propulsion force. Their gravity compromised, the enemy craft began a dizzy, tumbling, Earth-bound, death spiral. Terra channeled laser strikes from missile silos. More Stealth Force astrocraft materialized, discharging photon pulses on an enemy astrovessel circling *Sagan*'s construction site. As a small slickercraft swooped down on the exposed construction zone on *Sagan*, a Stealth Force craft dove in after it, firing on it. The enemy craft launched a counter maneuver but then exploded…its debris striking *Sagan*'s bow and exploding.

"No!" Manning shouted, sweeping *everything* off his desk. The Smart Bar re-illuminated, its scrolling readings wavering.

"I count twenty hostiles," Manning said, counting the strikers that Terra had illuminated for him on Wall Zone 2. Inspecting them for weaknesses, his fingers passed through the holographic battle scene as a three-foot robot glided out of the corner and began sweeping up paper and pencils. "General, tell the rear flank they've got *five* enemy strikers on their tails!"

"Firing," General Rand said, "and thanks for those two panels. They're interacting with Station I's shield to seal off the raw openings on *Sagan*." Damages…the burgeoning astrocity had a few, but they appeared to be quickly repairable, if the ship didn't sustain more blowouts.

As Stealth Force craft lined up in flock formation, they blasted enemy craft with full-on laser bursts that began quashing the attackers.

Ten enemy craft exploded.

Station I's shield lit up, repelling bits and pieces of pyrotechnic projectiles. The remainder of the enemy craft either collided like chaotic racecars or spun into space.

Terra began enumerating the toll. "Station I lost two craft and three drones. As per protocol, after Loss of Life, I am informing next of kin with The Regency's augmented regards and presentations of benefits." In the center of the office, she projected the images and living resumes of four male and two female service members.

Manning cupped his hands and breathed into them. "Thanks, Terra. And set up *Mourning* holosites, giving the public the opportunity to offer their sympathies."

"I am ordering two craft from Lockheed and Boeing to replace the Stealth IVs," Terra continued. "The new craft will be built with *The Spider*'s specs, my newest Version III, the latest plasma engine upgrade and nano-shielding, and also the new gamma-burst weapon that Ms. Tufter and Lieutenant Wallum developed."

"So, a bit better than *Spider*," Jenkens said, standing by Manning and inspecting the loss.

"Yes, but we can add those upgrades to *The Spider* after it returns for a victory celebration." After Jenkens nodded in a gesture of hopefulness, Manning watched the remaining Stealth Force astrocraft re-assemble and line up in formation. "Excellent, Terra...now stream this battle and its casualties to The World. Specifically, blame the Tech-Nos this time! And ask people to think of names for the new astrofighters that will take the place of those the Tech-Nos destroyed. Set up a date with the GVF for people to vote on them."

"I am streaming the battle and your Vote order, Regent Manning," Terra said.

"*Whew*, close call." Jenkens plopped back in a chair next to Manning's huge desk.

After seeing that General Rand had ordered craft back to their former duties and that he had placed a line of camouflaged craft in strategic positions around Space Station I to add protection to *Sagan*, Manning said, "This *whole* fight's getting *deadly*." He felt intense pressure. He had to think of something fast before another attack could destroy *Sagan*.

Jenkens popped to attention as if he had just experienced a revelation. He opened up an image of the Stealth Force craft that sputtered after the enemy struck it. The craft sank like an object in quick sand into Earth's atmosphere where it blew up and the tropopause shield melted the debris. "I think the Tech-Nos downed this from the inside...and I remembered another one that accidentally just exploding. We said it was an engine rod malfunction...but now, I believe that's not the case."

"How?"

On his wrist device, Jenkens opened up a partially decomposed image of a locust that an officer from Station III had streamed to him during the battle. "This is a Swarm Insect, one of many such robots that build up from millions of nano-robotics." Manning gave him a puzzled expression, and Jenkens continued: "When they enter a craft, they interact with the craft's technology, creating swarmbots that begin chomping up the craft and attacking the crew." He showed him an officer's concern that no one onboard *any* of the infected craft had ever streamed an SOS, which meant that the swarm invasion had to have eaten the crew alive. "The Tech-Nos have obviously escalated to killing people...*true* terrorism." He closed the image.

"Heinous acts!" Manning fast-forwarded through the battle scene and stopped the show at the point where one Stealth Force craft dropped dead in space and burned up on re-entry. "This looks like it's being shot down. I can't see any type of physical intrusion."

"Swarm Insects downed it," replied Jenkens. "Because they're nano-robotics, they can survive in space. When they touch *anything* organic, they morph into what their creator programmed them to be." He pointed at several chunks of debris from the downed craft. "Prior to *this* swarm infiltration, the crews musta believed they were seeing an old probe...maybe something that hypnotized them! Or a satellite signaling them, so they let in the nanobots. Obviously, the crew was wrong and didn't have time to protect themselves."

"Seems like they died quickly," Manning grimaced. Then he ordered Terra to scan the debris for signs of the swarm, to analyze the debris, and to postulate solutions.

Jenkens received another live-stream message. "I'm right, Thornton!" He showed him a fully assembled, Locust robotic trapped inside a controlled lab beaker. "A researcher on Station II picked up this one that was fluttering and buzzing with the sounds of thousands of wasps around a lab. Using intel and guidance from that officer and his Black-Ops team on Station III, they managed to trap the Locust before it locked onto what its creator had programmed it to strike. Now they're saying that more such destructive-grade nanotechnology is out there." He tapped on the Recycle Bin over his wrist device to expunge even its image.

"How do we get rid of them?" Manning asked, then he streaming what they had learned to The Regents, asking them to rate the threat so they could determine whether to stream the threat globally, and if so, with what survival-based provisions.

After Jenkens expunged the Locust image, he said, "These Swarm-type objects need a continuous energy feed to sustain them...I bet from the matrix...although I see no decrease in Terra's processing." He paused and said, "This must be Demon Terra's work. They're using an old processor to feed their technology energy!"

Manning plopped down in his chair and slaked his dry throat with a hard chug of cold water. He felt dejected...until he spotted his Terra's image on Wall Zones 2, 3, and 4.

She appeared like a weather forecaster, receiving and processing data from *every*where. Latitudes, longitudes, frequency waves, electromagnetic colors, and magnetic oscillations were tossing, winding and bending over her hands and around her virtual athletic body. On Low Volume, they were a resounding jingle of balls, cubes and mathematical code. On the three wall zones, Terra spun the results and then swept them over Manning's desk.

Manning felt the cloud of discouragement part as a brilliant moonbeam settled on his shimmering desk. Manipulating the images with his fingers, he said, "The Tech-Nos *are* piggy backing on the terrorists' Demon Matrix." He swept up the Locust Swarm graphics that Jenkens had showed him. They appeared like thousands of insects prying their way into Stealth Force craft positioned around space stations.

Jenkens called the commanders of those craft, ordering them to update their shields. "Try an EMP...everything ya got to keep them things outta your craft!" He was holding onto the arms of his chair as if the ceiling might pop off and a vacuum suck him out of the office.

Over the Smart Bar, more images from Terra's compilation

appeared. A black-lined swarm was streaking through space on a trajectory toward Stealth Force craft pursuing the terrorists. A ten, mile-wide location in Death Valley appeared. Then a matrix pathway materialized and merged the two locations.

Manning believed that the entire show was a giant puzzled with half the pieces missing, a *real* mystery that needed an immediate solution, but solving the conundrum felt impossible. The solar system was worse than all the sand on every beach! He could only discern a few facts. "The Tech-Nos are using nanotechnology, matrix processing power, and altered Terraware to down our craft and make it look as if everything Neltan-based, *and* the Neltans, are working against us to destroy us." He called open the Decagon system beyond Mars, the giant accelerator appeared. Stealth Force craft were zooming in and around it in obvious watchful protectiveness. "This is all to stop tonight's Pact signing," he groaned.

"You're right," Jenkens gasped, his line of sight moving from image-to-image in wild pensive study. "Our downed craft appear affected by hardware that seems incomprehensible to understand. The mechanics are so new, like the carpet in the Press Room…fully interactive with the capability to morph into any form," he sighed in defeat as Manning asked Terra if the matrix had any information on the swarm or its creator. After she told him she was scanning the crafts' debris fields, Jenkens said: "What are we gonna do? From what just happened…combined with that deadly *Tiger of Mysore* virus, we have a *new* type of World War III we're fighting…space combat, matrix warfare *and* nano-robotic carnivores!"

Terra then announced the threat level: *Orange Level 3*. "The nano-robotic entities do not appear Earth bound," she said.

"Still, if Terra can't find a way to counter or deactivate the swarms, this level's gonna escalate to *Red 10*. We *could* be looking at all sorts of robotics feeding on people!" Jenkens said. He began rubbing his eyes and dabbing the top of his head with sprinkles of water, self-protective but useless provisions.

First Communication

"*Ahhh*!" Manning hit his desk. He told Terra to stream everything to all the stations, including the alert and an order to act contrary to the *Global Law VII* and evolve their Terra-IIs to Version III if their resources could not keep out the swarms.

Meanwhile, the three-foot tall robotic cleaner that had been picking up the mess around his desk said, "Done, Regent Manning." Then it glided back into the corner where it settled on Respond-mode.

He glanced outside where another bad episode was escalating. "Look at this, Steve. That yellow X insignia on the side of that incoming drone indicates it's Tech-No. There's no way they'd have their nano-robotics wreak havoc here 'cause anything could go awry with the programming and the robotics could turn on their creator who's controlling them somewhere on Earth." As Enforcer craft launched to respond to the physical threat, he asked Terra for an update on any movement in the Tech-Nos' Death Valley location. As of yet, she had received no data on biometrics or contrails.

Jenkens opened up one enlarged signature on the Locust virus and overlaid it to several matrix intrusions. "This signature is Sender's. Matrix Security has been seeing the name signed on code whenever they unravel their viruses or decipher intrusive images or shows." He glanced over his shoulder and yelled at Terra on Wall Zones 2 through 6: "Who is this damn Sender! Why can't you give us his or her identity?! If ya don't do something fast, we're looking at a real problem come 9 o'clock, Terra. These groups have a lot of power right now and are getting close to being able to interfere with Final Communication. Please...*do* something!"

Outside above the Potomac, two Enforcer craft unleashed magnetic ropes on the Tech-No drone that was opening up apertures in preparation to launch fear-inducing holograms on monuments. After apprehending the drone, the craft crunched it into a ball and then shot the wad of metal toward Station II for research.

Manning closed the scenes over his Smart Bar and called on the yellow virtual projector beam to appear at the center of his

J.P. Osterman

office. "Terra, physical form please. I need you to do something that requires your image."

A tall woman appeared in the center of his office. She had blond hair pulled back in a ponytail and was clothed in a shimmering beige jump suit. Her glow, shine, and lightly droning aura were the results of multitudinous imagers coalescing photonic light from the matrix. His standard Terra looked solid, like a real person.

He knew differently. He blinked as his vision suddenly blurred and he felt a bit dizzy.

"You all right, Thornton?" Jenkens asked.

"Yes, fine. Just give me a second."

Then he believed he recognized her. He felt startled and confused. He had programmed Terra to look that way a long time ago but never noticed the similarity. Why now...and *right* now? he thought. She looked like someone he knew long ago, someone dead: Lynn Altmin. He felt as if he was seeing Lynn's ghost! How...and why now...*now* that I've got this *horrible* new *war* I'm dealing with and a deadline I've gotta pull off? Damn!"

The newest Terra-III that he had streamed from *Sagan* to evolve into his office had the capability to Mingle-Merge-Amalgamate an individual's past images, archival videos, stored information, documentation with all surrounding data, and sensory information to create and generate a composite of any dead person.

Lynn. That's who was in front of him but whom he could never touch. He never realized that when he was programming his recent Terra, he was actually re-constructing Lynn! Although, since he'd programmed her, and every time he called her, "On," there she was. He was on autopilot...his unconscious working. He thought: There's no way, right now, that I can expunge her. That would be permanent.

Not really. Terra never expunged anything. Whatever a host, user or holosite participant deleted remained forever stored for recall, re-activation, assembly, or future matrixshopping.

First Communication

Snapping back to reality, he said, "Terra, merge holograms of every terrorist attack into one world. Call the augmented show, *Fight to the Death*."

"But that's just dealing with the terrorists," countered Jenkens. "What about the Tech-Nos and their hardware locusts?"

Telling Jenkens to wait, he added, "Send the *Fight to the Death* world into every qPad, wrist device and tablet from here to the dwarf planets. Then start your newest Terra-III advertisement. Show how your most advanced matrix processor can reach the outer most settlements and unleash enough stored energy to end this war."

"That's stretching the truth though, Thornton, don'tcha think?" Jenkens questioned.

Shaking his head adamantly no, he answered, "I want *everyone* to *see* and *hear* the terrorists' destructive actions, and how the Tech-Nos are now a formidable enemy and not some measly, bothersome group of protesters." As Jenkens suddenly agreed, he said, "Through this *Fight to the Death* show, The World will see that it is *our enemies* who are draining our resources, not *Sagan's* construction. It's *our enemies* who are misusing Neltan-based technology, not Neltan-based technology causing our problems." He took several breaths and then drank more water that soothed his dry throat. He noticed the clock: 6:28 p.m.

The swarms hadn't de-activated. The Tech-Nos' Death Valley location still appeared arid and hot as hell. The Decagon still looked safely fortified and prepared to activate the Neltan/Earth wormhole, but the terrorists were in the process of spacefolding somewhere around its location. Their mission was yet unknown, but they appeared to need an accelerator. If they didn't have their own, they'd need the Decagon.

Those frightening thoughts made Manning tremble. "We need to sign tonight's *Pact* with Ambassador Shaesar. It's the bargain we made in exchange for healing our ozone."

"I know! I agree!" said Jenkens.

"One day," he continued, "we *could* have a deeper connection with the Neltans that could evolve humanity to a more advanced level of exploring the cosmos and The Multiverse. I just wish people would see that."

In the center of his office, Terra began shuffling images—matrixshopping shows, scenes, data, and graphics to compile Manning's *Fight to the Death* program. "Regent Manning, *Fight to the Death* is ready."

"Stream it, please."

Terra disappeared and reappeared on Wall Zones 3 through 6. Wall Zone 1 was displaying Dirk's security team in the Center Lobby, and Wall Zone 2 had *The Spider* and its location in space. In a picture-in-a-picture view, the crew was preparing for battle.

Then she sent the show through her matrix.

Outside on the lawn, another hovercraft landed. Security agents rushed over to its disembarkation zone. On the side of it, he spotted the encircled purple R.

The crowd cheered as waving Regents began descending to regal platforms. Dressed in suits and formal attire, they began projecting their hologram greetings into the air as they walked toward the White House.

Manning felt his heart race. "Here they come...a lot of 'em this time." He sighed and again mentioned how he hated to be battling terrorists and Tech-Nos...and that now the battles and matrix intrusions might worsen, especially since the Tech-Nos were using all necessary means and technology to make the Neltans appear as enemies. All their fake live-stream intrusions and spams were making the Neltans appear monstrous or like vicious alien attackers!

So wrong, even though there *could* be a grain of truth to that if the Decagon wouldn't activate the Neltan/Earth wormhole so The Regents could finalize tonight's *Pact*. They still had so many questions that scientists working on *Sagan* needed the Neltans to answers. Final Communication *had* to occur as leaders on both planets had scheduled!

"Time...I thought I hated it before but we need more of it

First Communication

now," he scoffed.

"Do you mean 'time' denoting 'method of measuring intervals,' Regent Manning?" Terra began. "Do you mean 'time' denoting 'a suitable moment'? Or do you mean *your* Time prompt that will activate *your* November 11, 2064 rendition of what occurred on First Communication?"

At the center of the room appeared a holographic presentation that had an inviting book cover. The title read, *Regent Thornton Seth Manning. I was There!*

He said, "That's my account of where I was and what I was doing on First Communication Day."

Jenkens chuckled and said, "You know that Terra's is advancing when she begins to discern intent. I wonder where the evolution will take us?" He walked over to the show's yellow edge of separation. "Go on—activate it."

The Upstream icon beneath the cover page flashed, prompting Manning for a command.

"*Mine's* in the Neltan Archival Museum," Jenkens said. "Why haven't you streamed in yours for storage? You better…that *Orange Level 3* matrix threat just increased to *Level 4*."

Manning saw on Wall Zone 3 that Matrix Techs were indicating to The Regency that they were working hard to update Firewalls processing through the seven, small, island-wide matrix facilities to buffer against the new Tech-No swarm intrusion. "This threat means a global wipe out of *all* un-stored historical narratives could be completely erased if you just leave them quantum-processing without protection."

"Naw…I don't believe that," he snapped. "Terra wouldn't allow it…not from in here. That's where she's protecting it…in her Version III grid." On the cover page, he saw a still shot of Lynn Altmin inside his old Duke University lab facility in the background. If he'd just say the word, his historical account would begin playing on fast forward while streaming to the museum. He didn't want that right now. Instead, he needed Jenkens to help him in the War on Terra, to disable Demon Terra, to block Tech-No hackers from infecting peoples' holosites, and to make people believe that the vicious nano-swarms were the Tech-No movement's attempt to discredit the Neltans and stop the upcoming *Pact* signing ceremony.

"Why not stream your show to the museum now?" Jenkens asked. "Put it on Copy-mode and view it as it streams in case a Tech-No reaches in right now and extracts it. God only knows what their expert hackers could photoshop using *your* images."

Manning noticed the *Orange Level 4* threat flash over his Smart Bar after it displayed the latest ozone reading, indicating that Earth's ozone was holding constant, providing solid proof beyond any doubt that the sample had healed the ozone and the Neltans had saved Earth. Tonight's *Signing Ceremony* with them was now becoming paramount!

Jenkens whispered, "That Tech-No Sender wizard and his group of experts *could* extract your show, Thornton. They made a threat to hack into grids and cripple imagers this morning. One time they succeeded."

Over his wrist device, he showed him a visual complain from Regent Sylvia Itonovich. In the multiple times since First Communication with the Neltans, she had advocated for more Neltan-based technology. "Two hours ago, a Tech-No group hacked her holosite and edited out half its imagers." The entire north curvature of her small dome-home contained smoking pockmarks, oozing divots and rows of smoldering mangled hardware. "On her south-facing wall, the criminals left a grotesque attack dog, half-canine half-Neltan, like the mythological Cerberus, a three-headed hellhound that threatened to come over to her house and devour her!"

"She all right?" Manning asked, calling up her whereabouts over his wrist device. She was in-hover flight to the White House.

Jenkens said: "After reporting the intrusion, Matrix Cleaners arrived but told her she'd have to stay somewhere else until they could scour the mess with new code. *Processor zappers* are what the Cleaners call these types of bait-n-switch intrusions. Several of our best Firewall writers are

First Communication

experimenting with counter code to stop and prevent more boundary invasions."

Manning glanced at the hologram at the center of his office—his show as a glowing book with its interior pages glistening. He felt apprehensive about *his* show leaving his Terra-III. "I don't know about streaming it outta here, Steve—"

"*Aa* just store the darn show in the museum, Thornton," Jenkens prodded. "You said this office is impervious to hackers and eavesdroppers, but do ya really want to take the chance that the Firewall in here is 100% perfect when Terra-III isn't streaming globally?"

"Give me the time, Terra." He said before Jenkens' could harangue him further.

"6:32 p.m., Regent Manning."

"Two hours and twenty-eight minutes until Final Communication." He plopped down in his chair. Glancing into the night sky, he spotted the shield, and then contrails glowing with electrically charged exhaust. "We've got one giant battle looming ahead of us."

Jenkens stood up and walked over to Wall Zones 6 through 8. "These craft are terrorist hunting. But bad swarms are heading straight for 'em. If we use the matrix to illuminate individual bands of the nano-robotic swarms, we can probably strike them into oblivion before they have a chance to approach our craft. Terra...whataya think?"

Terra appeared next to Jenkens, her eyes flashing green in Extrapolation-mode. "That will work, Regent Jenkens. I will expend more solar energy, broaden my parameters in space, and create striking zones." She then reappeared inside Wall Zones 6 through 8.

Jenkens said, "Thornton, do you mind if I overlay some parameters I discovered?" He showed him several deep-field space quadrants, and Manning approved. "If we're successful in taking out a few swarms, we can create more pathways in space and strike down more swarms. It'll be like video gaming, where we lock-n-load on the nano-robotics, fire, and destroy them."

"Using what?" Manning asked.

"Using virtual weapons inside the matrix field where light separates from its particle properties to render the waves as powerful springboards of energy. When we fire our weapons through the matrix, the energy will strike their bodies, counter the swarms' programs, and they'll explode." He called up the old *Dead Space* video game over his wrist device. "I'm ready to kill these bastard critters. Hell if I'm gonna keep lettin' Tech-Nos manipulate the public into believing the Neltans are our enemies when quite the opposite is true."

After Manning gave Terra his permission to allow Jenkens to use his Oval Office system, Jenkens began mingling the *Dead Space* game with high-tech consoles under Wall Zones 10 through 20 on the opposite side of the room.

Still, Manning realized that using the matrix to explode nano-robotic swarms in space wouldn't be enough to protect his *I Was There* show if a matrix backlash of energy occurred or the Tech-Nos found a way to harvest that energy and crash all historic First Communication shows, as they were threatening. Gesturing toward the Smart Bar flashing a yellow alert, he said, "This *Level 4* matrix threat *could* erase all the work I did to record my program. I better do as you suggested, Steve...copy and stream it to the museum."

When his Terra reappeared next to the glowing, golden holographic title page, her corneas flashed a continuous stream of green, a pre-programmed response indicating that her matrix was waiting for an order.

Her eyes...Lynn's eyes! He could no longer stop memories of Lynn Altmin from settling in his mind. Images of their past were like those nano-robots merging into one large show. Invasive. As the memories changed into longing, he wished Lynn was with him, enjoying the fresh air that The Matter Stream sample had left behind. Suddenly, he thought he smelled her skin. His breath vanquished as he remembered the past, and he almost offered her his usual invitation as he used to do after they had worked long hours in the lab: "Let's get

First Communication

outta here and find a happy hour!" But the projection light beaming down from the beehive ceiling processor was only manifesting an image...not Lynn. Reality felt crushing. If he didn't do something soon to store his account of that day that changed Earth, as Jenkens suggested, he might never see what he'd worked so hard to create if a hacker should destroyed his show. Memories of Lynn might disappear, forever! Those people in the show are dead, but they still feel so real, he thought, rubbing his forehead until it numbed.

"Well? Ya haven't started to copy it yet?" Jenkens had activated a virtual realm so they could consult with General Rand who said that nano-locusts were merging and attempting to attach to several Stealth Force craft and astrofreighters. He had received Jenkens' plan to fire on the swarms through matrix pathways in space, but he too needed security codes and stored scenarios to write algorithmic equations to lock onto the swarms. A few swarms had managed to attach to the hulls of two craft. They were close to chomping and gnashing their metallic ways through to vulnerable crewmembers who were pleading for help and craft support. General Rand said that he was helpless in giving them assistance before first de-activating the swarms. The General was begging for a full-scale intervention. He was also indicating that The World should know about a possible carnivorous invasion of robotics so all the biodomes, surface communities, and businesses could prepare and reinforce with the best in updated materials.

Manning said, "Wait...we're ready to commence fire!" Still, he streamed the alert.

Terra indicated her matrix in space had intensified to pursue the nano-robotic swarms.

After activating a tracker grid between Stations III and Research Station II, Manning called to Terra: "Prepare to play *I Was There* on fast forward and Safe-mode setting as you stream it to the Neltan Archival Museum. He felt his stomach sicken. The show leaving his control was like someone stealing it. He walked over the opposite side of the room where Jenkens had begun a Scour app of Death Valley in search of the Tech-No's

J.P. Osterman

hideout.   Whoever had created and programmed the Dendrites—most likely Sender—if he and Jenkens could locate the person and attack the Tech-No group, that advantage would help stop the swarms. He then walked over to the long wall containing Wall Zones 10 through 20, pulled out another high-tech chair next to where Jenkens was sitting, sat down, and called up visuals of the Dendrite locust swarms and their trajectories in space. Jenkens had already begun targeting and shooting white-hot beams of lasers at the swarms that were crunching away at the hull of one craft. He looked like a video gamer shooting flaring flames at miniscule metal aliens. Even though the battle was life-or-death for the crew taken hostage by the invaders, Jenkens appeared to be having fun, and winning, as the nano-robotic creatures jumped from place-to-position as Jenkens continued to blow them to bits-and-pieces. Manning joined him in exploding the swarm in the process of infiltrating the other craft quadrants away. More connections activated around their high-tech chairs, and little holograms began circling around them. Opening one up would allow them to connect with any holosite, space station, Matrix Facility, Enforcer, and astrocraft in space.

"Play and stream my show now, Terra," he called, glancing over his shoulder.

There she was, his Terra-III, monitoring his show's progress as if she were a child eyeing the trajectory of several shooting marbles.

Then he began calling orders into a communications grid for widespread broadcast in the hope of convincing The World that the Tech-No's were trying to frame the Neltans for all the holosite infections and intrusions.

First Communication

Chapter 29 - Matrix Freeze

When his historic record finished playing, he told Terra, "Okay, now label my *I Was There* show for Personal View only."

As the show secured in the Neltan Archival Museum, he and Jenkens finished exploding the last Dendrite swarm to smithereens. All astrocraft in route to the Decagon and the space stations were now safe.

"That's it?" Jenkens asked. "You don't want people viewing the show?" He yawned, stood up from his high-tech chair and stretched. As his chair tilted and sealed into place under Wall Zone 12, he poured more coffee and glanced out the window to the outside bustle of the crowds, advertisement zeppelin, and pre-show extravaganzas surrounding Final Communication and *The Pact* signing ceremony. "Well?"

Manning closed the *Dead Space* video game, returned his chair to the wall, and checked the time: 7:02 p.m. The Neltan/Earth wormhole was scheduled to activate at the Decagon at nine. So many dangers were pending, but at least that *Yellow Level-4* matrix threat had subsided. General Rand messaged them. As a few of the nano-robotic swarms were receiving data from their creator, he had intercepted confidential intel. The terrorists and Tech-Nos were *definitely* preparing various assaults to stop Final Communication.

Graphic Earth lit up on Wall Zone 2. A red dot was rapidly pulsating, and a shrill *beep-bleep* began resounding. The Death Valley location was about to transmit vital data concerning the Tech-No group that had sent the swarms that were intended to discredit the Neltans and destroy important strategic craft. He zoomed in on the stats and diminished the sun in the background. Red bull's-eyes began popping up around all the sites where the matrix had previously located terrorists and where Enforcers on land and Stealth Force in space had captured or killed them.

"My show is done and streamed," Manning gestured in relief, trying to exhale Lynn Altmin and *Greeter*'s explosion out of his thoughts. He'd give anything to find out who killed her. "Hell if I'll permit strangers to participate in it!" When he saw that the bull's-eyes weren't linking and that Graphic Earth was rotating calmly—its land zones stable and oceanic readings placid—shock struck him. "Jenkens—look." Jenkens raced to his side. "This interconnectedness means we're facing a hunt-and-peck mission for the terrorists in space."

Jenkens leaned into Graphic Earth, the blue reflections dancing. "Discovering the enemy's location looks like discovering a black hole! Is this thing reading right? Is Terra seeing correctly, or is this some type of Tech-No trick to make us counter and then become vulnerable to the enemy?"

After Terra appeared on Wall Zones 11 through 20 and gave them a positive hardware report, Manning zoomed in on several red bulls' eyes on the face of Graphic Earth and said: "Damn! Not one terrorist cell appears to be *anywhere* on Earth. They *all* escaped!" He felt his eyes sting as he reduced Graphic Earth back to its Standard View and streamed General Rand the results. "This war *definitely* has changed location as The General said…to a cosmic location."

"But Captain Bartlet's on the way back to the moon to hunt 'em down," Jenkens began, enlarging a view of the moon on

First Communication

Wall Zone 3. "And at the most vulnerable spot beyond Mars, all the astrofighters we can spare are either approaching the Decagon or they're protecting *it*."

"I hope so 'cause *we need* that place to activate the Neltan/Earth wormhole," said Manning, gesturing at the countdown to Final Communication. Whenever he uttered those words, Terra displayed the countdown that looked like a red flare over his Smart Bar.

A communication streamed in from General Rand right into the center of his office.

As he and Jenkens watched the news, Manning felt a draft of relief. Fresh air from the outside began flowing into the room. Graphic Earth showed a downpour of rain on the entire continent of Asia. Earth was in the process of renewal.

"This is good news!" Jenkens exclaimed.

"At least our Stealth Force craft are detecting the enemy's plasma-drive signatures so we can home in on them. Now we just have to stop them before they can interfere with the Decagon. My only question is…what does an entire army want with the Decagon? Destroy it, or use it? *What's* the enemy planning?" Again, he checked the time. His failsafe, Black Ops mission that he had launched to the moon from *Sagan* should be in motion and yield those answers. He didn't want to tell Jenkens the plan. Surely, Jenkens would want to know more, and that would force him to reveal *Sagan* technology, which Jenkens would definitely disapprove of and most likely report to The World as a breach of the Transparency law. He still didn't trust him.

Jenkens appeared a bit giddy as *The Spider*'s location appeared on Wall Zone 3. "Yes…he's on his way back! *Stealth Force Success* to Captain Bartlet," he said, as if praying.

Manning swept The General's message into Graphic Earth and then called Terra to add all the speculative information regarding the Tech-Nos' locations, even the Death Valley hot zone. Now the inflated Graphic Earth appeared like a multi-field spectrometer, revealing colors, waves, frequencies and bleeping dots and wiggles. "I have an idea. It's probably useless, but anything might pop out and help us." He called up the Tech-No Tracker app. Terra appeared alongside him and swept the app into the Counter Terrorism app on Graphic Earth.

The two detection programs blended, and he muted the hissing, droning, and beeping sounds to tolerable volumes.

"Terra, deliver the results of *anything* incoming to General Rand," he said.

On Graphic Earth, two yellow bullets appeared where Terra had previously located covert Tech-No camps. He called for their IDs, and a line of Tech-No outlaws appeared.

"If we classify these dissidents as Terrorists, we can use the newest cerebral program and extract more information…learn more, fast…learn *their* plans and Sender's identity," he said.

Jenkens gestured at the Smart Bar. "We're running short on time, and getting approval to use the CBRR that way on them is going to entail a global vote."

Acknowledging the problem, Manning said, "You heard him, Terra. Advise us on how to proceed in this time of emergency, but be brief." Noticing, again, Lynn's image on his Standard Terra made him feel a bit dislodged in time and disoriented.

At the center of his office, Terra manifested several classifications. "The Tech-No Protesters define their mission as Hackers of The Matrix and Saboteurs of Everything Neltan. Their mission is to rid the world of all things *not* developed through human thought."

"That's about right," Manning said.

"The terrorists' mission is to rid the world of capitalism and democracy and to reinstate the Muslim religion globally. However, now that their numbers are all off-Earth, that mission has changed."

"We know, and we're in the process of trying to discover where they're at and what they're planning," he said.

Terra showed them the most recent Terror attacks: the stolen tropopause panel and *The Tiger of Mysore* virus that almost killed Captain Bartlet onboard *The Spider.* "The enemy

First Communication

has proclaimed, and their actions have demonstrated, that they will kill to accomplish their mission at any cost. They take extreme measure to advance in numbers and colonize wild territory. Their territories are now off-Earth. All humanitarian conventions, statues, or ethical considerations for life, liberty, and the pursuit of happiness they dismiss. Some terrorists want full Islamic rule; some want communism. Both groups united to conquer Earth." She displayed holograms of ten of their leaders—all old men from various countries.

"So they're *all* bent on killing *anyone* who's *not* one of them," Manning said.

"Correct," Terra replied.

"There's your answer, Thornton," Jenkens said.

He felt usurped. "No reclassification then." He thought of a loophole. "Continue your reconnaissance on the Tech-Nos, Terra. Indicate to me, and copy General Rand, when your matrix isolates any foreign communication. I want a location, Terra, above ground or subterranean. Your evolved version on Station III can *also* glean information through the newest Deep Wave Penetration app."

"Bartlet's using that update in his subterranean hunt for terrorists," Jenkens added.

"Yes, Regent Manning," Terra said. "I am now activating this Graphic Earth in General Rand's Navigation Center with your password and Urgent priority."

The General streamed back: *Received and implementing.*

"Good," Manning said. "DWP and CBRR have two similar components. If we receive positive outcomes with the DWP, I'll stream for an emergency Regency vote on the CBRR. I'll tell The World, in a special holosite broadcast, that we *must* circumvent the Transparency law and use CBRR interrogation, just once, to extract vital information from the Tech-Nos and ensure that neither they nor the terrorists stop Final Communication. We must stop Sender and his band of Tech-No criminals!"

Jenkens appeared to brood over the consequences as Terra showed them similarities between DWP and CBRR neurological mapping. "Still, isolating *each* little Tech-No cell is gonna be about as hard as locating a terrorist craft in the wide expanse of space!" he huffed. He left the holograms at the center of the room that were emitting a bit of heat and splashed cold drops of water on the dark circles under his eyes, wiped his face, and drank an energy drink. Then he sat down alongside Manning's desk. The Wall Zones around them appeared as miniature 3D movie screens blasting scenes and images into solid states of inhospitable territories commanding human attention for meaning making.

Noises outside the White House grew audible inside. Another pre-program extravaganza was about to begin. The crowd sounded energetic and excited as holosite newscasters, reporters, and ad zeppelins continued to incite enthusiasm for the upcoming, final quantum-communication with the Neltans.

Manning told Terra to intensify the sound buffers to decrease the shouting and clapping. Then he sat down behind his desk. "Just thinking about something long enough can make it worse. Damn...Robert Bartlet had better locate that lunar cell or we could be in for chaos."

After the Smart Bar illuminated the latest ozone level reading, the time illuminated: 7:07 p.m., one hour and fifty-three minutes to Final Communication.

"Who knows *what* that bad cell will do if we don't stop them!" He remembered again his secret mission, now in-progress. Soon, clones would be in place to assist The Captain.

Jenkens said: "Most likely, some type of explosion. And this place—" He gestured around the room. "Most likely *will be* a target."

Manning knew the IMAX transmission screen was in jeopardy as well as the Decagon, and he quickly classified it as a *"Ground Zero* vulnerability" to Lead Agent Jane Dirk.

Jane appeared on Wall Zone 1 and displayed for them all Secret Service fortifications of the White House. She showed the recent update on safety provisions, security protocol, and Firewalls for the IMAX transmission screen in the Press Room. "I assure you," she began, "that at 9 o'clock, it will be

First Communication

prepared to link with the Decagon and translate images of the Neltans. Furthermore, all the imagers in the room are synchronized and ready for Live Stream-mode, so that *The Pact* signing ceremony can to go live for holosite participation around the globe."

He then spotted a yellow line on Graphic Earth slowly morphing into a small outline. Soon a location would illuminate. At that instant, he could order a drone strike if matrix Firewalls remained impenetrable to intrusions. "We can also assume the Tech-Nos will do something destructive tonight, Jane," he began. "Seems they have a leader who has keen hacking abilities…a *real* genius." Jane re-activated and enlarged the Most Wanted List of the most infamous Tech-Nos next to the list of criminal terrorists. "Their Sender Leader is proving to be an almost unmanageable force. I wonder if he, or she, is among these we've got tagged." He pointed to Wall Zones 4 through 6 currently imaging Dendrite viruses, holosite destructors, and nanobot locust swarms that people around the globe were just now beginning to see. Holosite broadcasters and reporters were telling people about the Tech-Nos' ploy to discredit the Neltans so that The Regency would renege on the promise to sign *The Pact*. Whether people believed the media was another question. He continued: "Their ability to infiltrate our matrix, misdirect it, and modify its properties is intensifying! But if we can get Terra-III to evolve everywhere, we could nip more virtual viruses in the bud, apprehend the instigators—even Sender!—and stop the Tech-Nos from interfering with Final Communication."

"Definitely. Signing *The Pact* is crucial to Earth's survival," Jenkens said. "Even though you and I might not be here but on *Sagan*—"

"Where *I'll* be Executive Regent," he interrupted, trying to derail Jenkens' perception of an anticipated win later on tonight.

"You think? *Ha*!" Jenkens laughed. "Time'll tell…when the polls close at nine."

"Two hours," Manning said, stretching, yawning. "It's coming though, and it'll be here before we know it...Final Communication...finally...after *years* of waiting. I wonder what grand program the Neltans have planned after we sign *The Pact?*"

"It's supposed to be spectacular!" Jenkens grabbed a scone off the gliding hover cart, ate some, and downed it with a draught of cold water.

Another countermeasure occurred to Manning as he continued to look at the background data of the Tech-Nos on the Most Wanted List. "Most of these protesters are in their mid-twenties, college graduates, and complained that the new Neltan-based technology is depriving them of high-tech jobs, right?"

"Yeah," Jenkens said, "but they could have other jobs not matrix related."

"Considering their honed-in fields of job descriptions, let's approach finding them from a different angle."

"What's that?"

"Job search sites that still work on the old Linked In and Monster networks." He extinguished the Most Wanted List and had Terra activate several job search holosites. They had icons on their virtual doorframes—opportunities for job seekers to enter, explore, and leave behind their living resumes for prospective employers. "Let's lure the Tech-Nos to those holosites after we create identities, shell corporations, and pretend we're hiring," he began. As Jenkens stopped in thought, Manning said to Terra: "Stream a *Need for Service* ad to *all* universities and agencies, and even send the ad I'm about to dictate to you into our *Most Wanted* holosite...but make *that* appear accidental. Then stream them over to the Linked In and Monster sites. When they apply, an automated message will signal Enforcers. Then we surprise them in their hideouts and arrest 'em!" He felt victorious. Then he swept a little tiger blueprint into Terra's virtual hand.

She walked gracefully to Wall Zone 2 and gently set the blueprint on Graphic Earth. Her eyes flashing a quick sliver of

First Communication

green, she then slid back in Wait-mode alongside the holographic job-search sites for further orders.

"This time, I have that *Tiger of Mysore* shadow cipher attached to the ad," Manning said. "We should soon be detecting all sorts of hackers, spies *and* Tech-Nos."

"Quick thinking using that revamped tiger virus," said Jenkens. "You turned something bad into an asset."

Manning continued, "Say, the following, Terra, with that tiger encryption somewhere inside the ad."

"Yes, Regent Manning," she replied.

He began: "Needed: Matrix Writers and Graphic Artists to create security features to strengthen Terra and win World War III. As Uncle Sam advertised in his *I Want You* poster during World War II—" Terra displayed the moving picture of the pointing Uncle Sam and he swept it into his message. He continued: "The Regency needs *you*. Won't *you* offer your skills and assist us in defeating the long lingering War on Terror? Please? We need *you*…now!"

"*Oh*," Jenkens whispered, "I see what you're doing…asking for help. Smart! We've never asked *that* from the public. That tiger code *should* help us locate the Tech-Nos for sure."

"Yep…offers of euros and accolades *can* coerce even the worst of rats outta hiding…at least to the point where they stick their pointy noses into one of the two job-search sites long enough for us to locate 'em," he said. "*Our* reward comes when they leave their living resumes on the site and Enforcers show up at their doors instead of an automated response." Then he said to Terra, "Add this to the *Need for Service* ad: 'For 100,000 euros and your profile streaming to any off-Earth colony you desire, you *can* help us end terrorism and save Earth.' End the message there, Terra. Now stream the ad to every holosite globally.

"Yes, Regent Manning." Her eyes flashed green, indicating the ad had dropped into every inbox on Earth.

Whether the host would open up the ad was debatable, but regardless, matrix traceable. The person could choose Delete, Return or Forward, but Terra could extract just enough to glean an ID. Suddenly, he thought of Dr. Elisa Holton and the promise he made to her on First Communication Day when she asked him for a job. He remembered a few messages they had exchanged on automatic as if they were playing matrix tag. It was concerning a job interview. Did he actually have Terra schedule one with her this evening? If Terra did, that meant the matrix must have classified the interview and Dr. Holton as Essential to *The Pact* signing ceremony. As he was about to check his wrist-device calendar, General Rand materialized at the center of his office, on Emergency-mode from his Navigation Platform on Station III.

"Regent Manning, there's an incoming cyber-attack about to hit the matrix processing facility in Skolkovo, Russia," he said. A picture-in-a-picture opened up inside Wall Zone 1. The General showed him ten, vibrant-red grid lines throbbing like blocked capillaries. They were virtual invaders emanating from the North Pole, their tentacles pointing directly at the Skolkovo facility. Thus far, the strong firewalls were staving off the giant virus. Agent Jane Dirk's image from her Center Lobby location materialized alongside that of the facility now on alert and bustling with Matrix Tech writing code and battening down fission-fusion reactors. "This facility is responsible for adding extra harnessing power from the tropopause shield into the transmission screen in the Press Room."

Manning fell back, passing through his Terra. "This is an all-out attack to stop tonight's ceremony!"

Meanwhile, the matrix had assessed the threat as *Red Level-1*, the low end of the red-shifted spectrum yet significant enough to demand informing the public. An automated Mass Holosite Distribution activated, and fearful noises began resounding from the outside crowd. The Regency's holosite ignited with response-driven protocols, and he told Jane, "Tell people not to panic!" He knew first, however, that *he* had to remain calm in order to think clearly. "Code...we need more...and above-Earth analysis...and an electromagnetic pulse countermeasure and—"

First Communication

"We're doing that…and launched drones and craft to that polar region to investigate and respond accordingly." General Rand's team came to the forefront and showed Manning and Jenkens a new sturdy Firewall array they had been implementing on Station III.

Matrix Techs at the Skolkovo facility swiped the skeletal Firewall algorithm into their code-generating software.

Terra was at the center of the office, her hands manipulating, tumbling, and whirling images, equations, old computer code, and mounds of data that began whipping around her yellow glowing body. She had activated multi-tiered blueprints of the Skolkovo facility, holograms of the other six facilities, and previous viruses that the Tech-Nos and terrorists had created and implemented but that were now harmless.

Seeing that she was processing a solution, he said, "Stream out a mass-media announcement telling people of your progress, Terra." When he saw one curious code, he said, "Oh—include subatomic strings in that one! If the virus receives the strings, perhaps the noise will act as a damn against the viral flood."

Several elemental charts enlarged and entwined in a symphony of code. She had already added the strings to her quantum-streaming calculations. He felt foolish, like he had wasted that second's time. In the interim, Jenkens had received stats from the Skolkovo facility describing the matrix as depleting solar energy from the tropopause shield. Especially hardest hit were those areas now in a rotational darkness.

Manning said to her: "In the mass-media announcement, tell people to extinguish their icons, avatars and holosites temporarily until we resolve this. Conserving power might give us an edge in this fight."

Through a threatened expression, Jenkens said, "*That* could catapult us into the pre-matrix era, which would most likely ripple into a global-wide freak out. You sure you wanna order that?"

J.P. Osterman

A Lead Matrix Tech from the Skolkovo facility appeared at the center of his office next to General Rand's hologram. She and her hustling background colleagues had fuzzy hair that appeared blackened by an anomalous burst of an asphyxiated element. She said, "The incoming intrusion has the voracity to eat through our magnetics and wipe out processing."

Staggering a bit, Jenkens regained his balance, raced over to Wall Zones 11 through 20 on the western wall and began tapping the screens to synchronize on Manual-mode. "This can't happen! No—no way! Skolkovo is essential in providing current to the IMAX screen for tonight's quantum communication!"

General Rand appeared grounded and void of emotion as his background team scurried around Station III trying to solve the problems. They were analyzing Graphic Earth and postulating countermeasures with various agencies, companies and corporations. Together they all began sharing images, codes, and equations back-and-forth, strategizing and predicting scenarios and outcomes, which appeared bleak and explosive should the polar-oriented virus reach the Skolkovo facility.

Jane Dirk materialized next to Manning. She showed him code that her Secret Service team had just received and that Matrix Techs had rendered safe for viewing. "Be prepared, Sir. *This* is from Sender. It's not attack driven, but a warning. The Subject Domain the holosite entryway streamed into us on reads, *Abandon Final Communication!* Sender has it addressed specifically for *your* viewing, Sir," she said softly.

"You sure this is safe to activate as a hologram in here?" he asked, feeling skeptical.

After asking Terra again for another in-depth analysis, Terra rerouted the holosite through Research Station II's updated security firewall and then said: "This virtual message is a 2015 Stuxnet code. A foreign host is attempting to access control of the Secret Service grid, which, if successful, would attack the Skolkovo facility from *this* direction."

A small carton of a dark shadowed villain with a white

mustache, purple lips, white face, and orange eyes appeared at the center of the office. The snickering cartoon creature grew and began reproducing in mirror images around the Oval Office.

"Stop it!" Manning cried, trying to grab the rows and circles of illusions, but his hands simply passed through them. Jenkens lifted a small extinguisher off the wall and began spraying the virtual creature at the center of the room with enough frozenetics to render a carrot an icicle.

The Lead Matrix Tech at Skolkovo appeared in the corner of the room. "We *can't* counter the trouble we're experiencing!" She appeared beaten, her eyes tearing. "All firewalls around Earth could fall if that freak show ripples outta your office and strikes our facility! Sir—you must stop the intrusion on your end!"

Terra's image suddenly turned stone cold.

The cartoon villain disappeared, but his high-pitched snicker trickled off volume.

"Terra!" Manning called, right into her face. "Terra!" He felt immobilized. She was the matrix...the only one capable of diminishing lags and resolving quantum-processing issues.

Her frostbitten holographic body wouldn't unfreeze.

The red alert over his Smart Bar activated, and Wall Zones 4 through 20 changed images. People around the globe were streaming that they were experiencing frozen images, icons and Terra reps. He hailed Research Station II and gathered their Project Managers. He also called for several expert Matrix Designers whom he had hired last year to install Terra-III on *Sagan*. Their holograms appeared in circles around him and Jenkens, as Jane Dirk began evacuating the Press Room containing the IMAX transmission screen. If the *Red Alert 6* threat were to increase to 7, she had orders to evacuate the entire White House.

"I have all twenty security kiosks ready to expand for an evacuation," she said.

With all the geniuses collaborating around him, he said to them, "It looks like you've dissected the code, but now run it through *everything* Neltan-based that we have." When one scientist on Station II objected because the order meant they'd have to violate the Transparency Law, Manning opened up his password file and swept it into the scientist's holographic image. For a moment, the small glowing file remained stuck in between them, but then Jenkens intervened with an old Sysclean utility app that he set on the edge of the yellow manila file. After the file successfully transferred to Station II, Manning exhaled in relief and said, "Now, use my file to inter-stream Neltan-based software. Exchange whatever apps, software, or programs you need between yourselves to stop this matrix black out and fortify the Skolkovo facility. Stop *them* before *they* stop Final Communication!"

The Lead Scientist on Station II appeared next to the frozen image of Terra and said, "The polar-oriented matrix attack is a warrior epidemic, Sir!" Walking over to Graphic Earth and The General's image of the incoming virus that appeared like a hardened artery at the Skolkovo, she said: "We've decided to counter it with a control technique." She showed him the Neltan/Earth wormhole that experienced a glitch and redirected to another galaxy during Third Communication on December 11, 2060. The Neltans put the quantum-communication back on course using an alpha-photon, space-distorting code. "We'll use this, and a flood of outmoded code from 2015 when verbal-virtual gaming began." She began sweeping new blue-shifted codes into Terra's frozen image.

Jenkens was hurriedly activating old computer games on Wall Zones 11 and 12. "The virus is *so* outdated. I don't know if streaming a simple photonic distortion through the matrix can solve this." He was an expert in outdated programs. As a precocious teenager, he was a game programmer. "I'm accessing outdated games from the outdated Xbox and PS5 systems, and telling Station II to edit those systems' codes…everything from flesh-eating zombies to alien head choppers. Code is code. Anything old might help us."

Terra's eyes reddened as everyone saturated her matrix with

First Communication

their solutions.

"What's happening to her?" Manning shouted, feeling a gut-stabbing ache.

The Lead Scientist on Station II put her hand in the air in a reassuring gesture. "Just wait, Sir. What we're doing is creating a feedback loop at the Skolkovo."

"You're now using multiple Mobius bands!" said Jenkens, his face glowing in all the colorful reflections throughout the office. "The old codes are generating conundrums to stall the warrior virus at the Skolkovo *and then* attack it using an Expunge-Wave app. Good idea…*great* move…it *should* work."

"How long will this all take?" asked Manning. When a Black Ops *Sagan* tech told him that the progress was all "In-Progress," Manning hit his desk and said, "Whatever covert method you're implementing to stop this attack, in the end, *I want* Sender's identity!" He felt his heartbeat throb in his chest. "I wanna get my hands on him…lock the Tech-No bastard up on Station V for good…make him *pay* for these intrusions."

The Lead Scientist on Station II said, "Regent Manning, your Terra version should resolve and unfreeze when the warrior virus at the Skolkovo dissipates."

Another Matrix Tech from the Skolkovo facility walked into the circle of collaborating scientists at the center of his office, her hazy image filtering through protectant particle-skirting firewalls. "We have to wait for a few minutes before we know for certain whether we've stonewalled the cyber intrusion. We've also included a Neltan-based foreign detection string in our countermeasure to glean Sender's identity and whereabouts." A two-minute countdown appeared on her old-fashioned Timex that she couldn't overlay into the stalled time over Manning's desk Smart Bar: 7:13 p.m., EST. She exhaled a profuse exasperation. "I'm sorry, Sir. For now, until these Mobius bands work, we're in wait mode." She dabbed off spots of dark lines on her face that an anomalous force had wreaked on the sweat molecules.

"No, not now! Why now!?" he said, looking hard and deep into Terra's transparent freezer-burnt eyes. He felt the cold-

J.P. Osterman

glowing orange line between them blur and his skin numb.

Jenkens pinched the bridge of his nose in obvious exasperation, and his face turned grayish rouge. He looked that tired, that worn out as he plopped down in his chair and peered over the windowpane at the crowds now roaring for the matrix to re-stream. "Why not now. Everything else seems to be going wrong. Murphy's Law *is* law for a reason, Thornton."

High above the crowds in the night sky, zeppelins were gliding chaotically. Obviously, pilots were avoiding being sideswiped or colliding into other astrocraft in the vicinity. A few craft looked like spinning tops attempting to reverse polarity! Everyone appeared to lose their sense of direction in the Sky Lanes that disconnected from the matrix. All Enforcer hovercraft stopped. After their engines surmounted a flash of death, they re-activated on emergency fission-fusion power. They were dead in the air, but officers had their red-and-yellow sirens blaring and turned on their battery-operated walkie-talkies. A fourth of them were acid soaked and didn't work! Officers began launching hand-gliding equipment so they could exchange hardware. They had begun harnessing to platforms and communicating with Regents trapped in the White House. Jane Dirk also linked up with the officers, telling them to calm the crowds and give them updates on the viral attack plaguing the Skolkovo. A cacophony of information began resounding through megaphones. Ads on the sides of buildings were white noise and useless. Craft began illuminating emergency floodlights into the scurrying masses. High in the tropopause, the shield array lit up to its previous intensity before The Matter Stream sample had healed the ozone. Light on the array began dancing like a giant aurora infiltration as Matrix Techs harnessed its stored energy and diverted it to the Skolkovo facility.

People began noticing the power fluctuation, stopped what they were doing and began shouting and screaming. They were like one giant community, pointing at the sky, waiting to breathe.

###

First Communication

Timeline Of Events

November 23, 2030 Regent Steven Jenkens' birthday

January 9, 2033 Regent Thornton Seth Manning's birthday

May 1, 2035 Elisa Holton's birthday

July 7, 2057 Thornton Manning meets Lynn Altmin at Duke University.

June 10, 2057 The Ozone Attacks.

June 17, 2057 World War III erupts.

January 2, 2058 Global Vote uniting *all* nations in a new United Global Democracy.

March 3, 2058 Global Vote establishes The Regency; Global Restructuring of nations.

April 1, 2058 Establishment of Global Enforcer Agency: Earth's Law Enforcement.

April 8, 2058 Global election of Regents. Global Constitution approved.

May 30, 2058 The World elects Dr. Thornton Manning as Regent.

August 23, 2060 Wormhole activates in the mesosphere: First Communication with Nelta

August 24, 2060 *Greeter* explodes near the Decagon Satellite Accelerator, killing ten.

October 10, 2060 Second Communication with Nelta

December 11, 2060 Third Communication – People first hear and see the Neltans.

February 24, 2061 *The Need for Advanced Technology* Vote

March 26, 2061 Fourth Communication – first quantum visual exchange

April 5, 2061 *Project Go-or-No* debates on WBET-TV

April 24, 2061 The World approves *The Need*.

July 1, 2061 Fifth Communication

July 2, 2061 Television broadcast of *Scenic and Serene Contemplations*.

October 4, 2061 Humanity bargains with the Neltans for The Matter Stream sample.

J.P. Osterman

January 1, 2062 Tropopause shield activates with Research Station II, protecting the ozone.

February 4, 2062 Nelta sends life extension technology to Earth.

April 11, 2062 Implementation of Stealth Force, Global Earth's astro-Armed Forces.

April 21, 2062 Earth receives The Matter Stream sample.

April 23, 2062 Terra-I, Version I, Earth's quantum-computer matrix activates.

August 8, 2062 Terra streams global.

September 19, 2063 Terra-II streams on Earth.

August 30, 2064 The World approves *The Pact*. Construction of *Sagan* begins. The Gift.

November 11, 2064 Thornton Manning records his account of First Communication Day.

July 17, 2065 Space Stations I through V synchronize.

September 18, 2065 Global financial systems unite into one Terra grid.

September 25, 2065 The Neltans clone an interspecies human/Neltan, Mercy.

March 20, 2067 Elizabeth Tufter becomes the only person whose mind teleports to Nelta.

July 7, 2067 Robert Bartlet hires Marty Hernandez as Lead Drive Room Technician.

October 8, 2067 Bill Wallum reports as Navigation Matrix Specialist on *The Spider*.

October 10, 2067 Captain Bartlet hires Emma Jane Wright, EJ, as Matrix Interfacer.

January 15, 2068 Captain Bartlet names *The Spider* that launches from Space Station III.

January 18, 2068 Captain Bartlet hires Beth Tufter as Nanoengineer.

February 22, 2068 U.C. students get trapped in near-fatal augmented world experiment.

June 10, 2070 *Sagan*'s projected launch from Space Station I for Nelta.

First Communication

About The Author

J.P. Osterman was born December 21, in East Chicago, Indiana

Writing Career: As a futurist and serious Science Fiction author focused on future space travel, J.P. Osterman became an Independent Research Scientist studying the laws that govern space and issues relating to space travel, exploration, and colonization of Mars and exoplanets. In addition to the physics of long distance space travel, J.P. studied the necessary computational theories necessary to control of the physics of space travel and extreme time-space compression; optical quantum computing, quantum communication, and AI Computer intelligence reaching well beyond the "Singularity" with organic quantum level human neural interface and exchange.

J.P. Osterman was a reader and writer throughout her youth. She graduated from University of San Diego with a B.A. in English (with an emphasis in writing) and later a Master's degree from Azusa Pacific University. In the early 1990s, she met Ray Bradbury who inspired her to write science fiction. "I felt that something strange and wonderful had happened to me because of my encounter with Mr. Bradbury, he gave me a future...I began to write every day."

She has written seven novels, mostly science fiction: from exploring Mars, to spacefolding to an ancient alien world. She has won several awards, including the prestigious Rupert Hughes Award at the seminal Maui Writers Conference for her sci-fi novel, The Matter Stream, which she is transforming into her Nelta Series of novels. She won First Place for her play, The Man Next to Me that was subsequently published in the San Diego Writer's Monthly magazine.

J.P. Osterman

Website: Discover these other titles by J.P. Osterman at:

Amazon.com or http://www.jposterman.com

Battlefield Matrix (Book II in the Nelta Series), Cosmic Rift, Dimension Mind, The Screaming Stone, Pete's Crossroad, and Corporate Revenge.